A Murder in Bath

An Inspector Naish Mystery

Chapter 1

Inspector Naish leant his forearms on the railings and rolled himself a cigarette while he contemplated the scene before him. Below him, the river ran past in full autumn flood between deep culverted banks a good twenty-five feet beneath the pavement where he stood. To his right, the river curved away out of sight, and to his left, a footbridge carried the pavement over the river linking the area of Widcombe with the city centre of Bath. On the city side of the bridge the footpath passed under Bath Spa railway station and, as such, was a popular route for commuters in the morning rush hour.

It was someway off that time at present, being just after half past five in the morning, and as such it was quiet in the vicinity of the bridge. Naish was acutely aware of the time, having been summoned from his bed by a telephone call from the desk sergeant at Orange Grove. The reason for his sleep having been interrupted was the current focus of Naish's attention, as he put a match to his cigarette before discarding it into the water below.

Ten feet below the deck of the bridge and right in the centre of the span hung a body suspended by the neck. The other end of the rope was secured to the lattice framework that formed the sides of the bridge. A little further along, to Naish's left, near the bridge, his sergeant was taking a preliminary statement from the milkman who had made the discovery as he drove his float along the riverside road on his morning round. A uniformed constable was stationed at each end of the bridge to keep any early rising members of the public away.

As Naish took the last drags on his roll up, Sergeant Newton came up and joined him.

'So, what does our friend the milkman have to say for himself?' asked Naish.

'Not a lot, I am afraid,' replied Newton. 'He came along the road here on his float, glanced to his right and noticed the body. He parked up where the float is now and ran round to the shops in Widcombe Parade behind us over there and phoned the station. After that, he walked up on to the bridge, more out of curiosity than anything else I think, but saw nothing of note other than the rope securing the corpse.'

'Any other witnesses?' asked Naish.

'No, none as yet. What do you want to do about recovering the body, Inspector? It will be getting busy around here soon.'

'Have you made arrangements to have the body taken to the mortuary?'

'Yes, an ambulance is on its way. I thought it would be quicker than getting the mortuary men to come out with their van.'

'Fine, I just want to take a close look at the scene and then we can get the body away. You had better get a few more men assembled. It is going to be hard work pulling that body back up and over the side,' said Naish as he walked on to the bridge.

Naish leant over the side of the bridge, but there was nothing noteworthy in what he saw. The body was suspended in the middle of the span by a general-purpose rope of a type in common use in a number of trades. As Naish knelt down, he could see where the end of the rope had been tied off through the lattice framework of the bridge side, just below the handrail. Naish was no specialist, but the knot used appeared to have been tied by someone with some knowledge of knots. It looked efficient and fit for purpose, rather than the collection of granny knots that a novice might have tied to suspend a heavy load.

'There is no note about,' said Newton, 'but perhaps we will find it in his pockets.'

'Note?' said Naish with a note of incredulity in his voice.

'Well, it's got all the hallmarks of a suicide,' said Newton. 'He comes out here, ties the rope off and jumps over the side.'

'Have you ever seen a hanging, Sergeant?' Naish asked, rhetorically. 'The length of the drop is crucial. If it is too short, the man will be strangled by the noose. If the drop is too long, it will decapitate him. I am no expert but, looking at the length of that drop and the size of the dead man, I would suggest that a drop of that length would have decapitated him. Now, we need to wait for the autopsy, but I would strongly suspect that this man has been lowered by the neck over the side of the bridge and left hanging there. We can only hope for his sake that he was dead beforehand.'

As Newton peered back over the side of the bridge to re-examine the scene in the light of Naish's observations, the ambulance drew up from behind the railway station and the driver and his assistant made their way over.

'Have you got all the notes you need for the case files?' Naish asked.

'Yes, I have everything. I don't think we need photographs and, anyway, by the time the photographer gets here we will be overrun by members of the public. If you are happy, Inspector, I will get the body in before we attract too much attention.'

'I understand your sentiments, Sergeant, but I don't think we are going to keep this from public attention. Too many people have passed by for that. Anyway, I have a suspicion that the purpose was to attract attention.'

'That's why I thought it was suicide, Inspector. Hanging in a public place is an angry gesture by the deceased, intended to send a message to someone who they have an issue with.'

'Thank you, Sergeant, but I do understand the psychology of suicide motivations. What I mean is that I believe that this body may have been put here not only to be seen but to communicate a message.'

'A message, to whom?' Newton asked.

'That's too early to say, as yet. It's too early to say if it's even right as a theory – but it's my hypothesis for the moment. Now you get your men together and go and haul the body up and whatever you do, don't cut the rope until he is on the bridge. We don't want the added ignominy of him dropping in the drink. I will want to have a look at him before they take him to the mortuary. In the meantime, I am going to have a smoke and wander over to the station.'

When Naish returned, the corpse was laid out on its back on the bridge. The ambulance men and two constables, still recovering from their exertions, were leaning against the sides of the bridge.

'Well done,' said Naish to the group, 'nasty business. Now then, Sergeant, what have you gleaned from the body?'

'Well, he is in a mess, to be frank, Inspector. His face is badly hit about and there are a couple of teeth that look as if they have been freshly knocked out. It looks to me as if he has been in a punch-up. He also has a few broken fingers from what I can see, so it looks as if he put up a bit of a fight. Not that he looks the sort of gent who would be handy with his fists – he is fifty if a day, and I would say a bit of a gent looking at his suit. I have been through his pockets and they are all empty.'

Naish squatted down next to the body and examined it silently. He then took up each of the man's hands and examined them in detail.

'There is no doubt that he has been roughed up, and badly at that. But I am not sure that he was defending himself. You might break one or two fingers with a strong punch, but you don't break all of them on both hands. No one would carry on fighting in that sort of pain. The other point of interest is that he has two fingernails missing on his left hand and three on his right. That doesn't look like a fighting injury to me.'

'Has he fallen do you think, perhaps slipped down a slope or such like and torn out his nails in the process?' Newton suggested. 'He has quite a lot of blood on the front of his shirt. While some has come from his face, it might also be consistent with him sliding face down over a rough surface – a roof for instance.'

'It is possible,' said Naish as he unbuttoned the man's shirt, ' but this, unless I am very much mistaken, is a stab wound.'

Naish lent back on his haunches to let Newton get a close look.

'You are right, Inspector – it is a stab wound, and a deep one at that, by the look of it. So much for my suicide theory.'

'Well, it is clearly a complex death and I think that we have done all that we can here for the moment. Once we have the police surgeons report and understand a little more about the order in which these injuries were inflicted, and what actually caused his death, then we can make a more informed start on our investigation. And now I think it is time for a cup of coffee and a bacon roll.'

'What about the process of identification of the deceased?'

'Well, the formal process of identification will need to be put in train, obviously,' said Naish, rising to his feet. 'But informally, I am certain who the man is.'

'You know him?' said Newton with a start.

'Oh yes. Unless I am very much mistaken, despite the bruising to his face, this is Edward Lynch – Ted to his friends and, indeed, to his enemies. He is a career criminal. Only petty crime, low level theft, simple housebreaking – you know the sort of thing. He has been around this city all his life, moving from one set of low lodgings to another, interspersed with short terms on the inside. He is not, as his suit led you to suppose, a gentleman, but he has always been a dapper dresser when he is in the money. I thought that he was still inside, but clearly not. Anyway, we can look into all of that back at the station after we have had that bit of breakfast.'

The clock of the nearby church was chiming seven o'clock and the crowds of frustrated commuters were beginning to build up at the end of the bridge.

'Right, Sergeant, get this body into the ambulance, have a quick last look around to make sure there is nothing we have missed and then get this bridge opened and let these good people be about their business. I will meet you in the cafe in Kingston Street when you have finished.'

Naish made his way off towards the railway station and passed through the archway by which a road ran out to the front of the station. A hundred yards up the road in a small side road on the left-hand side was a cafe of the traditional type. It was busy with people on their way to work but Naish squeezed into a small table in the corner. He ordered two bacon rolls and two mugs of coffee and while he waited for Newton to join him, he lit a roll up and mused on the interesting events of the morning.

The cafe was too public a location for them to discuss the case and so they chatted about general things as they ate their breakfasts. Naish's statement that it would be difficult to maintain any discretion about the crime was adequately borne out as they overheard snippets of conversation from the adjoining tables – already it was a topic of discussion and speculation. Having finished their breakfast, they made their way out of the cafe and up Manvers Street to Orange Grove, where the police station was located.

'Right,' said Naish as they came into the entrance foyer, 'go and rustle us up a pot of tea and bring it up to my office where we can make a proper start on this investigation. I am going to give the desk sergeant a couple of jobs to do.'

'Well, it appears that old Ted has only been at liberty for ten days,' said Naish, as Newton entered with a tray. 'I got his file from the records department on my way up. Anyway, he didn't waste any time getting himself into trouble, did he?'

'What was he in for?' asked Newton.

'Handling stolen goods this time. He got caught selling on a load of lead taken from a church roof over in Bathford. He got six months and served his sentence at Horfield prison. We can begin to trace his movements following his release with a visit to his last known address and see if he returned there.'

'So, he was out and straight back to crime then.'

'Difficult to say really. Men like Ted Lynch are so well known in the local fraternity that they attract trouble. He may have come out with every intention of keeping out of trouble but he only had to bump into an associate who needed a favour, or who made him an offer to good to refuse, and there you are, back in a life of crime. Sad, really, not being able to break free of it all. He may not have been one of this city's model citizens, old Ted, but he didn't deserve to end up hanging from a bridge.'

'I suppose it depends what he got himself mixed up in,' observed Newton.

'I know what you mean, but I just can't see Ted, after all these years of petty theft, getting mixed up with a bunch of heavies like that. Anyway, it's a fundamental mistake to begin speculating at this stage. What we need to do is to follow the facts and see where they lead us. We can start with that suit of his.'

'The label on the inside said that it was made by a tailor in Milsom Street, very upmarket, if it's the place that I am thinking of.'

'Well you can put visiting them on your list of things to be done. These establishments always keep records. I can't believe that he bought it new, but he may have picked it up second-hand.'

'It would still have cost him a few quid, even second-hand,' said Newton. 'He must have got his hands on some money quite quickly.'

'Either that or he had some salted away,' said Naish.

There was a knock at the door and the desk sergeant came in carrying a large ledger.

'I have been back through the incident records for the past ten days, Inspector, and there are only five cases that I can see that Ted Lynch might have been associated with. I have listed them here, but I brought up the book for you to double-check,' said the sergeant, laying the volume on the desk before Naish, open at the relevant pages.

Naish held the sergeant's handwritten list in one hand and referred to it as he made his way through the list of incidents that had been entered in the record since Lynch's release.

'I agree with you, Hancock,' said Naish looking up and pushing back his chair a little from the desk. 'These are the only fives cases that I can see Ted getting mixed up in, knowing his form. Can you chalk them up on that blackboard please, Newton?'

'The first two crimes on the list,' began Newton, 'took place in Larkhall on the Sunday night following Lynch's release on the previous Thursday. The first was after midnight at a house in Belgrave Road. The scullery window was covered with glued paper and broken, and the thief got away with a small amount of cash that comprised the housekeeping money that the housekeeper had left in the kitchen. Six silver picture frames were also stolen from a table in the hallway but other than that, the thief does not appear to have ventured any further into the house.'

'That sounds like Ted to me,' said Naish. 'Careful, almost cautious, and once he has got enough, he cuts his losses and gets away. No point being greedy and taking more than you can conceal in your pockets – never draw attention to yourself is the motto of the successful thief.'

'The second crime was reported at St Saviour's Church, a few streets away. It may have occurred before or after the break-in in Belgrave Road. The lock of the vestry door was picked, and a large amount of money was taken. It comprised all three of the Sunday collections and as such was largely coins. It must have weighed a few pounds, so I suspect that, if Lynch perpetrated both crimes, the one at the church came second.'

'I agree, said Naish. 'A careful guy like Ted would have made his way home with the coins if he had acquired them first. I expect that he came past the church, thought that, being Sunday night, there was just the chance that the collection was still in the vestry waiting to be taken to the bank on Monday, and just his luck, the verger hasn't secured it in the safe and he hits the jackpot, so to speak.'

'I happen to know that Lynch was a dab hand at picking locks,' said Hancock. 'He prefers to pick the lock rather than break a window if he can. If we looked at the backdoor locks at Belgrave Road, I bet they would show signs of being picked.'

'Right,' said Naish. 'Crime number three.'

'The third crime was at the picture framers in Broadway Parade over in Widcombe. It occurred sometime between half past eleven on the Tuesday night and two o'clock in the morning of Wednesday. The times were established by the local beat constable who noticed that the front door had been forced shortly after two.'

'Broadway Parade,' said Naish. 'Very near to the scene where Ted's body was found. What was taken?'

'A small amount of cash from the till and some tools, according to the record, not as lucrative as the first two jobs but then I suppose it's a case of speculate to accumulate with these opportunist thieves. The next crime is on the Thursday night, again about midnight, not far away in Prior Park Road. Once again, like the Larkhall job, entry is made at the back of the house. Again a window is covered with glued paper and broken in. This time the thief ventured across the whole of the ground floor, presumably finding nothing in the kitchen, again taking a few silver picture frames and a collection of silver snuff boxes.'

'He has a thing for silver picture frames,' said Hancock.

'They are the perfect item for a thief,' said Naish. 'Like I said, they fit easily into pockets, they are high value for their weight and if you can't pass them on as frames then they can be melted down and sold as an ingot – if you have the contacts of course.'

'Final crime,' continued Newton at the blackboard, 'two nights later, assumed to be on the Saturday night, although the scene was not discovered until early Sunday morning by the beat constable – a watch repairer on Broad Street. This time no cash, but the bodies of three watches that were being worked on at a bench – one silver, two gold – taken. Fortunately, everything else of value was in the safe, which was untouched.'

'Breaking safes was not one of Ted's lines, I doubt if he would even have tried the lock. His skills as a lock-picker were strictly limited. Anyway, Hancock can you follow up the cases with the respective officers and let me know if they have any suspects or have made any arrests. Newton and I will take a trip along to Ted's last known lodgings and see what we can learn there. Let's meet up back here at four o'clock for a cup of tea and see what we have achieved.'

The last address recorded in Ted Lynch's file was in Oak Street, an odd road that ran through an archway of the railway embankment that carried the main line into Bath. The house was on the far side of the archway where the road came to a dead end.

'It would pay to be hard of hearing living this close to the main line,' said Newton with a smile.

'Beggars can't be choosers,' said Naish. 'Anyway, they say you can get used to the sound of trains after a while and, from Teds point of view, it is an out of the way spot where no one comes unless they live here.'

As Naish knocked on the door, an express passed by overhead and although it was slowing for the station the ground still vibrated as it passed.

'Good morning,' said the lady of the house as she stood wiping her hand on her apron. 'Not today, thank you.'

'We are police officers, Mrs West,' said Naish before she could close the door in their faces.

'Ah,' she said in a knowing tone. 'Would it be about Mr Lynch?'

'It would, I am afraid. Might we come in?' asked Naish.

They were shown into the front parlour where the landlady offered them a chair.

'I am Inspector Naish. I take it that Mr Lynch has recently returned to lodge with you, then?'

'Yes, he wrote to me some weeks ago and asked if he might take up lodgings here again as he was "returning to the area". He appeared two weeks ago come Friday,' said the landlady.

'That would be a fortnight ago tomorrow, then?'

'That is correct. He packed up his property in a couple of trunks and left them in his room as he was going to be "away" for six months. I had an arrangement with him that whenever he was away that I would keep his room. If I could let it for the duration of his absence, then I would put his trunks in storage, and he understood that if I got a permanent let then he would need to seek alternative accommodation. I managed to let his room for three months of the six that he was away and so it was free when he asked to return.'

'You are aware of the circumstances that took Mr Lynch away on occasions, I take it?'

'Oh yes, Inspector, I know all about Mr Lynch's absences.'

'That never gave you cause for concern?'

'The way I look at it is that it is none of my business. Mr Lynch has always been polite, paid his rent on time, in advance usually, and never caused me any problems. What else could a landlady want?'

'Did his hours ever disrupt you?'

'Never. He was quiet as a mouse when he was here, and if he kept late hours, I never heard him come and go. I sleep like a log and have my ear plugs in – you need to with the railway outside your window.'

'Yes, I suppose that it helps being a deep sleeper, from both railway and tenant point of view,' said Naish with a smile. 'I am afraid that I have some very unfortunate news for you Mrs West – Mr Lynch was found dead this morning over in Broadway Parade.'

'Oh, my good God!' she exclaimed. 'What ever happened to him?'

'It is far from clear at this moment in time,' said Naish. 'I am hoping that you can provide me with some information that will help me understand his movements. You say that he returned here thirteen days ago. What has he been up to in the meantime? Did he go out every day? Did he have any callers or associates?'

'He turned up here, as I have said, on the Friday evening. It would have been about five o'clock and he went up to his room to unpack and arrange his things. I took his evening meal up to him about half past six, and as far as I know he didn't venture out until the Sunday morning about half past eleven. He didn't have what you would call a daily routine, but he went out most days and was home in time for his evening meal. If he was staying out, he would always let me know so that the food didn't go to waste.'

Mrs West caught Naish's eye as he looked knowingly at Newton.

'No, it was not what you are thinking, Inspector. The evenings when he stayed out were the evenings that he would be out taking a drop with his friends.'

'And where did he go to take a drop?' asked Naish in an apologetic tone.

'His usual haunt was the Golden Fleece, Inspector. Always has been as long as he has lodged here with me.'

'Thank you, Mrs West, I will make some enquiries there. Did he pay his rent regularly?'

'He was always good with his rent. He paid up for the month on the first Monday he was back with me.'

'How did he pay you?' asked Naish.

'Cash always, but I had to take it to the bank on the Monday because it was all in coins, nothing bigger than half a crown. It was a bit inconvenient, but he apologised saying that it was what he had saved up before he went away and had not had time to cash it all up. Still, I didn't complain. A month's rent in advance is a month's rent and not to be quibbled over.'

'Of course, Mrs West, I completely understand.'

'What was he wearing?' asked Newton.

'Well he was looking a little unkempt when he turned up, which was unusual for him as he was usually quite particular about his appearance. Anyway, by the middle of his first week back he was in a very dapper suit, lovely cut and very nice cloth.'

'What about callers?'

'He never brought people back and no one ever called on him, which is what made him such a good lodger. That was until last Monday night. It was not a problem, but it was unusual.'

'Who was it?'

'A clergyman. He asked for Mr Lynch and having checked with Mr Lynch I showed him up. They were in his room for about a quarter of an hour and then they came down together and went out.'

'What time was this?' asked Naish leaning forward in his chair.

'They stepped out at eight o'clock. I know that because the news was just beginning on the wireless.'

'How was Mr Lynch behaving? Was there any disturbance?'

'No, there was no disturbance or raised voices. Mr Lynch was perfectly at ease in the clergyman's company.'

'Describe the clergyman for me, please.'

'He was an elderly man, I would say, sixty if a day. He was slight of build and not very tall. He was very well-mannered though, as you would expect from a man of the cloth.'

'Well thank you Mrs West. You have been extremely helpful, and I am sorry that I have been the bearer of bad news. Now before we leave you in peace, would you show me Mr Lynch's room, if you please?'

Lynch's room was a bedroom on the first floor overlooking the street. The furnishing was simple: a cast-iron framed bed; a small washstand with a shaving mirror above it; an armchair and a chest of drawers. A cupboard in the wall provided a few more shelves and a place to hang clothes.

Naish and Newton began a systematic search of the room while Mrs West looked on from the doorway. The room proved to be a thin source of clues as to Lynch's activities but in the bottom drawer of the chest was a cloth cash bag which contained a large number of low denomination coins.

'The remains of the Larkhall collection, I would suggest,' said Naish holding up the bag before putting it in his coat pocket. 'We can check if this is the bag that the collection was in. Have you fared any better in the cupboard?'

'Not so far, just clothes and shoes, as you might expect,' said Newton as he pulled two trunks out into the room. 'Just leaves these two to go.'

The trunks were stacked on top of each other. Newton opened the top one which proved to be empty.

'Well we have something in this one,' said Newton as he opened the bottom trunk.

'What is it?' asked Naish, stepping forward.

'Nothing really,' replied Newton, with a disheartened tone in his voice. 'They look like artist's canvases to me.'

'From the Broadway Parade job,' said Naish, picking up one of the canvases and inspecting it.

'Four canvases with some ink drawings on,' said Newton. 'An unusual divergence from his usual acquisitions, wouldn't you say, Inspector?'

'I agree with you, but it all fits together from a factual point of view. What his motivations were in taking them is something we may get to the bottom of, or possibly not. For all we know, he had a buyer for them and that was the motivation for the burglary, or he just gathered them up in his opportunistic way.'

'I suppose so, but it is odd that the remains of the church collection and these four canvases are all there is to show for all the items he has stolen over the past days.'

'Very odd,' said Naish. 'I find it hard to believe that he has not got some of the proceeds of the thefts secreted away somewhere here. I cannot believe that he has passed on all those pieces of silver already, or that if he has, there is not some evidence of the cash he got for them here.'

'He might have had it on him and that was the motivation for his being assaulted?'

'I cannot believe that a man as cautious as Ted and who kept such dubious company would carry large sums of cash on him unless he had to.'

'Do you think he had a bank account?' asked Newton. 'He could have paid it in there.'

'He might have a savings account at the Post Office where he could keep some money on deposit for the times he was inside, but I would doubt he had a bank account. He would never use either for his day to day work. It's too risky for him to pay in cash or even large amounts of coins. Besides, he would rather have the coins as they would be easier to pass on at the pub, the bookies or in shops without exciting interest. If Ted were seen using notes in his regular haunts it would excite comment and attract the sort of inquisitive interest in his affairs that Ted was always keen to avoid,' said Naish sitting down in the armchair.

Chapter 2

'Hello, now here is an idea,' said Naish, who had risen to his feet and was now pulling back a corner of the square of carpet that covered the centre of the room.

The first two corners he pulled back revealed nothing but the floorboards beneath. However, having pulled back the third corner, he let out a cry of satisfaction. He knelt down and, taking a pen knife from his pocket, he began to lift up a floorboard. It was clear to Newton, who peered over his shoulder, that two adjacent floorboards had been cut through to form a small trap door about eighteen inches square.

'Got you, Ted Lynch,' said Naish with an air of satisfaction as he pulled a wooden box out from under the floor. 'I think you will find, Sergeant, that when you compare the list of silver items stolen from the thefts that we have under consideration, you will find that all or most of them are accounted for in this box.'

'I will need to check,' said Newton, as he knelt down to inspect the contents of the box. 'It may well be all of them. It could be that he decided to postpone selling them until he had exhausted his windfall from the church collection. As you said, Inspector, he probably didn't want to have much cash about at any one time.'

'Exactly, and the longer he delayed selling them on, the lesser the risk of a connection with the crimes. Although he might sell them on over in Bristol or even further afield, he could not risk that we might have circulated descriptions of the silver pieces to the trade.'

'What's that, more stuff under there, Inspector?' asked Newton, as Naish pulled some more items from beneath the floorboards.

'Well, these are the tools from the shop in Broadway Parade I imagine, although why they are under here I cannot imagine, as they hold no value.'

'Traceable to the crime scene though, I suppose, whereas the canvases are just too large to fit under there,' offered Newton.

'Two A3 sketchbooks appear to complete the contents of the hideaway,' said Naish, as he peered under the floorboards.

'Well, he wasn't going to sell these on – they have been used, sketches on every page. Why didn't he just ditch the canvases, the tools and the sketchbooks as worthless?'

'I imagine he brought the fruits of his crime back here to examine them in the light and, having found them to be worthless, concealed them until he could dispose of them in a manner that they could not be traced back to him. Criminals like Ted would rather hang on to something that could link them to a crime scene until it could be safely disposed of. Burn the canvases and sketchbooks and sling the tools into the river when he could do so discreetly.'

'Is my floor going to be safe, that's what is worrying me,' interjected an indignant Mrs West.

'Oh, I am sure it will, Mrs West. Nothing affecting the structure – a couple of nails and it will be as right as rain,' said Naish, reassuringly. 'I am sorry to impose on you, Mrs West, but this discovery will mean my remaining here a little longer than I had anticipated.'

'That's no trouble to me, Inspector. Would you both like a cup of tea?'

Mrs West scuttled away to make the tea and while she was gone Naish and Newton pulled back the rest of the carpet to check for any other underfloor hideaways that Lynch might have cut in the floorboards, but they found none. They even had time to sound out the floor in the cupboard and inspect the walls for any signs of impromptu safety deposits that might have been constructed, but finding none, they were able to reseat themselves and adopt a casual air as Mrs West returned with a tray of tea.

Having finished their tea and informed Mrs West that a constable would call round within the hour to collect the stolen items, Naish and Newton made their way out into the street. Rather than wait for a car to collect them, Naish decided they should walk back across town to the station.

'So, what struck you most about the collection of items in Ted's room?' asked Naish.

'The pointlessness of the canvases, sketch pads and tools, I suppose.'

'I thought I had explained the most probable reason for them being there,' said Naish, with a mild tone of exasperation in his voice. 'I will need to check the crime reports and the statements when we get back to the station, but in my opinion the odd thing is this: the items recorded as having been stolen from the various crime scenes that we are considering all exactly match what we have found in Ted's lodgings. The watch cases are clearly not there, and some of the photograph frames may be missing, but they may have already been sold on. However, in the case of the picture framers, it appears to me that there are some items that have been stolen which have not been reported. Now why would that be?'

'They were either of no value, and so the owner did not bother to report them, or else he did not realise that they were gone.'

'I agree that he possibly did not realise they were gone – a few canvases stolen from a picture framers may go unnoticed. It's odd, though, that he mentions the tools, which are also of limited value, but not the sketchbooks and canvases. Either way, I think it will be worth our while to visit the shop at some point and interview the proprietor and get to the bottom of it.'

The clock in Bath Abbey was chiming two o'clock as they arrived back at Orange Grove. Naish went back to his office and Newton set off into town to make enquiries at the banks and post office.

Having asked the duty desk sergeant to see if Hancock was in the station and, if he was, to send him up to his office, Naish made his way up the stone staircase to his office. He rolled himself a cigarette and began to survey the three blackboards that had been set up on easels around his office. This was his preferred method; to see the case developing visually. On one board was the chronology of the crime; on the second was a list of the people associated with the crime, from suspects through to witnesses and others of interest on the periphery of the case. The third was general information and a list of matters to follow up. Over by the fireplace a trestle table was set up for items of evidence on to which Naish had placed the sole item so far – the cloth cash bag found in Lynch's room.

'Come in,' said Naish, in response to a knock at the door. He had been expecting it to be Hancock but instead the door was opened by a young constable carrying a large cardboard box.

'The items from Oak Street that you requested to be collected, sir,'

'Ah yes. Set them out on the trestle over there, please.'

As the constable was making his way to the door, he paused in deference to rank to allow Hancock in. Hancock had with him a bundle of manila folders.

'The case notes that you asked me to review,' he explained, as he set them down on the evidence table. 'I thought we would need them for our meeting at four, so I brought them up.'

'Sit down and tell me what there is to know, then,' said Naish, who was sat behind his desk rolling his next cigarette with the remains of the existing one lodged between his lips.

'There is scant additional information other than what we have already learnt from the files,' began Hancock, lighting his pipe. 'Sergeant Dodd has been working on all the cases with a couple of detective constables and is making steady progress. With regards to the two burglaries out at Larkhall, all the statements that you would expect to have been taken have been completed. Enquiries have been made with those on the edge of the criminal fraternity known to deal in silverware and the like and also with the antique and jewellery businesses in the city. Two likely suspects known to the police have been interviewed but they both have convincing alibis and so no progress has been made in identifying a primary suspect. However, there is a witness description of a man seen about a mile away from Larkhall walking back along the London Road towards the town.'

'Is it credible?' asked Naish, discarding the butt of his cigarette in the ashtray and lighting the second roll up.

'I think it is. The timings are about right for someone who had committed the two crimes when they were estimated to have occurred and to be walking back into town, as we know Ted Lynch would have done. And the description matches Lynch.'

'Why did they not interview Lynch?'

'In fairness, because they thought, like us, that he was still inside, and this witness statement was only taken this Monday as part of their ongoing investigation.'

'Fair enough,' said Naish disconsolately. 'Anyway, knowing what we now know about Ted, it is unlikely that they would have been in time to interview him. It strikes me as odd that Ted would take such a public route along the main road into town where any number of witnesses might identify him, even if it was the early hours of the morning.'

'I agree, but I think he worked on the notion that there are no other routes back because he had at some point to cross the river. The

London Road was the only practical option open to him. I think he thought the chances of being observed from a window overlooking the road were remote and as an insurance against that he had, according to the witness, his coat collar pulled right up and his hat pulled down to partially conceal his face. The road is long and straight and so he would anticipate getting plenty of warning if a pedestrian or vehicle were approaching him and he would probably nip into a front garden and wait for the danger to pass.'

'So, what went wrong then?'

'Wrong?'

'Well, someone evidently saw him didn't they, so his plan, if that is what he intended, went wrong, didn't it?'

'Oh, I see what you mean, yes. The witness was a train guard making his way into work for an early turn of duty. He came up from a side alley where his lodging house is and walked right into the suspect's path.'

'Did he see his face?'

'Only partially. The witness apparently said good morning, as you would if you bumped into someone in those circumstances, but our man just grunted, kept his head down and walked on towards town. It's ironic because, according to the guard, if the bloke had been less abrupt it would not have provoked his suspicions.'

'So, what did the witness do?'

'Gave the bloke a couple of yards start so as not to have to tangle with him again and made his way to work at the station.'

'Which station? Green Park or Bath Spa?' asked Naish.

'Green Park, and, yes, I have anticipated your thoughts. If it was Ted heading back to Oak Street then the route they walked would be almost identical – and it was. The guard followed Ted over Cleveland Bridge, down St Johns Road, over Pulteney Bridge, then along Westgate Street and across Kingsmead Square, where the Guard broke off to go into the goods yard at Green Park with Ted heading on in a direction that could well have led him to Oak Street.'

'So why was there such a delay in this witness coming to light?' asked Naish.

'The guard was on a goods train that headed to the Midlands and from there he took over a train that went down to Bournemouth before taking over a train that terminated in Green Park. That's the nature of the work, apparently. So, it was only last weekend that he returned to Bath and saw a report of the burglary in Larkhall and, remembering his encounter, he came along to the Station here to volunteer a statement.'

'So, does that conclude where we are with the first two incidents?'

'Yes, that is the latest position and leads on to the next case that occurred at the picture framers in Broadway Parade.'

'So, what exactly is the nature of their business?'

'The main business is framing pictures – paintings, prints photographs and the like. The proprietor also restores old picture frames. They also display small collections of work by local amateur artists that are for sale.'

'Quite a comprehensive range of services, then,' said Naish beginning to roll another cigarette. 'Lucrative, I should imagine?'

'The premises are modest but from what I can make of the facts, yes, it turns a pretty penny.'

'Does the proprietor live above the shop?'

'No, the floors above the shop are given over to workshops and storage areas. The proprietor lives off the premises, but I have no information as to where.'

'Well, we can follow that up later. Have you got the list of the items reported stolen there?'

'Yes, a small amount of cash and a selection of tools. That's it.'

'Yet in Ted's room we have found two sketchbooks and four canvases not mentioned in the statement. Why?'

'Perhaps they were not noticed if they were taken from a larger pile of stock of such items. When it is apparent that you have been burgled, most people immediately check the obvious things like cash, and a workman would quite quickly notice if the everyday tools of his trade were missing.'

'Yes, I see that. Newton made the same points as you. It is just a loose end, but it needs tidying up. Where next?'

'The house in Prior Park Road was next. A few silver picture frames and a collection of silver snuff boxes are taken.'

'That ties in with our find at Oak Street, but obviously a detailed check will need to be made with the owners to ensure they are the items reported,' said Naish. 'Anything more?'

'No, the investigation there has turned up nothing more. Despite a large number of local residents being questioned, including the milkman and early morning postman, no one saw anyone in the vicinity of the crime. It's the same with the watch repairers in Broad Street, I am afraid.'

'So, five crimes, only one witness identifies a suspect and we have a strong belief that it was Ted Lynch. Despite the lack of progress on the other cases it appears inevitable from the items found in his room that all five crimes are down to our man. Well, the good news is that as a result of his death we have cleared up, in a single act, all five crimes. The Superintendent will be pleased to have his statistics so efficiently put back in the black, I am sure. However, it does not move us any further forward in understanding what happened to Ted, does it?'

'No, I am afraid that it doesn't, Inspector,' said Hancock knocking out his pipe in the wastepaper bin.

Naish and Hancock sat in silence for a while whilst Hancock refilled his pipe and Naish rolled yet another cigarette. As the abbey clock chimed a quarter to four, there was a knock at the door and Newton came in carrying a tray of tea.

'Good man,' said Naish, clearing a space on his desk for the tray. 'How did you get on with the banks?'

'The banks were all very cooperative. Unfortunately, they have no record of Lynch having an account under any permutation of his name that I asked for; so, unless he was using a pseudonym, I think we can be confident he had no bank account.'

'Sounds sensible to me,' said Naish. 'I can't see him going to the trouble of a pseudonym and, anyway, the false documentation he would need to acquire to support the pseudonym would be more cost and trouble than it was worth for a man in Ted's particular line of crime.'

'I tried the post office,' continued Newton, 'but again nothing, certainly not in this area anyway. The main post office in Bath has a record of the accounts opened by the surrounding sub-branches, but nothing beyond the Bath boundary. I thought that Lynch might prefer the discretion of being able to pop into a quiet local post office out in the suburbs where he was not known to conduct his financial affairs, but apparently not. However, I went into the main office of the local building society and he does have an account with them. Like the post office, they also have a few sub-offices and it appears he used the one up in Combe Down on a very occasional basis. I went up there to make enquiries and the balance of his account is thirty-four pounds and ten shillings, and the last activity on the account was a deposit of four pounds and three shillings two weeks before he went inside for his last stretch.'

'Good work. Then as far as we can tell, any cash stolen from these properties or generated by selling the silverware is, in all probability, spent.'

'I agree with your theory, Inspector, that he has been using the cash from the Larkhall church before selling on anything else. He has paid a month's rent, bought a second-hand suit and had a few nights on the beer. If we subtract all of that roughly from the average Sunday collection at Larkhall, I doubt we will be much adrift from what is left in the cash bag.'

'I will check that when I go out to Larkhall,' said Naish. 'I want the houses in Larkhall and Prior Park visited so that we can check the items we have recovered against what was stolen. Then we will know if he has or has not sold anything on. I know it's mundane, but we need to try and find a lead into what got Ted, the petty thief, into a world of murder. Hancock, I am bringing you in on this case, so it's time for a break from the front desk and time to dig out your civilian clothes – I want you to set about finding what happened to the watch cases. Visit the watch repairer, go over Ted's room again in case I missed them there and get around a few of the local antique shops, you know the ones, to try and see if they have bought anything like them. Right then, I think that will do us for today, Hancock you can update Newton on the latest information on the five cases we were just discussing while you are washing up the tea mugs together in the mess room. I am going to finish off my in tray then call it a day.'

'What is the plan for tomorrow then?' asked Hancock.

'Newton and I need to be at St Martin's first thing to meet the police surgeon and get his report on the cause of death. I suggest that you get on with matching the items we have recovered with the relevant owners and drop in at the watch repairers and Ted's room. Allowing time for lunch, I think it feasible for us to meet back here at two o'clock and see where we are.'

His paperwork finished, Naish put out the lights in his office and, having said goodnight to the desk sergeant, made his way out into the street as the abbey clock struck seven o'clock. He pulled his coat collar up against the cold of the night air and set off for The Volunteer Rifleman pub where he invariably took his evening meal on his way home from work. He always sat at one of the small tables alone and enjoyed the solitude after a day in the police station. He ordered his meal and sat with a pint of beer and a cigarette in hand, reading the evening paper.

'Well, it's a brutal attack in my opinion,' began the police surgeon, as Newton and Naish stood opposite him, the corpse on a slab between them.

'An attack – not a fight?' asked Naish.

'From what I can tell, this man put up no defence at all. Let me talk you through the injuries. The injuries inflicted appear to have happened in four stages. In the first stage, I believe that the deceased was bound to a chair. If you look at the contusions on his wrists you can see clearly where his hands have been bound together. However, further up his arms, here, on the back of his upper arms, you can see bruises on the inner side of the arm. Now, from my experience, that is consistent with him being tied to a high-backed chair, like a dining chair, with the hands tied behind the back of the chair. You can also see above the ankles similar marks left by a cord. The way the wounds have been rubbed deep into the skin on the wrists is an indication that he was struggling to free himself. The wounds on the ankles are less severe as an individual tied in this fashion cannot exert the same force to try and free their feet. It is also probable that the socks also protected the skin to some extent. It is my opinion that once this man was tied in this position, he was then struck violently across the face, probably with alternate blows to the left and the right, looking at the balance of the bruising on each side of the face. However, you will note that the injuries are more severe on the left of his face, including the displacement of three teeth, which indicates he was being assaulted by a right-handed man, who stood in front of him.'

Naish and Newton exchanged a glance that indicated their mutual disbelief at the violence of the tale unfolding before them.

'Now, the second stage,' continued the surgeon. It is difficult to discern, but from my examination of the wounds, it is my opinion that a very minor healing of the wounds that I have attributed to stage one was beginning to occur before the wounds associated with this second stage were inflicted. If you look at the victim's forearms you can see signs of bruising, but only on what would be the upper surface if you forced your arms flat on a surface, such as a table with the palms down. Now, I believe that the bruising is only evident there because his hands were being held down so that these injuries on his hands could be inflicted.'

The surgeon looked up and caught Newton wincing at the thought.

'I know, Sergeant, it is very disturbing to contemplate what was done to this man. It is clear from examination of his injuries that his fingers were broken with a hammer, probably in turn, as each blow is centred right on the middle joint of each finger. If you care to look here on his left hand you can see where I have exposed the fractures with a scalpel.'

Naish lent forward to peer closely at the wounds and smiled kindly as Newton declined the opportunity.

'In addition, as you can see, a number of the nails on his right and left hands have been removed. Again, from examination of the injuries, it is my opinion that the nails have been pulled out using a pair of long-nosed pliers.'

'You are clearly suggesting that this man has been tortured, Doctor,' said Naish, gravely.

'That is exactly what I believe happened to this unfortunate man,' said the surgeon, looking up from the body. In my opinion, the nails would have been extracted first, as it is, and I use the term in the sense of torture, a more slow and subtle means of inflicting fear and pain. I think that, because he resisted telling them what they wanted, they became more desperate and resorted to the violence of breaking his fingers in turn. I imagine they didn't break them all as, in all probability, he fainted from a mixture of trauma and pain.'

'Then finally they stabbed him as the coup de grâce,' said Naish.

'I think so. Either at the conclusion of this second stage or soon afterwards. The single stab wound to the heart was delivered at the third stage of injury and, of course, death was instantaneous.'

'You say to the heart, Doctor. Do you suggest that it was a precise act to insert the knife into the heart, rather than a stab wound that happened to pierce the heart?'

'I cannot be certain, of course, but it is a very accurate incision, passing directly between the ribs with no evidence of the blade having struck the ribs, as you would expect to find in a casual stabbing. The knife would have to be angled very precisely to miss the ribs and there is no bruising around the wound here, if you look. That suggests to me that the knife was inserted slowly and deliberately rather than in the usual manner of a stab wound inflicted in violence.'

'Then it truly was a coup de grâce?'

'Yes, I believe it was. You are dealing with some very violent men here, Inspector, in my opinion. Men who know their profession and are clinical in their approach. The fourth and final stage of this series of injuries is obviously the wounds inflicted by the ligature around the victim's neck. The nature of the wound and the absence of any fractures to the vertebrae suggest to me that he was lowered, postmortem, from the bridge where he was found hanging. As to why that was done is, I am afraid, a matter entirely for you to speculate upon, Inspector.

'You suggested that some healing of the wounds inflicted in stage one had begun to occur before the wounds associated with phase two were inflicted?'

'Yes, but only to a very minor degree. Some clotting had formed and the finest of scabs had begun to form on the cuts above his eyes.'

'That suggests to me that there was an interval of some time between the two events. In the true style of torture, he was left to reflect and or recover before they tried their powers of persuasion on him a second time.'

'Your theory is certainly compatible with the results of my examination of his injuries.'

'It also fits in with the timeline of his being abducted on the Monday, held captive until the Tuesday and being found in the early hours of Wednesday morning,' said Naish. 'Abducted, taken somewhere, tortured, left to think things over in a cell of some sort, tortured a second time, murdered and disposed of.'

Naish wandered off to the window and stared silently into the distance as he rolled himself a cigarette. The surgeon made to speak but stopped as he caught Newton's eye, which suggested Naish was best left in silence. Having finished rolling his cigarette, Naish tucked it behind his right ear and wandered back to the slab.

'I don't know if you are able to tell from your examination, Doctor, but my assumption is that the knife wound was inflicted immediately after the conclusion of the second period of torture. They realised that they were not going to get the information that they wanted and put him out of his misery.'

'I cannot make a definitive judgement as to when the knife wound was inflicted, Inspector, but I agree that your theory is the most probable sequence of events.'

'So, does that conclude your findings, Doctor?'

'Yes, I am afraid that that is everything that I can determine from my examination.'

'Nothing to be afraid about, Doctor. Your findings have been extremely thorough and will be of great assistance in this case. Now before we leave you in peace, I would like to take the suit jacket that the deceased was wearing with us, if that is in order.'

Having taken his leave, Naish went out to the front entrance of the hospital where the car was waiting for him. Whilst he waited for Newton, who was retrieving the suit jacket, he took the roll up from behind his ear and lit it as he stood in thought.

'I can hardly believe what I heard in there,' said Newton, as the car took them back to the station. 'It is unimaginable that a petty thief like Lynch should come into the sphere of such criminals. I mean these people are at a level of violence and professionalism that is rare even in the world of organised crime within metropolitan cities.'

'I know,' said Naish gravely. 'What is concerning me is what are they doing in a city like Bath, and even more mystifying is how a small-time crook like Ted Lynch, who has been inside for the last six months, got mixed up with them.'

'Do you think it is something to do with his recent term inside, something he was told by a cellmate or fellow prisoner, or perhaps some information he simply overheard?'

'It may well be,' said Naish. 'It could be he was even mistaken for somebody else, who knows. But I think it would be wise if you took a trip over to Bristol and went to Horfield Prison. Find out who he shared a cell with, who he associated with, even who he might have had disagreements with. We can then prove or discount the prison link. In the meantime, we will focus on finding how he got involved with these people. It may have happened in the brief time since he was discharged from prison or it may relate to something he was involved in before he went inside.'

'It may even go back years,' Newton offered.

'No, I don't think it will go back that far. The sort of people we are dealing with here don't bear grudges, in my experience. If you need to be dealt with or they are after revenge it is dealt with there and then.'

The car pulled up outside the station and Naish and Newton got out.

'Right,' said Naish. 'An hour for lunch and I will see you in my office at two o'clock.'

Chapter 3

'Apologies,' said Hancock as he came into the office at ten past two. 'I am a bit behind but getting round to follow up everything took longer than I anticipated.'

'It's not a problem,' said Naish, 'pour yourself a cup of tea and sit down. So, what have you learnt?'

'Well, I have been out to the house in Larkhall and the house in Prior Park and all the items of silver reported stolen from each address are present in the box you recovered from Oak Street. The housekeeping money from the Larkhall house, however, is either gone or amalgamated in the contents of the cloth cash bag. Then I went along to the watch repairer in Broad Street. He was able to give me a very detailed description of the three watch cases and also the hallmarks that were on each item. He apparently keeps a record of these for his own purposes.'

'That will be useful when we start to try and trace them when they get disposed of,' said Newton.

'Exactly,' said Hancock. 'I then went over to Oak Street and, having shaken off the redoubtable Mrs West, I spent an hour turning Lynch's room upside down and inside out, but I could find no more than you both did. So then I set off back into town to make a start on the antique and jewellery businesses.'

'You have worn off some shoe leather this morning, Sergeant,' said Naish with a smile. 'I imagine you have not put in that sort of mileage since you were a beat copper.'

'I know. I will be putting in a chit for a boot allowance before this case is over. Anyway, I did the three main auction houses in the town and two of the antique dealers – the one in New Bond Street and the one in Cheap Street – without any success. Then I went into that old jewellers in Northumberland Place and I had my first bit of luck. On Monday morning, about half past ten, an elderly clerical gentleman came into the shop and asked if they bought old silver and gold. The proprietor was non-committal but said he would need to examine the pieces first. He told me that he only buys pieces that he can renovate and sell on. He does not buy precious metals for scrap or to refashion into new items. The clerical gentleman produced three watch cases, one silver and two gold, from a felt bag and placed them on the counter. As he was doing so, he told the proprietor that he had brought them in on behalf of an elderly parishioner who was housebound and, having fallen on hard times, wanted to sell them, depending upon their being of some value. Because they were just watch cases, the proprietor had no interest in them and declined to purchase them. He did note that they were antique silver and gold because he read the hallmarks, although he could not remember them. The clerical gentleman thanked him for his time and replaced the items back in the felt bag. As he left, he asked if the proprietor knew of anyone else in the trade who might be interested in such pieces. The proprietor suggested a dealer in curios in the Guildhall Market. He tends to buy up old precious metals that have more value as scrap than as artefacts.'

'What is the description given for this cleric,' asked Naish.

'Mid-sixties, five foot six, round spectacles, clean-shaven, wearing black suit, black shirt with dog collar, black hat.'

'Very anonymising, clerical dress, and of course it engenders an air of trust. Was he at all suspicious of the man?'

'Apparently not,' said Hancock. 'Since the watch cases had only been stolen on the previous Saturday night, I assume the cleric was reasonably content that news of the theft was unlikely to have circulated and the three items would not attract suspicion.'

'It is unbelievable that it is not the same clerical gentleman who left Oak Street with Lynch on Monday evening.'

'According to Mrs West, it is,' said Hancock. 'That is partly why I am late. I went back over to Oak Street to recount the jeweller's description to her and they match as exactly as a verbal description can match.'

'Excellent,' said Naish. 'Get hold of the police artist and make arrangements for him to meet with the jeweller. It will move things on if we have an image of this cleric. Interestingly, you say that the cleric asked where else he might sell on the items and yet he did not ask for their value?'

'No, he did not,' said Hancock. 'I assume he only asked for the name of someone else in the trade who might be interested in them to add some verisimilitude to his pretence. Odd that he was given that dealer in the market, because that is just where I would have sent someone with those sorts of goods.'

'I agree,' said Naish. 'So, I would suggest that we are dealing with a man who knows the value of precious metals but who is not local to Bath.'

'Or he knows nothing of the precious metal trade, either,' interjected Newton, 'and he was just running errands for Ted Lynch.'

'Interesting thought,' said Naish. 'The main thing is we now have a proven link that Ted Lynch and this clerical gentleman were acting in some form of association and that it was, as far as we can tell, an amicable and trusting relationship. That would account for why Ted left with him so naturally on the Monday night. How they came into that association is something we need to look into as we go along. Right, Hancock, is there anything else to add to your account?'

'Only that on my way into the station I looked in at the Guildhall Market and spoke to the dealer. He denied any knowledge of the cleric and he didn't appear to me to be hiding anything, but you never know with these dealers, do you. Anyway, I gave him a description and asked him to let me know if he was approached.'

'I think he will do that,' said Naish. 'Since we are almost his next-door neighbours, I think he would rather help us out and have us owe him a favour than run the risk of us taking an unhealthy interest in the nature of his trade. I also think that the proximity of this station to the Guildhall market may have deterred our clerical friend from taking up the suggestion from the jeweller – to close to the police for comfort, he may have thought.'

'Well, that's it from me,' said Hancock, as he lit his pipe. 'What did you discover from the autopsy report?'

Hancock sat back and listened intently, as Naish related the grim details of the examination that the police surgeon had explained to him and Newton that morning.

'So, we need to create some hypothesis and cross-examine ourselves to try and establish a plausible theory of what brought Ted Lynch into association with these men. We will at least then have a framework to hang our investigations on,' said Naish.

'All right, then. Here is a starter for ten,' said Hancock. 'Did he unwittingly learn something while he was inside prison that made him a risk to these men or their business?'

'An interesting proposition,' said Naish. 'I would say that if that were so, and given the nature of these men, that they would not have bothered to torture him to find out the extent of what he knew. They would simply kill him in cold blood, regarding him as a minor player in their business.'

'Fair point,' said Hancock. 'I can see the sense of what you say.'

'Suppose they were concerned that he had divulged the information to third parties,' said Newton. 'They might torture him to find out who they were, so that they could deal with them as well as Lynch.'

'For me, that holds water if we assume that they were concerned that the third party he had shared the information with was a fellow prisoner,' said Naish. 'If they were concerned that he had, or was, sharing the information with associates since his return to Bath then, if I was them, I would simply follow him around his haunts, identify his associates and simply murder them in cold blood.'

'I agree,' said Hancock, 'but given the regularity of his visits to the pub from Mrs West's account alone, perhaps they believed that there were just too many potential confidants to make it practical to murder them. If that is the case, then they would need to identify exactly who they were going to target.'

'I cannot argue with the logic of that,' said Naish.

'Do you think he knew them?' asked Newton.

'He may well have known them when they confronted him,' said Naish, 'however, it would appear logical to me that he did not believe that he was at risk from them, or indeed anyone, whether he knew them or not. If he did, he surely would not have returned to his last-known address, as it would make him so easy to trace. You would either take alternative lodgings away from your usual locality, or even better, go to a different town altogether as soon as he was released.'

'If he did not know them but they knew that he was in possession of information that put them at risk, then they may simply have followed him from the time he was released from Horfield prison all the way back to his lodgings in Oak Street,' said Hancock.

'Two aspects of this matter puzzle me,' said Newton. 'Firstly, what can have been so valuable about the knowledge he had that he resists divulging it under torture, at least, we can assume, during the first phase of torture. Secondly, if he knew something valuable, why was he not pressing that to his advantage instead of returning to a series of petty crimes?'

'Those are interesting points that you make,' said Naish. 'However, it assumes that the information was something that he could profit from. The more we tease this out, the more I am convinced that the information he knew put others at risk and was not something that he could personally profit from.'

'Unless he decided to try and turn the information to his advantage and try his hand at blackmailing the person or persons at risk,' said Hancock.

'Again, that is possible, but then we return to Newton's point – why not focus on that instead of getting involved in petty crime?' said Naish.

'Perhaps because the blackmail was going to take some time to produce a financial return and he needed some cash to cover the short term,' suggested Newton.

'But as you just pointed out, he has got money in the building society, surely he would have used a little of that to cover the shortfall until the blackmail began to yield results,' said Naish.

'I think all these hypotheses are credible,' said Hancock, 'but on the balance of probability, I can't help but think that when Lynch was discharged from prison he was in a carefree frame of mind, and simply returned to his old habits in his familiar lodgings and returned to his old line of work. I don't think that he perceived any threat to himself whatsoever. From what I know of Lynch, he was not a man who liked confrontation at all. If he felt under threat then I think it would have manifested itself in his behaviour and people who knew him, like Mrs West, would have noticed it. Whether he acquired the information these men believed put them at risk inside prison or else in the short time since his release, I don't think he thought that knowledge put him at risk.'

'On reflection, I am happy to agree with that position,' said Naish. 'How about you Newton?'

'Yes, I think it is the most likely theory for the moment. Although some aspects of our discussion may also end up forming part of the background.'

'Right then, we agree. You see the benefit of talking these things out. I always feel that a rounder conclusion is reached as a result of cross-examination,' said Naish, lighting a cigarette with an air of satisfaction. 'Right, let's try and take this theory on a stage. I don't think Ted Lynch knew anything at all.'

'Go on,' said Hancock.

'Ted Lynch was no hard man,' began Naish. 'He would be intimidated if he was confronted by a couple of men in an alleyway. Men of the type we are dealing with here would only have to get him in a room and threaten him and I think that he would cough up everything they wanted to know almost immediately.'

'Suppose that the information he had was more valuable then we can imagine,' interjected Hancock.

'It may be that the information would put someone close to him in danger, his wife or a child,' added Newton.

'That may or may not be so,' continued Naish. 'The sort of terror that was inflicted on Ted Lynch was designed to break a man of iron will, to force him into revealing information that would lead to his own daughter being murdered, and that is my point. If this sort of torture would break a man desperate to resist it, then I don't see how a man as timid as Ted Lynch would have the tenacity to endure it, no matter how vital it was for him to maintain his secret.'

'We don't know that he did not eventually crack,' said Newton.

'I agree that we cannot prove that, but I cannot see it myself,' said Naish. 'I cannot believe that he would be able to stand up to the first stage. I mean, that is a horrifying prospect, being tied to a chair and systematically beaten for perhaps an hour or more. Blows to your head probably delivered in a slow deliberate manner, probably a period of questioning between each, so that the anticipation of the next blow alone is enough to make the average man crack. I imagine the quiet, measured interrogator appealing to Ted's better sense to tell them what he knew, then stepping back to let the silent hard man come forward once again to deliver the next one or two punches with clinical precision. But let us suppose that he did resist against all the odds. I have been giving that second stage of the interrogation some thought. If a man could still resist having some of his fingernails extracted with pliers and then, say, one or two of his fingers broken with a hammer – if you got that far, I mean if it were humanly possible to endure that sort of pain, then why would you suddenly crack because another few are broken, to me that does not make sense. If you were able to endure to that point, why give up then?'

'I agree,' said Newton, 'and it ties in with the surgeon's supposition that they gave up breaking his fingers because he probably fainted away from pain or the sheer trauma of the event.'

'That's my theory,' said Naish. 'He passed into unconsciousness and his persecutors, with all their experience of doing this sort of work, concluded that he did not know anything. At that point, one of them slid a knife between his ribs and pierced his heart to finish him off, as if he were a piece of meat. Otherwise, if they were as desperate to extract this information from Ted as their actions clearly suggest they were, then surely they would have thrown him back into his cell, waited for him to regain consciousness and begun a third stage of god knows what to try and make him speak.'

'I see what you say, and it makes total sense to me,' said Hancock. 'Then I suppose that, if the three of us are in agreement, we have a second working hypothesis. So, taking the two hypotheses together, am I right in saying that, on the balance of probability, Ted Lynch left Horfield Prison two weeks ago today; that he had either unwittingly acquired some information in prison or shortly after his release, and was unaware of the risks to which that information exposed him; or else he had no information at all, although someone clearly believed, albeit mistakenly, that he had such information. In either case, the fact is that those who tracked him down and tortured him were mistaken in their belief that he had such information, and this was attested to by the fact that he was unable to give them any information under torture, not because he resisted, but because he had nothing to tell.'

Both Naish and Newton nodded their assent.

'Then I will chalk that up on the blackboard,' said Hancock.

'Before we move on, I would like to talk through another aspect of the case,' said Naish, as Hancock wiped the chalk dust from his hands with a duster and resumed his seat. 'What was the purpose of hanging the body under the bridge once he was dead?'

'Well, it cannot have been to give the impression of suicide,' began Newton. 'Even a fool would know that the true cause of his death would be apparent as soon as the body was examined.'

'Even if they knew the true cause would be revealed, did it perhaps give them a brief interval in which to get clear of Bath?' suggested Hancock. 'They may have judged that by putting the body where it was and making it look like a suicide, together with the time it took for discovery, the summoning of the police, the subsequent recording of the scene and recovery of the body, that it would give them at least a couple of hours head start.'

'I think if that were the motive then it would have been more likely that they would have taken the body out of the city into woods or farmland, and buried it,' said Naish. 'These sorts of people prefer to carry out their work anonymously, if at all possible. Interrogate the victim, derive what they want to know, murder and then dispose in a discreet location so that, not only do they make a clear get away, but in all likelihood the body is never even discovered. No, this body was meant to be discovered, and not only discovered, but seen in the very public way in which it was placed.'

'We are back with the suggestion that it was placed as a warning or a threat to others associated with Lynch and this perceived risk to their activities?' asked Newton.

'If that is so, if there is a message in this hanging, then to whom is the warning or threat directed?' said Hancock.

'Well, this is my theory, and if we can all sign up to it, then it can be chalked up as our next working hypothesis,' said Naish. 'I think it is a warning to someone to stay away from their business, and the threat is that this is what will happen to you. They know the word will get around the criminal fraternity, not only in Bath, but for miles around. But if you know your adversary, then, surely being men of discretion as these men are, you seek out that adversary and you deal with him directly. I think that they have made an error of judgement here, because in sending out this blanket threat, for want of a better description, they have betrayed themselves. They have betrayed that they do not in fact know who they are looking for. They do not know who they are seeking or who their potential adversary might be. It also reinforces for me the theory that they got no information from Ted Lynch. He left them at a dead end. I think they are worried because they do not have an answer as to who is directing this and or why their business is at risk, whatever that business may be. There may be no who or why, but they cannot rest until they are certain. Why and what it is that they are afraid of coming to light is what we need to establish.'

'I can sign up to that. You see, that is why you are the Inspector,' said Hancock with a warm smile as he picked up the chalk and headed towards the blackboard.

'I agree as well,' said Newton. 'For me, the two points that follow on from that are – firstly, whatever that business is, it is clearly something of significance given the lengths they have gone to already, and secondly, are they actively looking for someone else in Bath now or have they changed tactics and are looking to cover their tracks for a while?'

'I agree that this unknown criminal activity is significant,' said Naish. 'As to your second point, I am not certain. I think they will at least be a little more circumspect in their activities for a while. Now then, as time is getting on, I think that you need to get over and conduct those enquiries at Horfield Prison tomorrow, Newton. I have got a list of things for Hancock and myself to work through. If you give Ted's suit jacket to Hancock, we can deal with that tomorrow while you are in Bristol. I know it is going to be a long day, but we need to press on before the weekend. So, let's aim to meet back here at six o'clock tomorrow evening. Agreed. Good. Hancock, I will see you here at eight in the morning, then.'

'All fine with me,' said Hancock. 'Just one last thing – do you think these men who murdered Lynch are the men whose nefarious activities are under threat, or are they acting for them?'

'That's exactly the question I have been asking myself,' said Naish, 'and, at the moment, I don't have an answer to it.'

'Well, I will chalk it up on the matters to consider list,' said Hancock, and having done so, took his leave along with Newton.

Naish sat back down at his desk and rolled himself a cigarette while he contemplated the blackboards before him.

The following morning, Naish was back at the station at seven o'clock. He stopped briefly in the foyer to speak with Newton who was setting off to catch his train to Bristol. Having asked the desk sergeant to rustle him up a mug of tea, he went on up to his office to plan out his day. He had finished making a list of the things that he wanted to cover and sat down in front of the blackboards. He was deep in thought when, at quarter to eight, Hancock knocked and entered.

'Trying to get this case straight in your mind?' asked Hancock.

'I was just playing around with the facts to try and make some sense of the motivations behind these people.'

'I know, it's interminable. I was thinking about it last night, but I let it go in the end. I think we need more facts to emerge and then hopefully it will begin to fall in to place.'

'That's very keen of you, thinking over work out of hours,' said Naish with a smile.

'Ah well, there you are then. I often think over work matters when I am up on my allotment, you see. Get it all out of my head during a bit of manual labour, then I get home with a clear mind. Anyway, I have brought you a mug of tea, although I see you have already had one.'

'Thanks,' said Naish, taking the mug and then lighting a cigarette. 'Now, this is what we are going to get done today. First job is to call into the tailors and close off that issue of the suit. Then out to Larkhall – I want to visit the church and perhaps look in at Belgrave Road. Then I think we will go across town to Broadway Parade and have a chat with the picture framer and have a look around his business. Once we have done that, we can see how the time is going on and then decide if there is anything else we can tick off before Newton gets back.'

'If we split the jobs between us, we could cover more ground in less time,' suggested Hancock.

'I know we could, but I want us to work together because we can use the rest of the time to talk through some of the grey areas in this case and perhaps find an opening.'

'That's fine with me,' said Hancock. 'I will go downstairs and arrange for a car to run us around.'

'Tell him to be out the front at ten o'clock,' said Naish.

'Ten o'clock? That is not exactly setting the pace.'

'Ten o'clock is when we are leaving to go to Larkhall. The first job is to walk around to that tailors in Milsom Street.'

'Walking,' said Hancock, with an air of mock surprise.

'No need to be impertinent, Sergeant. There is something else I want to do on the way. So, if you go and get your coat, I will see you in the foyer at half past eight.'

At half past eight, Naish and Hancock stepped out of the front entrance of the police station into the cold greyness of the October morning.

'Chilly,' said Hancock.

'I know, so I thought we could go and get a hot drink before we start.'

'Is the station tea not good enough for you, then?'

'It is, but I want to have some entertainment as well. Come with me.'

Naish turned right out of the front entrance and immediately turned right again through a high archway into a courtyard that was at the side of the station. They went through the courtyard to the rear entrance of the Guildhall Market. On the far side of the market was a coffee bar with a few stools up against a counter. They each took a stool and Naish ordered two coffees. Naish sat with his back against the counter and looked intently across the market.

'Good, I just caught his eye,' said Naish with satisfaction.

'Whose eye?' asked Hancock.

'Our friend over there, opposite. Barncy Jones, the trader in silverware and curios. I thought that I would gently remind him that we are taking an interest in his activities just in case any information comes his way.'

'Just through the coincidence of us taking a coffee break here, no thought of intimidation then,' said Hancock as he sipped his coffee.'

'None at all, but I think he may well reflect that he would be better keeping us informed on this one rather than us taking a regular interest in his work, don't you think? Oh look, he is coming over.'

'Good morning Mr Naish. Come round for a decent cup of coffee, have you?'

'Well, it was just that I fancied a change of scene, Barney. I was saying to Sergeant Hancock here that we should try and find somewhere regular where could take our morning coffee rather than be stuck in the station all the time. We were thinking that this might be the place, being so close to the station as it is, and the Superintendent always on to us to engage with the local community. But then we would be getting under people's feet all the time, wouldn't we and, as Sergeant Hancock said to me, with the station being so close, anyone who has anything to say would just pop in and talk to us wouldn't they?'

'It does get very noisy in here, Mr Naish, and there are probably far more classy places for a coffee in town and, as you say, the station is so close at hand for us traders. Very reassuring, I always say.'

'Thank you, Barney,' said Naish, finishing his coffee. 'I am glad we understand each other. Come on, Sergeant, let's go and see if we can find an alternative coffee venue – for now, anyway.'

They walked out of the market through the entrance on to the High Street and headed towards Milsom Street.

'I think that that was useful,' said Naish, with a smile. 'Now, back to the point of us being together. We need to think through the point that you raised last night. Are the men who murdered Ted the same men whose activities are perceived as being somehow threatened by something we assume Ted knew – or they supposed he knew – or are they a group of heavies brought in to carry out some sort of enforcement or retribution on their behalf?'

'The fundamental issue, as I see it, is what line of business are those under threat actually in. If it were robbery with violence, bank jobs and possibly blackmail, then probably they are one and the same men. If, however, it is a softer crime – fraud, deception or confidence work – then I would suggest that they were hired in to bring a set of skills that the business does not possess.'

'I agree with that,' said Naish.

'Of course, the risk is that you have to disseminate information about yourselves and your association with crime to a third party. That may not matter, of course, if you are already known within the criminal fraternity.'

'However, you do not have to reveal your secret or the nature of your business,' said Naish. 'The sort of thugs we are probably dealing with here just take on the task given them and don't ask too many questions why.'

'Yet in this situation, where questions need to be put during the interrogation, we have to assume that the thugs were taken into their employer's confidence to some extent. Firstly, to know what questions to ask and, secondly, to know whether the answers given were correct.'

'The trust needs to be reciprocal to some extent,' said Naish. 'The thugs also need to know they can trust their employers, so we can assume that they, or someone acting to introduce them to the thugs, was known to be trustworthy within the criminal world. There is a secondary advantage for the business in using an intermediary which is that it keeps the businessmen two steps removed from the thugs.'

Chapter 4

'Well, we can come back to this discussion later on,' said Naish. 'This, I believe, is the tailors that Newton identified.'

At the top end of Milsom Street was an alleyway between two shops that led through to a courtyard at the rear. Halfway along the alleyway was a sign directing potential customers to a stairway that led up to the tailors' premises. *Gosling and Sons*, proclaimed the sign in elegant hand-painted letters, *Gentlemen's Bespoke Tailors*. A bell rang as Naish opened the door at the head of the stairs. As no one appeared in response to the bell, Naish and Hancock wandered on in. It was the premises of a classic gentlemen's tailors, spread across the first floor of the shop below.

'Good morning, gentlemen. I am sorry to keep you waiting, but I was in the middle of a cut and I had to finish it off,' said an elderly gentleman with half-moon spectacles, pointing back towards a bench covered in chalk-marked cloth.

'I am Inspector Naish of the Bath police and I was wondering if you might be able to assist me in my enquiries.'

'Of course, of course. If there is anything that I can do to assist the police – what is it in connection with may I ask?'

'This suit jacket,' said Naish, reaching out for the garment that Hancock had taken from a bag. 'I believe that it was made by you and I am anxious to trace the gentleman who purchased it.'

'Oh dear, oh dear,' said the tailor, clearly distressed, as he took the jacket and examined the label on the inside breast pocket.

'There is no need for you to be anxious regarding any of your clients' said Naish, sensing the cause of the tailor's distress. 'I believe that the garment has been bought second-hand or third- hand after your client had disposed of it. Are you able to identify it?'

'I think so, but looking at the cloth it would have been made some years ago. If you will excuse me for a moment I will go and consult my records.'

After ten minutes the tailor reappeared with a ledger in his hand.

'I have traced the jacket and it was made up five years ago for a Mr Cowley, a regular customer of mine.'

'Can you give me his address, please,' asked Naish.

'The address is Tyning House, Belgrave Road, Larkhall.'

'Thank you. Do you think that you could write that down for me,' said Naish, flashing a look of disapproval at Hancock who had whistled under his breath. 'Thank you very much, Mr Gosling. You have been most helpful, and please rest assured that I shall treat the information with the utmost discretion.'

'Sorry about that,' said Hancock, as they walked back out on to Milsom Street. 'The minute he said the name Cowley, something rang a bell, and it was as he said the address, I remembered meeting Mr Cowley yesterday when I was cross-referencing the recovered items with their owners. I just couldn't help the whistle.'

'You would make a poor poker player, you would,' said Naish, ruefully. 'Anyway, it looks as if we are going to be paying a return visit to Mr Cowley and we may as well do it while we are out at St Saviours.'

'There is the car pulling up over there,' said Hancock, and they both climbed inside for the journey out to Larkhall.

'Well, this is the first connection that we have had in this crime,' said Naish, lighting a cigarette. 'That is, supposing that Ted bought it second-hand. If he was the third or even later owner, then we may just be left with a coincidence.'

The car pulled up at Tyning House and Naish followed Hancock up the pathway to the front door.

'Good morning once again,' said Hancock, as the housekeeper opened the door. 'I am sorry to have to trouble you once more – is Mr Cowley at home?'

'No, I am afraid that he has gone into town on business,' replied the housekeeper, dryly.

'Then it may be that you can assist me and my colleague here. May we step inside for a moment?'

The housekeeper gestured for them to come in and directed them into the hallway. Realising that this was as hospitable as the woman was going to be, Hancock continued.

'Do you recognise this garment?' he asked, taking the jacket from the bag. 'Please take it and have a close look.'

'Yes, I recognise it,' she replied, coldly. 'It is part of a suit that Mr Cowley had no longer any use for and asked me to dispose of for him.'

'When you say dispose of, did he give it to you to sell or to give away?' asked Hancock.

'He made no condition as to the manner of its disposal,' she said, becoming icier by the minute. 'I am not so situated that I need to supplement my income by the sale of second-hand clothing. I gave the suit to Orton, the gardener, who said it might be of use to him.'

'Have you ever heard of a man called Edward or Ted Lynch?' asked Naish, cutting in.

'No, never,' she said cutting him dead and immediately returning her attention, reluctant as it was, to Hancock, who she clearly assumed to be the superior officer.

'Is the gardener in today?' asked Hancock, replacing the jacket in the bag.

'He is, but you will need to go back out of the front door and round by the side gate.'

'Thank you,' said Hancock, feeling that the hospitality had gone as far as it was going to go. 'You have been most helpful.'

They found the gardener sitting by the side of a potting shed smoking his pipe. He started when he realised that he had company.

'No need to panic, Mr Orton,' said Hancock with a smile, 'it's not the housekeeper.'

The gardener clearly understood the nature of the comment as his expression changed from one of guilt, to relief and then to questioning.

'Nothing to worry about. We are police officers making a few enquiries and we were wondering if you may be able to assist us. The housekeeper said we might find you here. Do you recognise this jacket, by any chance?'

The gardener took it and it was clear to Naish that he recognised it immediately, despite making a pretence of continuing to examine it further than was necessary. His manner became uncomfortable and he glanced awkwardly between the two officers.

'We know that the housekeeper gave you the suit,' cut in Naish, sensing that it was better to cut off any chance of the man digging himself a hole by lying, as it would only make matters more complicated.

'Then why did you ask me, then?' said the gardener, becoming a little aggressive.

'Because we wanted to know if you were going to play straight with us and cut to the truth,' said Naish, equally combatively. 'Don't play games with me – you recognised the jacket straight away, so don't try and cover it up. How much did Ted Lynch give you for the suit then?'

The gardener almost did a double take at Naish, with a look of surprise.

'Right then,' said Naish striking a conciliatory tone. 'Why don't the three of us sit down on that bench over there and have a smoke while we get to the bottom of this.'

'I have done nothing wrong I promise you, gentlemen.'

'I am prepared to believe that,' said Naish, 'subject to you providing me with information that can support your claim. I take it that you are worried that Ted Lynch has put you in a difficult position.'

'I am not certain of that, but I think he has,' said the gardener. 'I know Ted from the Golden Fleece. We happened to be chatting in there on the Saturday lunchtime just after he came back to town, and he was going on about the state of his suit. By a complete coincidence, on that Wednesday, the housekeeper had offered me Mr Cowley's old suit together with some bits and pieces that I kept for myself. The suit was too big for me and, being a nice bit of cloth and well cut, I thought I could make a few shillings selling it on. So I wrapped it up and put it in this shed where it would be nice and dry.'

'Why didn't you take it home?' asked Naish.

'Because my wife would have made me take it to be altered to keep for myself and that would be my few shillings spending money up the spout,' he said sheepishly. 'Anyway, I told Ted about the suit and he said he would pop out with me that afternoon, and if he liked it, he would give me a fair price for it. So, after a couple of pints, we got the bus out here. I knew that Mr Cowley was out for the day and so I brought Ted round here to the shed. He tried on the suit, liked it and gave me a fair price for it.'

'What happened next?' said Naish.

'He began asking me about the garden and complimenting me on how good it looked, even though it was autumn.'

'So, you showed him around the gardens, I suppose?' said Naish, ruefully.

'I did, fool that I am.'

'And he asked you about the household, asked about general stuff – is he a good employer? what about his wife? oh, he lives alone, does he? oh, just a by-the-day housekeeper to help? That sort of thing, and without realising it, you have given Ted Lynch, the burglar, all the information he needs.'

'I know, I know,' said the gardener, desperately.

'Whatever possessed you to do it? I mean, you know the sort of reputation Ted had.'

'I know. He took me in, the swine, and I fell for it, thinking that he was just being friendly.'

'So, you turn up here for work on Monday morning and find the place has been burgled. Knowing that it is too much of a coincidence, you decide to keep quiet about the matter, fearing that you will get yourself sacked and possibly arrested by the police for complicity in the crime. Well, you will need to make an appointment with Sergeant Hancock here to come along to the station next week and make a full statement. If what you are telling us is the truth, we might be able to keep you from any charges related to the crime but, unfortunately, your lack of judgement in inviting Ted here will come to your employer's attention. I cannot avoid that, so you might want to think about giving notice and obtaining a reference before Mr

Cowley acts, but that is up to you. Anyway, give your details to the sergeant, as I say, and we will be in touch.'

'Did you not see him again in the Golden Fleece, then?' asked Hancock.

'No, I was away for a week. We went down to the wife's sisters at Weymouth, so I didn't see him again. Anyway, he would only deny it, wouldn't he, and if I had made any trouble, he knew that I would drop myself in it anyway, so I had to lump it. Anyhow, when I got back home, I avoided the Fleece for a while, but then on the Thursday after I got back, I saw that he had been found dead. So I kept mum and carried on with my old routine.'

'What was being said about him at the Golden Fleece, then?' asked Naish.

'Not a thing. I went back in on the Friday night, but everyone was quiet about it. He was never mentioned and so I never asked. Good riddance, I thought, if you really want to know.'

'What a fool,' said Hancock, as they made their way out on to the pavement and got back into the waiting car.

'I know, but that is Ted Lynch all over, charming and beguiling all in one. He may have cultivated the image of lovable rogue, but underneath it all, he was a selfish and calculating thief. That's the nature of the beast. Anyway, it's good news for us. We have closed off the matter of the suit and as a bonus we have the answer as to why, with all of Bath to choose from, Ted picked this house for his first job. Very neat, I like that. Right, here is the church.'

The church was open and so Naish led the way in through the front doors. Inside, there was an unexpected amount of activity. Two ladies were cleaning the pews while several others, in ones and twos, were gathered around pedestals arranging flowers in preparation for the services on Sunday.

Naish asked one of the ladies where he might find the vicar and was directed to a doorway that led to the vestry. He knocked at the door as he entered and found the vicar talking with two more ladies about altar linen. The vicar was a man in his late thirties and six feet in height.

'Well, that rules out any possibility of our clerical friend being the vicar,' said Hancock, in a whisper.

Seeing the ladies' eyes wandering towards the door, the vicar turned and, seeing the two men, walked over with a welcoming smile.

'Can I help you, gentlemen?'

'I am Inspector Naish of the Bath police and I am making enquiries into the recent theft of the weekly collection.'

'I am pleased to meet you, Inspector. I had met with your Sergeant Dodd who took the details of this most regrettable matter.'

'Yes, Sergeant Dodd is progressing the investigation, but I have an interest in the case because it potentially crosses over into another case that I am looking in to. If I might impose on you, I would like to ask you a few additional questions.'

'Of course, Inspector,' he said, and seeing that the two ladies were leaving, he closed the door after them.

'What amount is the average collection that you anticipate by the end of the three Sunday services?'

'I would say it would be between seven and eight pounds. If I was to refer to the ledger, I could calculate an exact average over the past weeks, if you wish?'

'No, your estimation will be fine, thank you,' said Naish, looking at Hancock for a response.

'That figure tallies with my calculation, Inspector.'

'We have recovered an amount of money which is all in coins and in a cash bag identical to the one that your verger described to Sergeant Dodd. We have made some rough calculations of the known expenditure of the man we suspect of the theft, and taking that total from the estimation that you have provided, I am certain that the money that we have recovered is the residue of the stolen collection. The monies in our possession total two pounds eighteen shillings and eight pence, so, unfortunately, a considerable amount has been spent by the culprit.'

'That is very distressing,' said the vicar, 'but I am glad that you have apprehended the culprit and recovered some of the money given for God's work. I will explain the situation to my archdeacon. I assume that you will be retaining the monies as part of your investigations?'

'I will have to for the time being, I am afraid, as they form part of our evidence. Do you have any assistant clergy in the parish?' asked Naish.

'I usually have a curate assisting me, but the last one left two months ago to take up his own living as the vicar of Bathampton and his replacement is not due to take up his duties here until the end of the month. I am fortunate to have two lay readers to assist me, but other than that, I am here alone.'

'Can you describe the two lay readers to me, please?'

'I can do better than that, Inspector, I have a photograph of them over here on the wall, taken back in the summer to mark the anniversary of the church's dedication.'

Naish and Hancock peered at the photograph and exchanged despondent glances. The age and build of the two men who flanked the vicar and his curate in the photograph were clearly not capable of being mistaken for the clerical gentleman who they were seeking. Naish thanked the vicar for his assistance and having assured him that Sergeant Dodd would keep him abreast of developments, he and Hancock made their way back out to the car.

'Well, that's another loose end tied up,' said Hancock.

'I know, but tying up loose ends is not going to solve this case for us. We need some firm leads. Right then, what next?'

'How about something to eat?' said Hancock, optimistically?

'How about we get across to Broadway Parade first, and then get something to eat in a pub. Then we should be ready to visit the picture framers about two o'clock?'

Naish and Hancock sat in the window of the Old Jupiter pub, each with a pint of beer and a cheese roll. Across the road from them was the picture framer's premises.

'Unassuming sort of place,' said Hancock.

'These places always are. All the ones at the higher end of the market are in the shops in town. However, looking at Dodd's notes, it is washing its face. I think we go in with an open mind and get a feel for it. Looking at the front door, I can see what attracted Ted to it – nothing too substantial, from what I can see from here, and the nearest street light some way away. I think we will have a wander around the block and have a look at the back as we go past, then go and introduce ourselves.'

A narrow road passed behind the shops, which each had a small yard at the rear with a gate that opened on to it. Naish and Hancock stopped at the rear of the picture framer's shop and casually surveyed the scene, while affecting a discussion as they respectively rolled a cigarette and lit a pipe.

'That rear door looks very substantial,' said Naish. 'I can see why Ted took the front door.'

'Nothing much else to see,' said Hancock. 'General accumulations of waste from the business. Still, we can have a closer look once we have introduced ourselves, can't we.'

They carried on until the service road brought them back out on to the other end of Broadway Parade and then they walked back along to the shop. Naish flicked his dog-end into a drain while Hancock knocked out his pipe on his heel, and they went inside.

In the window was a small collection of framed pictures for sale. The walls at the front end of the shop were covered by a mixture of samples of picture frames consisting of right-angled corners, formed of the various styles of wood available, and examples of mounts and surrounds. Towards the rear of the shop was a glass-fronted counter containing artist's materials for sale, and on the top of the counter sat a till of antique design. Beyond that, at the rear of the shop, was a workbench where the frames were made up.

The proprietor, a thin grey man in his mid to late sixties, was leant over the bench measuring up as the shop bell rang and he came forward to the counter.

'Good afternoon, gentlemen, may I be of assistance?'

'I am Inspector Naish of the Bath police,' said Naish, presenting his identity card. 'I am making enquiries related to a theft from your premises and I was hoping to have a look around and ask you some questions, if that would be in order?'

'I understood that Sergeant Dodd was investigating the burglary. It is him that I have been dealing with. I have already given him a statement and, as you can see, I am extremely busy.'

'I have read your statement, Mr Emery, and very informative it was,' said Naish, adopting an ingratiating rather than combative tone, which the proprietor's attitude had initially roused in him. 'If you are busy, I am happy to take a look around on my own so that you can get on. I doubt I shall get lost.'

'If you really must,' Emery continued, 'the stairs to the upper floors are over there, at the rear of the workshop.'

Naish and Hancock climbed the narrow stairs up to the first-floor landing. There was a room to the rear and a room to the front. Both rooms were clearly used as stockrooms. In the rear room there were racks filled with lengths of all the timber samples in the shop and shelves full of the various mounts and surrounds laid out flat. In the front room were vertical partitions separating panes of glass and another bench with tools for glass cutting. On one wall were two sets of shelves that were filled with stock items of artist materials. Having looked around and found nothing of interest, they made their way up to the second floor. The second floor was one large open-plan area and was completely empty. Evidently the walls had been recently painted, because the room smelt of emulsion paint and on the floor was a new covering of linoleum that went up to the skirting boards.

'Odd,' said Naish.

'What is?' said Hancock.

'The walls have been painted and a new floor covering has been put down, yet the skirting boards and the ceiling have not been painted. If you were decorating a room, surely you would finish all the painting before you put down a new floor covering?'

'I agree. Even if you were going to do the ceiling later, you could cover up the lino, but to not do the skirting is, as you say, very odd.'

They made their way back down to the workshop. Emery was dealing with a client and so, without waiting to ask, they opened up the back door and made their way out into the yard at the rear.

'You were right about this rear door,' said Hancock. 'Very sturdy – mortice lock and two dead bolts. That's not going to give way easily.'

'Someone has been having a fire,' said Naish, surveying the contents of a large metal dustbin with holes punched in the sides to form a brazier.

'It would fit in with the decorators burning up their rubbish.'

'There is a lot of timber in here,' said Naish, who was stirring through the ash and debris at the bottom of the bin.

'Offcuts from the picture frames?' offered Hancock.

'I don't think they are. They are half-inch by half-inch planed timber. All the picture framing timber is gilt or painted. Might be something from a bigger frame.'

'Is that an offcut of the lino there in the bottom,' said Hancock, reaching into the bin and retrieving a piece about five inches by an inch. 'No, it's not lino, but it is similar to lino, some sort of fabric with a gloss finish to one side.'

'Anyway, let's get back and have a chat with the genial Mr Emery,' said Naish.

'I understand that you reported to Sergeant Dodd that two items had been stolen from your shop in the recent burglary, a small amount of cash from the till and a selection of tools. I assume, from the till here on the counter and your work bench over there?'

'Yes, that is correct,' said the proprietor, in a less irritable tone. 'Have you made any progress in recovering them? The loss of the tools is a great inconvenience to my work.'

'We think we have recovered both items, Mr Emery. I will have someone bring around the tools we have in our possession for you to identify. If they are yours, then they will be returned as soon as they are no longer needed for evidential purposes. The cash has, in all probability, been recovered, but has been subsumed into a larger pot of coins that the thief has accumulated, so it is difficult to discern at the moment whose money is whose. Are you certain that these are the only items that you are missing? Have you checked your premises thoroughly?'

'Yes, most thoroughly. I told Sergeant Dodd so when he asked me the same question.'

'It is odd, but among the items found at the thief's residence were some sketchbooks and some canvases. It would appear that, of all the premises that were burgled by this thief over the period of time in question, yours is the most likely to be the source of such items. They could, of course, be the property of an amateur artist, but none of the other properties has reported them as having been stolen. So, unless there has been an additional theft that has not been reported to the police, I am left with the notion that they must have come from here.'

'If this is the case, Inspector, then I will go and recheck my stockroom upstairs and see if I have made a careless mistake.'

Emery disappeared upstairs and Naish stepped back out into the rear yard for a smoke.

'I am relieved to say, Inspector, that my stock is complete, and no items are missing. So, the items did not come from my shop.'

'Then I will need to explore the possibility of an unreported crime,' said Naish, checking Hancock with a glance. 'Well, thank you for your time, Mr Emery. As I promised, I will send a man round with the tools for you to hopefully identify.'

They made their way out of the shop and across the road to where the car was waiting for them.

'The sketchbooks never came from stock,' said Hancock, as they got in the car. 'The ones we recovered had brown cloth covers – all the sketchbooks in his stock were blue card covers.'

'I know that, and it was interesting that he was keen to reiterate that they could not be from his shop.'

'Do you think he knew the sketchbooks had been used?'

'If they were taken from that shop then they must have already been used, because, even if Ted Lynch had become a competent artist in the prison art group, he didn't have time to do that amount of drawing in the time since his release, did he? Also, if someone asked you to go and check stock items, what would be your first response?'

'To ask what items I was being asked to account for, to save time. What size sketchbooks? A5, A4, or A3, perhaps even the rough size of the canvases?'

'Exactly, and Mr Emery did not do so. Now I know the amount of stock he holds is not great, but I still think that it is a question I would have asked with two men waiting for an answer downstairs.'

'So, what do we infer?'

'We infer that we have no proof to question Mr Emery's story, but there is something odd in his manner. He is uneasy about something. He tried to front it out with that show of irritation when we first went in, but I am left with a sense that he is uneasy. For now, we can do no more than leave it there.'

'And the upstairs room that has been half-decorated, we didn't question him about that.'

'I know, but we will, at some point, go back to that. I sensed we have gone as far as we need with today's visit. Now then, I think it is time to rustle up a pot of tea. If you sort that out, we can spend the next hour recording what we have learnt on the blackboards, by which time Newton should be back from Bristol.'

As Hancock was pouring the tea, there was a knock at the office door and the police artist came in carrying a folder.

'If you are free, Inspector Naish, I have the drawing that I have created from the description given by the jeweller in Northumberland Place.'

'Excellent, come on in and let us have a look,' said Naish.

'Well, he is not anyone I recognise' said Hancock. 'How about you?'

'No. He is not anyone that I can ever recall coming across over the years.'

'I have done a second sketch without the glasses, in case they were a disguise,' said the artist. 'I know how effective glasses can be in disguising the features.'

'Good work,' said Naish, 'but I still don't recall the man. The jeweller is confident that this is our cleric?'

'Oh yes, Inspector, he was most complimentary about the likeness. I finished it a couple of hours ago and, as you were unavailable, the desk sergeant suggested that I take it along to Oak Street and show it to a Mrs West who apparently may have seen the man. I am pleased to report that she identified this as the man who called at her premises on the Monday evening.'

'Excellent,' said Naish, with a smile. 'If you ever give up being an artist, you might consider becoming a detective. I will arrange for someone to take formal statements from the jeweller and Mrs West to record their positive identifications of this man. If you would be good enough to get those sketches to the printer, I would like half a dozen copies made in colour, I think. When can they be ready?'

'If I get around there now, Inspector, I would hope to have them back by Monday evening.'

'That will be fine. Have them sent up as soon as you have collected them.'

The artist collected up the sketches and replaced them in the folder, and, as he made his way out, he stepped to one side to let Newton enter.

'The wanderer returns, and right on time, I believe,' said Naish, as the abbey clock chimed six.

Chapter 5

'So how was your day in prison?' asked Naish.

'Very useful, I think,' said Newton, sitting down at the desk. 'The governor passed me on to the chief warder, who gave me all the assistance that I needed to look through the various logs that are kept, and, I have to say, meticulously so. First of all, I looked through the records to see who Lynch had shared a cell with. Then I went through the individual files of each of those men. Lynch had three cellmates during his six months inside, and it didn't take me long to see that the first one was the most interesting. On his arrival, Lynch was placed in a cell with a man named Thomas Edwards, and they remained together for three months until Edwards was released at the end of his sentence. They were a similar age and got on amicably according to the chief warder. According to his file, Edwards was a small-time confidence trickster – small scale fraud and deception stuff, nothing elaborate in nature or involving large sums of money. That was until his last offence, the one that got him put away for five years.'

'Five years,' exclaimed Naish. 'That's a long stretch for a petty fraudster. What did he do?'

'He targeted two elderly spinsters who lived together and deceived them into making a donation of two hundred pounds to a mission that provided food and shelter for orphaned children in the north of England. The charity, of course, did not exist, and the matter only came to light when the ladies' bank manager became suspicious of such a large transaction on their respective accounts. Anyway, the significant fact was that, when the police began to look into the matter, the ladies reported that the man who claimed to represent this charity was bound to be respectable because he was a clergyman. Investigations were made and Edwards was found to be the bogus clergyman.'

'Brilliant,' said Naish. 'Do you have a description of this Edwards?'

'Better than that,' said Newton. 'There was a copy of the photograph taken at his prison induction on the file. I have it here.'

'Got you,' said Naish, with satisfaction. 'The artist impression is on its way to the printers at the moment, but that is, without doubt, our man. Take a look, Hancock.'

'I agree, that's him,' said Hancock. 'So, is he a Bathonian then?'

'No, apparently not. He was from Gloucester, born and bred, and, apart from his times inside, he never left the city.'

'Gloucester's answer to Ted Lynch, by the sound of it then,' said Hancock.

'What brought him here then, I wonder,' said Naish, rhetorically.

'I don't know the answer to that,' said Newton, 'but, out of the blue, he came here immediately or, very soon, after his release from Horfield, and took up lodgings in a furnished room at the Rose and Laurel in Lymore Road out at Twerton.'

'How do you know that?' asked Naish.

'Because in the 'post out' records there was an entry for a letter sent from Lynch to Edwards at that address, three days after his release.'

'So, do we simply assume that Edwards decided that things had got too hot for him in Gloucester and, having heard from Lynch that Bath was a pleasant enough place to go to earth in, he relocated here. Or had he and Lynch hatched some scheme that they could work on together once Lynch was released?' said Naish.

'Well, according to the chief warder, the rumour on the wing was that Edwards was looking to relocate away from Gloucester. The publicity surrounding his last case had given him a notoriety that would make him too much of a focus of attention with the local police for him to return to the quiet anonymity that he had previously enjoyed, and under which the petty crook likes to conduct his business. So, I would say definitely yes to your first theory. As to the second, we can only suppose that such a plan might have been agreed between them. If we had the letters, then we might know a little more.'

'I don't think the letters would be enlightening, even if we found them. Men like Ted Lynch don't put their plans and schemes down in writing. Anyway, whether it was planned or a coincidence, we know at least that they were associating together right up until Ted's last hours.'

'Shall I chalk up a visit to Edwards's lodgings on the list of to dos?' asked Hancock.

'Yes, we need to get out there first thing Monday. You and Newton can do it as soon as you are on duty, then come up and brief me,' said Naish. 'So, I assume that you are both off now for a weekend of domestic bliss? Well, don't let me stop you, it is getting late. Give your good ladies my apologies for keeping you, but I think it has been worth it. We have made some progress today.'

Naish stayed sat as his desk for another hour after Hancock and Newton had taken their leave, making notes and re-reading statements. Finally, he pulled his notebook out of his inside jacket pocket and began to make a list of things that he planned to get done in the morning. Weekends held no appeal for Naish, and, having finished his jottings, he closed up his office and made his way over to The Volunteer Rifleman for his evening meal and a couple of pints.

The alarm clock woke Naish at six o' clock on Saturday morning and, having washed and dressed, he went into the kitchen. He put the expresso maker on the hob, and while he was waiting for it to boil, he rolled and lit himself his first cigarette of the day. He then poured out the contents of the pot into a cup and sat at the kitchen table, rolling himself another three cigarettes that he put in his tobacco tin. Having finished his coffee, he pulled on his overcoat and, closing his flat door behind him, he made his way down the broad Georgian staircase and into the street outside. He walked around the curving pavement of the Circus and turned down Gay Street and then across town to the station at Orange Grove.

As he came opposite the Guildhall, he smiled to himself and, instead of walking on around to the front entrance of the police station as had been his plan, he went into the Guildhall Market. It was just a quarter past seven and Naish knew that, although most of the stalls would not yet be open, the café in the market would be. His purpose was twofold: firstly, despite his usually finding tobacco and expresso a sufficient breakfast, this morning he had a yearning for a bacon roll; secondly, he thought it would do no harm to remind Barney Jones of their conversation yesterday morning. Although it would be too early for Barney, he knew that word would get back to Barney via the grapevine – a far more effective method of making the man uneasy, thought Naish. He bought two bacon rolls, but not wanting to over egg the pudding by eating in the market, he had them wrapped to take away.

'Good morning, Sergeant,' said Naish, with a smile. 'You are due off at eight, aren't you. Had a busy night?'

'I am, Inspector, and it was, I am afraid. What brings you in here this chilly morning?'

'No rest for the wicked about sums it up, Sergeant. Here, cheer yourself up with a bacon roll.'

'Why thank you, Inspector, that's very good of you.'

'No problem, Sergeant. Enjoy your day off,' said Naish, and made his way up to his office.

Having finished his bacon roll and lit one of the cigarettes from his tin, he telephoned down to the general office and asked for a constable with a car to be ready at the front door at eight o'clock. Naish then spent some time sketching out a cross section of the picture framer's building on one of the blackboards and then sat making some notes as he contemplated it. As the abbey clock chimed eight, Naish gathered up the picture framer's tools and made his way down to the waiting car.

'Right then, Constable. First stop – the Rose and Laurel, Lymore Road, Twerton.'

Naish went around to the rear of the pub and found the entrance door to the private quarters above. Having pushed the electric bell for about fifteen seconds, he stood back to see what reaction he might get. After a few moments, the door was opened by a portly lady. It was clear from her housecoat that she had not been roused from sleep, but it was also clear from her manner that she had jobs to be doing.

'Not today, thank you,' she snapped.

'I am a police officer, madam,' said Naish, feeling that he should perhaps consider a change of career if his demeanour was so suited to door to door sales work.

'Oh yes,' she replied. Her manner did not thaw, but her tone indicated a reluctant engagement.

'I am trying to ascertain the whereabouts of an individual who I think may be able to help with some enquiries that I am making.'

'Well if you come along at opening time, my bar parlour is usually full of the sort of men who I am sure would interest you in any number of enquiries,' she said, with the hint of a smile. 'Come on in and go through to the kitchen if you want.'

'Thank you,' said Naish, and made his way inside. 'I understand that you let rooms?'

'That is correct. I have three spare rooms that I let out on a regular basis.'

'Would one of them be let to a Thomas Edwards, by any chance?'

'Yes, I have a lodger by that name.'

'He has been with you about three months, I believe?' said Naish.

'Yes, he has, actually. He has been a good lodger, regular with the rent and a good customer in the bar, if you know what I mean – he likes his cider.'

'Is he in now?'

'No, he is not. I have not seen him since about two o'clock on Wednesday. He is usually very regular in his habits, ever since he arrived. Out every morning about nine, except weekends of course, then back about four o'clock. He would have his meal in his room, then he would be down in the bar from six o'clock right through to closing time. Then on Monday, after his evening meal, he went out about seven o'clock without coming down to the bar. I know that he got back about half past ten, because, by a coincidence, I was going along to the cellar and came across him as he came in at the back door.'

'Was he all right?' asked Naish.

'He was all right physically, as you might say, but he was not his usual, happy-go-lucky self. In fact, he looked as if he had seen a ghost, or something that had unsettled him. I asked him if he was going to step along to the bar for a tot of brandy, or something that might calm him a bit, but he said he would be going on up.'

'Did he resume his old routine on the Tuesday?' asked Naish.

'No, not at all. He stayed in his room all day. I knocked his door about ten o' clock, being worried that he might be unwell, but he assured me through the door that he was fine and was resting. I took his meal up at six and he took it in, and I know he finished it all off because he brought the tray down with the plate wiped clean. He then went on into the bar as usual, but he was hitting the cider very hard. As I told you, he liked a good drink every evening, but he was what I always call a happy drinker. Drink raised his spirits and he was always good company in the bar parlour. Yet that Tuesday he was just drinking for drinking's sake. He sat alone in the corner of the bar and got through twice his usual number of pints.'

'Although he sat alone, did anyone come in and join him? Were there any strange faces in the bar that night?'

'No, it was just a normal Tuesday trade for me. Everything just as normal except for Mr Edwards behaving strange. A couple of the regulars who had taken a shine to him went over to ask after him, but he was not in the mood, so they left him to his own devices.'

'So, did he go up to his room at closing time?'

'Yes, he did, a little unsteadily. I watched him up the stairs and by the time I had locked up, his light was out, and I went off to bed myself.'

'So, what happened Wednesday? Did you see him at all?'

'I did not trouble him with breakfast, which I usually serve at eight o' clock, thinking he would be lying in late. He eventually came down at half past one in the afternoon. I was cutting some sandwiches in the kitchen and he came in looking a little sheepish. I offered him something to eat in lieu of his breakfast, but he said no thank you, he was not feeling hungry and was stepping out for some fresh air. I told him what I was cooking for his meal that evening and he went off out.'

'Was he carrying anything, a case or a bag, that might suggest that he was going away for a few days?'

'No, he just went out with his overcoat on as he did every day.'

'What response did he make when you told him what you were cooking for his dinner?'

'He said "Oh", in a vague manner. I didn't read anything into it, as he was looking very green about the gills. He crossed the road outside and walked off down Lansdown View. That was the last I saw of him.'

'Well, thank you, Mrs, ah … '

'Wilson, Mrs Wilson.'

'Well, thank you, Mrs Wilson. You have been most informative. Would it be possible for me to have a look at Edwards's room? I am happy to do it on my own. I appreciate I am keeping you from your chores.'

'No, not at all Officer … I am sorry, I didn't catch your name either.'

'Naish, I am Inspector Naish.'

'I do have a few things to get done before opening time and, being a widow, I have very little help, although my cellar man will be here in a while. But I am not too busy to give you any assistance you need. He is not dangerous, is he?'

'I have nothing to cause me to believe that he may be,' said Naish, 'but I will be questioning him formally when I eventually track him down.'

Mrs Wilson led Naish up the stairs and taking a key from her pocket she opened the door to Edwards's room. The room was sparsely decorated but clean. A bed, a small table, and an armchair were the only furniture. There was a small washstand with a china bowl and a shaving mirror before it in a corner next to a cupboard which Naish took for a wardrobe.

'The bathroom is along the passageway,' offered Mrs Wilson.

Ten minutes was sufficient time for Naish to search the room and conclude that there was nothing of interest to be found. He tried the handle of the wardrobe which was locked.

'I have a key to that, Inspector,' she said, pulling another bunch of keys from a pocket beneath her housecoat. 'I tell my lodgers that I don't have a spare. It makes them feel they have somewhere private, as it were. I never use it ordinarily, but if they up and leave, I want to be able to get into my own cupboards, don't I.'

'I understand,' said Naish, taking the key that she held out from the bunch.

As Naish opened the door, he was confronted by a rail of clothes that filled the whole width of the cupboard. The shelf above the rail was filled with various boxes and other items of clothing. Half the floor space was occupied with a boot rack, and on the other half stood a small wooden cabinet with three drawers which were secured with a single lock. Naish began with the shelf, taking down each item and examining it before handing it to Mrs Wilson to put on the floor. One box he asked her to put to one side before he continued with the hanging clothes on the rail. It was the usual assortment of clothes that Naish expected, but towards the end, he took down a hanger that held a suit cover. Opening it, Naish inspected the contents with satisfaction and asked Mrs Wilson to put it aside with the box. His examination of the shoe rack was unremarkable but again he took one pair of polished black shoes and asked Mrs Wilson to put it aside. He then tried the first of the drawers to find that the cabinet was locked. Naish looked around at Mrs Wilson who smiled sheepishly and, having reached into another pocket, produced a small key ring with three keys on it.

'I take it that this fits the cabinets in each of your lodger's rooms?' said Naish, with a smile, and she nodded that they did.

The top drawer contained collars and cufflinks and other small items. Naish took two of the collars from the collection and, handing them to Mrs Wilson, asked her to put them aside with the other items.

'Why, these are dog collars,' she exclaimed. 'The ones that the minister wears. What is he doing with them?'

'When I have finished with these drawers, I will explain,' said Naish.

The second drawer also took Naish's interest. There was a selection of papers of no apparent importance, but Naish set them on the top of the cabinet to take away for closer reading. The only other item of interest was in the bottom drawer: a post office savings book with a number of banknotes placed between the pages. Naish got to his feet and, having counted the notes and replaced them between the pages, let out a soft whistle.

'Twenty-five pounds, a very tidy sum,' he said.

'Good lord,' said Mrs Wilson. 'What's he doing living here with all that money to his name?'

It was the same question that Naish had silently been asking himself but, tactfully, he kept his thoughts to himself.

'Mrs Wilson, I am going to be here for another half hour or so. I suggest that you get on with whatever it is that I am keeping you from and I will finish off what I have to do.'

'Yes, I will be getting on, if you are sure. Would you like me to bring you up a cup of tea?'

'That would be very welcome. There is a constable in the car out the front – perhaps you would be kind enough to ask him to come up here and make him a cup of tea as well.'

With Mrs Wilson gone, Naish took a cigarette from his tin and sat back to read through the papers he had found. There was nothing obviously of interest to the case and he turned his attention to the post office savings book. He recounted the notes. There were five new five pound notes and Naish made a note of the serial numbers in his notebook. He flicked through the pages which indicated that Edwards had held the account for at least the last eleven years, judging from the date of the earliest transaction. The opening balance was a pound, but it rose fairly quickly to an average balance of about fifteen pounds, with regular deposits matching occasional withdrawals. The twenty-five pounds was clearly placed in the book with the intention of making a deposit, as there was no indication of such a sum, or amounts totalling twenty-five pounds, having been recently withdrawn. There were also periods of inactivity on the account which Naish was confident would match the periods of Edwards's imprisonment. The serial numbers on the notes were consecutive, so he had received them as a single payment as opposed to having accumulated them. He was mulling over where Edwards could have acquired such a sum in the period since his release, when he heard steps in the passageway outside.

'Here is your tea, Mr Naish,' said Mrs Wilson, as she followed in the constable who was carrying a tray. 'I put on a plate of biscuits for you as a treat,' she added, with an engaging smile at Naish.

'Thank you,' said Naish, a little embarrassed, and frowning at the constable who had given him a knowing smile.

'You were going to explain to me about that outfit and the dog collars in that wardrobe,' continued Mrs Wilson.

'Yes,' said Naish. 'Constable, get that suit out of the suit cover and hold it up. Now, did you ever see Edwards wearing this outfit, or did you ever see him, perhaps, with an overcoat on that might be covering this outfit. You know, black trousers and shoes and the hat, the rest covered by the overcoat?'

'No to the first one, but yes to the second. I would not swear on the good book that he was wearing it under his overcoat, but he did occasionally go out dressed as you say. It was unusual, because he usually wore brown suede shoes and light-coloured trousers, that is why I noticed. It was also the only time he had that black hat with him as well, though if he had the black hat, he was usually carrying it.'

'Keep hold of the hanger a minute and let me check the pockets. Ah, here we go,' said Naish, with satisfaction. 'Three watch cases – one silver and two gold.'

Naish gave them to the constable along with the papers, the post office book and the cash and, declining Mrs Wilson's entreaties for him to have a second cup of tea, ushered the constable along the passageway and downstairs to the front door of the pub, which Mrs Wilson had unlocked to let the constable in.

'Thank you, once again,' said Naish. 'Please keep Edwards's room locked and as soon as he returns, please telephone the police station on this number.'

'What shall I say about his things?'

'You can tell him that they are with Inspector Naish and that he can come down to the station in Orange Grove and collect them whenever he feels like it.'

The constable, having closed the items in the boot, started the car and Naish climbed in beside him.

'Nice woman that, Inspector,' said the constable, with a respectful but playful smile. 'A widow lady too, so she says.'

'Thank you, Constable, but I am not in the market for widows at the present time,' said Naish. 'Now then, next stop is the picture framers in Broadway Parade.'

The shop bell rang as Naish opened the front door, and the proprietor looked up from his work at the bench with a weary expression that said, *not the police again, to what do I owe the pleasure of this visit.*

'Good morning, Inspector Naish and what can I do for you?' the proprietor managed to say, in an ingratiating tone which, combined with the forced smile, did not entirely convince Naish that his visit was welcome.

'I am sorry to trouble you,' said Naish, untruthfully. 'I have brought along the tools that I believe to have been stolen from your premises for you to formally identify. Tedious, I know, but it ties up some loose ends for me. I have a simple witness statement with me. It only needs to record that you formally identify the tools as being exhibit six in my evidence log and a quick signature, if you can give me ten minutes of your time.'

'Very well,' the proprietor said, with a weary tone that conveyed his reluctant acquiescence. 'We can use the work bench as a desk, if you care to pull up a stool.'

'Thank you,' said Naish, with a smile, and he took the tools from the bag and laid them out on the bench.

'Yes, these tools are undoubtedly mine and I will swear to that.'

'Thank you, then if you will be good enough to read through this statement and sign it at the bottom, we have that piece of business concluded.'

'I assume that you are taking the tools away with you?'

'I am afraid that I must. I realise the inconvenience, but process is process,' said Naish, gathering up the tools and replacing them in the bag. 'That is an interesting painting you have on the bench.'

'It is only a print, Inspector. A limited edition of a watercolour by a local artist. I have five that need to be framed by Monday.'

'It looks as if they are very talented, but then I am not really an arbiter of great art. Do you have any talent as an artist yourself, Mr Emery?'

'Sadly, I do not have any artistic ability at all.'

'You do not even dabble at painting or even sketching? I should have thought that your daily association with art would encourage you?'

'It sustains my interest in the works of others and gives me an eye for what is good and bad in artistic terms, but, sadly, artistic talent is a natural gift – it does not come to one by osmosis. If that were the case, then, as you say, my day to day exposure would render me a second Michelangelo.'

'I see your point. Sad but true, I suppose. Unfortunately, a talent for crime is often developed in men by nothing other than osmosis. Luckily not in my case, however, or else I should be the second Professor Moriarty.'

'Indeed,' said Emery, with a smile that suggested a slight thaw in his frosty demeanour.

'Might I delay you just five minutes longer?' said Naish, sensing the thaw himself. 'You will think my memory poor, I know, and I should have made some notes yesterday, but would you mind if I walk through your premises again? I find it helps me to develop my theories if I walk them through in the location that they have occurred.'

'Oh, very well,' said Emery, reverting to his irascible persona, 'if you must. But I must get on with these frames or it will be five o'clock, another day gone, and I will not have finished the order off.'

'Oh, absolutely, please don't let me delay you. I am more than happy to find my own way about, you won't know I am here, and, as I say, I will be out of your hair before you know it,' said Naish, anxious to avoid a precise time.

Naish went back to the front door and began to enact what he suspected to be Lynch's actions on the night of the burglary. Having found a small amount of cash in the till and the tools on the ground floor, he goes upstairs. Naish made his way past Emery at the work bench and went up the stairs to the first and then second floor. Having had another cursory look around on both floors, he sat down on the stairs between the first and second floors. His purpose was twofold. Firstly, he was running through in his mind the endless possibilities of what Lynch's movement might have been that night and how the sketchbooks and canvases fitted in; but without many facts, the possibilities were difficult to distil down to a single likely one. Secondly, he was keen to see if Emery would follow him about or else come looking for him after a short while. But Emery did neither, and Naish could hear from the workshop at the bottom of the stairs the sounds of him working away at the frames. He took his tobacco tin from his pocket and rolled himself three more cigarettes. Placing them in his tin, he eventually made his way back downstairs.

'Well, thank you for your time once again, Mr Emery,' said Naish, as he came back into the workshop.

'Not at all,' said Emery, whose attention remained focused on the joint he was trying to glue in a frame.

'I will see myself out,' said Naish, and closing the shop door behind him, he walked back to the car.

'Do you fancy earning some overtime tomorrow, Constable?'

'Why yes, Inspector, I am up for that.'

'Good lad, because I am going to need a driver tomorrow as well, looking at how this case is going. Right then, on the strength of that, I will buy you some lunch. Let's step over to the Old Jupiter over there – I fancy a roll and a pint of beer. How about you?'

They sat in the window seat of the pub and ate their lunch in silence. Naish appeared deep in thought, and the constable, who was unaccustomed to lunching with a detective inspector, did not feel it appropriate to intrude on his thoughts.

'Fancy another pint?' asked Naish, coming out of his reverie.

'Not for me, thank you, Inspector.'

'I am not used to having the police in,' said the landlord, nodding towards the constable, 'nothing to worry about I trust?'

'Not at all,' said Naish, 'and sorry about the uniform, but we needed to grab a quick lunch.'

'Are you on to that burglary over the way there at old Emery's?'

'I have been over there this morning, yes,' said Naish, sensing that the landlord was about to become conversational. 'Do you have much to do with him – fellow traders and all that?'

'I don't have much to do with him and he is a bit of an odd one. I see him coming and going, not that I watch him, of course.'

'No, I understand, but you can't help noticing your neighbours can you,' said Naish, taking his beer. 'Look, I can see you are busy now. How about I look in later and chat with you? You never know, you might have seen something that is important to my investigation.'

Naish sat back down with the constable and took a couple of sips from his pint.

'Right,' said Naish 'let's be getting back to it.'

'Not finishing your beer, Inspector.'

'No. We have things to do.'

Chapter 6

'Well that might be a useful opening, or it might not. Either way, I will be going back to the Old Jupiter and having a chat with the landlord to see what he knows of the genial Mr Emery. Now then, Constable, to the Golden Fleece. This is an investigation and not a pub crawl, I promise you,' said Naish, with a smile.

The Golden Fleece was situated in a small cobbled square and, so as not to draw attention to himself, Naish told the constable to go back to the station and he would call him when he was ready to be collected. Being a Saturday afternoon, the Golden Fleece was doing a good trade and Naish made his way through the throng to the bar where two barmaids were serving the customers, while the landlord, George Jenkins, sat on a stool behind the bar watching proceedings. Naish caught his eye and he got up and came over.

'Good afternoon, Mr Naish. A social call rather than a professional one, I hope?'

'Hello George. It's professional I am afraid, but no need for alarm. I will have a pint of bitter, please.'

'Can we keep it discreet please, Mr Naish? I don't want to alarm my regulars if the police are taking an interest around here. No offence meant, you understand.'

'I understand completely, and none taken,' said Naish, taking the beer and overtly handing over payment. 'I would put it about that I was only here to discuss a technical matter on your licence application, that sounds credible enough to me.'

'Thank you, Mr Naish. Now, what is it I can do for you?'

'I am looking into the death of Ted Lynch,' said Naish, lighting a cigarette. 'I know that he has been a regular in here for the past few weeks since he was released from prison. He had got himself mixed up with some very serious players, I don't know how, and I don't know what as yet, but I need to find out more about his associates. I understand that it puts you in a difficult position with your clientele, but I have always played fair with you and now I need some help.'

'I understand you, Mr Naish, and everyone was shocked by what happened to old Ted. He was coming in here regularly as you have said. He was just like his old self, happy-go-lucky, always sharing a joke and always stood his round. He just mixed in with the usual crowd in here idling the time away – cards, darts and placing the occasional bet, you know the sort of thing. However, since he was found hanging under that bridge no one has mentioned a thing. Not mentioned him and not talked about how he was found. No gossip, no speculating, silence – and I mean nothing – and if there was anything to hear in here, then you know that I would know about it.'

'Then if hanging him under that bridge was meant to be a warning to others, it has worked.'

'Oh, it has worked all right. The rumour soon got around about what they did to him – breaking his fingers, beating him up and all of it. Oh yes, it shut up everyone. There are some hard men in here as you know, Mr Naish, but even the hardest of them, for all their bravado, aren't saying anything. I don't know who these people are, and I don't want to know, but they have certainly put the fear of god into people round here.'

'If, as you say, they have put the fear of god into the people round here, it suggests to me that you think these men are not from around here?'

'That may be so, Mr Naish, but while I am willing to help you, I really don't want to get into all that.'

'I understand that, George. Well, let's keep to basics. Why don't you go and get your cellar book and put it on the counter – it will add credence to the pretence of our licencing discussion.'

While the landlord went off to collect the book, Naish turned on his barstool to look casually about the room while lighting a cigarette. He was aware that his presence had attracted the attention of the locals. It would be going too far to say that he was so obvious that he might as well have been wearing uniform, but he had certainly sent a message to those in the criminal fraternity, most of whom knew him personally and if not personally, then certainly by reputation. His message was, I am on the case, you all know that, and I am not intimidated.

'So, who was Ted associating with, then,' continued Naish, as the landlord spread the ledger on the bar.

'No one particular, from what I could tell to be honest. He just came in here drinking and having a good time, as I say, with the locals. You know them, Mr Naish, and what they are all capable of. Let us say we share a lot of the same customers. I can spot a mile off when they are colluding on some scheme or other, but I did not see Ted up to any of that in here.'

'What about this man, then?' said Naish, discreetly taking the prison photograph of Edwards from his inside pocket and placing it on the ledger.

'Why, that is Tom Edwards,' said the landlord. 'He came in here with Ted the first night he came back from being away. He mixed in with Ted and all of the locals, but I have not seen him since Ted was murdered.'

'So, we are talking Saturday, the 6th of October, then, if I have got it right?'

'Yes, that is right. About seven o'clock I would have said.'

'So, Ted is back in Bath on the Friday and he has met up with Edwards almost immediately. Did they come in together or was one here before the other?'

'No, they came in together. I know that for a fact because I served Ted and said it was good to see him again. He introduced me to "this friend of mine, Tom", as he put it.'

'Interesting,' said Naish, stubbing out his cigarette. 'It would appear not to have been a coincidental meeting, then. I would love to know what that pair were up to. Did Ted ever try and pass off anything that he might have acquired in here?'

'No, Mr Naish, certainly not to my knowledge. All my regulars know the rules of this house. Their business is their own business and I don't ask questions, but I am not being used as a marketplace for stolen goods. They all know that, and if I catch them at it then they get barred. However,' said Jenkins, looking to his left and right, 'Ted did make me a kind of odd offer. I have a niece at art college and I was chatting about her the other evening to Ted. Then he came in a few nights later and said he might have some drawing books and things that I could have for her. He said that I could have them for nothing, so I said thanks and left it at that.'

'When was that?' said Naish.

'Let me think – yes, it would have been on the Wednesday. I remember now because it was the same night as he turned up in his new suit.'

'So that would be Wednesday the 10th?' said Naish, looking at his notebook.

'Yes, that is right. Then a couple of nights later he comes back in and apologises, saying that he had checked the items and found that they were no good as they had been used. Typical of Ted was all I thought, nothing as simple as it sounds.'

'When did he tell you that they were no good?'

'It was two nights later, so that would be Friday evening.'

'Friday the 12th,' said Naish to himself, as he made a note in the book. 'Did he offer you anything else, tools for example?'

'No, nothing, Mr Naish. As I said, I won't have them trading their wares in here and they certainly don't offer them to me. I think that Ted simply saw it as a friendly gesture. As I told you, he didn't want anything for them. So he said, anyway.'

'Do you know a man called Orton,' said Naish, changing the subject, 'a gardener?'

'Yes, I know Dick Orton. He comes in two or three times a week to escape from that wife of his. I think she has a spy in all the pubs out his way.'

'Did he have anything to do with Ted as far as you know?'

'They would exchange words now and again if they were up at the bar together. Oh, and I think Ted bought a suit off him. Very pleased with it, he was, thought he was Beau Brummel in it.'

'So, no one has been asking questions about Ted either before or since he disappeared. Are you absolutely sure of that?'

'No, not a soul. I swear on that, Mr Naish. But there has been a new face in here occasionally. I don't know him, and he just comes in from time to time, takes his drink and sits over there by the door. He usually has a second, makes them both last about an hour. Sits there making out he is reading the paper and then he leaves. Same drill every time.'

'You say "he makes out to be" reading the paper?'

'I have been in this game long enough, Mr Naish, to spot someone who is faking it. I knew straight away that he was not a copper, but I thought that he might be a private detective or some such thing. Having seen him a couple of times, I am not so sure.'

'Does he have a regular time?'

'No, never, and I don't give him the opportunity to think that I am taking an interest in his affairs. He does not look the sort of bloke that you want to cross, if you know what I mean.'

'I understand. If you see him again at any time, call the station straight away and let me know. If I am not about, ask them to get a message to me straight away, day or night.'

'Very well, Mr Naish, I will see what I can do. Would you be staying for another pint?'

'No, George, I am fine. I will be getting out of your hair and will let your regulars settle themselves back down. Remember, anything at all, get in touch. Well, thank you George for your time,' said Naish, in a louder voice just sufficient that a few regulars in earshot could hear and pass on the subject of their conversation. 'I will drop the licencing paperwork in the post for you.'

With that, Naish got up and turned to go. As he walked towards the door, he saw Orton the gardener sat with a group of men playing cards. Naish did not say anything, but he made sure that he caught Orton's eye squarely before the gardener could avert his gaze. Naish smiled to himself as he went outside. He walked up into York Street where he knew there was a telephone box from where he could call the station for the car to come and collect him. Having made his call, Naish went into his tobacconist just off York Street and bought eight ounces of his rolling tobacco. The tobacconist weighed out the tobacco from a stone jar and, having wrapped it up, handed it to Naish.

'Are you due a cigar, Mr Naish?' he asked.

'Not yet, I am afraid,' he replied, with a smile. 'My current case is someway off the cigar time, but I will be in sometime soon, I assure you, just as soon as I get to the bottom of it.'

As he came out of the shop, he saw the car pull up for him.

'When I didn't see you, Inspector, I thought that you might have popped in for a couple of ounces of your usual.'

'It was a few more than a couple' said Naish, with a smile, as he got in. 'The way this case is going, I have just bought eight ounces. Right, run me round to Broadway Parade. It will be getting on for opening time in half an hour and I can catch the landlord of the Old Jupiter before he gets busy with customers. Once you have dropped me off, you can get on home.'

'I am on duty until six o' clock, Inspector.'

'Well, you are working for me today, and as far as I am concerned, the day is over. So, if I were you, I would get on home. If anyone asks, just direct them to me. Then I will see you for that bit of overtime tomorrow in my office at eight, sharp.'

The constable dropped Naish in Broadway Parade at half past four, and to fill the thirty minutes before opening time, Naish walked down to the bridge where Lynch had been found hanging. He stood, thoughtfully, by the railings from where he had first surveyed the scene, and pondered over a cigarette.

'Good evening, officer,' said the landlord, as he opened the front door. 'Come on in.'

'I didn't introduce myself earlier. I am Inspector Naish and, as you correctly assumed, I am looking into the burglary from Mr Emery's premises across the road. Has he told you anything about it?'

'No, he is not much of a one for conversation. Keeps himself to himself, as you might say.'

'Do the shopkeepers have much to do with each other around here?'

'We have a business association that meets every month, and most of us belong to it and most of the traders attend it regularly, but I have never seen old man Emery at any of them. I pass the time of day with him if I pass him on the Parade, but it's only pleasantries.'

'Do all the traders live above the premises along the Parade?'

'Why do you ask?'

'I am trying to narrow down why his business might have been targeted over another and whether or not the proprietor living over the premises may be a determining factor in a thief choosing to burgle one shop over another – less risky if the premises are unoccupied, you understand.'

'Oh, I see. Most live over the business, yes. I should say the majority of them, in fact, but not old Emery. But he does keep strange hours.'

'In what way are they strange?'

'Well, he does not live over the shop. I know that for a fact because I usually see him locking up about half past ten each night and making his way home. He lives over in St Mark's Road.'

'That is a late hour for a shopkeeper. Is that every night?'

'Every night, regular as clockwork. Monday through to Friday, but not at weekends.'

'I suppose, keeping the hours of a publican, you are around to witness his comings and goings?'

'Exactly, not that I am nosey. But you can't help noticing, living and working right opposite a bloke, can you?'

'Business must be booming in the picture framing business, then. So, does he keep the shop open till those hours, then, if he is working in his workshop at the back of the shop?'

'No, the shop is always closed at half past five, sharp, and he does not work downstairs after closing up. The shop is in darkness, but the lights are always on upstairs. I assume that he has a workshop up there where he does the majority of his work in the evenings.'

'When you say upstairs, which floor are you talking about?'

'I don't know exactly, I have only been in his shop half a dozen times in as many years and never upstairs, so I don't know where his main workshop is. There are lights showing from the windows on the first and second floor, although the blinds are drawn across the windows. Obviously, in the summer they are not on until later in the evening, but at this time of year, as soon as the lights go out in the shop, the lights go on up there until half past ten when he goes home.'

'Always half past ten?'

'There or thereabouts. Sometimes a bit before and sometimes a bit later, but generally half past ten.'

'I might look in one evening, then. I think that my visits during the day sometimes irritate him, probably because he is busy. He may be more amenable in the evening.'

'He is always an irritable bloke, so I doubt you would find him in any better humour in the evening than in the morning. Anyway, you would be wasting your time now. He hasn't been working late this week. First time in years I saw him shut up shop on the Monday night at half past five and off he went home. It's been the same every day this week. He may be having some work done in there, for all I know, because there was a decorator in there all day Wednesday from first thing and first thing Thursday, although they finished up about three o'clock on the Thursday.'

'Was the van out the front all day then?'

'No, it was around the back of the shop parked by his backyard. I saw it when I was out walking the dog.'

'So, on Monday, for the first time in years, Mr Emery changes his evening routine, and on the Wednesday and Thursday, he has the decorators in?'

'That's about the size of it. It may be that he has been having his upstairs workshop spruced up and he will return to his usual routine next week. So it might be worth you looking in on him one evening next week, if you want to catch him.'

'Do you know who the decorators were by any chance. Did they have their name on the van?'

'No, they didn't. I only knew they were decorators because I happened to see them a couple of times going to the van as I passed by with the dog. Oh, and once they were sat out the back having a smoke.'

'There were two of them, then?'

'Yes, there were and grim looking coves they were as well.'

'Could you describe them and or the van? Did you notice the registration number?'

'The van was a blue Bedford – deep navy blue colour – but I didn't notice the registration number. It was very new, and I remember thinking to myself that they must be doing well for themselves in the decorating line, having a work van like that. The two blokes were not from round here, but I would recognise them again if I saw them, I am sure.'

'Well, thank you for your help, and a very enjoyable pint of beer. If anything else occurs that you feel noteworthy, please contact me at the station in Orange Grove.'

Naish made his way out into the street and walked back across the town. He was feeling hungry and in need of his evening meal, but instead headed back to the station.

'I have a couple of things that I would like you to look into for me tonight,' said Naish to the desk sergeant. 'Something to while away the hours.'

'Certainly, Inspector. They say there is no such thing as a free bacon roll.'

'I want you to look at the files and find the details of all the blue Bedford vans that are registered in Bath. Hopefully, it should not be too long a list. I need the registered keeper and their address, including ones that are registered to businesses. Secondly, I will need a list of all the painters and decorators in the Bath area – hopefully the local gazetteer will provide you with that list. Can you also put a note up on the general notice board for any of the beat constables who have knowledge of a blue Bedford van on their patch to come and speak to me. Oh, and while you are at it, can you look up the records for a Thomas Edwards. He moved to Bath about six months ago. See if he has come to our attention in any way at all – crimes, cautions, drunk and disorderly – anything at all. I also want the details of his terms of imprisonment over the past eleven or twelve years, if you can track them down as well. One last thing and it's a very long shot – when you check the records over the last six months, just check there were no men of the cloth that came to our attention.'

'What a vicar or the like you mean?' asked the sergeant, incredulously.

'That's exactly what I mean. Very unlikely, I know, but have a look.'

Naish then made his way on up to his office, lit the fire in the grate and spent the next hour or so writing up the various notes that he had made in his notebook in the course of what had been a long day. Eventually, as the clock on the abbey chimed eight o' clock, Naish put on his overcoat, locked up his office and wandered off to the Rifleman's for his evening meal.

Naish woke at six o'clock and, having washed and dressed, went into the kitchen and put the expresso maker on to boil. He sat at the table and jotted a few notes on a scrap of paper as a rough agenda for the day, the first item being to get into the station just before eight to catch the desk sergeant, and see what progress he had made with the tasks that had been set for him the previous evening.

Naish was just pouring his second cup at five to seven when the telephone rang. Naish started; he very rarely received telephone calls at his flat, so he assumed it must be business, and if it was business at this hour, it must be unwelcome business. It was the desk sergeant calling to say that he was needed urgently, as a body had been discovered in town. The details were unclear, but the desk sergeant told Naish that he had sent the constable around to his address with the car, and he would be with him in a matter of minutes.

Naish swigged the last dregs from his cup, gathered up his tobacco and notebook, pulled on his overcoat, took his hat off the stand in the hall and made his way down to the front door, which he opened just as the constable was pushing the bell.

'Good morning, Inspector,' said the constable. 'I am here to take you to see the body at Monmouth Place. Did the sergeant telephone you?'

'He did telephone but told me no more than you have just done – what is going on?'

'The sergeant took a call from the beat constable, who was reporting that he had found a body in a trench in Monmouth Place. That is all that is known, at present. As we knew that you were coming into work today, we thought it best if I collected you with the car and took you straight to the scene.'

The car drew up in Monmouth Place and Naish got out to be greeted by the beat constable and two other constables who had been directed to assist at the scene.

'I have sealed off both ends of the street as best I can, Inspector, but fortunately there aren't many people about at this time on a Sunday.'

'Very good, Constable. Now show me what this is all about, will you.'

'Well, Inspector, the gentleman over there by the pub was walking his dog along the pavement and as he went past the roadworks here, the dog started to pull towards that trench dug in the road. He pulled at the dog's lead to get him away but the dog resisted and the lead slipped from the gentleman's hand, upon which the dog starts digging at the ground, and by the time the gentleman had got under the barriers to get the dog by the collar, the dog has exposed what looks like the leg of a body buried in the trench.'

By the time the constable had completed his report, they were alongside the trench in question. From the pipes stacked on the opposite side of the road, it was clear that the trench had been dug for the replacement of a mains water pipe. The roadworks were surrounded by wooden barriers on to which were hung paraffin lamps that glowed red in the dawn light. The trench was about three feet wide and twenty feet long. It was clear that the work was nearing completion, because the trench had been refilled to within a foot of the road surface with gravel, on to which a final layer of tarmac would be laid to complete the repair. It was through the gravel at about the centre of the trench that the lower part of a human leg was protruding and, from what Naish could make out, it looked like the leg of a man.

'Right then, you two,' said Naish to the two constables nearest to him. 'Bust open that tool store over there, find yourselves some spades and gently start to uncover the body.'

'What can I do, Inspector?' asked his driver.

'Get on to the station and tell them I want at least another two men out here to secure the area, and I want the police surgeon to attend. You can go and get him in the car. Oh, and we will need some means of getting the body to the mortuary. Tell the desk sergeant that I know it is Sunday, but this is urgent. If he has any problems let me know.'

The constable disappeared towards the car to start the tasks allocated to him while, unnoticed, an elderly man came down the street from the opposite direction.

'Oi, what the hell are you doing with that tool store,' he shouted, as he came into view. 'Leave the bloody door alone, I have got a key here. What the hell is going on?'

'I am Inspector Naish from the Bath police, who are you?'

'I am Bert Rose and I am the lamp man,' he exclaimed angrily. 'I have come down here to put out the lamps and see that the barriers are all secure and I find you lot busting into the tool store – what's the game?'

'Have you got a key to the store, Mr Rose?' said Naish, calmly.

'I have, if it is anything to do with you lot.'

'Mr Rose, if you give my constables the key, they can help themselves to a couple of your shovels and then, while they are doing that, I can take you over there out of the way and explain what is going on,' said Naish, as he drew Rose away from the trench.

Having calmed the lamp man down, Naish had learnt that the work on the main had been completed on Friday and the trench had been filled with the gravel on the Saturday. The tarmac was due to be relaid first thing on the Monday morning. Naish lit a cigarette and wandered back to see how the constables were getting on.

'According to Mr Rose, the main is about three feet down,' said Naish, 'so there is not much depth of gravel covering him. Be careful – once you have got most of the gravel off the top of him, I want to have a look.'

After half an hour, the body was uncovered sufficiently to see that it was face down. So, on Naish's instructions, the constables carried on with the exhumation until all the gravel around the corpse had been removed, leaving just the body face down in the bottom of the trench, laid on top of the main. Naish got down into the trench, but with the face still in the gravel and the trench side making it all but impossible to turn the body over, he was just climbing back out as the police surgeon arrived at the scene.

'My God, it is a resurrection,' said the surgeon, with a smile.

'Not much chance of that,' said Naish. 'This man will need more than a miracle to get him back to the land of the living. Care to take a look?'

The surgeon peered over the side of the trench.

'No, it's too confined for me to do anything meaningful down there. If you are happy, Inspector, I suggest that the constables get the unfortunate man up on the pavement and then I can have a proper look at him. I take it that this is no casual drunk who has just fallen in?'

'This is no accident,' said Naish. 'This man has been buried under that gravel which has just been removed. The gentleman over there was walking his dog and it appears to have sniffed him out, which is odd, because from what I can work out, he was only buried in here less than twenty-four hours ago.'

As they talked, the two constables had managed to lift the corpse on to the pavement and roll it on to its back.

'Well, there is no doubting who he is, then,' said Naish. 'That is Thomas Edwards – associate of Ted Lynch, lodger at the Rose and Laurel and sometime impersonator of clerical gentlemen.'

'That's as may be,' said the surgeon, 'but just like the last corpse, he had been the victim of some brutal treatment.'

'So, he has,' said Naish, kneeling down beside the surgeon to take a closer look. 'That looks like an identical stab wound to the chest, just as we found on Ted Lynch. What are those holes on his chest and neck, stab wounds?'

'I should say, at a first glance, that they were burns, Inspector, but I need to conduct a proper examination in better light than these street lamps afford.'

'I need the results as quickly as possible. When can I come up to St Martins for the report?'

'I can do you a favour, Inspector. My wife is away for the weekend and she has organised for me to lunch at her sister's. It would be a favour to me and a favour to you if I have to ring her up and say that I have a murder to deal with and must reluctantly give my apologies. So, I can carry out the autopsy this morning and meet you at the mortuary this afternoon at two o'clock.'

'That would be most helpful,' said Naish. 'I will see you then.'

Chapter 7

It was getting on for nine o'clock as the corpse was put on a stretcher and placed in an ambulance. Naish checked through his notebook to make sure that he had all the details that he needed, before handing over the scene to a day shift sergeant and the two constables to record the scene, arrange for appropriate photographs to be taken and then return the street to the normality of a Sunday morning. This completed, he climbed back into the car to resume his intended schedule for the day.

It was half past nine as Naish walked into the foyer of the station. The night-shift desk sergeant was dressed in his civilian clothes chatting with his day-shift counterpart.

'You are very late after your shift, Sergeant,' Naish remarked. 'No home to go to?'

'I was hanging on to catch you, Inspector. I have the answers to most of the questions that you set me to look into last night. I assumed that the information may be even more important, in light of this morning's events, and I thought it would be easier to talk you through the information than just hand you my report.'

'Thank you, Sergeant, that is very considerate of you,' said Naish, with genuine appreciation. 'Come on up to my office. Constable, can you get a tray of tea sorted and bring it up please.'

'So, what news of the blue Bedford?' asked Naish, sitting himself at his desk and rolling a cigarette.

'Well, there are no records of a blue Bedford van registered in the city. Quite a few of various other colours, seventeen in fact, but none that are any shade of blue. Did you have a registration number or even a part of one?'

'No, the witness didn't note the number plate, unfortunately.'

'It was just in case it had been resprayed recently. So, if it has, then the only way I can see us finding out is to get someone around the spraying shops and make some enquiries. It won't be a big job as there are only three of them. The list of painters and decorators, however, is a somewhat bigger list. There are twenty-three of them listed in the gazetteer. I have written them all out on a separate sheet attached to my report. Most of them are one-man bands, if their business names are anything to go by, but then a lot of them probably employ a couple of men to work with them, so I am not sure how we can narrow the list down other than visiting them in turn.'

'That will be a dockyard job,' said Naish, 'and it will need to be done in the evening to have any chance of catching them at home, otherwise it's a waste of time. I will have a think about that later. Did you put that note up in the general office?'

'Yes, I did, and I have put it on the list of matters for the duty sergeants when they conduct their morning and evening briefings to the beat constables.'

'Excellent, how did you get on with Edwards?'

'I telephoned Horfield prison and got the history of his imprisonment. Again, I have written it all out on a separate sheet attached to my report.'

Naish got up and went over to the evidence table as the constable knocked and entered with the tray of tea.

'Put it over there on my desk and pour us all a cup – have one yourself,' said Naish, as he located the post office book belonging to Edwards. 'Now then, Constable, sit down with your tea and compare the dates in this post office book with the dates on this piece of paper while I finish off with the sergeant.'

'I went back in our records to the first date of his release and I can find no record of his having come to the attention of the police, not even an application for a dog licence. I even set one of the constables to looking back a further two years just on the off-chance he had been here before, but there was no mention of him at all. Did he use an alias, at all?'

'Not that I know, but he did masquerade as a clerical gentleman on occasions, to my certain knowledge.'

'Ah, hence your asking me to check the records for a man of the cloth. No, sorry, not a single mention of such a person coming to our attention.'

'Well, thank you for your endeavours, Sergeant. How are you getting on, Constable?'

'Well, Inspector, I would say that they match pretty well. All the transactions coincide with the periods of his being on the outside, and there are no entries for the times he was inside.'

'Good,' said Naish. 'We will make a detective of you yet. Now on that blackboard over there, I want you to chalk up a table to show how they compare. Right then, Sergeant, I have taken up enough of your valuable time. I suggest that you get on with your day off and make sure you put down a couple of hours on your overtime sheet. I will sign it off for you.'

The sergeant disappeared and Naish wandered over to the blackboard where the constable was finishing off the table of dates.

'So, do you deduce anything else from the post office book constable? Let me give it to you as I found it,' said Naish, replacing the banknote back inside the book.

'He was presumably going to pay the money in,' offered the constable.

'Good. Other than the fact it was tucked in the book, how can you deduce that?'

'None of the withdrawals made since his release date six months ago come anywhere near twenty-five pounds, so it must be an amount he was going to pay in?'

'That agrees with my reading of the facts. So far so good. You will also notice that the serial numbers on the notes are concurrent, and so it is fair to assume that they were given to Edwards as a single transaction.'

'It is a very large sum. Do you think he stole it?'

'I doubt it,' said Naish. 'Men like Edwards would never pay in stolen notes, particularly ones of such a high denomination. They would most likely buy something with them for a couple of shillings and then pay the change in to the post office – much less likely to attract attention. Do you see any significance in the last transaction on his account?'

'On Friday the 12th October, he withdrew two pounds from his account – that was nine days ago,' said the constable, struggling a little to offer more insight.

'Don't look sheepish, lad, you have done very well. Let me tell you what I think. If he needed two pounds on that Friday, then it is improbable that he had yet come into possession of the twenty-five pounds. Clearly you would not withdraw two pounds if you already had twenty-five. Indeed, if my other theory is to be believed, he would be trying to spend two pounds using the five pound notes in order to try and break them up. Now, I know from our friendly widow up at the Rose and Laurel that Edwards was last seen at two o'clock on Wednesday the 17th of October and, as far as I know, she was the last person to see him alive. Clearly, someone else did, but we have yet to track them down. So, Edwards must have come into possession of the twenty-five pounds between the Friday and two o'clock on the Wednesday, because he left his post office book at the Rose and Laurel where I found it yesterday, and he had not been back there.'

'But he must have intended to come back later to the Rose and Laurel, either on that Wednesday or later in the week, or else he would have taken the cash and the post office book with him. With that amount of money, he could have done a runner and replaced all his possessions for a fraction of the money he had to his name.'

'Good, very good,' said Naish. 'I agree that wherever it was that he went on that Wednesday afternoon, he clearly intended to return to his lodgings.'

'Did he steal the cash from somewhere do you think, Inspector?'

'He may have done, but as far as we are aware, no such loss or theft has been reported to us, and none of the burglaries that his mate Ted Lynch perpetrated realised such a sum. I know for a fact that he was in the Guildhall market on Monday the 15th at half past ten trying to sell on the three watchcases that Lynch had stolen from Broad Street, but he didn't make a sale and, anyway, they were worth nothing like a fiver let alone twenty-five.'

'So, he didn't have the twenty-five pounds at that time, either,' offered the constable, eagerly.

'It may be the case, but that is supposition, as we have no facts to determine one way or the other. A good supposition, but that is one of the first rules of detective work – don't start to build theory off your own supposition. Don't look so crestfallen, lad, you are doing all right for a novice. At this stage the best we can say with any certainty is that Edwards received the twenty-five pounds as a single payment, and that, on Friday the 12th, he had no expectation of his windfall. It is also a reasonable certainty that he received the money between late on the Friday and midday on the following Wednesday. However, I also know that Edwards didn't leave the Rose and Laurel all day on the Tuesday nor on the Wednesday morning. He spoke with a few regulars in the bar briefly on the Tuesday night and he may have sneaked out without the landlady knowing, but I think it unlikely. So, although I can't prove it, it appears highly probable to me that he didn't acquire the money on those two days. That narrows it down to between Friday and Monday night.'

'It all makes sense to me, Inspector.'

'Good. Right then, I am going to write some of our musings up on my blackboards and tidy up my notes for an hour. I suggest that you get yourself something to eat. Meet me out the front at two o'clock and we can go up to St Martins and find out the results of the autopsy on Edwards.'

The afternoon was bright and warm as they drove up the Wellsway out of town up to St Martin's hospital.

'Have you ever been to an autopsy, Constable?' asked Naish, as he threw the butt of his cigarette from the car window.

'No, I never have, Inspector.'

'Well, you are welcome to come along with me if you have the stomach for it, rather than sit in the car.'

'Well, you are up against some very unpleasant men, Inspector,' said the surgeon. 'Are you any nearer catching them?'

'I am getting there,' said Naish, somewhat optimistically, 'but there is still some way to go.'

'Well, I hope you catch them quickly before they make it three in a row.'

'Has it been perpetrated by the same men, do you believe?'

'I cannot say who was there and contributed to his injuries – that needs a piece of detective work – but I am certain that he was killed by the same man. The knife wound in the chest once again, you see,' said the surgeon, indicating the area. 'If I lift back this section of skin and flesh that I have opened up, you can see that the knife has passed straight between these two ribs without even scratching them and then pierced the heart, as you can see there, inside the chest cavity.'

'Death instantaneous?' asked Naish.

'If not instantaneous then within a minute, I should say. However, he has been tortured prior to death, as was the first victim. But the nature of the injuries is different.'

'Different, in what way?'

If you look at the arms and wrists, you can see the same pattern of injury as was present on the first victim that I believe is consistent with his having been tied to a high-backed chair without any padding.'

'The dining chair again?' said Naish.

'Very probably. This time there are no marks on the ankles but the victim was wearing those boots over there on the table, so that would account for it.'

'He may not have been tied at the feet.'

'I doubt that they were not tied, as his assailants would need him to be very securely restrained for what they were about to do to him.'

'Those stab wounds to his chest you mean?'

'They are not stab wounds, Inspector, they are burn marks left by what I believe to be a poker. If you look at the marks, they have been scorched into the flesh and the edges of the wounds are almost cauterised. If you both look closely, I will cut away a little of this wound with my scalpel. There, you see.'

Naish winced at the thought and looked around to make sure that the constable was not about to faint away. He was impressed to see the young man following the surgeon intently with no suggestion of squeamishness.

'So, another case of torture to extract information, you feel?'

'The injuries are consistent with that theory. However, in the case of the first victim, I got a sense that the two assailants began slowly with their attempts at persuasion with the punches to the face, then the nails, and finally the breaking of the finger joints. But in this case, I have a sense that they cut to the chase straight away. I think that there may have been a brief attempt at simply threatening the man. If you look closely at his cheeks, here and here, you can see evidence of two very slight singes to his skin. I suggest that, once tied to the chair, they then held the red-hot poker right up close to his face to intimidate him, so close as to singe but not burn the skin. If that is so, judging by the burns, they only did it twice before driving the end of the hot poker into his chest – you see now why they would want him firmly bound. The burns appear to have been done in stages. Some of the burns are very severe and some not so. It would be consistent with the poker cooling and then being returned to the fire.'

'So, they burnt him two or three times and then reheated the poker, you believe?'

'That theory would match the evidence of the injuries. Given that there are eighteen such injuries, it is reasonable to suppose that there were about six periods of torture.'

'He may well have fainted away.'

'Indeed, he may have. He may have passed out completely and they then simply delivered the coup de grâce, as in the case of the first victim. He may have told them what they wanted in the misguided belief that they would let him go before they in fact killed him. Unfortunately, the opportunities for speculation are endless.'

'So, all it is safe to say is that he was bound, threatened with the poker held to his face, burnt eighteen times and then stabbed through the chest.'

'That is exactly what the evidence of my examination will corroborate, Inspector.'

'When did he die?'

'Now, that is interesting. The last victim had been dead no longer than twenty-four hours after he was found. With this man, it is nearer three days.'

'Well, I know that he was not placed in the trench where he was found until sometime after five o'clock on the Saturday evening, and most likely, given the location, it would have been in the early hours of Sunday. So his corpse was stored somewhere for around thirty-six hours.'

'I would also suggest that, given the state of the decomposition on the internal organs, the body was stored in an ambient temperature. It is this which caused the body to attract the attention of the dog.'

'The decomposition was fortunate, then, as was the presence of the dog, otherwise the body would never have been found. Monday morning and the tarmac gang would have arrived, and the disposal would have been perfect. Well, thank you, Doctor, for coming in today. It has helped me to keep one step nearer to the criminals than would have been the case if we were doing this tomorrow. I hope your wife is suitably understanding.'

Naish sat in thoughtful silence as the car travelled back to the station. He dismissed the constable and went back to his office for an hour. Being a Sunday, there was no food on offer in the Rifleman's and so it was the one day of the week when Naish fended for himself. Having had a pint, he wandered back to his flat in the Circus to cook himself dinner.

Naish entered his office at five minutes past seven and was surprised to find Hancock sat on a chair in front of the blackboards, deep in thought and smoking his pipe.

'Well, you are up and at it very early. What brings you in at such an hour?' said Naish.

'Well, I didn't want to be behind the pace this morning, as I am aware that someone has been at it all the weekend without a break.'

'Who might that be, then,' said Naish, as he hung his coat up.

'The Chief Superintendent might think he is in charge of this station, but I have not been the senior desk sergeant here for twenty years to not know what makes this station run and what is going on every minute of every day, whether I am on duty or not. They all know to keep me abreast of what is going on. You could have called me, in you know that, don't you? I understand that this is no ordinary case. Newton has a young family and needs time away, but I have no such ties. I might make out that I get some grief off the wife, but she knows the score. So while it is not for me to lecture an Inspector, please, if there are ever things to be done, let me know and I will be in here to assist you.'

'Understood and thank you,' said Naish. 'So, what do you make of the new information?'

'You have clearly been very busy, but it would be good if you put it all in context and gave me some sense of your thoughts and conclusions.'

'Of course, but to save me repeating myself, perhaps we can wait for Newton and run through it all together.'

At eight o'clock, Newton appeared and Naish got down to the process of recounting his work over the weekend. He found it useful rather than tedious, since it gave him the opportunity to review the events in his own mind, and the steady flow of questions from his two colleagues acted as a means of testing the theories he had formulated in his own mind in the course of the weekend.

'Well, that is one of my jobs taken care of' said Hancock, rubbing the task to visit the Rose and Laurel off the blackboard.

'You are a very lucky man,' said Naish. 'I was very nearly eaten alive there – the widow landlady took a shine to me. I suggest you watch your back if you ever end up in there.

'The gardener from Larkhall is due in this morning. I pencilled him in for eleven thinking I would be up at the Rose and Laurel first, so I have a couple of hours spare until he comes in to give his statement.'

'In that case, I want you to get round the three spraying shops in the city and find out if any of them have resprayed a Bedford van blue in the last few years. That will close off that piece of work. Another thing, when that gardener comes in, give me a heads-up. I will let you get started but I want to be in at the end – I have something I want to try and work on him.'

'I will send someone up to get you when I am coming to the end, then,' said Hancock. 'Anything else?'

'No, that will keep you busy until lunchtime. Look back in here after you have finished with the gardener,' said Naish.

The phone rang as Hancock was leaving and Naish picked it up.

'Newton, there is a message at the front desk for me, nip down and get it will you,' said Naish.

Naish got up and took Edwards's post office savings book back over to the evidence table so as to keep things in order. He lit a cigarette and opened one of the two sketchbooks. He had not given them anything other than a cursory glance until now, he realised, and began to turn the pages slowly as he smoked. The sketches in the first book were mainly single line drawings without any detail but were clearly street scenes of Georgian buildings. In fact, the more he looked at the sketches, they appeared to be the same building drawn from a number of different vantage points, but the same four elevations were evident throughout the book. His cigarette nearing the butt, Naish took both the sketchbooks back to his desk and, having discarded the butt and rolled another cigarette, began to examine the second book. The sketches in the second book were far more detailed and, even to an artistic incompetent like himself, it was evident that they were the work of someone with talent. The sketches in the first half of the book were all detailed studies of elements of the building: porches, windows and various pieces of architectural stonework. It was when he came to the later drawings in the book that Naish suddenly realised that the building was the Assembly Rooms in Bennett Street, and the reason that the less detailed sketches had stirred his memory was that the Assembly Rooms were just around the corner from his flat in the Circus. He passed by the building most weekends when he stepped along to his newsagent.

'I have got your message,' said Newton, breaking in on Naish's contemplation. 'Sealed envelope marked addressee only.'

'What do you make of those?' said Naish, pushing the sketchbooks across his desk towards Newton as he opened the envelope.

'Studies of some Georgian buildings, I should say,' offered Newton. 'Done by a pretty competent artist. All unsigned.'

'Did they say who brought this note in?' asked Naish.

'Yes, a young lad put it on the front desk. Said he was told to say it was for Mr Naish and legged it. Is it anything of interest?'

'It is a handwritten note signed BJ, who I take to be our friend Barney Jones from the Guildhall market. He is tipping me the wink to say that two men have visited his stall and were asking if he knew of an elderly cleric who dealt in silver and gold watches, as they had some that they wished to sell.'

'Do you want me to get hold of Jones?' asked Newton. 'It must be the men who did for Edwards.'

'No, not at all,' said Naish. 'I don't want Jones put at risk by us being seen around him. He is sticking his neck out for me here. The first thing we need to do is to get an artist impression of these two men.'

'But how do we get that from Jones without contacting him?'

'Because I am going to get it from the gardener after Hancock has interviewed him. I know that he has seen what I believe to be one of these men in the Golden Fleece. I may be wrong, but that is my first port of call. I don't want Barney Jones as the next corpse in this case. Now, about those sketches. They are by a competent artist, I agree, and I am certain that they are all of the Assembly Rooms. We have got an hour before I am due in with Hancock and the gardener. Go and get a car and we can take a quick trip round to Bennett Street to test my architectural discernment.'

'Sergeant Hancock says he is ready for you to step down to the interview room if you are free, Inspector,' said the constable.

'As you were, Sergeant,' said Naish, brusquely, as he walked into the interview room without pausing to knock and took up a chair in the corner of the room.

'Please continue to read through your statement,' said Hancock, coldly, as the gardener glanced uneasily over at Naish. 'Sign it there at the bottom when you are content.'

'Before you go, Orton,' said Naish, rising from his chair and walking over to the interview desk, 'I need a favour from you. You see, I think that you have seen someone who I am very interested in. Someone who has recently started drinking in the Golden Fleece.'

'Not me, Inspector, I keep myself to myself.'

'Don't take me for a fool,' said Naish, curtly. 'You know the man I mean, the man that you have all noticed in there. Comes in, sits alone, has a couple of drinks, and is obviously on the lookout for someone.'

'Can't you ask someone else, then. I don't want any trouble. If he is as well known as you say, then ask them.'

'It's my business who I ask,' snapped Naish. 'I can't ask the landlord or his staff as it would be too obvious and this man, if he was going to take umbrage – if he was, I stress – would know who had spoken to me. You are different. You are a no one in there. You sit with that group of friends that I saw you with in there the other day, but you are a face in the crowd. He won't be watching you and he won't suspect you.'

'But I sold that suit to Ted Lynch, didn't I, Inspector,' Orton pleaded.

'But he wasn't in there when you did, was he?' Naish bluffed.

'Even if he wasn't, I really don't want to get involved. I couldn't describe him, honestly I couldn't.'

'So, he wasn't in there when you sold the suit to Lynch, you admit that. So you have nothing to fear.'

'I won't do it, I tell you,' said Orton, becoming defiant.

'If you don't agree to cooperate with me here and now, Orton, then I will come and visit you at your house and make the same request in front of your wife. I would be interested to know what she would think, selling that suit and pocketing the money, getting involved with the man who burgles your employer, and drinking behind her back among the low company in the Golden Fleece. Really, I don't think that your life would be worth living, would it. Now that's better, you know it makes sense,' said Naish, seeing the reluctant look of acquiescence on Orton's face. 'Sergeant Hancock here will make you a cup of tea and I will send the police artist along. A couple of hours and you can walk out of here and no one knows the difference. Not the man you identify, not the regulars down at the Fleece and, best of all, not your wife. But just you take care with the information that you give to the artist. You try and give a false impression and I find out later that you have, then I will get you put away. Understand?'

'I understand, Inspector,' said Orton.

'I know it is difficult for you, but if you mess it up, as I say, I will have you for perverting the course of justice and that is an inside stretch.'

'Well, you certainly put the wind up him,' said Hancock, as he came back into the office. 'Anyway, it did the trick. He is down there now with the artist and they should be finished in an hour or so. I have left a constable with them to get Orton's statement verifying his identification of the man. The artist says he will bring the finished sketch up for you to see.'

'That all sounds good to me. It's a shame that his sketch of Edwards is of no use now,' said Naish.

'I know,' said Hancock, 'the copies from the printers are due back this afternoon as well.'

'Money down the drain there, then. Don't let the superintendent know about that,' said Naish, with a wry smile. 'So how did you get on with your visits to the spraying shops?'

'Not so good on that front, I am afraid, ' said Hancock. 'None of them can recall respraying a Bedford van. The closest was one that had had a front wing resprayed following a minor collision about six months ago, and that was red.'

'So, we are left with the conclusion that this van, if it is working in Bath, is registered somewhere else,' offered Newton.

'Or else these decorators are from outside Bath and travelled in to do the work,' countered Hancock.

'Given the number of decorators in the city that we know about, it seems a bit extreme to get in an outside firm to undertake a simple redecoration job,' said Naish.

'Perhaps they were an acquaintance or a family friend,' said Newton.

'Either way, there are so many permutations of vans and decorators that the work involved in tracking them all down and cross-referencing the links between them does not, at this time, justify the potential outcomes. I am happy for now to leave the van and the decorator leads where they are and wait and see what comes along. I have a hunch that we might just find that the sketch that Orton has just constructed may turn out to resemble one of the decorators, but let's wait and see.'

'That makes sense to me,' said Hancock. 'So, what is next on the agenda?'

'Well, while you have been busy, Newton and I have been considering architecture,' said Naish.

Chapter 8

'While you were interviewing Orton, Newton and I had a look through the two sketchbooks. It was remiss of me not to have studied them in more detail before, not that they contribute much to the case, but it is a cardinal mistake not to examine every piece of evidence with equal rigor. Anyway, I thought that I recognised the Assembly Rooms from the sketches and so Newton and I took a trip up there in the car. My hunch proved to be right – they were, indeed, studies of the Assembly rooms from three viewpoints, it would appear. What the artist found to dislike about the other elevation, I could not deduce, but there you are. Another little piece in our puzzle.'

Hancock had made his way over to the sketchbooks on the table as Naish was speaking to follow his observations with the drawings before him.

'Looking at these canvases, I would say that two of the elevations, as you call them, are what have been very lightly sketched on to them. They are so faint that they don't grab the eye or make any sense. But if you look at them with the sketchbook open at these detailed drawings, I would say that our artist has chosen these two elevations as the subject for his paintings. I assume that is the purpose of transferring them on to the canvases.'

Naish and Newton came over and stood either side of him.

'I have to say that I agree with you,' said Naish. 'There are only the merest marks made, I suppose to give the sense of the painting without the sketch marks, whatever they are – pencil or charcoal I suppose – showing through on the final painting.'

'I agree,' said Newton. 'But I don't think that it is pencil or charcoal. It looks like a very fine ink line to me. If you look in the bottom corner of this one, it looks to me as if someone has tried to rub out the marks without success. You see that the canvas is scuffed but the ink line remains.'

'The artist would not have done that though, would he,' said Naish. 'But I know who did. I will bet anything that it was Ted Lynch trying to rub them out, so that he could give them to George Jenkins at the Golden Fleece for his niece. It ties in with the story that George told me. Poor old Ted couldn't even get that right, when all he wanted to do was do the bloke a favour.'

'Something else is odd about these canvases, I reckon,' said Hancock, continuing to examine them. 'They are not a standard size, from what I can see. I am no expert, but from my limited knowledge canvases and sketchbooks are sold in established sizes. These sketchbooks, for an example, are A3. You get A3, A4 – you know, foolscap paper size – A5, all the way up to A1. If you hold this canvas over this sketchbook it is not quite A3, but it is clearly bigger than A4, as you can see if I hold this notepad over it.'

'So, the point is?' asked Newton.

'I think Hancock's point is that we are not dealing with an amateur artist here. If he or indeed she were an amateur, then I would have thought that they would have transferred the sketches that they made in the A3 sketchbook on to an A3 canvas, or some other established size. The non-standard size suggests a bespoke canvas made to the artist's particular requirements.'

'Exactly,' said Hancock. 'If you look at the back of these canvases, they are very well made. They have not been knocked up by anyone. This is the work of a craftsman.'

'There is an art shop in Green Street,' said Newton, anxious to try and contribute to the conversation. 'I am sure that they will sell premium canvases, so I will make a comparison of the craftsmanship.'

'Good idea,' said Naish. 'But don't take these along, just get an idea. I will give some thought as to where we go to get our thoughts on the canvases' production verified, but I don't want to do it in this city as word may get around.'

'Is that a problem, given that we don't see a particular relevance to the case? More of an academic discussion, I would say,' said Hancock.

'I am not so sure. I don't know what I am not sure of,' said Naish, with a wry smile, 'but we have two men dead already and there is an aspect of this case that we have not pinned down yet, so I want to play our cards very close to our chests for the time being. Something that is connected to the crimes Ted Lynch committed is at the root of this, and the more that I mull it over in my mind, the more it appears to come back to the picture frames in Broadway Parade. What it is, I don't know, but my instinct tells me that is where the answer lies.'

Newton and Hancock both nodded their assent to this theory.

'Right then,' said Naish, 'as we are working so well at developing theory and hypothesis, let's spend a bit of time thinking through the night of the burglary at the picture framers. As you see, I have sketched out a rough plan of the cross section of the building, so if one of you goes and gets a tray of tea, we can give it our best attention.'

'I will go and get the tea,' said Hancock. 'By the way, Inspector, just for the record, it is clear to me from your sketch that, whoever else we may suspect of being the artist, it is clearly not you.'

'Right then,' said Naish, as Hancock poured out the tea. 'I don't want to spend forever on this, but I want to get straight in my mind how Lynch came to have possession of these two sketchbooks. And the canvases, for that matter.'

'Well, my understanding,' said Newton, 'is we have reached agreement that he forced the front door and then closes it shut behind him so as not to attract attention. I think that he probably worked by the light of the street lamps outside the shop. The windows are large and are not to his favour in terms of being seen from a passer-by, but conversely work to his advantage, as the street lights mean he can keep the use of a torch to a minimum.'

'Excellent,' said Naish, 'go on.'

'So, he works quickly, as every minute he is in the ground floor area he is at risk of being seen. In keeping with what we understand of his method of work, he will want to try and get cash or some small-sized high-value items that he can conceal in his pockets or under his coat, so that he does not attract too much attention on his walk home to Oak Street. But his plan does not work out, and all he can find on the ground floor is a small amount of cash in the till. He also finds a small number of low-value tools. My guess is that he puts the cash in his pockets straight away and leaves the tools to one side, planning to take them with him on his way out as a last resort if he finds nothing else of value. So, reluctantly, he makes his way up on to the first floor where he finds nothing but materials for making picture frames and a small stock of artist's materials. He goes up to the second floor and finds nothing but empty rooms. So, realising he is on to a loser, he decides to cut his losses and go back downstairs and make good his escape, reluctantly taking the tools with him as a consolation prize. As he is making his way out, he remembers his conversation with George Jenkins and, seeing a couple of sketchbooks and some canvases, he picks them up, most probably on the first floor among the stock of artists materials, and makes off into the night with the consolation of having helped a mate as some compensation for an evening's work of poor returns.'

'That is faultless, well done,' said Naish. 'That is the most credible interpretation of Lynch's actions that night, given the facts as we know them. The issue for me is, were the sketchbooks and canvases on the first or second floors?'

'Sorry to be dense,' said Hancock, 'but why is that important?'

'I am not certain that it is, at the moment, but it intrigues me,' said Naish. 'They do not fit in naturally with the contents of the ground floor and they don't fit in with the contents of the first floor. And, anyway, we know that these sketchbooks are a different style to the ones that are in the stockroom.'

'Well, they hardly fit in with the contents of the second floor,' said Hancock. 'There is nothing on that floor to fit in with.'

'There is not, now,' said Naish, 'but it is plain that the second floor has only recently been decorated.'

'It may well have been, but it does not mean that there was necessarily anything there before,' said Hancock, with an air of frustration. 'It may well have been empty for years and the proprietor just decided to give it a spruce up before putting it to some future use.'

'Yes, but the landlord of the Old Jupiter over the road tells us that, every weekday night, the proprietor, after closing up the shop, went up on to the first and second floors and was there until around half past ten.'

'We only know that the lights were on, that is no proof that he sat up there or did anything else up there,' retorted Hancock.

'But it is reasonable to suppose that he was engaged in some activity that took him between these two floors,' said Naish. 'There is a second workbench on the first floor, for a start. I believe that there was something up on that second floor that was, in some way – even if remotely – connected to his evening activities, and it intrigues me that the area has been decorated and that now he is no longer working there in the evening.'

'Something's been cleared out, you mean,' said Newton.

'I think it has, and it has been done in a hurry. That decorating job is a bodge to end all bodges – a blind man could have done a better job.

That work is not the work of any self-respecting painter and decorator, and that leads me to my suspicion that we won't find the two men in the navy blue Bedford van in any list of professional decorators in the Bath gazetteer, or any other gazetteer for that matter.'

'Hence you think that one of them may resemble the artist's impression that Orton the gardener has provided for us,' said Hancock.

'Exactly,' said Naish, 'and it is why I am drawn to the hunch that it is Lynch's burglary at the picture framers that has caused him to become embroiled in this murky matter.'

'This is a very long shot, I know,' said Newton, 'but is it just possible that the second floor of the picture framers was where Lynch and possibly Edwards were taken and tortured. It could be that the hasty redecoration and new floor covering were to hide the scene of the crime. I mean, there must have been a reasonable amount of blood, certainly on the floor, if they were both stabbed there. It is possible that some arterial bleeding spurted on to the wall and had to be painted over to hide the scene of the crime.'

'It's a credible theory' said Naish, lighting a thoughtful cigarette. 'It certainly deserves further thought. The chair and the means of heating a poker, together with a surface on which Lynch's fingers were broken, could all have been removed. The rear entrance is discreet enough for both bringing the victim in and removing the corpse, possibly using the van. The biggest problem with your theory is the noise. Both victims would have made considerable noise – I know I would if I had been subjected to either of the sessions that the police surgeon detailed to us. There is the pub opposite and, even after it has closed, there may be other residents who might overhear. Have a discreet look into who lives over the shops, if you can.'

'But it works as far as what has happened in terms of the recent witness statement of the landlord of the Old Jupiter, doesn't it,' said

Hancock. 'The picture framer uses a workshop on the first and second floor for his nocturnal activities, whatever they are. Somehow yet to be explained, the premises are taken over as the location for the torture of Lynch and Edwards. The resulting mess caused to the decor of the room requires the bodged redecoration of the room, presumably by members of the gang who conducted the torture, or else their close associates, resulting in the workshop no longer being available, hence the absence of the proprietor in the last few days.'

'I agree that it is a very plausible line of thought,' said Naish. 'However, you must both admit that it needs some considerable work done on it in terms of evidence and facts to enable us to hang our hats on it. For all we know, he may simply have used the upstairs to catch up with the backlog of work from his business. Either way, I suggest that you write it up on the board over there, Newton, and we can work on it if further evidence comes our way.'

'I think that we should go down there and have a thorough examination of the second floor and see if there is any trace of that evidence,' said Hancock.

'I agree with that, but not just yet,' said Naish. 'Let me explain why.'

'If we go into that shop again now, we are going to provoke suspicion. Even if we just go over old ground, the proprietor is going to get suspicious that we are after something else, let alone if we go in there and start turning the place upside down, lifting floor coverings and the like. He may or may not have knowledge or information related to Lynch or even Edwards. He may be involved in something deeper we have yet to uncover, but at the very least, as a bare minimum, even if he did not cause these matters to come about, he must at least have a knowledge of something going on in his own premises. Now, I am concerned that if we give any hint of our interest he will clam up. He might even do a runner, for all I know, so, for the time being, I am anxious to not shut down the one potential lead we have in this case. We have to play a waiting game – I don't know what we are waiting for, if indeed it is anything at all – but wait we must. I think the best line is to have the premises put under surveillance, just in case there is an attempt to move anything else in or out of the building. Newton, I also want you to look into this man. I want to know his family history, the history of his time in Bath and anywhere else, and also his financial status, banks, the lot. If he has a secret, I want to know it. Hancock, see what can be done about the surveillance but, given the front and rear entrance, it may be difficult. You can use the time there to try and establish the situation as regards residents who may have been in earshot, if the interrogations were, in fact, carried out there. Also, I am not keen in using a room opposite as a vantage point – I don't trust the discretion of the traders in the Parade. Also, find out if Emery has resumed his old routine yet. The last thing this case needs now is another corpse to contend with. Right then, if you two get on with all of that, I will take over with the canvases and I will pick up the Green Street visit for you, Newton.'

'Right then,' said Naish, as he poured out the tea, 'it's getting late. Newton, tell us how you have got on this afternoon. What have you learnt about Mr Emery?'

'He moved to Bath twenty-two years ago. He came from London and he bought his house in St Mark's Road at that time. He also bought his shop in Broadway Parade at the same time, in fact, he completed on the shop before he completed on his house.'

'So, did he move here for the business and subsequently settled on a home nearby, or vice versa?' interjected Naish.

'He would have been in his thirties or forties at that time,' offered Hancock. 'He could also have been looking to move to Bath and, having found a business that suited his needs, he located and purchased a house conveniently close by. But the opportunities for speculation are endless, really, unless we interview him.'

'It is interesting that you mention his age,' continued Newton. 'He is sixty-three now, so when he moved here, he was forty-one. Not young, but he was clearly well set up at this time, as he bought the business premises in Broadway Parade outright. He owns the whole building, freehold, and he had a fifty percent mortgage on the house on St Mark's Road, which, three years later, he pays off in a single transaction.'

'Those are considerable sums of money,' said Naish, with a whistle of surprise. 'Clearly, he was doing all right for himself by the time he arrived here at the age of forty-one. Either business was booming, or had he inherited money?'

'I cannot trace where his money came from, but it does not look like a single inherited sum. His bank does not have records prior to his time in Bath, but he opened his account at Lloyds in Milsom Street with an opening balance of five thousand pounds.'

'How much?' exclaimed Naish.

'His balance is now ten thousand five hundred and fifty, and that is his current account.'

'Does he have other accounts, then?' asked Naish.

'No, but he also owns a number of properties in Bath. In fact, he owns six other properties in total and the deeds are with the bank. What is interesting is that these are not slum dwellings, either – two town houses in Camden Crescent, one house in Lansdown Crescent, two houses in Daniel Street and one in Duke Street. I have not got accurate values as I have not had time to speak to an estate agent, but even to laymen like us, it is clear that he has amassed a considerable fortune for a simple shopkeeper.'

'A fortune that is so vast, that it beggars belief as to why he is still working. I mean why would you? You are certain that he is the sole owner of these properties, he is not just a partial shareholder?' asked Naish.

'No, the deeds are quite clear, and his bank manager was quite clear, that Mr Emery is the sole owner of these six properties and of the balance of his account. It is also interesting that he has acquired these properties at intervals over the years, the last one being purchased three and a half years ago.'

'So, has he had a series of inheritances from a line of aunts and uncles, for example?' asked Naish.

'He may well have had, but there is no evidence to support that assumption. All that his bank manager knows is that Emery purchased the houses and brought the deeds into the bank for them to hold in a safe deposit box, where Emery kept them along with the deeds to his house in St Mark's Road and his shop. Where the money for the purchases came from, I have not been able to trace, but what I do know is that if he inherited a large capital sum which he then used to buy property, that capital sum was never paid into his bank account with Lloyds first.'

'So, he may have a second bank account?' offered Hancock.

'If he has, as far as I am able to tell he does not hold it in Bath, at least not in his name.'

'If he were to have inherited the money, it may well be that the solicitors acting for the executors held the money in their client account and paid it directly to the vendor of the property,' said Naish. 'That would be reasonably normal practice. That is assuming, of course, that it was inherited money. As yet, we have no means to prove that, let alone where these considerable sums came from. What were the intervals between these purchases?'

'The first house, the one in Lansdown Crescent, was purchased in 1938. The second, a house in Camden Crescent, was in 1942, then in 1947 he buys two houses in Daniel Street. In 1949 he buys his second house in Camden Crescent, and his last, the house in Duke Street, in May 1950, three and a half years ago.'

'No particular pattern then,' said Naish, 'but it would not be unexpected if he was to make another such purchase sometime soon.'

'Unless his line of rich family has finally been exhausted,' said Hancock, with a smile.

'As I have said, we have no means of knowing that to have been the case at all,' said Naish. 'However, I am not sure that we have the means to look further into the source of this money. If it is inherited money, then we can search the probate records of his family members – if we can identify them – without his knowing what we are up to, but it is another dockyard job.'

'Why don't I just try and trace one or two of them,' said Newton. 'If the inheritance theory stacks up, then at least two of them must have left him significant sums. That is supposing, of course, that he does have any relatives at all. I understand your concern about wasted effort, Inspector, but in this case I think that the potential benefits outweigh the effort. I am happy to take it on.'

'I am happy to let you get on with that. I think that you should get up to London and visit Somerset House. It's no good trying to do this sort of job using local records and then after all your effort find them incomplete and the job not done. No, Somerset House is the place, especially if he was originally from London. Whilst you are up there it would be worthwhile to look in at Scotland Yard and see what information they have on our friend Emery. I will telephone a contact that I have there, to make sure that you have all the assistance that you need. If you get the first train in the morning, you can be back here by Wednesday evening with the job done, hopefully. If you are going to run over, just keep me informed. If you get a blank travel warrant, I will sign it for you and trust you to fill in the details. Don't do the Ritz or that will be my pension gone west,' said Naish, with a smile. 'Now then, Hancock – what of your afternoon?'

'Well, the good news is that Emery has returned to his shop. However, he has not resumed his old routine in the evening. I hung around until half past five and I saw him lock up and then followed him along to his house in St Mark's Road. As for a location to set up a surveillance position opposite, I don't see much opportunity for that. The Old Jupiter is out, as we don't want to involve the landlord. Anything beyond the Old Jupiter does not give a clear view of the picture framers, and the two or three shops are, as far as I can tell, unoccupied on the first and second floors. They also have attic rooms as well. I went into each of the three shops that are potentially suitable for use and spoke with the proprietors on various pretexts. I am not sure that I would trust any of them. One was too nosey, one was clearly a gossip and the last was, at best, surly. I think that any approach would be difficult and, even if it were successful, I think the chances of maintaining any discretion are nil.'

'Not too promising from the surveillance point of view, then,' said Naish. 'Any chance at the rear of the premises?'

'No, and I don't think it would give us much by way of information. The majority of the movements in and out of the shop are clearly made through the front shop door. However, there was one interesting feature about the occupants of the premises around the picture framers – there are none. At least, not after six o clock, when the last of them shuts up for the night. The two shops either side have no one living above them, the three shops opposite I have just described. The Old Jupiter is the only one nearby where the owner lives over, and, from what I can make out, he sleeps at the rear of the building. There are quite a few other shops in the Parade where the proprietor lives over, but not in the ones within reasonable earshot of the picture framers.'

'So, if Newton's theory that the second floor may have been a place of interrogation is correct, then the risk of the victim being heard was limited to a chance passer-by in the street outside,' said Naish, thoughtfully. 'So, all in all, not a bad afternoon's work, Sergeant.'

'How about your afternoon, Inspector?' asked Hancock.

'Very interesting, very interesting indeed,' said Naish, rolling himself a cigarette. 'I took a walk round to the art shop in Green Street and had a look at the pre-made canvases that they sold. Interestingly, as has already been mentioned by Newton, the canvases we have appear to be a darker and finer cloth than those being sold – they were bright white and relatively rough in terms of texture. Interestingly, even the most expensive range that they sell has a frame that is made of what I would call cheap wood. It is planed, not sanded, and is formed from pine sections that are about a half-inch square. I imagine it is bought in lengths and cut to size. The jointing is also quite basic, a simple joint cut and then pinned with a metal staple. Although it is a good quality shop, it was obvious that it had nothing like our pieces over there on the table. So I took one of the canvases over to Bristol to an auction house in Clifton that specialises in fine art. They were extremely illuminating on the subject. It was the view of the expert there that the frame for our canvas has been handmade. At first he thought that the wood that had been used had been stained to give it an appearance of age, but on closer examination he was of the opinion that it was wood from an old frame that had been cut down and reused to form this frame. His other interesting observation about the frame was that it was, in line with the thoughts of our resident expert Hancock, a bespoke frame made to a specific size, presumably to the exact requirements of the artist.'

'Well done me,' said Hancock, with a smile.

'Don't overdo the modesty,' said Naish, with a wry smile. 'As for the canvas, it is apparently a high-quality cloth. It is not possible to tell the age or estimate a time of its manufacture, but it has clearly not been used before. Apparently, it is not uncommon for artists, particularly if they are poor, to reuse old canvases. The colour of our canvases that we were puzzling over is the result of it having been prepared for painting with a sort of size – a common process, apparently, for artists with a pretence to being taken seriously. However, he was intrigued by one feature, and that was that the outline of the building drawn on the canvas had been done before the sizing had been applied. In his view, an artist would prepare the canvas and then usually apply a coat of white paint as a sort of base, before beginning the subject he was painting. Clearly this process would hide from view any original sketch used as an outline for the painting. The way our artist has gone about it would mean that, once the white base coat was applied over the size, the drawing he was going to use as the outline of his painting would be lost from sight.'

'Perhaps he wanted to make sure that the thing he was going to paint would fit on the canvas,' offered Hancock.

'I asked that question myself, but I used the word subject rather than thing,' said Naish. 'That's your budding reputation as an art expert gone. The expert thought it would be very unusual, as an artist would usually do a number of detailed sketches in the same size as the planned painting in order to get the proportions correct. The bespoke canvas would then be commissioned to accommodate the painting that had been planned. The expert was of the view that to do it in the manner I suggested would only be done if the artist had a fixed-size canvas that he had to fill and wanted to check his proportions before starting. In this situation, the artist is governed by the size of the canvas, whereas in our case, and apparently in the case of all professional and serious amateur artists, the canvas is made to accommodate the painting.'

'So, we have an anomaly with the circumstances before us,' said Hancock.

'Such would appear to be the case,' said Naish. 'Anyway, it's food for thought, and talking of food, it is getting late. I suggest that we sleep on it for now. Newton, you need to be getting away. I will see you back here in forty-eight hours. Hancock, I will see you for tea and a smoke, first thing tomorrow.'

Chapter 9

'What have you got there?' said Naish, as Hancock came into the office.

'These are the sketches from our police artist. He brought them up yesterday afternoon, as promised, but we were all tied up with various things, so he left them at the front desk. I just picked them up as I came in.'

'What do you think of them?' asked Naish.

'Well, these here are of the late, unlamented Tom Edwards, and whilst they are of no use to us anymore, they are helpful from one perspective.'

'Which is?'

'Which is that it gives us an ability to judge the quality of our artist's skills. I would say that these sketches of Edwards are a very accurate depiction of the man we now know. So it follows that this sketch of our friend from the Golden Fleece should hopefully be of equivalent quality.'

'True, but the quality is also dependent upon the accuracy of the one giving the description isn't it. So, if, come the end, this sketch does not look like the man we eventually track down, then we will know that Orton has been deceitful, and, if he has, then I will have him just as I threatened him.'

'So, where do we go with this sketch?'

'I want to keep it in a very discreet and limited circulation for now. Get a couple of colour copies made as soon as you can. I think that in the first instance, we need to take it around to the landlord of the Old Jupiter. We know that he saw this man. Hopefully, he was one of the men at the back of the shop. He is not at risk from the gang, as far as I can tell, and so we can get a quick verification of the picture little risk. Although, he will need to be warned to keep his silence or else he will be putting himself at considerable risk.'

'We tell him that after he has identified the picture, I take it?' said Hancock, with a wry smile.

'Absolutely. All is fair in love and police work. I also want Barney Jones to have sight of it, but he is at risk and so we need to consider a discreet means by which he can view the picture without drawing attention to our association with him. The same goes for George Jenkins at the Golden Fleece. Then I think it would be useful to show the picture to Mrs West at Oak Street and the landlady at the Rose and Laurel. It may well be that these men have called on them, or been near them, without them realising it. That will also potentially give us an idea of the gang's interest in Lynch and Edwards. I think we can do that without exposing them to any risk at all.'

'That sounds good to me. In the case of Barney Jones, I know one of the cleaners in the market. I think I can arrange for an envelope to be dropped off at his stall without attracting any attention, and then picked up again at a later time.'

'That's a good scheme. I have already established a reason to call again on George Jenkins in the spurious matter of his licence renewal. If you prepare me an envelope identical to the one for Jones, then I will take it around to him. In his case, he can sign it while I wait, or I will just ask him to post it back. I suggest that you fill out a witness statement form that simply confirms that they have positively identified the man. In Jones's case, that they came to his stall and made the said enquiries regarding the watches, and in the case of Jenkins, that he identified the man as the solitary drinker in his pub. More detailed statements can be made once all this is over, but a statement of positive identification will suffice for now.'

'Right, I will get that done as soon as the printers are open. What else were you wanting done today?'

'As soon as you are back from the printers you can be dealing with the Jenkins and Jones papers. While you are doing that, I will get the car to take me over to the Old Jupiter and then I will take a chance on dropping in on Mrs West and Mrs Wilson. I think that with a fair wind we should both be back here for a cup of tea and a smoke by eleven o'clock.'

'Right, Inspector. See you at eleven. Watch out for Mrs Wilson.'

'I have arranged for the Jones envelope to be dropped off in the next hour. If Jones works with us, the reply envelope will be picked up about three o'clock this afternoon. The envelope for you to take to Jenkins is there on your desk.'

'Thank you. It's good news from the Old Jupiter. The landlord identified the man as one of the two that he saw at the rear of Emery's shop, so we have a positive connection between the thug, the blue van and the redecoration work.'

'How about Mrs West and Mrs Wilson?'

'Mrs West did not recognise the man at all, so at least we know he has not been sniffing around Oak Street. She has not had anyone else making enquiries either, which is reassuring. I asked her to let us know if anyone called making enquiries of any nature. I also took with me the sketch of Edwards and she positively identified him as the cleric that left her house with Ted Lynch. As for Mrs Wilson, she had never seen the man, but by a lucky coincidence her cellar man was hanging around in the bar and she asked him if he had ever seen the man. Very interestingly, he said that he had. On the Monday night, if you remember, Mrs Wilson had met Edwards as he came in through the back door at about half past ten. Well, it transpires that the cellar man was out in the rear yard and, having finished stacking some crates of beer bottles, he was sitting quietly on them having a crafty smoke. He saw Edwards come back into the rear yard of the pub in the company of the thug in the sketch. They exchanged a few words that he was unable to hear and then he saw the thug give Edwards what looked like a small brown envelope, which Edwards opens and looks into as if to check the contents. He then put the envelope in his pocket and the thug goes on his way, and Edwards goes on into the pub where Mrs Wilson sees him.'

'Did they see the cellar man?' asked Hancock.

'No, and it may be fortunate for him that they didn't. Because I think that things could have turned out badly for him if he had revealed himself as an unwitting witness.'

'You think he was paying Edwards off?'

'I am certain that he was paying Edwards off for delivering Ted Lynch into their hands, and I think the sum involved was the twenty-five pounds that we found in Edwards's post office book. I can't prove it, at the moment, but I am certain that that is what has occurred. It is only a small piece of the puzzle, but for the first time we have a significant number of pieces that fit together.'

'You are right. They do fit together, and it all looks very logical. It just needs fitting into the wider puzzle of how and why it was done.'

'I agree, but like you, I have a feeling that that is what happened on that Monday night. Why and how, I don't know yet, but as sure as eggs is eggs, Tom Edwards was coerced, either willingly or unwillingly, to betray his cellmate Lynch into the hands of this gang, who I believe went on to torture and murder him in the course of the next thirty-six hours or so.'

'It looks like he was a willing associate, given he took what we believe to be the blood money,' said Hancock. 'They would betray their own mothers some of these bastards.'

'He may have accepted unwillingly,' said Naish, 'knowing that, if he didn't take the job and the money, he would most likely end up dead himself. Either way I agree with you – it's a low thing to do. But there is no honour among thieves, as the saying goes. The significant thing to me is that the serial numbers on the banknotes now provide an indelible link to the crime. Eventually, if we can identify some of our thugs' known associates, and then look into their financial affairs, there is the strong possibility that we can link them to the notes and hence to the crime. But we are getting ahead of ourselves again.'

'Maybe, but you have to admit, you have made a leap forward with that information.'

'I agree,' said Naish. 'So, what should we do next, Sergeant Hancock?'

'I have been wondering if it might be worth using the gasman ploy on our friend Mr Emery.'

'For what reason?' asked Naish.

'Because I want to have a close look around on that top floor. Now we know that it was definitely one of the thugs in there involved in the clear-up redecoration, it adds weight to Newton's suggestion that it could have been the location where Lynch and Edwards were done away with. If we got the opportunity to re-examine the area knowing what we are looking for, we might be able to rule the idea in or out.'

'I see your point. Get in without Emery being aware we are taking an interest in him again, you mean?'

'Exactly. It gets us the information we need and it deals with your concerns about provoking his suspicions.'

'So, who would play the gasman?'

'I suggest young Constable Miller.'

'The lad who has been driving me about recently?'

'That's him. Bright lad, shows a lot of promise. I will give him a complete briefing if you are happy.'

'Go on then, but we can't risk any cock-ups here. One foot wrong and Emery will be on to us.'

'I will take care of it,' said Hancock.

'The other thing that I have been going over and over in my mind is who owns those sketchbooks?' said Naish.

'Yes, that question had occurred to me as well. If Emery is not an artist, by his own admission, then clearly they belong to someone else.'

'Someone who has left them there or someone who frequents the place who we have not seen up to now. It could well be that someone joins Emery at the premises after hours, upstairs above the shop.'

'But for what purpose?'

'Perhaps he wanted some of the drawings in the sketchbooks mounted in frames – they are certainly good enough. Perhaps not good enough for the retail trade, but good enough that an artist proud of his own work would wish to display them at an exhibition or else his own home.'

'So, your hypothesis is that, for some reason, Emery has let this person use his workshop to frame his own work?'

'It is, indeed, only a hypothesis,' said Naish, lighting a cigarette.

'It could be that he lets this person in by the back door and leaves this person with the use of his premises while he lets himself out via the back door, returning just before half past ten. He lets this person out by the back door once again, and then leaves by the front door as the landlord of the Old Jupiter reports seeing.'

'It's an ingenious theory,' said Naish, 'and it would account for the facts as we have them. The main counter argument, of course, is the nocturnal activity has been going on for some time and yet the sketchbooks are still intact.'

'There may have been a third one that he has already completed,' offered Hancock.

'It would support our hypothesis, but I think we are grasping at straws to keep it afloat, if I am honest. It all hangs on whether Emery is lying.'

'Lying?'

'Lying about his lack of artistic skills. If he is lying, then the sketchbooks could possibly belong to him. Then our hypothesis of the second man falls apart.'

'But why would Emery lie about having an artistic bent? What would be the problem with that?'

'I agree with you, I cannot see any reason to play down such a talent, but you have to admit that if they are his sketchbooks he does not appear very concerned about the loss of them. In fact, he has in effect denied all knowledge of them.'

'Then is it this mysterious other person who owns them and is either unaware that they have been stolen from Emery's premises or else is not fussed about the fact?'

'Or is he, in fact, extremely troubled by the loss of them and is prepared to go to extraordinary lengths to track down the thief, Ted Lynch, torture and then murder him in order to recover them, and, having failed in that, he is prepared to do the same to Tom Edwards.'

'But why?' said Hancock. 'What in the world can be so valuable in these two sketchbooks that someone would go to such lengths – it's just not credible.'

'Then we are either wrong, and wrong by a wide margin, or else there is something else in this matter that we have failed to recognise or understand.'

'Then is there something, a fact, a clue or an item of evidence that, if we had it, could make sense of this business?'

'It could well be, and if it is one of those things that we need to make sense of the case then I am concerned that we may never get to the bottom of it. Let us assume that there is some element of truth in this hypothesis of ours – not all of it – but let's assume that our general theme is somewhere on the money. I agree with you that there is an apparent disconnect between the value of these sketchbooks and the crimes that have been committed as a consequence of their loss. If that is the case, what you and I have got to do is understand what their value is. They are, to you and me, of little intrinsic value, but to the owner who produced them they are clearly of sufficient sentimental or material value to kill for. So, what is the value?'

'Do they contain a message, not a code exactly, but some message conveyed by the drawings – is that their value? Are they plans for a building that is a potential target of a burglary? Is there something, a message or the like, concealed in the spine or in some sort of invisible ink on the pages? I know that it is sounding far-fetched, but I really am struggling to see this one.'

'You and I both,' said Naish, with a reassuring smile. 'I think we go with this. Let's send the sketchbooks for detailed analysis. If nothing comes back, then we have to stop the theorising about the sketchbooks and refocus our investigations on another part of this case that gives us some sort of foothold that gets us somewhere towards solving it.'

'That sounds like a plan to me.'

'Right, you make some phone calls and try and identify a suitable laboratory or facility that might be able to assist us. I am going to have a lunchtime pint and a cheese roll over at the Golden Fleece and deliver the envelope to George Jenkins. I will see you back in here at two o'clock.'

'Well, that was a worthwhile lunch out,' said Naish, as Hancock entered the office.

'What did he have to say?'

'He said nothing about it at all in the pub. I slipped the artist's impression over the counter to George in a bundle of other papers and he took them out the back to examine them. As I was finishing my lunch, he placed the papers back on the bar for me, did some business of signing one or two signatures on a blank piece of paper for show – to any customers who might have been watching – and I left. I have just been looking through the bundle and I have located the artist's impression which he has signed and a copy of his statement of identification also duly signed. All very satisfactory.'

'Well, if this is what I think it is, hopefully we have had a reply from Jones as well,' said Hancock, handing Naish another envelope. 'It was dropped off by the market cleaner just before I came back through the foyer.'

'A second piece of good news,' said Naish, handing the statement to Hancock to read. 'So, we have everything that we had hoped for regarding our friend the thug. He is one and the same man as identified by all our witnesses. Progress at last. Time for a smoke and a cup of tea to celebrate, don't you think?'

There was a brisk knock at the door and the desk sergeant came in without waiting for a response.

'Sorry to barge in, Inspector, but there is something going on that I think may be of urgent interest to you.'

'What?' said Naish, with a cautious tone in his voice.

'There is a fire in progress in Broadway Parade – the picture framer's shop. Going like a train, so I understand.'

'I knew it was too good to last,' said Naish. 'When did the fire break out?'

'Local constable phoned it in about five minutes ago, at half past two, and said that the fire brigade was just pulling up. We had a second call from the brigade asking for assistance with closing the road about two minutes later.'

'Your somewhat vivid analogy would appear to be very apt, Sergeant,' said Naish, as he stood up and looked out of his office window. From the direction of Broadway Parade, a large plume of black smoke was rising into the sky. 'It is indeed going like a train.'

'Shall I get round there?' asked Hancock.

'It would be best if you can. You won't be able to do much until the fire is out and some sort of investigation can then begin, but it would be best to have an informed eye at the scene. Let me know when it's worth me coming down to start asking some questions.'

After Hancock had gone, Naish lit a cigarette, glanced at his watch and picked up the telephone.

'Can you send up someone with a copy of the city gazetteer. If it is someone with a good knowledge of the city shops, that would be even better.'

Naish put down the phone and returned to his cigarette. After ten minutes there was a knock at the door and an elderly constable came in.

'Ah Davis, sorry to have you put to running errands, but I asked for someone with a good knowledge of the city. So I have struck lucky with you.'

'There aren't many people I would say could better me for knowledge of the city's topography, Inspector, but I would say you were one of the few that are my equal.'

'Kind of you to say so, Davis, but it is a while since I have walked the beat and so you may have the edge on me for current knowledge. Now what I am after is a list of the high-end dealers in art and antiques in the city – not the ones aimed at the tourists and the amateur collectors – I am after the ones that supply the serious trade.'

'Well, for antiques I would say that you are looking at Frazer's in Old King Street and Dobson's in Queens Square.'

'Yes, I would agree with that,' said Naish, offering Davis his tobacco tin. 'For fine art I would suggest the Byfield Gallery in Wood Street?'

'I would agree with you there, Inspector,' said Davis, pushing Naish's tin back across the desk and lighting his cigarette. 'None finer. They come from London and all places to their showroom. There are a couple of other quality ones, but they are in the next division down, so to speak, in my humble view.'

'No, I concur with you. Can you do me a favour and get me the name of the top man at each of the three we have agreed on, so that I know who to ask for if I take a wander round to them in the next few days.'

'Of course, Inspector, I will have it for you within the hour. I will also jot down the names and contacts for my two second division players, if that is of any use?'

'Yes, that will be useful if the first three draw a blank. I may not be here in an hour because I need to take a wander down to that fire in Broadway Parade. If I am out just leave it on the desk will you.'

'Come in,' said Naish, stubbing his cigarette out as Hancock came in. 'Fire out, then?'

'It is, and the brigade are beginning to damp down inside. I have had a chat with the senior fire officer. A good man who I think you know as well – Station Officer Hazel.'

'Yes, I know him all right. What are his thoughts?'

'Too early to say yet. I have explained a little of our interest in the premises and that we need to have his report as to the supposed cause. He said that if we give him an hour, he should be able to give us at least his preliminary thoughts on the matter. So, I thought I would come back and have a cup of tea and we could walk back together to meet him at half past four.'

'Fine,' said Naish. 'Anything else worthy of note catch your eye? How about Emery?'

'Nothing of note. I spent the first three quarters of an hour mingling with the crowd to see if anyone was taking an unusual interest, but I didn't spot anyone, just the usual collection of idlers and loafers that you get hanging around at these events. As for Emery, there was no sign of him at all.'

'But it's the afternoon of a trading day, was the shop not open?'

'I put that to our old friend the landlord of the Old Jupiter and a couple of other shopkeepers who had been evacuated by the blaze. Apparently, he was seen this morning going in and out a few times, but no one has seen him since just after two o' clock when he returned from lunch.'

'So, he was open for business when the fire started?'

'It would appear so.'

'Is he inside the building, then?'

'Too early to say. He has not been seen by any of the witnesses that I spoke to, but that is not to say that he didn't get away, perhaps out of the backdoor. The firemen who went inside didn't find anyone as they were fighting the fire, according to Hazel, but they need to do a thorough check to be certain.'

'Have you been around to his house?'

'That was the next thing that I did. I went around to St Mark's Road and knocked at the door but got no reply. I had a wander around the back, but I could see no sign of him.'

'Did you not try and force an entry?'

'I thought it a bit previous, to be honest, not having a real justification and no warrant. I thought that I might leave myself a little exposed to criticism, to be honest.'

'Fair comment,' said Naish, ruefully. 'Right, let's have that cup of tea and a smoke then we can set off for Broadway Parade.'

'What was Davis after, if you don't mind my asking?' said Hancock.

'I was picking his brains about the quality art and antiques dealers in the city. It occurred to me that if Emery is the one making these high-quality picture frames, then it is possible that he is doing so for a quality market. Clearly his own shop is not in that bracket, and so I thought that I would just take a wander around to the best ones and have a sniff about.'

'Sounds a sensible thing to do. As you say, he must be making them for someone. If it's not a private client, then it may be a top-end dealer.'

'Just another line to try and get us that bit further in this business. Anyway, it will have to wait for now until we have dealt with this damn fire.'

Naish and Hancock came down the front steps of the station, crossed Orange Grove and walked down Manvers Street towards Bath Spa railway station. Dusk was giving way to darkness in the late autumn evening, but a pall of steam and light smoke was still visible in the sky above the railway station roof. They walked through the tunnel under the station and then crossed the river by the bridge where Lynch had been found hanging and then along to Broadway Parade. There were a considerable number of people gathered at the cordon that closed off the end of the Parade; a few were sightseers, but the majority were commuters pausing to watch while considering the best diversionary route that they could take as a result of this unexpected change to their evening routine. The constable on duty at the cordon lifted the rope to enable Naish and Hancock to pass. Two fire engines were still at the scene and the firemen were still coming and going from the shop dealing with the last remaining embers. Naish recognised station officer Hazel standing on the opposite pavement surveying his men's activities and wandered over to chat with him.

'Good evening, station officer. Anything to report, as yet?'

'Good evening to you, Inspector Naish,' said Hazel, taking off his helmet and wiping his brow. 'As you can see, it was quite a severe fire, but we managed to knock it down quite quickly.'

'Any sign of the proprietor inside?'

'The elusive Mr Emery? No, there is no sign of him, so I have reported to my control room that fact. The fire was intense enough but not of sufficient duration to have consumed a body, so he must be somewhere else, as far as I am concerned.'

'Good news,' said Naish. 'Have you any idea how it started? I assume that, given the time of day, it was not arson.'

'As you say, this time of day in an occupied premise is not a usual time for an arson attack. However, on first examination, I am not convinced that it was accidental. If it was, then it involved the accidental spilling of an accelerant.'

'Petrol, you mean?'

'Paraffin for a heater would be the more usual flammable liquid to find accidentally spilt and causing an intense fire, but having had an initial look around, I think it may well be petrol, given the severity and speed of the fire development.'

'Well, I went through the property recently as part of an enquiry that I am making, and I can assure you that I didn't see any paraffin heaters in the place, if that helps your deductions.'

'Interesting,' said Hazel. 'Let me check with my leading fireman and, if everything is stable, I can take you inside and we can have a look round and compare our thoughts.'

'Well, given what we know, it's a certainty that it is a case of arson,' said Hancock, 'but for what purpose? Why now? Unless there was something that we failed to see in there, I cannot for the life of me see what they hoped to conceal by setting fire to the place. It can't be the building itself, so it must be something in it. And if it were an item, surely the best thing to do would be to take it away somewhere remote from the building and burn it discreetly there.'

'Perhaps it was meant as a message or a threat,' said Naish.

'But with what purpose? If they wanted to threaten Emery, they know where he is in his shop and, given that they tracked down Lynch and Edwards in more difficult circumstances, it wouldn't be beyond the wit of the worst amateur to follow him home one evening to a house he owns just five hundred yards away. It doesn't make sense.'

'It may be that they wished to remain anonymous.'

'But Emery knows them – he had the thug twins decorating his shop.'

'He did. But you are assuming that the people who did this are the same people.'

'You mean that someone else has got involved in this business?'

'I don't know, but if it was meant as a threat, and we are still surmising that, then it would make sense of the facts, wouldn't it?'

'I see your point.'

'As I see it, there are only three options. First, that Emery set fire to the shop for reasons we do not yet know. Second, that Emery left the shop either voluntarily or under duress, and that person or persons set fire to the shop, either to conceal something or else as a threat. Third, that Emery caused the fire accidentally and fled.'

'Well, I rule out the third, personally, even more so as, if it were the case, surely Emery would have made the first call to the brigade. Five calls were made, and he was not one of them – I have looked into that already.'

'Very efficient, Sergeant,' said Naish, with a smile. 'My gut instinct is that we are dealing with option two. The only matter in question is, was it for reasons of threat or concealment? Anyway, let's wait and see where the facts take us shall we?'

As Naish finished speaking, Hazel reappeared at the shop doorway and beckoned for them to come over and join him.

Chapter 10

Naish and Hancock followed Hazel through the doorway. The front door of the shop lay in pieces to one side as a result of the brigade forcing entry. The ground floor was badly smoke- damaged and the walls were running with soot-stained condensation caused by the heat of the fire, which could still be felt in the building. The front window was still intact, but there was a lot of debris and water across the ground floor which Naish and Hancock attempted to navigate, stepping in the shallower areas of the water which had accumulated from the fire hoses.

'I am not sure how you would like to conduct this investigation, Inspector,' said Hazel. 'Would you prefer to take a look around yourself first and form a view before I give you my thoughts on the fire development? Or shall I talk you through the building as I see it?'

'I am happy to be guided through by you, station officer. This is an area of your expertise, not mine. If I need to pause or have any additional questions, I will call out.'

'That's fine with me. Then I think we can start the story here at the foot of the staircase,' began Hazel. 'I think that we are dealing with professionals here – professionals but not experts.'

'So, this is not an accidental fire, then?' asked Naish.

'It is certainly not accidental,' said Hazel. 'Whilst there is a lot of smoke damage throughout the building, there are two main areas of burning. If you look up this staircase, here, which goes up to the first floor, you can see that quite a severe fire has occurred. This area of the fire has caused the damage to the first floor and the ground floor, but the main area of burning is on the staircase itself. Now, if you look here, where my men have swept the stairs clear of debris, you can see quite clearly an area where the wood has been burnt more deeply than that around it.'

'Almost as if it has poured down the stairs,' said Hancock.

'That is very perceptive,' said Hazel, 'because that is exactly what has happened. A liquid, and, from the smell of it, I would say it was petrol that has been poured over the stairs and then set alight. Because the petrol has ignited first and burnt most intensely on the surface of the floor, it has scorched a pattern of itself into the wood. It is a classic indication that a flammable liquid has been used. Now, there are some situations where the presence of a flammable liquid might be anticipated, a paraffin heater in the home for example. However, given that you did not see a paraffin heater in the premises, there is no such explanation for such a liquid being here. Small amounts of turpentine and white spirit have been found in two containers in the workshop area over there, but they are not of sufficient quantities to have done this and, interestingly, they have not been used in connection with this fire as they are both nearly full.'

'Hence the assumption this is not Mr Emery's doing,' said Hancock.

'I am not saying that it was not the work of the proprietor or that he was or was not involved, only that the flammable liquids that he used in connection with his business have not contributed to the fire.'

'Is it not odd that other areas of the ground floor have not been doused in fuel in a case of arson?' asked Naish.

'It is unusual, but it may have been that the intention was to destroy the building and, if that was the case, then it would make sense to ensure that the staircase that links the entire property was the main source of the fire. It would then have spread throughout the building, the staircase acting like a chimney. The fact that all the doors off the staircase are opened may be deliberate or it may be coincidental.'

'On my previous visits to this property the doors off the staircase were always left opened,' said Naish.

'Now, if you follow me carefully on up to the first floor landing, we can look at the second area of burning.'

'So, these doors were open when your men came up the stairs?' asked Naish, as he looked about himself on the first floor landing.

'Yes, they were and that is why these rooms have suffered so much damage.'

'Smoke and heat damage in the main though, I would suggest?' said Naish.

'Yes, that is right. There is very little evidence of direct burning,' agreed Hazel. 'Now here, at the foot of the stairs to the second floor, you can see this second area of burning on the staircase almost identical to that on the stairs we have just looked at. The main difference here is the severity of the fire. If you look again at the pattern of burning here, it is much deeper.'

'Might that be due to the fact that, presumably, this fire was lit before the one below it, as the arsonist made their way out of the property, and therefore it burnt longer? It was also, I assume, put out later as your men made their way up the staircase into the building,' said Hancock.

'That is very true,' said Hazel. 'It may well have contributed to this deeper scorching, but I don't think it is the complete explanation. I think it is also the result of far more fuel having been used here. On the staircase below, the burn pattern caused by the fuel looked as if it had been poured from a can as a person walked backwards down the stairs – that left behind that narrow spill pattern down the centre of the staircase. If you look on these stairs, the fuel has covered almost the entire surface of every tread. There are only a few small areas in the back corners against the risers, here and here, for example, where the fuel has not extended. Now, if you tread carefully and come up to the second floor, there is one more area to look at.'

Naish and Hancock followed Hazel up on to the second floor. The open area was less dark than the staircase as the evening light was visible through a couple of areas of the roof where the fire had set light to the roof timbers and the brigade had cut open the roof to extinguish the embers.

'If we stand to the side here, we can see what I want to show you without stepping on the evidence too much,' said Hazel. 'This is the only other area that has been ignited using a fuel. As you can see once again, there is the classic pool pattern across the centre of the room where the fuel has been poured. Again, the fire has been very severe, and the damage is quite extensive, destroying that large skylight and even penetrating the roof, as you can see.'

'Do you mind if I walk across to the far corner?' asked Naish.

'Certainly, Inspector, it's safe enough to walk on.'

'Can I borrow that torch of yours, station officer?' said Naish, as he went over and sank on his haunches. 'Despite the fire, it is interesting that the lino floor covering has survived in all four corners of the room. These far corners at the opposite ends to the staircase are the best preserved.'

'It is not unusual, Inspector,' said Hazel. 'Unless the oxygen can get around an object it will not burn. The upper surfaces are often badly burned but when lifted you find the underside completely undamaged.'

'That is what I am hoping,' said Naish. 'Now, can I please ask that, as soon as you are content that the fire is extinguished, your men ensure that the roof is sheeted up and made weather-proof, and that, once we have left, no one else comes up into this second floor. It is important to my enquiries that what remains is left undisturbed.'

'Of course, Inspector, I will see to it, you may rest assured.'

'Thank you. Then perhaps we can conclude our discussions as to the origins of the fire, and then I can explain to you how I see it fitting in to the case that I am investigating.'

'Well, now that I have shown you the relevant areas, Inspector, I think that, if you are in agreement, I can talk you through the remainder of my theory over at the Old Jupiter, where the landlord has been good enough to provide tea and coffee for my men.'

'So, station officer,' said Naish, lighting a cigarette and throwing the match into the fireplace in the bar parlour, 'what do you conclude from what you have shown us?'

'It is my conclusion that a deliberate act has caused the fire. That fact is plain to me by the clear evidence of accelerants, in the form of petrol, whose distinctive burn patterns you have seen,' said Hazel, warming his hands around a mug of tea.

'But you suggest that you discern something more in terms of the arsonists' actions and intentions?' asked Naish.

'Yes, Inspector, I do. As I said earlier, I believe that a number of things have been done to give the impression that the fire was not arson. However, schoolboy errors in the lack of understanding of the burn patterns that accelerants leave, draw me to the conclusion that this fire was planned by someone with a professional criminal background but one who is not an expert in the use of fire as a means of destroying evidence,' said Hazel, as he watched the confused expressions on the faces of the two policemen. 'Let me explain myself in more detail. I know that the fire was deliberately set, and it was set by someone other than the proprietor. I believe that this time of day was chosen with the deliberate intention of trying to make the fire appear accidental. Arson, as we know, is most commonly committed at night when the property is unoccupied and the fire has the greatest chance of taking hold of a building and achieving the arsonists' objectives. The manner in which the petrol has been applied to various areas of the building is also of interest. I think that there was a real intent to destroy the top floor of the building.'

'The second-floor area, you mean?' said Naish.

'Exactly. That is the only place in the building other than the stairs where fuel has been applied.'

'Yet, there was nothing to destroy, as far as I can tell,' said Naish. 'When I last visited the premises and went up onto the second floor, it was completely empty of any furniture or fixings.'

'Well, that tallies with my examination post-fire,' said Hazel. 'There is no evidence of anything having been there of any substance since, even with the severity of the fire, furniture or light fixtures and fittings would have left some remnants of their existence.'

'What about something like a picture frame?' said Hancock. 'You know, a canvas stretched on a light timber frame. Surely a fire of that magnitude would have destroyed something like that to ash?'

'Yes, in all probability, an item such as you describe would indeed be rendered down to nothing more than ash. I have not done a fingertip search of the floor, but I can do so if you wish. It may be that a mere fragment of such an item could be discerned in the debris.'

'I think that it would be worthwhile doing such an examination when we revisit the building tomorrow,' said Naish. 'Please continue with your deductions about the arsonist.'

'Accepting the points raised, the application of such an amount of accelerant, in my view, confirms the intention was to destroy something on that second-floor level. The heavy application of petrol over the upper staircase would also lead me to suppose that the arsonist, knowing a little of the physics of combustion, concluded that, if the stairs were also involved in a well-developed fire, then the staircase would cause a chimney effect. This would draw in more air and result in an extraordinarily intense fire on that second floor, and that was in fact what happened, as you saw from the way the fire broke through the roof structure. If we had not arrived so promptly, then the upper floor and roof would, in all probability, have been completely destroyed by the fire.'

'So, if the arsonist had not tried to be so keen to give the impression that it was an accidental fire occurring in the afternoon, and had, in fact, committed the act at night, then their objective would have been certain to succeed?' said Naish.

'Undoubtedly so, Inspector – almost too clever by half, you might say.'

'Indeed,' said Naish.

'I believe that the more scant application of petrol on the lower staircase was simply to give the impression that the whole building was affected by the outbreak of fire and mask the true target of the attack which was the second-floor area.'

'Could the more scant application simply be that the arsonist realised that he was running out of petrol as he came down the lower stairs, presumably pouring out the petrol as he went?' said Hancock.

'It may account for it, but I am not sure. If he ran out of fuel unexpectedly, then you might expect to see the application of fuel on the upper portion of the lower staircase be as heavy as that on the upper staircase, and the application get scanter and scanter towards the last few stairs, or have stopped on the last few stairs altogether. That is not the case, and I believe that the arsonist kept back sufficient fuel to carry out his intention to set a fire of some size on that lower staircase. It was because he was less concerned with creating the impression of a fire that spread throughout the building, than making sure that the second floor was totally destroyed, that accounts for the lesser application. I appreciate that I am speculating on the psychology of the arsonist, an area that I am not qualified to opine on, but that is what I believe was planned and what subsequently happened.'

'Well, thank you, Hazel, you have given me plenty to think about. Given that it is getting on for eight o'clock, I think that we should adjourn for tonight and arrange to meet at the station in Orange Grove first thing tomorrow morning, if that is convenient for you?'

'That will be fine with me, Inspector. I can get my second-in-command to cover me on the appliances and I will be at your office at eight o'clock sharp.'

'So, what are you thinking, Inspector?' said Hancock, as they walked together back to Orange Grove.

'I am thinking that if the purpose behind the fire being set was as Hazel supposes, then it may just be that Newton's theory is right.'

'That the second floor was the scene of the torture of both Lynch and Edwards?'

'It adds up from a logical sense, based on the facts and information we have, but that's why we need to get back round there tomorrow morning and carry out a thorough examination of that second floor. It the redecoration and new floor covering were intended to hide indications of a crime, then we have to hope that some of that evidence still exists under the lino.'

'From what Hazel said, there is the possibility of something being there but, given the intensity of the fire, I am not all that confident, personally.'

'Well, we have got to hope, haven't we? This is a case where it is only hope and speculation that appear to hold the theories together most of the time, facts and hard evidence being so short in supply. You need to get a couple of good detective constables together tomorrow morning and they can do the heavy work for us. We also need to go over the place, inside and out, again.'

'If that's what you want. You want evidence of the arson attack, I assume?'

'I do, but I am also looking for a poker, a hammer and a high-backed chair. It is clear to me that if Newton's theory holds water, then these items must have been in place on the second floor. Now, they may have been removed elsewhere some time ago, but if they weren't, then they may well be still there. They are small enough items to be tucked away out of sight in a cupboard or a drawer, and we have not done a fingertip search of the premises at any time. They clearly weren't in the fire, as the poker and the hammer would have survived in part, and, from Hazel's assumptions, the fire would have been unlikely to render down a piece of timber furniture like a chair to nothing but ash in that intense but short fire.'

'So, they may still be there?'

'Yes, or there may be evidence that attempts have been made to destroy them at the scene – in the backyard for instance. So we need to have a good look, then we can turn one piece of speculation into fact and prove they are or are not there, and whether it is or is not the scene of the torture and murder of our two victims.'

'Well, here's hoping,' said Hancock, with a dry smile, as they arrived back at the station steps. 'If you are done for the day, I am off for supper with the wife.'

'Have a pleasant evening and give my apologies to Mrs Hancock for the lateness of the hour. I will see you here in the morning.'

At eight o'clock the following morning, Hancock and Hazel were stood shoulder to shoulder at the head of the staircase on the second floor, while Naish was in the far corner of the room perched on a stepladder that he had found. From his vantage point, Naish was directing two detective constables who were preparing to lift the floor covering back.

'Right then, gentlemen,' said Naish to the two. 'As you can see, the central area of the floor covering had burnt away and the boards are deeply charred, but now that you have swept it clean, have we found anything of interest in the debris?'

'No, Inspector, there is nothing of interest other than unrecognisable pieces of timber and plaster which I assume fell from the ceiling as it burnt through.'

'That sounds feasible to me. However, if you place it all in that sack and pass it to Sergeant Hancock, then he can label it and add it to our collection of evidence. Now then, let me get down from here a moment and have a look at those boards.'

Naish climbed down from the steps and knelt at the edge of the central area of burning which had left four crescent shaped pieces of floor covering in each corner. He spent ten minutes on his hands and knees moving methodically to examine each square foot of the floor, occasionally stopping to scrutinise an area in greater detail using a magnifying glass.

'Well, I can make nothing from this area at all' said Naish, rising to his feet with a groan. 'Would you care to make an examination yourself, Hazel, and see if there is anything that I have missed?'

'No,' said Hazel, after ten minutes or so spent on his hands and knees, 'other than it being consistent with a classic pattern of burning caused by the application of an accelerant, I can find nothing more than yourself, Inspector.'

'Fine,' said Naish, returning to his stepladder. 'Hancock, if you have completed the note-taking for that part, then I think we will move next to the first of the corners.'

The two constables used a spade to slide under the edge of the lino and prise it from the floorboards. However, the lino had been loosely secured to the floor if indeed it had at all, and, to the constables' surprise, it came away from the boards remarkably easily. They rolled it up as they went, staying on the lino and rolling it back towards them to avoid disturbing what evidence may be concealed beneath it.

'Is it bloodstains we are looking for, Inspector?' asked one of the constables.

'That is certainly one possibility, but I am keeping an open mind.'

The first corner was now clear, and once the roll of charred lino had been put to one side, the floorboards were clearly visible. Although they were wet with water from the fire hoses, they were otherwise undamaged.

'Just what I told you, Inspector,' said Hazel. 'It is surprising how a floor covering can protect the boards from damage.'

'It is surprising, indeed,' said Naish, as he descended from his steps once again and knelt by the revealed floor surface. 'Unfortunately, there is no indication of anything at all. The boards appear clean and unmarked to me, no sign of anything at all.'

'Let me wipe them over with this rag,' said Hazel, kneeling beside him. 'No, you are right, they are as fresh as the day they were nailed down and, looking at them, they are the original boards.'

The second corner was in the same condition as the first. Naish, somewhat dejected, lit a cigarette and, as there was now sufficient space to be out of the way of the constables, abandoned his steps and leant against the wall next to Hazel.

'This one is a bit trickier, Inspector. It appears to have been glued down in this area,' said one of the constables, as he peered under the edge of the piece of lino they had begun to lift with the spade.

'Hang fire,' said Naish, moving forward and peering under the lino at the adhesive substance that held it down. 'Right, gently as you go, keep easing it up but keep it flat. I don't want it rolled, if we can avoid it.'

After ten minutes of levering with the spade and the additional assistance of Hazel and Hancock pulling around the edges, they had freed the triangular piece of lino. It was about five feet long on the two edges that were against the right angle of the corner, with a concaved curve on the third edge burnt into it by the fire.

'Lay it with the adhesive side up, over there in the first corner we cleared,' said Naish. 'What have we here then – a glue do you think, Hazel?'

'I don't think it is glue,' said Hazel, kneeling at the edge of the floorboards which had been revealed. 'If you look at the floor, as opposed to the underside of the lino, I think you get a better idea. I think it is paint, Inspector. Do you mind if I scrape up a small amount with my knife?'

'Not at all, carry on. Are you sure it's paint? It looks more like a pattern to me, there is such a variety of colours,' said Naish, peering at the floor intently.

'It's a very random pattern of colour, if you ask me,' said Hancock. 'Do you think it was a pattern on an older floor covering that the new lino was placed over. That would have to be the explanation, because the new lino that we saw with our own eyes just after it was laid was grey.'

'When I say paint,' continued Hazel, as he wiped the blade of his knife clean, 'I don't mean decorating paint. Imagine an artist's studio – an easel placed somewhere about here – and what you have all over the boards are the splash patterns that would accumulate as the artist worked. I would suggest that, given the amount of paint, it would have been used for a considerable time.'

'It accounts for the random pattern,' said Naish.

'I think that the lino was applied when the paint was dry – it may be a number of years since it was used as a studio – and the heat of the fire has melted the oil paint and it has formed an improvised glue between the boards and the underside of the lino.'

'I think you have hit the nail on the head, station officer,' said Naish. 'I am not sure it is what we hoped to find or that it goes anyway to making this business any clearer, but it would appear that you have explained what we see before us.'

'I think it might be best if we reserve judgement until the other corner has been cleared and then we can have a look at the floor as a whole and review our theory,' said Hazel. 'I also think that we should get this paint analysed to be certain that it is what we think it is.'

'I agree,' said Naish. 'We can get a few samples sent to the laboratories for testing.'

Half an hour later and the final corner had been cleared. It also revealed the same residue of paint as had been found in the third corner. With the whole floor uncovered, Naish directed his four colleagues to stand in the first corner that had been uncovered, as he moved across the floor and related his theory to them.

'I have reflected on your excellent observations, Hazel, and I have to say that it provides a compelling explanation of what we see before us. I suggest that if we look at these two areas of paint splatters, then it is apparent that they indicate that two easels were set up in this area of the floor comparatively close to each other. If, in your imagination, you infill the areas of burning, then you are left with two areas where the concentrations of paint are extremely dense. In fact, if you look at the floorboards between the two areas there is, in fact, a lesser accumulation of paint that almost forms the two into a figure eight.'

'It would make sense that the easels were positioned there,' said Hancock. 'From my recollection, it is where the skylight let in the natural light, and I also thought it unusual that there were more light fittings hanging from the ceiling in that part of the room. The provision of light for an artist makes sense to me.'

'It would also enable our artist to work on until half past ten at night in the winter months,' said Naish. 'Now, going back to proof, we need to get the paint deposits photographed and then sent for analysis. I also draw your attention to the nails around the edge of the room and the corresponding holes at the edge of the unburnt portions of linoleum. It demonstrates to me that they were the means of fixing the lino down and not any adhesive applied over the paint. So, it takes us back to a number of fundamental questions, doesn't it?'

Naish glanced over at his three police colleagues but since none offered a response, he continued as if his appeal had been rhetorical.

'Who is the artist? What is Emery's involvement? And how long ago was this last used as an artist's studio?'

'You suggest that the redecoration, although recent, may have simply been done to deal with an untidy area of long-standing?' asked Hancock.

'I agree that it would appear uncannily coincidental, but it is a point that needs to be proven. We cannot simply speculate. No matter how compelling the circumstantial evidence may be, we need to establish the facts.

'Then finding Emery is fundamental to answering all three of your questions,' said Hancock. 'I would add a fourth question to yours, as well – where are the paintings that have been produced here? I mean, there must be a few to account for, the amount of drips and splashes on the floor.'

'I agree, your question undoubtedly needs to be answered as well,' said Naish. 'The one thing that I think we can discount is that this was the scene where either Lynch or Edwards met their ends – there is nothing here to suggest it to me. I think that we can take a break now for a smoke and a cup of tea. After which, I want you, Hancock, to ensure that this scene is properly recorded and your two constables to start a fingertip search of the rest of the building for the poker, the hammer, the chair and anything else we can link to the facilitating of torture. And when I say fingertip, I mean top to bottom, every nook and every cranny. Right then, tea.'

Once the tea break was over, Naish set Hancock and the two constables the task of searching the building for the items he had described. Having thanked Hazel for his time, he set off alone back to Orange Grove. With Hancock and Newton both occupied, he intended to take an hour to reflect on the case and consider these latest developments. He sensed that he needed to understand the issues that the fire had raised in his mind and then set some new objectives for the case, if it was not to stall. In order to assist him, he took a slight diversion along York Street and into Church Street to his tobacconist where, in addition to taking two ounces of his usual rolling tobacco, he bought himself a half-corona cigar.

'Not your usual celebration cigar, Mr Naish,' observed the tobacconist, with a smile.

'No, it's not, because I am not there yet,' said Naish, ruefully. 'But I am hoping that this might assist my thinking and aid me in finding a solution.'

Naish cut across the abbey courtyard back to the station and, having given instructions to the desk sergeant that he was not to be disturbed for an hour, he went up to his office, locked the door and made up the fire. Leaning back in his chair, he lit his cigar and began to think.

Chapter 11

Naish's contemplation was broken by a knock at the door. Having stubbed his cigar out in the ashtray, he went over to unlock the door.

'Locking yourself in, Inspector?' said Hancock, as he entered.

'I just needed some time to reflect on things without being disturbed,' explained Naish. 'What is the news from Broadway Parade? Did the search uncover anything?'

'Nothing I am afraid, Inspector. No poker, no hammer, in fact nothing that could be associated with the process of the torture as we understand it. The building has been searched from top to bottom – and I went over it again myself – but there is nothing to be found. The yard at the rear was just the same, not even a trace of anything in that brazier other than the debris that was there before.'

'I don't know why I expected anything other,' said Naish, with a sigh. 'This case has been notable for failing to give us many easy breaks. So, we are no further forward in identifying the place where Lynch and Edwards were tortured and done to death, and not only that, but we have turned up an additional unwanted minor mystery, instead, in the guise of the paint under the lino.'

'Sorry, Inspector, but that's how it is. I was looking for anything that might have been associated with painting as well – you know art equipment and the like – but there was nothing of that ilk either.'

'Most of the things that I can associate with painting from my limited knowledge would burn down to nothing.'

'Brush stocks and metal paint tubes were all that I could think of that would not,' said Hancock, 'but, as I said, I went through the debris in the brazier and there was not a trace.'

'May have been taken away or even sold on,' said Naish, ruefully, 'if they existed in the first place. Only Emery can help us to progress that line of enquiry.'

'I agree, Inspector. Oh, and by the way, there was a telegram at the front desk from Newton to say that he will be back here between five o'clock and half past, depending on his train.'

'Come in,' called Naish, in response to a knock at the office door. 'Yes, Jones, what are you after?'

'I have some good news from Broadway Parade, Inspector, if you have a few minutes,' said the constable, hesitantly.

'If it is good news, then I can give you as long as you want,' said Naish, with an expectant expression on his face. 'Come on in and sit down, lad. What is it?'

'Well, Inspector, after Sergeant Hancock and Constable Wilson had left the scene, I stayed on to wait for the carpenter who had been called to board up the shop. While I was waiting, I was out in the backyard having a quick smoke when a vagrant came by. Not realising that I was the police he asked me if I could spare some money or a cigarette. I gave him a fag and as I was lighting it for him, he started on about the fire and what a bad thing it was. He says to me that it went up in a flash and that flames were pouring out of here and there and he had never seen a fire like it. So, I asked him if he witnessed the whole event. It turns out that he did because he had been dossing down in an empty garage on the opposite side of the road which runs past the yards at the back of the shops.'

'So, what did he see that was significant?' cut in Hancock, sensing that Naish's patience was running a bit thin.

'He described the whole event to me as he saw it from his vantage point and, cutting to the chase, the only bit he saw which we have not had in any other statement from a witness is that, just before the fire really took hold, he saw two men coming from the back door of the shop. They were not running, but in his view clearly moving with a purpose. They came out of the yard and went twenty yards down the road where they got into a blue Bedford van and drove off.'

'Is he certain,' said Naish, his attention suddenly captured by the constable's narrative. 'Where is he now?'

'He is certain, Inspector, and, although he is a drunk, he was not drunk when he was recounting his story to me and his account would seem to suggest that he was not drunk when he saw what he says he saw. From the sound of it, he had recently woken having been sleeping off an early morning session on the cider. I have him downstairs in a cell.'

'Have you arrested him?'

'No, he was more than pleased to come along. I offered him something to eat, a chance to get his head down in the warm for a few hours and, if he was cooperative in making a statement, I would give him the price of a drink when he left.'

'Good lad, well done,' said Naish, rising from his chair and patting the constable on the shoulder. 'Go and get yourself a cup of tea and, when he has finished here, Sergeant Hancock will come down with you and take the man's statement.'

'You look a bit more enthused, Inspector,' said Hancock, closing the door after the constable.

'If this goes where I hope it goes, then we have a link between the clearance and redecoration of the second floor and the arson attack. If our vagrant friend down in the cells also identifies the artist's impression of the thug, then we have a second confirmed link between his activities at the picture framers and the paying off of Edwards for what we assume to be the delivery of Lynch to the gang and his subsequent death,' said Naish.

'Looks like progress at long last?'

'It is progress, without a doubt, but we are still a long way from understanding what it is that has brought these men together. That is the vital thing to understand.'

'As far as I can see it, we need to get hold of Emery and, or, one or both of the thugs and put the screws on them. I can see no point in being restrained now.'

'I agree with you,' said Naish, 'but I have a strong sense that if we understand how vital Emery is to unlocking this mystery, then it is highly likely the gang know that as well.'

'You think that he will go the same way as Lynch and Edwards, then?'

'Well, only time will tell, but it does account for his disappearing off the face of the earth as of yesterday afternoon, doesn't it?'

'But why have they not just done away with him before now?' said Hancock. 'They had to track down Lynch and Edwards, but Emery was sat there in plain sight from what we know of the situation, so why not just do away with him quietly and bury him miles away in the countryside?'

'I can only assume that there was no necessity to dispatch him at the time. As to what we know of the situation, as you put it, my only assumption is that we do not, as yet, fully understand the complexities of that situation, and, as a result, we do not understand why events have unfolded as they have. It may be that Emery is not dead. For all we know, he may have made good his escape and be in hiding somewhere.'

'Well, I looked in at his house once again on my way back here and it looks to be completely unoccupied to me. Shall I arrange for a search warrant? Unless of course you wish me to go around and see if perhaps there is a window conveniently broken round the back?' said Hancock.

'No, this is no time for cutting corners, we need to do this by the book and apply for a warrant. I don't want to find vital evidence there that is ruled inadmissible due to improper practice. Get the warrant into the court this afternoon, as soon as you can get someone to do it.

'Right, I will go and get someone on to the application now and then I will go and interview the drunk and get his statement. I should be back up about two o'clock, if that suits you?'

'That's fine with me – I will see you back in here then. Yes, Davis what can I do for you?' said Naish, as Davis came in as Hancock went out. 'Have you got me that list of art and antique dealers yet?'

'I have, Inspector. It is set out on this report sheet here, all in order for you. But I have something more important, I think, as well – it is something that young Constable Burton has to report. Come in lad, come on in and tell the Inspector.'

'Come on lad, what is it?' said Naish, peering up at the nervous young man over the top of the sheet of paper that Davis had placed before him.

'I have seen that blue van that you requested information on, Inspector,' said Burton.

'Where and when was this,' said Naish, looking up suddenly from the sheet of paper.

'Yesterday, Inspector. I saw it when I was on the beat in the middle of the city,' said Burton, as he began to remove his notebook from his breast pocket. 'Knowing it was of particular interest to you, I noted the exact details down.'

'Good lad,' said Naish, taking up a pencil to make notes.

'The first time I saw it was at half past nine yesterday morning. I was walking down Stall Street towards Southgate and the van was coming up the street towards me. Just as it came alongside me, it turned left into Beau Street. I watched it as it went to the end of Beau Street, where it turned left out towards James Street West and disappeared from view. I was tempted to run after it, but I was not sure if you wanted observation only, so I left it at that.'

'Did you see who was in the front of it? Was it one or two men?'

'There were two men, Inspector, both wearing those light brown coats that you see storemen and delivery men wearing. The driver did shoot me a glance but made sure he did not make eye contact with me – a bit shifty he struck me. His mate just stared straight ahead, minding his own business.'

'Was either of them this man here?' asked Naish, holding up the artist's impression that he had on his desk.

'Why, yes – that is the spit of the man on the passenger seat, Inspector, I would swear on that,' said Burton.

'So, where did it come from?' said Naish. 'Had it stopped in Stall Street or had it come in from a side turning?'

'The first that I saw of it was as it came towards me on Stall Street, as I have said, Inspector,' said Burton, hastily referring to his notebook for further prompts. 'There was a delivery lorry parked up on the pavement on my side and the van appeared from around it into my view. I did not see it come around the bend at the bottom of Stall Street immediately before it appeared around the lorry, so it may have been parked or it may have come out of a side turning.'

'That would be Abbeygate Street, then,' said Naish. 'That is the only turning on your left as you walked down Stall Street that the van could have emerged from, unless it was either parked up behind this delivery lorry or came around the bend at the bottom and escaped your view.'

'That is right, Inspector. I am sorry that I was not more observant,' said Burton, a little crestfallen.

'Nonsense lad, you have done an excellent job. I know men in this station who would not have noticed half of what you saw. Did you get the registration number?'

'Yes, I did, Inspector, and I have sent it off for checking.'

'Just the job. So when did you see the van again?'

'That would have been at a quarter past two that afternoon,' began Burton.

'Where are we now?' interrupted Naish, impatiently.

'It was in Lower Borough Walls this time. My beat goes in a circle around the city and I was making my return leg back towards the centre. I go back round Stall Street, along York Street and back here to the station. I had stopped outside The Lamb and Lion to deal with a drunk asleep in the alleyway at the side. As I was dealing with him, I happened to look back out on to the street and saw the van going along Lower Borough Walls back towards Stall Street. Well, I left the drunk and ran down the alley and followed in the direction the van had taken, but by the time that I had run round and could look up the length of Stall Street, the van had disappeared.'

'How fast was it going? asked Naish.

'Not fast, Inspector, just going along like normal, so I thought that I might see it at the end of Stall Street as I came around the bend at the bottom. I ran up as far as Beau Street to see if it had gone back along there, but there was no sign and I ran along to the end to look up James Street West, but it was not in sight there.'

'What about Abbeygate Street off Stall Street, then?' asked Naish.

'I went back there last, Inspector, knowing that it only runs around into Abbey Green and it's a dead end. So, I thought that I would leave that until last, as they would have to pass me by to get back out. However, when I walked around there, the van was nowhere to be seen, I am afraid.'

'Nothing to be afraid about, lad. You have shown considerable intelligence in acting on your feet – your actions were very logical. Come over here both of you and sit down in front of the blackboards,' said Naish, as he crossed the room. 'Now, here we have a street map of the city centre that I have been using to plot some events in this case. We can use it to look in detail at the area around Stall Street where you saw this van. Now, what interests me is that these sightings occurred on the same morning as the arson attack on the picture framers in Broadway Parade. They were clearly on the road before the time that the fire started around two o'clock in the afternoon, and this would give them time to make any preparations such as buying the fuel. The return time is certainly interesting because it would tie in with the fire starting, them being observed leaving the rear of Broadway Parade and it would allow them just enough time to drive back for you to see them at a quarter past two.'

'It all sounds very plausible, Inspector,' said Burton.

'Indeed, it does,' said Naish. 'Now the other point of interest is that, as far as we know, there have been no reported sightings of this van since it was last seen at the time that the second floor of the picture framers was redecorated last Wednesday and Thursday, so it would appear that it is being used exclusively in connection with these crimes. The most interesting thing for me is to determine whether it was a simple coincidence that this van happened to pass through Stall Street twice yesterday, or was it departing and then returning to the place where it is garaged. It appears to me that it is no coincidence that it disappeared so quickly from your view, Burton, when I would have thought that a lad with your turn of speed should have been in time to round the corner and see it before it disappeared from view, either at the end of Stall Street or Beau Street. That leaves only one conclusion – that it is garaged somewhere in the vicinity of Stall Street or the few dead ends that lead off Abbeygate Street up to Abbey Green.'

'That sounds like the most logical deduction,' said Davis.

'So, we can put our heads together and narrow down the options by working our way round the streets using this map,' said Naish. 'Now, you two know this area as well as I do – where are there facilities to garage a van?'

'Well, I think we can rule out Stall Street, for a start,' said Davis. 'Unless my recollection is wrong, I can think of no garage or side alley off Stall Street at all.'

'I agree,' said Naish, as he noted Burton's nod of agreement.

'Beau Street is the same, other than Bilbury Lane, which runs off it, but there are no places off there that are suitable either, so I suggest that we rule that out as well,' said Davis.

'So, we are left with these three streets here, then,' said Naish pointing to the map. 'Abbeygate Street, which runs off Stall Street and runs up into Abbey Green, which just runs round the green outside the Golden Fleece and then back on itself into Abbeygate Street. The only other possible location is Swallow Street, which runs from Abbeygate Street up to York Street, here. So, we have a choice of three. Any observations?'

'Well, I walk those streets perhaps two or three times a week, and I cannot think of anywhere off Abbeygate Street or Abbey Green where you could park a vehicle off the road – it's shop fronts, the pub and houses all the way round. So that can only leave Swallow Street.'

'In my recollection there are a number of garages on both sides of Swallow Street,' said Naish.

'That's correct, Inspector, I have never counted them, but I will step along as soon as you have finished and take a look if you wish,' said Burton.

'Not just yet,' said Naish. 'I do not want these men to become suspicious that they are being watched. A number of leads in this case have vanished before my eyes already and I cannot afford this pair to take flight. I will set up some covert surveillance when I have thought through the best way to go about it. In the meantime, what you can do, Burton, is to get yourself round to all the petrol stations within a mile's radius and see if they sold canned stock to the occupants of a blue Bedford van between half past nine and two o'clock yesterday. If they did, get a statement to that effect and take this artist's impression with you to confirm an identity if you get a lead. You will need to get a statement to confirm that as well, so check with one of the detective constables downstairs before you set off. In the meantime, whenever you are on your beat around that area, keep out of Swallow Street and if you see the blue van again, make your observation of it discreet. Under no circumstances challenge the occupants – they are a desperate pair, do you understand?'

'Yes, Inspector. All understood.'

'Good lad, now get along,' said Naish, closing the door after him. 'Well, that was very useful, Davis. His diligence has taken us a good deal further in this case but, by God, he may have had a lucky escape. I need you to urgently change that briefing note for the beat constables to say they are only to observe the van with discretion, and on absolutely no account approach or challenge these men. I have no direct proof, but I have a strong suspicion that they have been complicit in or even committed two murders already. Young Burton had a lucky escape, there. If he had caught up with that van, I do not care to contemplate the result. I also want Swallow Street taken off the beat for the time being. I don't want any chance of these men becoming suspicious. It may be too late already, if these men did see Burton haring after them. They may think that we are on to them, but we have to hope not.'

'It all hangs on whether they are using Swallow Street,' said Davis.

'I just can't see a feasible alternative, though. Can you?'

'No, I cannot. But I just hope we are right.'

'Well, we have nothing else to go on, so I am hanging my hat on it for now,' said Naish. 'Thank you for this list, once again. I will make a start on it when I get a moment. Keep an eye on Burton, by the way, and send him up when he has finished with the petrol stations.'

As soon as Davis had closed the door behind him, Naish pulled on his hat and coat and headed out of the station in the direction of Swallow Street.

On returning to his office at ten to two, Naish was surprised to find that Hancock and Davis were already sat waiting for him. They half rose as he entered, in deference, but he motioned them to return to their seats as he hung his hat and coat on the stand in the corner.

'There have been some interesting developments then, Inspector,' said Hancock.

'There certainly have. I take it that Davis has brought you up to date?'

'He has, and in great detail.'

'Good. Then we can press on without wasting any more time. What news from our drunken friend downstairs – is he credible?'

'He certainly sounds credible to me. He may be a drunk, but he is nobody's fool. A good man fallen on hard times, by the sound of his tale. Anyway, I have his statement and it bears out everything that he told the constable.'

'That is reassuring,' said Naish, 'where is he now?'

'I let him go and promised him a half bottle of whisky if he reported back here in a few days' time, in case we needed anything else from him. It was the best idea that I could come up with to keep in touch with a vagrant of no fixed abode,' said Hancock, with a smile.

'How about the application for the search warrant at St Mark's Road?'

'That has gone in and it should be heard by the magistrate's tomorrow morning.'

'Excellent. Well, I have just taken a stroll along to Swallow Street. I know, I know,' said Naish, seeing Davis's look of surprise, 'disobeying my own orders. I wanted to just be sure how many garages there were down there, and I thought that, rather than ask someone else, if I went and it went wrong then I would only have myself to blame. Anyway, it is done and there was no one about to see me.'

'So how many were there, Inspector?' asked Davis.

'Six. Two on the side that backs onto Stall Street and four on the other side.'

'Doesn't the other side back on to the buildings on one side of Abbey Green?' asked Hancock. 'The side where the Golden Fleece is?'

'It does,' interjected Davis, 'although I am not sure that they are connected to or part of those buildings.'

'Either way,' said Naish, 'there were six potential premises that we need to consider, all with double doors without windows, so it is impossible to see if they are occupied. But they are all capable of garaging a van.'

'So, do you want some sort of surveillance put in place?' asked Hancock.

'Ideally, yes, but I cannot see anywhere where the observer would not be obvious, and there are no windows that overlook the length of the street. As I have said, I am concerned that anything obvious would make our friends suspicious.'

'How about my new friend, the Broadway Parade vagrant?' suggested Hancock.

'What, use him to do the surveillance?'

'I don't see why not. As I said, he is nobody's fool and, odd as it sounds, I would trust him as an informant. In light of nothing better, he may be the least worst solution. He would not look out of place in a doorway wrapped up in some old blankets.'

'Suppose they challenge him?'

'I would think he would be highly convincing, myself. He looks the part, he smells the part and he has sufficiently few teeth. If we dressed a constable up, they might see through that and I would understand your concerns, but he is the genuine article and the worst that might happen is that they would tell him to move along or else. That might end his activities, but he would have fulfilled his purpose by default.'

'All right, you have convinced me. I just hope to God that they don't knife him,' said Naish, lighting a thoughtful cigarette. 'Can you get hold of him before he is due to return for his bottle of whisky? I would prefer to have him at it as soon as possible.'

'I think that I will be able to find him for you. I gave him a couple of bob as he left and he said that, being in need of a drink, he was heading off to the Grapes in Westgate Street. I will send someone down there later to gather him in and after another night in the cells, I will sit him down tomorrow morning and set him to the task.'

'Come in,' called Naish. 'Yes, what is it?'

'I have got the information you asked from the petrol stations, Inspector,' said Burton.

'Blimey, you were quick about that. What have you found?'

'It was just luck that the second station that I called at had served the driver of the blue Bedford with three cans of petrol,' said Burton. 'They pulled on to the forecourt, the passenger got out and got the three cans out of the back and the attendant filled them. He paid up and drove off. The attendant identified our man from the artist impression, and I have his statement here for you, Inspector.'

'Good lad. Have they used the station before?'

'Yes, they have. The attendant can remember filling the van on two separate occasions in the past three weeks.'

'So, they are not just doing local mileage then, by the sound of it,' said Naish. 'Did he get a look inside the van?'

'He did not I am afraid, Inspector. He was stood to the side of the van to operate the pump and our suspect brought the cans over.'

'Never mind, but well done for asking the question,' said Naish. 'Right then, gentlemen. If we are all done here, I am going to have a chat with Sergeant Hancock.'

Naish closed the door after Davis and Burton and went over to one of the tables near the blackboards. Having turned through a collection of maps on one side of the table, he selected one and brought it over to his desk.

'This is the biggest scale ordnance survey map that I can find covering the area that we are interested in, and the scale is good enough that the outlines of the buildings are shown. My ad hoc surveillance of Swallow Street was somewhat more detailed than I revealed to our colleagues earlier,' said Naish, taking his notebook from an inside jacket pocket. 'I trust Davis emphatically, but a young lad like Burton, being impressionable, may not be able to contain himself in the midst of canteen gossip and I want as little known of this operation as is possible.'

'I understand completely, and I will keep my business with the vagrant as a personal matter between you me and Newton,' said Hancock.

'Now then,' said Naish, referring to his notebook, 'I am going to shade in the buildings that I have noted down as the garages with this coloured pencil. What I need you to do, before our meeting with Newton in an hour or so, is to take this map around the corner to the Guildhall and pay a visit to the rates department. I want to know who the owner is. If it's rented, then to whom is it rented, and, thirdly, who is it that pays the rates on the premises.'

'Do you want me to stay there while they do it?'

'No. If you set them to the task and then make an appointment to go through the results with an officer from the department, that will be fine. I want the answer within thirty-six hours and if there is a problem with that, let me know and I will get it sorted out.'

Naish sat down in a chair opposite the blackboards and rolled himself a cigarette. He spent the next hour amending the information on the boards and cross-referencing statements until he was content that he had every aspect of his investigation up to date. Satisfied, he was sitting back and rolling himself another cigarette to have one final review of the information, when there was a knock at the door and Newton looked in. Naish didn't speak and motioned for him to take a chair. After ten minutes, Naish glanced at his cigarette and seeing there was no possibility of relighting the minute stub, tossed it into the bin and turned to Newton.

'So how was the trip to London. Fruitful, I hope?'

'It was, Inspector. I think you will consider the journey worthwhile. I have unearthed some interesting information – would you like me to set it out for you?'

'I am expecting Hancock back in a short while, so let us wait and we can go through it together. In the meantime, let me run through a few developments that have happened in your absence.'

Chapter 12

'So, the wanderer returns. You have missed all the fun here, running off to London,' said Hancock, with a smile.

'I have appraised Newton of what he has missed. Sit yourself down and let's get on, or the pubs will be closing by the time we are finished.'

'The information from the ratings department will be ready by four o'clock tomorrow and there is no news on the van registration as yet, other than it is not registered in Somerset,' said Hancock, as he drew up a chair.

'That is interesting,' said Naish. 'Now then, Newton – the floor is yours.'

'Well, my trip to Somerset House was not very productive, I am afraid, other than to prove a negative in that, as far as I can tell, Emery has not inherited any money at all from relatives. I took some information from the local records here at the Guildhall, and together with that at Somerset House, I was able to identify his parents and a number of his aunts and uncles. I think it reasonable to suppose that if large sums were inherited, then at least a significant percentage would come from close, older family members,' began Newton.

'It sounds logical to me,' said Naish. 'One might inherit from one or perhaps two people who were not close relations, but one would need a connection to a large, wealthy family to inherit the multiple sums that Emery appears to have come into.'

'That was my line of thinking. I identified three of five brothers and sisters on his mother's side and four of six brothers and sisters on his father's side, and none of them left him anything at all, as far as I can tell. In addition, it does not appear that the family have any wealth at all on the scale that would be needed to provide for the sums we believe that he has come into. One or two of the uncles held positions in banking and local government, but none of them, nor his father, were captains of industry or landed gentry.'

'I thought you said that you had good news,' said Naish, wryly.

'Well, its good news in that we have been able to close down one line of our enquiries, but there is also what I hope you will regard as good news that does move the case forward. I also did some research with the land registry department, and I have found out that, although Emery is the owner of each of the properties that he owns in Bath, they were all previously owned by a company called Derwent Holdings.'

'Derwent? That's in Cumbria, isn't it?' interjected Hancock.

'It is,' said Newton, 'and I will come back to that in a moment. 'The interesting thing is that, according to the land registry, Derwent Holdings owned each of the properties for only a month to six weeks on each occasion before they were sold on to Emery.'

'A tax dodge?' said Hancock.

'Money laundering is another distinct possibility,' said Naish. 'Was there any record of the price Emery paid?'

'There was and it appears to me to be a reasonable market value almost equivalent on each occasion to what Derwent Holdings paid for it,' said Newton.

'Except we know that Emery never had those sorts of sums in any bank account that we are aware of,' said Naish. 'Just because a price is stated, there is no proof that any money actually changed hands, is there? Not unless we can look in to the financial affairs of Derwent Holdings or find a hidden bank account of Emery's.'

'Well, I don't think that we will get far looking into the financial affairs of Derwent Holdings,' continued Newton. 'I went along to Companies House, as well, and made some enquiries about them. It would appear that it is an offshore company, with its offices registered in Switzerland.'

'Well, we are getting into deep waters here,' said Naish, with a whistle.

'I agree, Inspector, and I am afraid that that was as far as my enquiries into Derwent's background could go. I also got along to Scotland Yard and met up with your contact there. Chief Inspector Hobbs was very helpful, and I spent some time with him. The upshot, however, does not move things on. Derwent Holdings is not known to the Yard, as far as their records show, and Mr Emery was not known to them either.'

'So, although he never came to the attention of the police, we are certain that he did come from London, aren't we?' asked Naish, in a questioning tone.

'Oh yes, that is a fact, Inspector. I took the address that I had for him in Lambeth along to the Borough records office and he was clearly living there for at least ten years prior to his move to Bath. It was a similar set up to what he has now in Bath. A ground floor shop from which he ran a picture framing business with rooms above. It appears that he lived and worked there. The only difference was that he owns the property in Bath and the premises in Lambeth were rented from a company that ran a large picture gallery in Westminster – Cotman Holdings was the company name.'

'You must have worn off some shoe leather on your trip,' said Hancock, with a smile.

'One last thing that I managed to do before I caught the train home was some more research with the banks. While I was discussing Emery's bank account with Chief Inspector Hobbs, he offered to get a check done on Emery with the banks in London. He has an Inspector in the fraud office who liaises with the banks regularly. I took him up on his offer, but the upshot was that, other than the account at Lloyds which he clearly transferred to the Bath branch, Emery appears to have no other bank accounts registered in his name.'

'If it is money laundering, though,' said Naish, 'it may well be that he is canny enough to have an account set up in another name or even a holding company of his own.'

'He may have, but, from his statements at the Bath branch of Lloyds, we have no records that he has paid or received money from such a body. There are plenty of transactions with a multitude of names, as you would expect from a business, but none of them are for sums of more than a few pounds.'

'Well, your trip was very productive then, I would say,' said Naish. 'It has thrown up a lot of useful food for thought, discounted a number of theories which can enable us to focus our efforts and has thrown up very little chaff. The Superintendent will consider your excursion money well spent, I am sure, when he goes through my budget with me at the end of the month. Right, it's getting late and I know that you have homes to go to. If you can spare me ten more minutes, I will set out what I want doing next.'

'Fine with me,' said Hancock.

'Tomorrow morning, Hancock, I want you to get your vagrant friend set up around at Swallow Street.'

'That is fine. I have had him rounded up from the Grapes, as I said, and he is down in the cells now.'

'Good. Now then, Newton. I want you to collect the warrant from the magistrate's court first thing in the morning, get along to St Mark's Road and make a thorough search of the house. Take a couple of men with you to help and I want it done with fingertips, from top to bottom. Right, gentlemen. If there is nothing else, I will see you back in here at midday tomorrow. I thank you and wish you a good evening. Please give my apologies, once again, to your good ladies for the lateness of the hour.'

Once they had gone, Naish picked up the list that Davis had given him and set off to The Volunteer Rifleman for his dinner. Over dinner, Naish examined the addresses of the businesses on the list and planned a circular walk home to the Circus by way of each of them. It was cold but dry as he stepped out of the pub. He enjoyed the occasional brief return to the nocturnal work he had enjoyed as a constable on the beat in the city. He thought it may provide him with some useful information if he could have a close look around each of the premises under cover of night while they were unoccupied, in preparation for the more formal visits that he had planned for his morning.

At half past nine in the morning, Naish made his way into Dobson's sale rooms just off Queen Square. A few other customers were browsing the items on display, some of whom were clearly from the trade.

'Good morning, sir. May I be of assistance?' enquired a middle-aged man in a smart suit.

'Thank you,' said Naish, 'I was hoping that you might be able to help me. I am the executor of the estate of a distant relative and I have two matters that I need assistance with. It is not a field that I have any experience in you see but since you appear to deal in paintings and works of art, I thought that you might be able to assist me. Would I be right?'

'Well, we are primarily an auction house, Mr ... sorry, I did not catch your name.'

'Bennett,' said Naish.

'Well, as I say, Mr Bennett, we are primarily an auction house and we have two main branches to our work. We have auctions of antiques and collectables, and we have auctions of fine art. Today is a viewing day for a sale of antiques and collectables and, as you can see, the sale room is laid out with an array of such items. These are the most popular of our sales. The other, the sale of fine art, happens every quarter and is a smaller affair, but tends to attract a more discerning type of client who specialises in collecting first-class paintings and sculpture. They are either private collectors or the owners of sale rooms looking for good quality works to sell on. Does that help you see if we can fit your needs, Mr Bennett?'

'I think that it does, certainly in the first part. You see, not only am I the executor of the estate, I am also a beneficiary of it as well, and, as such, I was hoping to buy myself a good quality painting as a keepsake.'

'Might I ask how much you were thinking of spending? I have no wish to appear impertinent, but it might help me to direct you to which of our sales could make the best use of the sum that you have.'

'Five hundred pounds,' said Naish, unemotionally.

'Then I think that you would be better suited to the works that come up in our fine art sale, sir. The next one will be in January. If you wish to leave me your address, I will ensure that you are sent a catalogue and an invitation to one of our private viewings.'

'Thank you,' said Naish, with an inward smile of satisfaction that his assumed persona had clearly been accepted by the assistant. 'And you are?'

'Mr Sharp, sir, I am the senior auctioneer. Here is my card.'

'Ah, you are not Mr Dobson, then?' asked Naish.

'Oh no, sir. Mr Dobson is the proprietor and managing director. You will have the chance to meet him at the private viewing in January. He tends to specialise in the fine arts area of the business these days.'

'I see,' said Naish. 'Well, I shall look forward to that. The other enquiry that I have is about making a repair to an oil painting that is part of the estate.'

'What is the nature of the damage that the painting has sustained?' asked Sharp.

'It is an oil painting, about three feet by two and a half feet, and the wooden frame on which the canvas has been stretched has split on one of the long sides.'

'That is quite unusual,' said Sharp. 'Do you know the age of the painting?'

'The canvas is dated eighteen eighty-two.'

'That is interesting, but the frame might be even older, of course. It is not the sort of work that we usually undertake. As I say, we sell, rather than restore, works of art and this sounds as if it might be a job for a specialist.'

'Is there anyone that you would recommend?'

'The only reliable firm dealing in that area of work in Bath would be Byfield Fine Arts in Wood Street. Otherwise I think that you may be better served looking for a restorer in London.'

'Well, thank you for your advice and thank you for the invitation to your January viewing day, Mr Sharp. My address, by the way, is Flat Three, number 35, The Circus.'

Well pleased with his work at the auction house, Naish stepped back out into the street and walked just out of sight of the entrance to roll himself a cigarette. Aware that the smoking of hand-rolled cigarettes might be in conflict with the persona of the gentleman he had just passed himself off as in the auction rooms, he had no wish to be inadvertently seen by Mr Sharp. As he rolled his cigarette, he saw a red Bedford van pull up at the side of the building and two men, one young the other older, got out of the van and began to unload some items of furniture from the van in through what was clearly the storeroom door of the auction house. They were unremarkable other than for the fact that they both wore brown storemen's coats of the type that Burton had described. In a change to his plans, Naish walked down towards where the van was being unloaded in the hope of seeing inside the storeroom, thinking that he might, by some fluke, see a blue Bedford van stored in there. But as he came within five yards of the back of the van, the two men emerged from the storeroom and closed the doors behind them and, without a glance at Naish, got back in the van and drove off. Naish was frustrated by the turn of events but carried on down the street for a while, pausing to stare into the windows of a random shop before retracing his steps back up the street and continuing his walk along to Wood Street.

Naish's survey of the Wood Street premises the previous evening had suggested to him that it was a gallery for the more discerning client. It had that sparsity of paintings hung for display that always struck Naish as being a hallmark of establishments that were or liked to imply that they were dealing in items of particular note. Now that the premises were open for business and he was able to step inside, his first impressions were confirmed. Even the carpet on the gallery floor was of excellent quality. Not only were the works of art few in number but there was a noticeable lack of clients in the gallery. Perhaps, thought Naish, eleven o'clock was too early for discerning folk to be about.

'Good morning, sir. May I be of assistance?' asked a well-dressed man, who had appeared in response to the shop bell that had rung as Naish entered.

'I hope that you may be able to do so,' said Naish, in a slightly off-hand manner, intended to counter the superior tone that the man had adopted.

'Certainly,' said the man, a little more demurely.

'I was hoping to speak with Mr Williams – I understand he is the proprietor,' said Naish, using the information he had been given by Davis. 'You were recommended to me by a gentleman at Dobson's.'

'I am afraid that Mr Williams does not deal with sales on a day to day basis, Mr … ?'

'My name is Bennett,' continued Naish, half-looking past the man as he spoke, as if to give the impression he regarded him as irrelevant. 'You are?'

'I am Mr Miles, sir, the general manager. As I say, Mr Williams deals in specialist sales made to order for specific clients. I am sure that I can accommodate you in anything that this business is able to provide for clients. What is it that you are looking for?'

'I am the executor of the estate of a distant relative and I have two matters related to paintings that I need some assistance with.'

'If you would care to come over here, Mr Bennett, and take a chair at my desk, I will take your coat and send for some coffee and perhaps you can tell me how we can help,' said Miles.

'One item in the estate is an oil painting,' said Naish, leaning back in his chair, his confidence growing in the role of Bennett as he realised he had taken Miles in. 'The painting is an oil about three feet by two and a half feet. I did not note the artist, but it is dated eighteen eighty-two. The frame on which the canvas is stretched has been damaged on the right-hand side – one of the long sides. The wood is badly split, but I have no knowledge of how it was sustained – it may have had a blow to it.'

'Is the picture in a frame?'

'No, it is not,' said Naish, 'so, in addition to wanting some advice as to whether it could be repaired, I was also looking to purchase a suitable frame to mount it in. Is that something you might be able to assist with?'

'I am certain that we will be able to help you. In addition to selling paintings, we also do restoration work, both restoring and, where necessary, repainting quality works of art, and we also restore frames. However, it would be necessary for us to examine the work closely before we could give you an opinion as to what exactly we could offer to do to assist you.'

'That is very reassuring,' said Naish. 'The work is not currently with me in Bath, but I will arrange to have it delivered to my home and then I can bring it in for you.'

'If it makes matters easier, I would be happy for it to be delivered straight to us here, then our restorer could examine it and, if you are in agreement, undertake the repairs.'

'Is the work done in-house or do you send it away to a specialist?' asked Naish.

'All the work is done in-house, sir, by our own restorer.'

'You mean here on these premises? I don't wish to be pedantic. I would be happy for the painting to be delivered here, but I would not want it to leave this building, even to go elsewhere in Bath. I am very aware of my responsibilities as an executor, you understand.'

'I completely understand, and I can assure you that all our restoration work takes place at our workshops within the premises here.'

'That is very reassuring. I will make the arrangements and telephone you when I know it is about to be dispatched, if that is acceptable to you?'

'That will be fine,' said Miles. 'Now, was there another matter you indicated that we may be able to assist you with?'

'Yes, there is, but it is by way of being a more personal matter. You see, I am also a beneficiary of the estate and I was looking to use the generous bequest that I have been made to buy for myself a quality piece of art, by way of both a keepsake and also as an investment.'

'Then you have come to the right establishment, Mr Bennett. Might I enquire how generous your bequest is?'

'Fifteen hundred pounds,' said Naish, casually revising the figure, having noticed a couple of the price tags as he had walked to Miles's desk.

'I am sure that we will be more than able to help you to find the right piece,' said Miles, becoming almost obsequious.

'Well, I am very grateful to you,' said Naish, rising from the chair. 'I am afraid that business means that I am pressed for time today. When would it be best for me to come and look at some paintings?'

'We have a small private viewing for a selected number of clients tomorrow evening at seven o'clock, if you are free?'

'That would be fine for me. I shall look forward to it,' said Naish.

'There are a number of other pieces that we will be showing then that are not on display in the gallery yet. As it happens, you will get the opportunity to meet our Mr Williams, as he will be hosting the evening.'

'Excellent,' said Naish, as Miles held the door open for him, 'I shall look forward to it.'

Naish turned left along Wood Street and headed back towards Orange Grove. Once out of sight, he paused to take a roll up from his tin, light it, inhale deeply and resume his walk, pleased with his morning's work.

'Right then, gentlemen. How have your respective mornings been? I have to say that I have made a little progress in my line of enquiry, but more of that later. Pour us all a mug of tea, Newton, and let's get down to it. Off you go, Hancock – how did you and your new-found friend get on?'

'All in hand, Inspector. He was pleased as punch to have had another warm night in the cells and some breakfast under his belt. I gave him the brief and set him on his way. I took the liberty of taking a stroll down Swallow Street an hour later and spotted him in his blankets in a doorway halfway down – just the spot to see every coming and going.'

'Will he stick to it?'

'I think he will. I have agreed payment on completion of the task, and he was pleased with that. I have also arranged for another vagrant, also known as constable Burton, to drop by once or twice a day and deliver some food for him. I also just mentioned to him that if he let me down and did a runner, I would hunt him down to the ends of the county and fit him up for every petty crime that I had outstanding on the books. I think that may have been the final encouragement,' said Hancock, with a smile.

'Yes, there is nothing like an unvarnished threat to focus the mind,' said Naish. 'So how about you, Newton – how did the search at St Mark's Road go off?'

'I knocked at the front door once again, but the place was still deserted and there were a couple of pints of milk on the doorstep, further suggesting that Emery had not returned. We made entry by a small window next to the back door, and I sent a constable in to open up the back door. We did a quick sweep of the house to make sure that he was not either hidden or else dead somewhere in the house, but there was no sign. While they did that, I went through the post on the door mat, but it was just a collection of bills, a few trade magazines and the usual circulars. The main items of interest were two handwritten notes from a Mrs Carson enquiring as to Emery's whereabouts, and a suggestion that he had left without giving her notice of the fact. I took it that Mrs Carson was probably a cook, housekeeper or the like and I sent Constable Wilson off to make some enquiries in the neighbouring houses, assuming that, if she was a housekeeper or some domestic, then the staff in the nearby houses may be acquainted with her. Half an hour later, Wilson came back and was able to confirm that she was indeed the housekeeper, but they had no notion of where she lived.'

'At least it confirms our suspicions that his absence was an impromptu one,' said Naish. 'The milk, as you say, supports that theory. Two pints would be about the right amount of milk to have built up at a bachelor's residence in the two days he has been away.'

'As you say, the milk and the two notes from the housekeeper are in keeping with the length of his absence. Coincidentally, the milkman arrived while Wilson was off making the enquiries about the housekeeper. Jones and I had made a start on the detailed search in Emery's study and Jones went to answer a knock at the front door. It was only when he had been gone about ten minutes that I went out to see what he had got into and saw him in conversation with the milkman. I left him to get on with it, supposing he was getting a quick statement to cover the milk deliveries and to confirm the absence of Emery.'

'You say you supposed,' said Naish, a note of concern in his voice.

'I meant that I supposed he had just gone to get the statement, not to get into idle conversation with the man. I did challenge him about it later, saying that there were more important things to get on with. He apologised, saying the man was more than willing to give a statement, but he had a number of questions himself – presumably worried about delivering more unwanted milk and concerned as to how his outstanding account was going to be settled.'

'It sounds like Jones needs to understand who is supposed to be interviewing who,' said Naish, sternly. 'Anyway, back to important matters. How did the search go on?'

'The three of us completed the ground floor within an hour. I had Wilson and Jones working together and I followed behind them, repeating the search to make sure that nothing was missed, but I could find nothing of interest other than a file containing his banking paperwork which only concerned what we know already.'

'Was there a chequebook?' asked Naish.

'There was, but the stubs were all for minor amounts to tradesmen for household matters and the occasional one for cash for himself, again for small sums – presumably for small change – but nothing at all to link him to the business. Just a normal domestic scene that might be the home of any bachelor.'

'What about the rest of the house?'

'I repeated the process again on the first and second floors, again nothing to report. The second floor was easy, as it was unfurnished, but not like the second floor of his shop. It looked to me simply that he had no need of the space in such a large house and never used it. It was obvious that it was cleaned and dusted occasionally. There were no cobwebs or dust up there, just bare boards and a few rugs on the floors and not a stick of furniture. The attic was the same, apart from a few suitcases and travelling trunks stored up there, but they were empty as well.'

'So, other than some things that confirmed what we already know about him, there was no fresh evidence to be had?' said Naish.

'I am afraid not, Inspector.'

'Nothing to apologise for, Newton, that's just the way it goes sometimes.'

'I was going to go back round there tomorrow morning and see if I could catch the housekeeper. I put a note on the front door addressed to her and asked her to be there at nine o'clock. I thought she would be there reasonably early, but if she isn't, I will get a constable to hang around until midday on the off chance she turns up.'

'That's fine,' said Naish. 'I will meet you here in the morning and walk around with you. I should like to cast an eye over the scene myself and get a better feel for our Mr Emery.'

'I have some other things for discussion,' said Hancock. 'The analysis of the sketchbooks has come back but there is nothing surprising to report. They are what they are – two books containing sketches. Best quality paper, apparently, and done in a mixture of charcoal and pencil, but there is nothing else. Nothing down the spine, nothing of the nature of a chemical that could be wetted or exposed by another chemical to reveal a covert message. They even went over each page with a strong lens but could find no trace of a message in a micro font on the pages or within any of the drawings.'

'Any more bad news?' said Naish, with a wry smile.

'Interesting, rather than bad,' said Hancock. 'The registration of the van, as we know, is not a Somerset one, but apparently the checks that have been run on it show that it was the registration of a Ford Popular that was scrapped two years ago.'

'Anyway, of linking it to our suspects?' asked Naish.

'Apparently not. The last registered keeper of the Ford was a vicar in Northampton. It looks to me as if it was just picked up at a scrapyard and passed off into the criminal fraternity, as these plates sometimes are.'

'It, at least, supports our view that everything to do with our two thugs is clearly of criminal intent,' said Naish. 'It is interesting to see the lengths that they are going to in order to avoid detection. As we have said, they are clearly professional criminals.

Chapter 13

'Come in,' called Naish, in response to a knock at the door.

'Sorry to disturb you, Inspector,' said the desk sergeant, 'but I have just taken a telephone call from a Mrs Carson. Apparently, she has read the note that Sergeant Newton left on the door at St Mark's Road and left a message to say she would meet him there any time this afternoon.'

'Give her a call back and say that we will meet her there at half past two,' said Naish. 'While we are out dealing with that, I have a task that I want you to get done this afternoon, Hancock, if you have time.'

'If it's urgent, I can fit it in, Inspector.'

'I would give it to a constable to do, ordinarily, but in the circumstances, it needs someone with a bit of finesse. I am not blowing smoke in your ear – let me explain.'

Naish gave Hancock and Newton an account of his trips to Dobson's and the Byfield gallery that morning and related, in particular, his observations of the two men in brown coats with the red Bedford delivery van.

'I want you to go around to Dobson's and Byfield and the others on this list and find out if any of them use a blue delivery van and have delivery men who wear brown warehouse coats. Use the pretence that you are making enquiries about a hit and run involving such a vehicle and see where it goes. If you can talk your way into that garage come storeroom at Dobson's, even better.'

'Not wishing to question you, but are you sure you want them to know that the police are interested in those two things, given their closeness to our investigation?'

'I understand your concern, but I am happy for it to come out in that way. If they have anything to hide, it might put the wind up them mildly, but it does not betray what we are really after. What is important is that I am kept well away from association with either Byfield or Dobson's, at the moment, given my involvement as Mr Bennett.'

'I understand, leave it to me,' said Hancock.

'Right then, Newton. A quick mug of tea and a smoke and we can set off to meet with the redoubtable Mrs Carson,' said Naish.

The front door of Emery's house was ajar when Naish and Newton arrived, and a gentle tap at the knocker produced the housekeeper.

'Mrs Carson? I am Sergeant Newton and this is Inspector Naish. Thank you for taking the trouble to contact me.'

Mrs Carson led them into the sitting room and showed them each to a chair.

'I hope this is about poor Mr Emery. I have been worried about him so much.'

'It is about Mr Emery,' said Naish. 'What can you tell me about him?'

'Well, as you may have heard, he has a shop over in Broadway Parade and it burnt down two days ago almost to this time.'

'Is that so,' said Naish, cutting across Newton before he could speak. 'I had heard something of it, was there much damage?'

'I don't know about that, but what is worrying me is that, following the fire, Mr Emery has not been seen since. I spoke to the man who runs the shop next door to his and he reassured me that he had not been in the shop at the time, but I am still worried sick about him.'

'I understand completely,' said Naish, gravely. 'If you give me some background to the case I will, of course, look into the matter for you. Sergeant – stand by to take some notes, will you.'

'Thank you so much, Inspector,' said Mrs Carson.

'Now, tell me a little bit about Mr Emery. What sort of a man is he?'

'He is a very considerate employer and ordinarily he is a very calm man of regular habits. But in the last few weeks he has not been himself. Nothing particular, but he was always on edge and not settled, as he usually is when I see him.'

'And when do you usually see him, Mrs Carson?'

'I come in every day except Sunday at half past seven and set the fires in the grates and prepare his breakfast. He goes off to the shop at a quarter to nine as regular as clockwork. If he is coming home for his lunch, he always lets me know and, if he is, I leave a sandwich under a cover in the larder for him. Then, having tidied round the house, I leave at half past ten to go to a lady who I do for. I come back here at seven o' clock and set the fires again to warm the house through for when he gets home.'

'Does he not come home for his evening meal, then?' asked Naish, innocently.

'No. He works on into the evenings every day except for Saturday – I wonder he doesn't waste away. I occasionally see him as I leave of an evening if he is early, but more often than not I don't, except for Saturdays of course. I always leave him something for a cold supper and then I leave about half past eight with everything set for his coming home. That is his routine, day in and day out.'

'And when he is home what are his interests of an evening? Does he listen to the radio for example?'

'Whenever I have seen him, he has his supper and when he has finished, he sits in that chair over there and reads. A great reader he is, and always books about art. You can see the shelves in here and in the drawing room are filled with them. He also loved his paintings – those over there are his particular favourites – and he is very particular about them. He won't have me dust them or touch them in any way. He always sees to them himself – very valuable I suppose.'

'These paintings over here?' asked Naish, getting up and walking over to a collection of pictures in gilt frames hanging together on the wall.

'That's them,' said Mrs Carson.

'Did he ever tell you anything about them?' asked Naish.

'No, not at all. Not that I would be interested anyway. They are nice enough to look at but not something that I would want to know about, if you know what I mean.'

'I understand you completely, me neither,' said Naish, with a smile. 'Now, Mrs Carson, as you may know, I have been granted a search warrant for this house, as Mr Emery's disappearance had been reported to us by another concerned person just before you got in touch with us.'

'Oh, who?'

'Just a concerned fellow trader, but the main thing for you to know is that I will look into this matter for you and I will be in touch as soon as I have some information about Mr Emery. In the meantime, I am going to secure the premises and you need not come back here until I get in touch with you, as you may disturb something that I may be able to use as evidence, you understand? Now, you give your address to my sergeant and we will be in touch as soon as there is anything to know, and in the meantime please don't worry yourself. I am sure all will be well,' said Naish, with conviction.

Newton, having showed Mrs Carson out, returned to the sitting room to find Naish still contemplating the paintings.

'These three are very interesting,' said Naish, pointing to three identically sized canvases hung together in a group. 'Have you heard of Turner?'

'He is an artist, isn't he?'

'Indeed, he is,' said Naish, turning to him with a pained expression. 'I meant, what do you know of him as an artist.'

'Nothing – other than that he is – I am afraid, Inspector.'

'I don't know much either, but I know that he is an artist of great renown. These three paintings here are scenes of Bath and appear to be by him. I assume they are reproductions because if they aren't then I imagine that they are of significant value – I mean big money.'

'They look like the abbey to me, Inspector,' said Newton. 'Perhaps Mr Emery is even wealthier than we already believe.'

'These other artists are not known to me,' said Naish, jotting the names down in his notebook, 'but then I am not an expert.'

'Perhaps we could get someone from one of the galleries to give us some advice on them,' said Newton.

'No, we can't do that at the moment as it might compromise my involvement with them as Mr Bennett. I think I might look in at the Victoria Art Gallery in the Guildhall and make some enquiries there, in the first instance. Anyway, I think we are done here. Let's lock up and get back to Orange Grove for a cup of tea.'

Naish stood on the front steps rolling a cigarette as Newton sorted through the keys Mrs Carson had given him to lock the front door.

'You're a bit late on your rounds, milko,' said Naish, with a smile, as the milkman came up the steps.

'I am not delivering,' the milkman grunted, 'this is the time of day I get round to chase up my bad debts.'

'Bad debts,' said Naish, in an interested tone. 'Is Mr Emery a bad payer, then?'

'And what might it be to you?' said the milkman, continuing his gruff manner.

'I am Inspector Naish and I am interested in the whereabouts of Mr Emery, as you know.'

'I don't' know nothing of the kind.'

'But you spoke to one of my officers earlier today.'

'You have got your facts wrong, mate – I haven't been here yet today. He hasn't been taking in the milk in the last two days, so I gave him a miss when I went past at six o'clock this morning. I have come back now to try and get hold of him, because he owes me a week's money.'

'You went past at six o'clock, you say?'

'That's right, six o'clock.'

'But one of my officers took a statement from you after nine o'clock, because they didn't get here until then,' said Naish.

'Look, mate, I don't want to get into an argument with you. I just want my money. I haven't been here yet today, I tell you.'

'Is this the milkman you saw earlier, Newton?' asked Naish, as Newton came down the steps, having locked the door.

'No, Inspector, that's not him.'

'At last,' said the milkman, with an air of exasperation.

'My apologies,' said Naish. 'Are there any other milkmen on this round?'

'None at all,' said the milkman, continuing to be tetchy. 'There is only me who serves this house. Another dairy has a couple of houses further up the street but, other than that, it's my round.'

'Then we urgently need to find out who Jones was taking a statement from this morning, don't we?' said Naish to Newton, clearly annoyed. 'And just as importantly, what it was that Jones told him.'

'Yes, Inspector,' said Newton.

'Once again, I apologise for the confusion, but I will have to ask you to give your details to the sergeant here, who will contact you to take a formal statement at a later time. We are investigating the disappearance of your customer, Mr Emery, and your information will be needed as evidence to help us construct a timeline, you understand.'

'All right,' said the milkman, a little less surly, 'just as long as the confusion is cleared up.'

Naish wandered back up towards the front door and lit another cigarette while Newton took the details.

'As soon as we get back to the station, I want Jones and you to sit down with the police artist and get a sketch done of just who it was you saw this morning masquerading as a milkman. As soon as it is done, get hold of Burton and bring him and the sketch up to me, along with Jones. Understood?'

'Yes, Inspector,' said Newton, deferentially. 'I will get it sorted out.'

'You were quick about it,' said Naish, as Hancock came into the office, 'or have you not started?'

'All done and dusted. I got Davis to run me round in a car. It only took five minutes at each place, so it made sense to go by car.'

'So, what is the answer?'

'Well, none of them have a blue Bedford, and that includes Dobson's.'

'Did you get in at that side door?'

'Yes, it was easy because I just went around and banged on the door until someone answered. I just played the innocent and said I didn't want to trouble the shop floor, but as they were directing me round, I got a clear view of the whole floor area and there was no vehicle.'

'What about the coats then?'

'Now the coats were different. Lots of differing answers, but in terms of your top three, it was yes at Frazer's in Old King Street, a yes at Dobson's in Queen Square and a no at Byfield's. Your second division list I have marked up with yes's and no's.'

'Who did you speak to at Byfield's?'

'A Mr Miles. He said he was the head man there, so I took his word for it.'

'Did any of the people you spoke to at any of the premises appear uneasy?'

'I can't say that they did. I went in, explained the nature of my enquiry, they gave a measured and helpful response – apart from the Miles bloke, he was a bit sniffy – and I made a note of their replies in my notebook. A thank you and I was on my way.'

'Well, at least we have ticked that line of enquiry off. If that's the finished list, put it on the evidence table over there.'

'There you go, step inside,' said Hancock, opening the door in response to a knock. 'Newton, Jones and Burton to see you, Inspector.'

'Sit yourselves down. Where are we with the sketch?'

'The artist is just finishing it off and he will bring it straight up, Inspector,' said Newton.

'Have you shown it to Burton yet?'

'No, Inspector, I just collared him to come up, as you asked.'

'Come in and join us,' said Naish, as the artist poked his head around the door. 'Bring it round here and let me have a look at it first. Excellent, excellent. Now then, Burton, step round this side of the desk and have a look at this drawing. What do you think?'

'It's him, Inspector, I would swear to it,' said Burton, with slight astonishment.

'If I cover up his milkman's hat, does that make it clearer?'

'It does, Inspector, and if his coat were brown, he would be the spit of the driver in the blue Bedford in Stall Street.'

'Just as I thought,' said Naish, with an air of satisfaction, as he pulled another sketch from the clutter of papers on his desk. 'So now we have our two thugs. Thug one, here, and thug two, here. Now then, Burton, I want you to go along with the artist gentleman here and get our milkman here redrawn without the hat. Just as you saw him, understand?'

'Yes, Inspector.'

'Right then, off you go and bring it up to me as soon as it is finished. Now then, Jones, tell me the details of what our bogus milkman was after.'

'He said that he was keen not to waste time and money supplying milk to a customer who had gone away, and did I know when he would be back. I am afraid that I was a little indiscreet because instead of just saying no, I didn't know, I suggested that he had done a runner.'

Naish rolled his eyes towards the ceiling and reached for his tobacco tin.

'He just came across as so genuine that I confess he took me in, Inspector,' continued Jones. 'He asked when he was last seen, had he left a note, had he taken anything with him, were the house contents just left as they were – questions like that. It sounds so obvious now when I list them all off, but he kind of slipped them in to the conversation as we went along.'

'Did he ask anything about Emery's shop?'

'He did, Inspector.'

'Did that not strike you as suspicious?'

'I am afraid it didn't, in the context in which he asked. He told me that he also delivered a pint at his shop every other day and was wondering what the police had been so interested in there, and did I think that he should stop delivering there as well?'

'Well, he took you in well and truly, didn't he?' said Naish, with a sigh of disappointment. 'I was going to say that I assume you didn't tell him anything about our interest in the place, but your body language tells me that you have.'

'He asked me if we had made any progress with the burglary a while back.'

'You mean to stand there and tell me you discussed the matter with him – a complete stranger? What did you tell him? I want the truth, now, all of it, because if I find out later you have lied to me, I will have you sacked.'

'I told him we were still on the case and … '

'And what?' demanded Naish.

'And that we were also suspicious of what he was up to after hours in the premises.'

'Well, therein lies the answer as to why the place was torched. They clearly thought that they had satisfactorily covered up whatever evidence existed on the first and second floors, but your insight clearly put the wind up them and they decided to try and eradicate the evidence along with the building. I am in a real dilemma with you, Jones. On one hand, I cannot believe that you could be so naïve, yet, bizarrely, your ineptness has caused this gang to reveal their hand as a result of your indiscretion.'

'I am so sorry, Inspector, I don't know what to say,' said Jones, clearly distraught.

'All right, no point wringing your hands now. What's done is done,' said Naish, sensing that the man had atoned sufficiently for his error. 'Just take it as a lesson and make sure it is never forgotten. Now, on your way.'

Jones closed the door after him and Naish joined Hancock and Newton on the chairs by the blackboards.

'Well, he is a cool customer, our milkman, I will give him that, and there is clearly more to him than mere thuggery,' said Naish. 'But what interests me most is that, clearly, our grim duo are as surprised as we are that Emery has done a bunk.'

'That struck me as well,' said Newton. 'And it would appear that they do not mean him any harm.'

'I am not sure that we can infer that,' said Naish. 'They may just be choosing their moment, or he has done a runner because he felt threatened.'

'He may know what we can only suppose – that these two murdered Lynch and Edwards,' said Newton. 'That might account for his recent unease, which Mrs Carson noticed.'

'He may think or know a good many things, but we can only work with the facts that we have, the facts that we can produce evidence to back up,' said Naish. 'I think it unlikely that they mean him harm. They have had at least two occasions where they could have done him in. At the time of the redecoration and the time before the fire. Emery clearly knows them. He may not trust them, but he clearly allows them to do what they want in his premises. Certainly, the redecoration is the most illustrative example of that. He is in the shop while the work is being done and, while we do not know his thoughts about it happening, he clearly acquiesced to it being done.'

'You don't think that it was Emery who wanted the work done?' asked Newton, slightly surprised.

'It has to be a possibility, I think,' said Naish. 'The other telling thing to me is that, if either of you had commissioned that redecoration, I don't imagine either of you paying up when you saw the standard of the finish, do you? That suggests to me that Emery was told that the work was going to be done – whether he agreed or just acquiesced, we do not know – and he accepts the completed work for what it is. Which tells you what?'

'That someone else paid for it?' said Hancock.

'Not only that someone else paid for or arranged the work, but that that someone told Emery and our two thugs that it was going to be done.'

'Who?' asked Newton.

'I would suggest someone that they all know and whose instructions they accept.'

'A boss?' said Hancock.

'Certainly a controlling mind,' said Naish. 'I suggest that it works like this: the controlling mind decides the work is to be done; he tells the two thugs to get it done; he tells Emery it is going to be done. We assume that Emery accepts, willingly or unwillingly – the unwilling option being managed, I imagine, by the clear threat that the two thugs will be unleashed on him if he argues.'

'If we follow that theory, then the implication is that both Emery and the thugs both work for this controlling mind,' said Newton.

'They do and they must therefore all know each other and be in whatever this business is, together,' said Naish, lighting a satisfied cigarette.

'But what is this business?' asked Newton.

'Ah, I am afraid that that matter is still in the dark for me. We need to begin to draw them together and I have a suspicion that these two holding companies, Derwent and Cotman, are in some way all or part of that connection.'

'So why do you think he has chosen to go to cover now?' asked Hancock.

'I don't know that either, I am afraid,' said Naish. 'Something must have changed. Perhaps, as Newton suggests, he discovered that they had murdered Lynch and Edwards.'

'You think he was in the dark about that, do you?' asked Hancock.

'Emery does not appear to me to be the sort of man who would be at ease if he were party to murder,' said Naish. 'Something petty, perhaps, but he has not got the nerve for serious crime, in my view.

If we take my theory about the controlling mind a step further, the thugs have one role and Emery has another role. I think it is also likely that, while they know of each other, they do not understand fully the role of the other. Emery understands the thugs are there to do the enforcing and strong-arm stuff, but he probably is not aware of the full extent of their activities. The controlling mind only lets them know as much as is necessary to allow the scheme, whatever it is, to function. Whilst the thugs' role is fairly plain, I imagine that the thugs know less about Emery's role.'

'Just like us, then,' said Hancock.

'Unfortunately, that appears to be so – for the moment, at least,' said Naish.

'Come in,' called Naish.

'A package for you, Inspector,' said the desk sergeant.

'Thank you, Sergeant. Can you put in on my desk,' said Naish.

Naish left Newton and Hancock to update the blackboards and create a schematic of how the relationship between the controlling mind, the thugs and Emery might function. Meanwhile, he sat back down at his desk and, having opened the large manila envelope, he sat and examined the small packets and the written report that it contained.

'Tea, Inspector?' asked Hancock, breaking in on Naish's train of thought.

'Yes, put it there and come and sit down.'

'What have you got there, then?' asked Hancock.

'It is the report of the analysis of the samples of paint that we took from the floorboards, and the results are very intriguing, I have to say. These five glass trays are the samples that were tested, and the report goes into the detail of the chemical composition of each of the samples and while I am sure that is fascinating for a chemist, the overall conclusion is what interests us. It appears that this style of paint has not been in use for decades. Apparently, the clearest indication of this is that some of the chemicals used to create the pigments are no longer commercially available. In addition, it appears that the ratio of pigment, oil and other elements is not exactly the same in each case – close, but not exact.'

'Does it offer a conclusion to account for that?' asked Newton.

'Not exactly, but the suggestion is that the slight inconsistency might have been caused by the paint having been blended by hand.'

'What, mixed up to order you mean?' said Newton.

'That would account for it, wouldn't it?' said Naish. 'If you buy a tin of paint from a hardware shop, made in a factory on a production line, you will get exactly the same ratio of ingredients in every tin, at least in that batch. But probably, unless the machine is altered, every batch will have the same ratio. But if you could be bothered to grind down the pigments blended in the oils, and whatever else it is you put in to paint, you would, no matter how careful you were, always have a slight variance.'

'But who bothers to mix paint up by hand these days? Anywhere you go it's all premixed – even artists buy it made up in those little metal tubes,' said Newton.

'So, could this paint have come from an old canvas?' said Hancock, drawing thoughtfully on his pipe.

'Go on,' said Naish. 'How do you see that working?'

'Suppose that our friend Emery is restoring paintings on those easels up there on the second floor. All the scrapings over time build up on the floor.'

'That's a lot of scraping and a lot of canvases,' said Naish, dubiously.

'So, he has been at it a long time,' said Hancock.

'Some of these restorers use chemicals to strip back parts of a canvas they are going to repaint,' said Newton. 'That would potentially form a substance similar to those peelings of paint you get where you use paint stripper on the woodwork at home. Over time it could just get trodden into the surface of the floorboards. Just a thought.'

'Taking that thought one stage further,' said Naish. 'It might be that, having stripped the paint from parts of a canvas, Emery then mixes up paints in a manner that replicates the consistency of the original paint and repaints the surface to give an imperceptible repair.'

'That works,' said Hancock, 'as long as it was done over a period of time and, of course, it can't be Emery, as he is not an artist.'

'Well, we know that someone has been using that second floor for a considerable period of time and as for Emery, I have two views on that,' said Naish. 'If we believe him, then we are back to the theory we chatted over the other day, that someone else is using that second floor. The theory fits the facts, but only on the assumption that Emery is up to something else at the same time that our other friend is at work up there.'

'Remember that we have evidence that there were two easels stood together up there. Perhaps they worked together,' said Hancock.

'It may well be so,' said Naish, 'but I am coming round to the idea that perhaps Emery is just a liar. If we accept that hypothesis, it makes sense of both Emery's evening ritual and the witness sightings of the activity in the building every evening. It was at one time possible that he let himself out at the back of the shop and went home while the other party used his premises, but we now know from Mrs Carson that that is not so.'

'Interesting idea,' said Hancock.

'Then the sketchbooks could well be his as well,' said Newton.

'Exactly,' said Naish. 'Why he denies it, we have yet to fully understand, but it all fits in. However, before we all run off with it as revealed truth, let us just remember that it is just a hypothesis. Some of it could be supported with the facts that we have but it needs some more meat on the bones.'

'Shall I chalk it up on the board?' asked Newton.

'Yes, it certainly needs to go under work in progress,' said Naish. 'Where are Lynch's shoes, by the way?'

'His shoes?' said Hancock, surprised. 'In the storeroom downstairs with all his clothes and other belongings from Oak Street, I think.'

'Nip down and get them for me, will you?' said Naish. 'Newton, go and make another pot of tea while he is at it.'

Fifteen minutes later and they were reassembled in Naish's office. Newton poured the tea and Hancock reloaded his pipe, while Naish sat as his desk examining Lynch's shoes with a handheld magnifying glass.

'Now, that is interesting,' said Naish, putting the lens and a shoe on his desk. 'Take a look at the soles of the shoes yourselves with the glass, but I should be happy to put money on the fact that this substance here on my blotter which I have scraped from between the treads is paint. Now we need to get it off to the laboratory as soon as we can to confirm it, but I would say they are the same sorts of colours as what we have in these samples in the five trays.'

'You may well be right,' said Newton, peering at the sole and then the scrapings on Naish's blotter. 'Difficult to be certain, because there is a lot of dirt in the treads as well.'

'But when you spread one of these scrapings out flat on the blotter with the edge of this penknife blade, you see something of the colour come to light. You see?' said Naish, demonstrating with his penknife.

'You are dead right,' said Hancock, leaning over Newton's shoulder to observe the demonstration. 'But what do you infer from it?'

'What I infer from it is, that it proves that Lynch was up there on that second floor on the night that he burgled the shop. It proves that he went right up to the easels that were there.'

'How do we know they were there?' challenged Hancock.

'They must have been there, because they were being worked on at the time and because Lynch stepped in the wet paint that was surrounding them. It all fits,' said Naish.

'So, do you think that he stole one, or both, of the paintings that were under restoration and that is why he was pursued, punished and then hung out as an example to others?' said Newton.

'It would account for the facts of this case better than any theory we have come up with so far, don't you think?' said Naish.

'They must have been very valuable pictures to provoke that sort of a reaction,' said Hancock. 'I am not saying it isn't so but – to take one of your phrases, Inspector – it needs a few more facts to take it from the hypothesis stage.'

'I agree,' said Naish. 'Not least among the facts we need to consider is, where the devil did the paintings get to? Not only that, but if Lynch was stealing to order then he got short-changed because – from all we know about him in the days after the burglary and from his financial affairs – he didn't get paid for his trouble.'

Chapter 14

Their discussion was interrupted by a knock at the door.

'I have the redrawn sketch for you, Inspector,' said Burton.

'You are sure that this is as accurate as you can recall?'

'It is, Inspector. That's as best as I can recall him, given the time that I had to take him in.'

'Right, make sure that you sit down with Sergeant Newton tomorrow and sign off a witness statement. Now get on home.'

'I was going to suggest that someone takes that sketch around to the witnesses who have already identified thug one,' said Hancock.

'Yes, the landlord of the Old Jupiter for one, and George Jenkins, Mrs West and Orton need to be on the list. I would prefer that you did it rather than delegate it. I could do without another mistake after the Jones debacle,' said Naish.

'Consider it done. I will get a message to George Jenkins and arrange to meet him somewhere discreet.'

'Good. Well, listening to the abbey clock, it's a quarter past six, so I suggest that you two get on home. I will see you both back here first thing in the morning.'

Naish was rolling a cigarette at his desk the following morning, when he looked up with a start as the door of his office was simultaneously knocked and opened.

'Sorry to burst in, Inspector, but I think it's urgent,' said Newton, as he came in followed by Hancock, a little more calmly.

'What is it?' said Naish, with a tone of concern.

'A break-in has been reported at St Mark's Road, Inspector,' said Newton. 'The postman phoned it in to the front desk ten minutes ago.'

'Get the car and let's get round there now,' said Naish, taking his coat from the stand. 'Is the postman still there?'

'No, he said he had to get on with his round, but he gave his details to the desk sergeant and said he would look in again after his round.'

'What did he say when he phoned in?' asked Naish, as the car drove out towards Widcombe.

'He just said that the front door looked as if it had been forced open. He didn't go inside, apparently, but he called out a couple of times and, having got no reply, left and came away to phone the station.'

'So, he didn't go inside, then?'

'It would appear that he didn't, Inspector, but I will verify his exact actions when I take his statement,' said Newton.

'Well, it's clear that the door has been forced,' said Naish, looking at the damage around the lock of the front door. 'Take a look around the back, Newton, will you. You forced entry the other day, so see if you can see any damage caused since you broke that rear window.'

'Those circular marks around the lock look like the end of a sledgehammer handle has been used to knock the hasp off the lock, to me,' said Hancock.

'I agree,' said Naish, peering at the marks closely.

The door had been pulled back so that it just stood ajar. Naish pushed the door open gently with the end of his index finger revealing the damage to the hasp in the door frame that Hancock had predicted.

'Not the work of our friend Emery, I imagine,' said Hancock. 'Firstly, he would have used his keys and secondly, he doesn't have the build to swing a sledgehammer, in my view.'

'He may have been here, though,' said Naish. 'He may have been brought by our two thugs.'

'But he would still have used his keys, surely?' said Hancock.

'I suppose it depends whether he was brought here unwillingly. He may not have been co-operating, assuming, of course, he was here in the first place. My inclination is that he was not.'

'Nothing to be found around the back,' said Newton. 'The boarding-up panel is still firmly in place on the window I broke, and there is no sign of any other damage.'

'Well, this doorway is not overlooked is it,' said Naish. 'In the dead of night, it was as good a point of entry as any, I suppose. Let's look inside, shall we?'

'Well, it does not appear to have been ransacked,' said Hancock, as they stood in the hall and looked into the rooms that opened off from it.

'Have we made an inventory of the property yet?' asked Naish.

'No, I had a constable assigned to get it done today,' said Newton.

'How do you want to play this, Inspector? Work together or take a floor each,' asked Hancock.

'Newton and I have been here before, so we have a rough idea of the layout and what was in each room. You two get on with the upper floors. The attic and second floor are virtually empty, so it should not take you very long. I will get on with the ground floor,' said Naish.

Naish went into the sitting room first, and immediately one of the motivations for the crime was apparent. Three of the paintings in the collection that hung on the wall were missing, their absence accentuated by the three darker squares on the wallpaper, each surmounted with a small brass hook. The other pictures in the collection were untouched, as far as could be seen. Naish got out his notebook and checked off the names that only confirmed what he already knew – that the three missing pictures were the scenes of the abbey by Turner. Naish went over the rest of the room in detail but, as far as he could tell, nothing else had been moved or taken. He then made his way out into the hall and carried out the same examination of all the other rooms on the ground floor. He was just coming back into the hallway from the kitchen as Newton and Hancock came back down the stairs.

'Everything appears to be intact, as far as we can tell,' said Newton. 'There are a few ornaments and a couple of silver picture frames that I would have thought would have been standard pickings for a petty thief, but they are all there.'

'Are you sure?' asked Naish.

'As sure as we can be, Inspector,' said Hancock. 'I moved a couple of ornaments and they left a dust mark on the surface of the table, so I would suggest that, as there were no marks, nothing had been taken. The contents of the drawers also appear untouched. Again, nothing of the disturbance that you would expect to find following a systematic turning-over by a professional thief.'

'How about any pictures on the walls?' asked Naish.

'No, nothing missing, no empty hooks or the like,' said Newton. 'The only thing that I noticed was that one of the floor mats has been disturbed – most likely one of them tripped over it in the dark.'

'Well then, I have found the sole purpose of the burglary and it was not opportunistic. Come in here and have a look,' said Naish, as he led them into the sitting room. 'As you can see, three of the paintings have been removed and they are the ones by Turner.'

'The ones that you pointed out yesterday,' said Newton.

'Exactly those ones,' said Naish. 'The rest of this room and the rest of the ground floor are exactly as you found the rest of the house. Nothing else has been touched and some of the items would be just the sort of thing that a thief would have taken if this were an opportunistic theft.'

'Why only those three?' asked Hancock.

'I don't know for certain, but my guess is that they are the most valuable – but I find it impossible to believe that they are originals. They would be out of the range of even Emery's pockets, I should think,' said Naish. 'I think that I need to bring forward my visit to the Victoria Art Gallery and see what I can find out about all these artists in Emery's collection.'

'Stolen to order, do you think?' asked Newton.

'It may be the case,' said Naish. 'or they may have been stolen on the orders of someone.'

'There is a chance that it may have been Emery who came to get them himself,' said Hancock, 'and he brought a stronger man to break in. Perhaps he thought that we might have changed the locks.'

'But we haven't, have we,' said Naish. 'Once he got here and found the original locks that he has keys for, it makes no sense to break the door down.'

'Unless … ' began Hancock, 'unless he was wishing to disguise the fact that it was him …'

' … and smashed the door in for effect,' said Naish, finishing the sentence with a smile.

'But if the theft of the three paintings was the sole purpose of the burglary, why did he or they go upstairs?' said Newton.

'How do you mean?' said Naish.

'The disturbed mat,' repeated Newton. 'I don't say that it is suspicious in itself, but it indicates that someone went up there, and, if they went up there, they presumably went through the entire house. Why, I do not know, but I just think it is odd if they came with the sole purpose of removing the three paintings.'

'Take me up and show me,' said Naish.

'As you see, Inspector, there is one of these large rugs in each of the unoccupied rooms on this floor,' said Newton. 'I imagine that they are just put down to dampen the noise. The one in the front room has been rucked up a little, as if someone has scuffed it up in the dark.'

'Makes sense, if they were using a small torch to avoid being observed from the houses opposite,' said Naish. 'Where is the entrance to the attic? Perhaps they were after something in those trunks and cases you said were stored up there.'

'It may be so, but I have already checked up there and the cases do not appear to have been moved. That is not to say that our visitor did not go up and check them,' said Newton. 'The stairs to the attic are behind that small door over there on the landing.'

'If they were going to check the contents of the cases, it doesn't make sense that they blunder about in these second-floor rooms, tripping over the mat and whatever. If they knew the cases were up there, then they would go straight to them, I should have thought,' said Hancock.

'Well, we could carry on with this speculation until the cows come home,' said Naish. 'What we need to do is get on with what we do know, for now, and establish some facts. You two need to start knocking on some doors up and down this street and see if anyone has seen anything. Check the tradesmen as well as anyone who makes deliveries in the early hours. I am going back to Orange Grove and I will send a couple of constables along to help you. It's half past nine now. Let's aim to meet up in my office at two o'clock. That should give you sufficient time to do the door to door stuff and get yourselves something for lunch.'

The car dropped Naish back at Orange Grove, and once he had detailed the desk sergeant to allocate a couple of constables to assist Hancock and Newton, he set off around the corner to the Victoria Art Gallery.

Naish climbed the broad staircase that led to the main public gallery on the first floor. It was typical of the style of many Victorian municipal galleries; a large single room of generous scale, with walls lined with dark wood panelling. Down the centre of the room were a number of glass display cabinets exhibiting various artefacts in silver and ceramic. These were interspersed with wooden benches upholstered with leather that faced the walls to enable the visitor to sit and contemplate the paintings that hung opposite.

There were already a few other visitors in the gallery silently making their way around the gallery, pausing occasionally to look more closely or read the printed labels at the side of the paintings. Naish affected to join them as he took in the place. At the far end of the gallery was an elderly gentleman dressed in a uniform who was clearly the guard. Naish quickened his cursory inspection of the paintings and stopped at the painting nearest the guard and feigned interest long enough for a couple of visitors to pass out of earshot.

'Good morning. I was wondering if it would be possible to speak with the curator of the gallery,' said Naish.

'I am afraid that the curator is not available to visitors unless it is by prior appointment, sir. I have a little knowledge of the exhibits and there are some information sheets provided if that would be of assistance to you?' replied the guard.

'My enquiry is not about the works of art. I am a police officer and I would like to speak with the curator as part of an investigation that I am making. It does not involve the curator personally, you understand,' said Naish, keen to avoid confusion.

'Well, if it is a police matter, sir, I could go and see if she is in her office – only, I am not supposed to leave the gallery unattended, you see.'

'Well, as I am a police officer,' said Naish, showing the man his identification. 'How about you leave the gallery under my supervision for a few minutes while you go and see if she is able to see me.'

'That will be fine, Mr ... ' the guard peered more closely at Naish's identification, 'Inspector Naish. I will go and see if Miss Whiting is in.'

Ten minutes later the guard reappeared followed by a stout woman of middle age. She was dressed elegantly, more for a social event than business, thought Naish.

'Inspector Naish, Miss Whiting,' said the guard, by way of introduction, before wandering back to his chair.

'I am sorry to have disturbed you, Miss Whiting, but I am seeking some advice regarding an investigation that I am making.'

'Then perhaps it would be best if you come along to my office, Inspector, where we can talk more confidentially.'

'Thank you,' said Naish, relieved at Miss Whiting's amiable reaction. He was not a man who was easily intimidated but she had the presence of a school mistress and, for some unaccountable reason, he had almost feared getting a sharp rebuke.

'What is the nature of your investigation, if I might ask?' said Miss Whiting, closing the door.

'Part of it involves some works of art and I was hoping that you might be able to give me some advice. I have the names of some artists here, if you will take a look,' said Naish, handing her his open notebook. 'There were nine pictures hung on a wall in a house. There was one painting by each of the first six artists listed and three by the last artist, Turner. The three paintings by Turner have been stolen and the six paintings by the other artists have been left behind.'

'The first six artists on your list are all minor artists from the eighteenth and nineteenth centuries. They are all competent and well-regarded artists working in oil. However, as I say, they are competent rather than gifted artists and therefore, while they are collectable, they are not valuable. Not without value, you understand – people collect their works and they appear with some regularity at auction – but they do not command the prices that the great artists command. Do you follow?'

'Absolutely,' said Naish, a little wrong footed by the final question that left him feeling as if he was in the presence of his old school mistress.

'Turner, however, is one of the greats. I assume you have heard of Turner?'

'Of course,' said Naish, keen not to appear a dullard, 'but only by name. I am afraid I know little about his work.'

'Turner's work is highly collectable and the paintings command very high prices indeed – well beyond the pocket of all but the wealthiest collectors. We have an example of his work here in the gallery.'

'Do you,' said Naish, a little surprised.

'I will show it to you when we have finished here if you would care to see it. Going back to your enquiry, Inspector, if these paintings are by *the* J.M.W. Turner, then their value – compared with the works of these other six artists – would explain why they had been stolen and the others left hanging on the wall. If one desired, one could purchase six paintings by the other artists on your list for a fraction of the value of one of the Turners.'

'That is very interesting,' said Naish.

'Of course,' said Miss Whiting, continuing her lecture, 'it all depends on it being J.M.W. Turner and not just another artist of similar competence to these other six who happens to be called Turner. You say that the paintings were all hung together?'

'Yes, they were all on one area of one wall in a group of nine. Three in a group to the left, a small space, then the three by Turner in the centre, another small space, and then a final group of three.'

'It appears odd to me that someone fortunate enough to possess such fine works would hang them in the company of such dross, if I might use the expression. It leads me to the suspicion that they may well just be works by another Turner. It is of course conceivable that the owner did not understand the value of the paintings in their possession but that someone else did – a visitor or an employee, perhaps,' said Miss Whiting, warming to her role as detective. 'Where were the paintings hung? Were they in an establishment that looked as if the owner might be able to afford three paintings by J.M.W. Turner?'

'They were in a modest home,' said Naish, keen to regain control of the discussion. 'But the occupier may have knowledge of the art market. I value your observations, Miss Whiting, particularly the points you raise concerning the incongruity of the paintings being among these other works.'

'If you would like me to view the remaining paintings, then I would be happy to do so and give you my opinion based on the works themselves.'

'That would be very helpful,' said Naish. 'Would this afternoon be convenient?'

'I think so,' said Miss Whiting, consulting her desk diary. 'Yes, I am free after three o' clock.'

'Excellent. I will send a car to collect you from the front door at three o' clock. The house is in St Mark's Road in Widcombe, so it will only take an hour of your time, hopefully.'

'It is a shame that you do not have more detailed information as to whether it was J.M.W. Turner. That appears to be the key to me,' said Miss Whiting, returning to the role of detective.

'They were scenes around the abbey, from what I could make out,' said Naish. 'Clearly, the surroundings have changed, but the abbey itself was, I thought, fairly obvious.'

'He painted a number of abbeys and other religious buildings,' continued Miss Whiting. 'Come and take a look at the Turner in the gallery and you can see what you think.'

Naish followed Miss Turner back out into the foyer and into the gallery where they stood before the painting.

'This is it. "Bath Abbey by J.M.W. Turner, painted before 1793." The point of interest, of course, is that you say the works that were stolen were painted in oil. This, of course, as you can see, has been executed in watercolour. It is a view of the west wall and entrance door viewed from the left. He did, of course, paint in oils, but not this scene.'

'The paintings were in this style,' said Naish, 'but not from this point of view. One was this scene, but as if the viewer was to the right of the abbey west wall. The second was of what would be the south façade, as if the viewer was stood in York Street, and the other was of the north and east walls – a corner view, as if the artist was stood in Orange Grove. I am no expert, but looking at this watercolour, all

I can say is that the finish of the three paintings was not the same. It was glossy and had a varnished type finish like this painting here, for instance.'

'Well, that is most definitely an oil painting, Inspector. So, you have a real mystery on your hands, then,' said Miss Whiting, with relish.

'It is a mystery, in its own way, but it is part of the much bigger mystery that is the case itself. I had been hoping to eliminate the strands of mystery with my investigations, not add to them. Anyway, Miss Whiting, I thank you for your assistance,' said Naish, spotting an opportunity for escape. 'You have been most helpful. I will see you this afternoon just after three o'clock in Widcombe.'

Naish breathed a deep sigh in the fresh air outside. He walked across Grand Parade, leant on the stone balustrade, lit a cigarette and stared down at the weir in thought.

Naish was surprised to find Hancock in the foyer as he returned to the station.

'You are back earlier than I expected.'

'I know. We had got most of the door to door stuff done out at St Mark's Road when I got a message to say that the rates information about Swallow Street was ready.'

'I had forgotten to ask you about that,' said Naish. 'I thought it was due in yesterday evening, about four o' clock.'

'It was, but they ran into some complications, apparently, in identifying the payee.'

'Complications? I can't believe that paying the rates is that complicated a process.'

'Ordinarily, it is not. But in this case there was some lack of clarity as to the payee. Anyway, they have got the answer to the question and now that they have got it, you and I can perhaps understand why the payee might have wished to mask their identity.'

'Go on,' said Naish, intrigued. 'Who was the payee?'

'Cotman Holdings,' said Hancock, with emphasis.

'That's the holding company that Emery rented his gallery in Lambeth from, isn't it?'

'That is right. They also owned a large picture gallery in Westminster, if you recall.'

'I do,' said Naish, as he climbed the stairs to his office. 'Things are starting to have a form in this case after all, aren't they? It's still all a bit unclear as to how they all link up, but something is forming, like an image becoming clearer as a fog lifts.'

'It is still all a bit too foggy for my liking,' said Hancock.

'Mine as well,' said Naish, 'but we are making progress, I can feel it in my water. Anyway, what is the situation at St Mark's Road? Are we still on for a two o' clock catch-up with Newton?'

'It may be sooner if he gets the last bits completed. With four of us at the job things went quicker than expected.'

'All right. Well, save the detail until we are all sat down. I need to be back at Emery's house for three o'clock as I have arranged for the curator of the Victoria Gallery to come and give us some advice on his painting collection.'

'What shall we do about this Cotman information?'

'I think that we need to go back to the rating department and ask if Cotman Holdings are paying business or domestic rates on any other properties in Bath.'

'That will take some time.'

'It may well take some time, but we need to know. It's the easiest path to identifying someone behind this mystery entity. I suggest that it is broken down. Do they pay the rates on any of the premises in Abbey Green that back on to Swallow Street?'

'The rank of buildings where the Golden Fleece is, you mean?'

'That's them. Next comes any property associated with art, auction and the like. Then the rest of the business market. Leave the domestic until last. Oh, and see if they can give an estimated timescale to get it done once they have calmed down,' said Naish, as Hancock set off on his task.

Naish was rolling himself a cigarette to enjoy with his mug of tea when Hancock and Newton knocked at his door.

'Do you ever eat, Inspector?' said Hancock, with a smile. 'Tobacco is not a food substitute, you know.'

'Well, it keeps me going until the evening,' said Naish. 'If your concerns were really a request to eat your sandwiches in my office, then the answer is yes, if we can crack on at the same time.'

'Fine with us,' said Newton.

'So, what have we learnt from the morning's work at St Mark's Road?'

'Very useful, I think,' said Newton, 'although it took some digging about to piece it all together. The first piece of information didn't come from St Mark's Road at all but from our friend, the tramp, in Swallow Street. Burton took him some breakfast at half past six this morning and he told him that he had seen the blue Bedford van leave the garage about half past one this morning.'

'How can he be sure of that?' asked Naish. 'In my experience it is a very unusual tramp that has a watch.'

'He heard the clock on the abbey strike half past just after the van had left the garage and disappeared out of view.'

'Who was in the van, then?' pressed Naish.

'Well, that is the interesting part, Inspector. He identified the two thugs, having been shown the artist's impressions of them as part of his brief before he left the station. He is certain that it was them and will swear on it. However, on this occasion they were not alone. According to our friend, they were accompanied by another man. A gentleman, so he says, to judge by his dress and the way the two thugs deferred to him. Once they had the van out in the street and the doors shut behind them, the gent climbs into the passenger seat while thug two jumps in the back.'

'Can he identify this gentleman?' said Naish. 'Was it Emery?'

'That's the strange part of it,' continued Newton. 'He describes this man as tall, slim and elderly, but with the poise and manner of a gentleman. That does not match up with Emery, as I would say he was of average height, slightly stooped and his best friend could not describe his bearing as that of a gentleman – more of a grocer, I would say.'

'But it was dark,' said Naish. 'He may have been deceived?'

'According to him, he had a clear view of them, including a glimpse of his face. I got Burton to take a photo of Emery that we took from his house to show our friend and he swears that it was not him.'

'Very interesting. We need to get the tramp back into the station as soon as possible and sit him down with the police artist. I don't care how clear his view of this man was, I want some pictures of him. We need his face, as best he can recall, and a full length of him standing. It is a long shot, but we need anything that we can to try and identify this man, or at least narrow his description down so as to eliminate certain types of people.'

'You think he is our controlling mind, then?' asked Hancock.

'It looks very much like it to me,' said Naish. 'If it is not Emery, then it must be the man controlling the thugs – the man they regard as the boss.'

'I will get him in as soon as we have finished here,' said Newton. 'Burton can deputise in his costume as the tramp's companion and source of food.'

'So, what next, then?' asked Naish, impatiently.

'Well, up at St Mark's Road we started the door-to-door stuff, and the neighbour opposite reports that he was disturbed at about two o'clock this morning. He was woken from his sleep so is a little vague as to what it was that woke him, but it may well have been the blows that were made to open Emery's front door, from the discussion that I had with him. However, the main evidence is that, despite what woke him, he got up and went to look out in the street, and parked in the road opposite his house, just up from Emery's house, was the blue Bedford van.'

'Can he identify the men concerned? Did he get the number plate?'

'No, he did not see anyone at all, but he could make out that the driver was in the van for the entire five minutes that he watched. He gave up in the end and went back to bed, assuming that nothing untoward was going on.'

'Well, it is clear, despite the lack of detail in what he saw, that the van is sufficient circumstantial evidence to link the three men at Swallow Street with the theft at St Mark's Road. Excellent work, well done, the pair of you.'

'But there is more to add,' said Newton. 'We finished the door-to-door enquiries and no one else had seen or heard anything at all. We were having a chat on the pavement outside Emery's house with a couple of the tradesmen who deliver, when a bloke came past. He was an engine driver who was just returning to his home further up beyond St Mark's Road. Luckily, two uniformed constables had joined us, otherwise I think he would have passed us by, not realising that we were police officers.'

Chapter 15

'"Good morning, gentlemen," he says, "no trouble at Mr Emery's, I hope?" I told him that we were making enquiries into Mr Emery's whereabouts, and did he know him. "Yes, I know him – only to say hello to in the street. I have known him for a year or so, ever since he framed a picture for me at that shop of his. When you say his whereabouts, I am not sure what it is you mean." I told him he was a missing person and we were making enquiries. "Missing?" says the engine driver, "Well, he wasn't missing when I saw him this morning."'

'Was he sure of that?' said Naish, surprised.

'Apparently, he was going down St Mark's Road on his way to Green Park Station at three o'clock in the morning and he saw Emery coming up the road towards him and go up the front steps of his house,' said Newton.

'Did he speak to him?'

'Apparently not, because he was about twenty-five yards away from him and he didn't want to call out in the small hours. Other than being surprised to see him at that time of the morning, he thought nothing untoward.'

'Well at least we know Emery is still alive. We need to get on and try and find out where he is living,' said Naish. 'We need to think through these two witness statements in more detail. Were the trio looking for the paintings or for Emery?'

'Well, we know from the activities of the milkman impostor that they know he is not living there at the moment, and as recently as three o'clock this morning they still have not found him. My guess is that they may still be after him,' said Hancock.

'I am not so sure,' said Naish. 'If they were only after Emery, the two thugs would have dealt with it in my view. I believe that they came specifically for the pictures, and the third man was needed to identify the three paintings, in particular.'

'It makes sense,' conceded Hancock.

'The interesting thing is what Emery was doing there an hour later. I cannot believe it was coincidental, and so he must have known that they were going to go to his house that night and he waited until they had completed their work before going into the house himself.'

'So, Emery was not after getting the three pictures himself, then?' said Hancock.

'I am not sure. I cannot prove that, but I sense not,' said Naish. 'If – and it is an if – Emery knew that they were going to steal his paintings, surely he would have tried to get there first. If the trio are after the three paintings alone, then it accounts for the fact that the rest of the house is undisturbed. Getting possession of these paintings is clearly paramount and, being professional thieves with a clear purpose, they do not pocket any of the bits of silverware, for example, as a petty thief would do. It's in and out, job done. They go in, start with the most obvious rooms, find the paintings very quickly, the boss identifies the three that are needed, they are taken down – perhaps wrapped in a sheet or something they have brought for the purpose – down the steps, into the van and gone.'

'And they do it without Emery's consent because they haven't got the keys and need to break the front door in,' said Newton. 'It all adds up.

'But why is Emery there at three in the morning? What is the purpose of his visit?' asked Hancock.

'Well, I suspect that the answer to the first part of the question is that he went there in the early hours in order to avoid being seen, which would confirm our suspicion that he is in hiding. The answer to the second part of the question, I am not so sure about,' said Naish.

'If your hypothesis about the actions of the trio is right, and I agree that it is,' said Hancock, 'then they did not venture beyond the ground floor. So, it must have been Emery who went upstairs and tripped over the mat.'

'Lynch, Lynch, Lynch,' said Naish.

'Lynch?' said Newton. 'What about Lynch?'

'Just a thought that occurred to me,' said Naish. 'Right then, if that is everything for now, I think that we should get up to St Mark's Road and then we can send the car back to collect Miss Whiting at three.'

'Can we pick her up on the way?' asked Hancock.

'I can't see her on the back seat with you two,' said Naish, with a smile. 'It would be a bit of a squeeze.'

'Large lady, is she?' said Hancock.

'Handsome,' said Naish, and saying no more, he took his hat and coat from the stand and went out to the front steps to wait for the car.

'Time for a smoke before Miss Whiting arrives?' said Hancock, as they climbed the steps to Emery's house.

'Not for me,' said Naish, looking at his watch. 'I want to test something before she arrives. Help yourself if you want to grab a quick puff.'

'No, I will give it a miss,' said Hancock. 'I am not missing out if you have got the scent of something.'

Newton and Hancock followed Naish up the flight of stairs to the second floor. Naish motioned for them to wait on the landing while he quickly surveyed each room from its doorway.

'This is just how you left it up here, I assume?' Naish asked Newton.

'Yes, this is how it was,' said Newton, having quickly repeated Naish's scan of the rooms.

'Right, come in here,' said Naish, leading them in to a large room that overlooked the front of the house. The floorboards were bare around the edge of the room and a large mat about ten feet by ten feet covered the centre. 'The mat here that is rucked up on this corner is the one you say shows someone has been in here.'

'That is how I see it,' said Newton.

'Right, then. Hancock, you kneel at that corner, and Newton, you kneel at that corner. Good. Now then, I want you to roll the rug up towards me.'

As the roll came towards Naish, he stepped over it on to the bare boards and knelt down with his penknife in his hand.

'There it is, just as I thought. Thank you, Ted Lynch.'

'What have you got?' asked Hancock, brushing the dust off his hands.

'An improvised safety deposit box beneath the floorboards, if I am not mistaken, in the Ted Lynch style. It was when you said that, logically, the trio would not have any need to come up here that it was clear, by default, that it must have been Emery. But Emery must have known that the room was empty, and it seemed unlikely that he would trip over his own mat, especially as the light from the street must have given the room a modicum of light. It was the rucked-up mat that cast my mind back to Lynch's rooms.'

One of the floorboards was cut to form a cover between two joists and Naish used the blade of his knife to lift the board up.

'Not exactly a crock of gold,' said Naish, peering into the space beneath. 'If there was anything here, it would appear to have been taken.'

'What were you expecting to find?' asked Newton. 'It is not exactly a large void.'

'It depends what you fill it with,' said Naish. 'If it were full of ten pound notes, for example, it could contain a fortune. Anyway, we appear to have just these two keys.'

Two small hooks were screwed into the side of one of the joists that the boards rested on and a key hung on each. Both were mortice keys, one about an inch and a half long, the other about three inches long.

'These keys are interesting,' said Naish, now lying prone on the floor to scrutinise them. 'Whatever else he took from here, last night, he didn't touch the keys. There is a small amount of dust on the tops of each and a very fine cobweb between the larger key and the joist.'

'So he came for something else,' said Newton.

'Or else he came just to make sure they were still here,' said Naish.

'It seems a lot of trouble and risk to come just for that,' said Hancock. 'Besides, he took the chance that if they found him, he would reveal his hiding place.'

'They may know that he has a hiding place,' offered Newton, 'but then, why not take the keys and have them safe in his possession?'

'Because I think that he is worried that they might find out about his hiding place. Clearly, by their actions last night, if they do know about these keys or whatever else was in here, they don't suspect that this house is the repository for them or else they would have turned the house over completely to find them. By coming here – possibly at risk to himself – Emery knows that they don't, as yet, suspect his house to be that repository. Whether he came up here to check that the keys were safe or to collect some other item or items, we will have to wait and see.'

'If the reason that he came up here was to check that the keys were safe, that would suggest to me that he is concerned that the trio have inside information about this safe-deposit box,' said Newton.

'If that is true, then it follows logically that he must have had a confidant who could expose that secret, I suggest,' added Hancock.

'You may well be right,' said Naish. 'However, what it does prove to me is that some enmity now exists between the gent of the trio – the boss as it were – and Emery. Now, to me, that is not an impression that I have discerned in their relationship before.'

'So, what has changed, do you think?' asked Newton.

'At the moment, I am not sure,' said Naish, taking the keys off their hooks and standing up. 'This smaller key looks like an ordinary mortice key to me – too small for a door, but it would fit a cupboard or a trunk, for example. This larger one is without doubt a safe key and that is interesting. Whatever else there was at Emery's shop, there was definitely not a safe and our search here shows there is not one here.'

'Do you want me to take them round the locksmiths and see what I can find out?' asked Hancock.

'Yes, get on with it this afternoon. There are only three or four locksmiths that I can think of in the city. Newton, you can go and do some research on who supplies and fits safes, at the same time,' said Naish, as their discussion was interrupted by a knock on the front door. 'Ah, Miss Whiting has arrived. You two have had a lucky escape there.'

'Not another Mrs Wilson?' asked Hancock, with a smile.

'On your way, Sergeant,' said Naish, 'on your way.'

'Good afternoon, Inspector,' said Miss Whiting, clearly enthused to be there.

'Come through into the sitting room please, Miss Whiting,' said Naish, directing her with a wave of his hand.

'So, these are the paintings,' said Miss Whiting stepping back in order to survey them before approaching closer.

'Yes, these are the six remaining paintings that I described to you earlier. What do you make of them?'

'I will need a few minutes to examine them in detail,' she replied, without diverting her gaze from the canvases.

'If you have no objection, I will sit over there and smoke a cigarette or two while you carry out your inspection,' said Naish, and receiving no response from the distracted Miss Whiting, he sat down and took out his tobacco tin.

'Very interesting, very interesting,' said Miss Whiting, emerging from her absorption.

'What do you make of them?' asked Naish, rising from the chair and rejoining her beside the paintings.

'Well, I can confirm that they are all genuine paintings by the minor artists that we discussed earlier in my office at the gallery. They are not of outstanding quality, but they are competently executed. I have seen finer examples by at least four of the artists but, as I say, these are all competent pieces, and it may well be that the gentleman who owns them was able to afford them because they commanded a slightly more modest price than truly outstanding examples might well do.'

'Can you tell me if any of them have been restored in any way?'

'Restored? Why do you ask that?'

'It is just a line of enquiry that I am following in connection with some of these works of art and I was keen to know from an expert such as yourself if they had been restored in any way.'

'I see. You think that, if restored, they might also be more aligned to the owner's pocket?'

'Exactly,' said Naish, untruthfully, but keen to divert the discussion away from such matters as Miss Whiting returned to her scrutiny of the canvases.

'I would say that they have not been restored in any way at all,' said Miss Whiting. 'However, I would suggest that you would need to have them examined by an expert using a microscope to be completely sure. But I would be surprised if I were proved wrong.'

'So, they are what they claim to be,' said Naish, keen to move the conversation on. 'The works of minor artists, competently executed and in no way restored.'

'Yes, I think that summarises what I have said,' said Miss Whiting, a little irritated at the unnecessary summary. 'However, I am still intrigued by the three paintings that hung here.'

'Ah yes, the Turners,' said Naish, pleased to have moved on.

'I have been making some enquiries since we met this morning. In particular, I had a most informative telephone conversation with a professor of fine art at the University of Bristol. I was intrigued by your description of these three canvases of Bath Abbey in oils in the style of the watercolour that I showed you in the gallery this morning.'

'Yes, it was very interesting to see the similarities,' said Naish.

'The professor was aware of three oils by *the* J.M.W. Turner that came to market about ten years ago. They had apparently been in a private collection for many years, possibly since shortly after they were painted. Regrettably, they were acquired by another private collector and have again disappeared from public view.'

'You think that these may be the paintings that hung here?' asked Naish.

'No, I do not,' replied Miss Whiting, bluntly. 'The paintings were on display prior to the auction for about six months at a London gallery, where academics were able to view them along with serious potential buyers.'

'It was not a public exhibition, then?'

'No, I would describe it as an invitation only exhibition. As I say, academics and serious potential buyers. However, Professor Andrews was invited to view them on a number of occasions during this brief period. The most important fact he reported to me was the size of the canvases – the three Turners that he viewed were at least twice the size of the canvases that have hung here, to judge from the shadow the sunlight has left of them on the wallpaper.'

'Could they be prints of these paintings?' asked Naish.

'I think it very unlikely. I am not aware that they were copied, although photographs were taken for the catalogue.'

'Not in colour, I imagine,' said Naish.

'As a matter of fact, they were. Although it is expensive, given the significance of the sale, the gallery catalogue did contain colour photographs of the paintings.'

'So, an amateur artist may have painted the paintings that hung here from the photographs.'

'I think that that is the most likely explanation. However, it is going a little bit far to have signed them as the artist. A copy is one thing, but to suggest it is by the hand of another is quite a different matter, as you will understand, Inspector.'

'Indeed, it is – if, of course, the purpose is to deceive another into believing that they are something they are not. If the purpose, as here, was to keep them as a private collection, then I think it would be viewed for what it was – especially given that their size is so much smaller than the genuine pictures are known to be.'

'Yes, I see your point and I accept your professional view.'

'Is it possible to view the catalogue by any chance, given that ten years have passed?'

'I hope that it will be. The professor kindly consented to revisiting his archives to see if he still has the catalogue in his possession. He is going to ring me this evening and let me know.'

'Perhaps you would be good enough to leave a message at the station for me if I am not there,' said Naish, giving her his card. 'Another thought occurs to me as a novice – how did a professor of art from Bristol get to see the exhibition, and more than once, you suggest?'

'That is simple. Professor Andrews is a foremost authority on the work of Turner and so he was invited to view the collection. Whilst it was of great academic interest to him as a scholar, the gallery, of course, had an ulterior motive in inviting the academic world to view the exhibition.'

'Which is?'

'Given the length of time that these paintings had spent in private ownership, there was, of course, some nervousness as to their provenance. Collectors and those who also buy art as an investment are naturally cautious of such paintings that appear, one might say, out of the blue. There were a number of letters and documents that accompanied the paintings from the artist and others known to be associates of Turner at the time the pictures were painted, but the endorsement of the academic world is always useful in providing additional assurance.'

'Professor Andrews was happy to give his endorsement then, I take it?'

'Oh yes. Indeed, the whole academic community was of the view that they were among the best examples of Turner's work that they had seen.'

'May I ask what price the paintings commanded?'

'It would have been in the tens of thousands, Inspector, but I will ask Professor Andrews if he recalls the auction price paid when I speak to him on the telephone later. I do hope he has the catalogue – it will be fascinating to see if the scenes are the same as the ones that you saw hanging here. I speak as an academic, of course.'

'Of course,' said Naish. 'Well, Miss Whiting, you have been extremely useful once again. Your information has been invaluable. If you will come along with me to the car, I will have you taken back to the gallery.'

'You will need to be quick unless it is very important,' said Naish, as Newton and Hancock knocked at his office door. 'I need to get home and assume the part of Mr Bennett. I have been invited to a private viewing at the Byfield Gallery and it starts at seven o' clock.'

'Well, I think it is important,' said Newton. 'Can you give us an hour?'

'If one of you can get a pot of tea organised, I will forgo my evening meal to hear what you have to say. Looks like tobacco will have to sustain me once again,' said Naish, with a wry smile.

'Well, my part of the tale will not take long,' said Hancock, returning with the tea tray and putting it on Naish's desk. 'I have been around to all the locksmiths in the city and they are all of the same view. The smaller key is a mortice lock of a size suitable for a cupboard or a piece of office or workplace furniture. It is too large for a cabinet or a piece of quality furniture like a desk or a bureau. It is an original key not a copy, apparently. The second is definitely a safe key from a Chubb safe and, given its size, they estimate it is a safe of some size and not a safety deposit box. Again, it is an original and not a copy.'

'None of them have ever been asked to make a copy of them?'

'They cannot be certain about the mortice but could not recall cutting such a key recently – obviously they do a fair amount of such trade. But the safe key is a definite no. They would not touch such a job as they cannot get hold of the blanks – it's a job for a Chubb dealer.'

'And if, of course, they did make a copy of such a key, they would not be admitting such to us.'

'I understand what you say, Inspector, but I think that all the locksmiths I spoke to are reputable businesses. They have enough legitimate work and, of course, reputation is everything in that line of work. One hint that the police had concerns about the nature of your trade, and they would, in all likelihood, be finished.'

'I take your point. Right then, Newton – how did you fare?' said Naish, glancing at the clock on the wall.

'Jenkins and Hall in Midland Road sold the safe to Emery. They were able to identify the safe from the serial number on the key. It is an upright Chubb safe, four feet high, two foot six across and two foot six deep.'

'I assume, from those dimensions, that he had it installed somewhere other than his home, hence our not finding it during our search,' said Naish.

'Apparently not. Jenkins and Hall installed the safe at Emery's home in a cellar. The work was done in conjunction with a firm of builders who were converting the coal cellar into a storage area under the house.'

'But there was nothing to indicate a cellar from what I saw. What about Mrs Carson? Does she know anything about this cellar?'

'No, she does not. I rang her up after I got back, and she has never seen a cellar or any entrance to it. I just passed it off and said that I must have been mistaken.'

'When was the safe installed?'

'In 1934. Two years after he moved to Bath.'

'Do we know the builders?'

'No. I did ask that question but, according to Jenkins and Hall, they are no longer in existence. Emery gave detailed instructions as to the installation of the safe to Jenkins and Hall and they provided the builders as sub-contractors. The records of the account for the work show only two basic pieces of work – to install the safe in the cellar and to floor out the attic.'

'Well, it is an interesting situation,' said Naish. 'Clearly the other mortice key is the lock to the cellar, wherever it is. Good work, we can follow it up on Monday. It must be assumed that Emery has the duplicate pair of each key, but at least we have the house secured. All the same, Hancock, can you arrange for a constable to babysit the house until Monday morning. I don't want anything going awry over the weekend. He can use the house, no need to stand guard outside all the time. I take it there were only two keys for the safe?'

'Yes, Inspector. Only two were in the records of Jenkins and Hall.'

'Right then, you two – off and enjoy your weekends. I am off to mix with the well-heeled of the art collecting world. I will tell you all about it on Monday.'

Unintentionally, Naish arrived a fashionable five minutes late for the private viewing. He could see through the windows that the majority of guests were already inside, but a small queue was still at the front door waiting for a doorman to check their invitations off on the guest list. Naish reached inside his jacket pocket and handed his invitation to the doorman, handed his coat to a girl dressed as a maid and took a drink from another as he made his way into the gallery. It was crowded but not overcrowded, just enough to make one feel that one was at an event of some desirability but with space enough for people to see and be seen.

Naish was suddenly aware that in such a gathering he might just be recognised for himself. He was a man who eschewed receptions for local business and local councillors, as far as he could when they were arranged by the superintendent. He was unmoved by the pressures put on him to attend – not being a careerist he was immune to being coerced – but he knew most of the local dignitaries even if they did not know him. Fortunately, from his initial scan of the room, he was unable to observe anyone who might recognise him or, indeed, to recognise anyone that he had ever arrested. Mr Williams was ensconced in the centre of the room in front of what were presumably the star exhibits of this evening's viewing, and a number of well-heeled people stood around in a circle listening to him. Miles was circulating, doing a light touch flit around the room; just enough niceties to make individuals welcome without getting tied up with any of the bores. Naish saw from the corner of his eye that Miles had spotted him and was heading his way. Having not caught his eye, Naish feigned interest in a small bronze figure on a display pedestal.

'Good evening, Mr Bennett. It is a pleasure to see you here this evening. Does this fine piece of sculpture interest you?'

'It is very charming,' said Naish, 'but painting is more my passion.'

'I understand. I had the opportunity to explain to Mr Williams your interest in acquiring a painting of note that would be both a reminder of your relative and be a sound investment, and he is confident that he can identify some works that you may wish to consider.'

'Thank you, that would be very helpful. I was also wondering if there might be an opportunity this evening for me to be shown some of the frames that you might be able to supply to hang my restored painting in. I appreciate that is not the real purpose of this evening's viewing, but I thought it would be opportune as I was here – if that would be convenient?'

'Of course, I will show you a selection myself. Unfortunately, our samples have been relocated to the workshop this evening to create space for the viewing, but if you are happy to come through to the workshops, I will be pleased to show you. Mr Williams is going to give a short talk on the paintings on display in a moment or two, so perhaps when he has concluded his remarks, I can take you through.'

'Thank you,' said Naish. 'I will get myself another glass of wine and listen to Mr Williams.'

'I will come and find you when it is over,' said Miles.

Naish smiled to himself. He was reasonably certain that if he were not the potential customer with fifteen hundred pounds to spend, Mr Miles might have put off his request to view the frames, but money talks, he thought to himself, and leant his back up against a wall and settled down to listen to the speech.

Naish was pleased that he had got himself another glass of wine, as it gave him something to distract him during the twenty minutes that Mr Williams held forth on the subject of the paintings. The great and the good appeared to hang on his every word, but Naish quickly bored of the subject and instead studied the audience. He was just wondering when he would get the chance of a refill, when the talk concluded, and he found Mr Miles at his elbow.

'If you would care to step this way, Mr Bennett. I think that now would be an ideal time to go through to the workshop – unless you would care to sample the finger buffet?'

'No, no I have already eaten,' lied Naish. 'Now would be fine.'

'It is just at the back of the shop, if you will follow me,' said Miles, leading Naish behind the counter in the corner of the gallery and through a doorway into the workshop. 'These are the display mounts – as you see here, only a right-angle section of each type of frame, but sufficient, I hope, for you to get an impression of the moulding and the colouring of each.'

'Yes, this is most helpful,' said Naish. He peered intently at the twenty or so examples on the display stands, but at the same time he was able to take in the whole extent of the workshop itself. There were five large workbenches across the room, each set aside to a particular task, from what Naish could make out. 'You have an extremely extensive workshop here, I see.'

'Yes. As I said, we pride ourselves on undertaking nearly every aspect of our craft here on the premises – craftsmen, all of them.'

'I don't wish to put you to any trouble,' said Naish, 'but as we are here, would you be able to show me something of how you would undertake the repair to the wooden frame that stretches the canvas of my damaged painting?'

'Well, as we are here,' said Miles, reluctantly, 'of course, it would be a pleasure. If you step over to this bench here, I can give you an explanation of the process.'

Chapter 16

'This is an example of what we can provide in terms of restoring the frame of a canvas, as you see with this painting here. This is a somewhat more extreme situation than that of your painting, but it demonstrates the principles. The frame that stretches this canvas is, as you can see, riddled with woodworm, and so we have removed the picture from its display frame and then the canvas has been removed from the wooden frame it was stretched on. What we have here is a replacement frame to stretch the old canvas on to.

'A new frame or a restored frame?' asked Naish. 'It looks exactly the same as the original frame.'

'That is very perceptive of you,' said Miles. 'This is actually a new frame that has been constructed using the wood joints and techniques that would have been used in the original frame. The wood can be aged to give it an authentic appearance. Once the canvas has been re-stretched and pinned into position, it is impossible to tell that a replica frame has been used. However, this is made using our preferred technique, which is to use reclaimed timber from a redundant frame.'

'It is, in fact, really as good as new, then,' said Naish, 'given it has been constructed using contemporary wood and contemporary carpentry techniques. Your craftsmen are true artisans.'

'They are indeed, Mr Bennett, and depending on the outcome of our assessment of the damage to your painting, I am reasonably confident that we will be able to match a piece of reclaimed timber of the age of your painting and effect an undetectable repair.'

'Fascinating and very reassuring,' said Naish. 'This work is done here on these benches, then?'

'The repairs such as I describe are carried out here, and such would be the case with your picture, as I promised. The only work we do not do here is the construction of a complete frame. We have a local craftsman who makes entire frames bespoke to our requirements. However, the frames are brought here, and the restoration is all undertaken on our premises, as I said.'

'I never realised how interesting the work was,' said Naish, keen to deflect any suspicion as to his curiosity and make sure that it was clear that his interest was solely the result of Miles's explanation of a hitherto obscure art.

'Oh, there are endless skills required in the work, each fascinating in their own part, but each making a vital contribution to the final piece.'

'Is this a restored frame or a bespoke one from your local craftsman?' said Naish, picking up a frame from the far end of the bench that he had been keen to make a detailed study of since he had spotted it.

'Ah, that is a bespoke one ready for this canvas laid out here,' said Miles, stealing a look at his watch. 'My, the time is getting on. I have no wish to cut short our impromptu visit to the workshop, but I did promise Mr Williams that I would introduce you to him before the evening ended, and so, if you will join me, I think we had better make our way back to the gallery. If you wish to take a more detailed look at the choices of frame design, it will be a pleasure to discuss the options with you on another occasion.'

'Of course. I will look in sometime next week at a convenient time but, as you say, it would be a pleasure to meet Mr Williams and see what pieces he has to suggest for me to consider,' said Naish, following Miles towards the door. As he followed, he put his hand in his pocket, and closing his fingers around some loose change, he drew it from the pocket and scattered it behind him on to the floor with a clatter. 'Ah, blast. I have dropped my change.'

'What was that,' said Miles, jumping at the sound, and turning to see Naish stooping to pick up the coins and shuffling back towards the far side of the workshop as he collected them up.

'A stupid mistake. I was trying to find my handkerchief. I do apologise. There, I think I have gathered up most of them. Ah, the last few are over there,' said Naish.

His pursuit of his last coins had taken him back to the most extreme corner of the workshop. During his conversation with Miles he had noticed in the corner a small area where there were a group of metal lockers, presumably for the use of the workshop staff. As Naish stood up and feigned to be checking his coins, he was able to confirm what he had thought he had seen from across the room. One of the lockers had been left with the door half open, and it was this locker that Naish wanted to see up close, because hanging on the inside of the door was a brown storeman's coat.

'If you have retrieved all of your loose change, Mr Bennett, we really must be getting back to the gallery. I would not want you to miss your meeting with Mr Williams.'

'No, indeed. I am looking forward to meeting him, and I would not want him to think anything was amiss by my absence.'

'Good evening, Mr Bennett. It is a pleasure to make your acquaintance. I am Mr Williams, the managing director of the Byfield gallery. I thought for one minute that you had had to leave us early on some account.'

'No, not at all, I was just in conversation with Mr Miles on the subject of a replacement frame for my damaged painting,' said Naish, keen to avoid mention that he had been through to the workshop.

'Ah yes, Mr Miles explained the circumstances to me. I will leave him to attend to you on that matter if you don't mind. My field of expertise lies more in the acquisition of fine art for the discerning customer. Perhaps you could tell me if you have any particular interests, subject, artist or period, that sort of thing.'

'I am afraid that I am something of an innocent in these matters,' said Naish. 'It is only my recent bequest that has opened my thoughts towards acquiring a painting.'

'In that case, let me be your guide. Perhaps if we take a look around the paintings here this evening, we can get a feel for where your tastes lie.'

It was a quarter past nine when Naish eventually left the Byfield gallery, and he was relieved to be out in the fresh evening air, cold as it was. He was beginning to quite enjoy his role as Mr Bennett, but he was constantly on his mettle so as not to drop his guard – a casual word or phrase could give his game away. However, despite the mental strain and the claustrophobic atmosphere in the gallery, he reflected that, on the whole, his evening's work had been remarkably fruitful.

As Naish arrived at the station at half past seven the next morning, he was surprised to find two tramps in discussion on the front steps.

'Good morning,' said Naish.

'Good morning, Inspector,' replied the younger tramp.

'Well, Burton, I have to say you make a convincing tramp,' said Naish, having done a quick double take. 'Your companion is our associate from Swallow Street, I assume?'

'He is, Inspector. He came in yesterday evening to sit with the police artist, as you requested, and after a warm night in the cells, while I was deputising for him, I am pleased to say he is ready to return to his post.'

'And you, yours, I imagine,' said Naish, with a smile.

'Indeed, Inspector. As soon as I have the artist's impressions, I will put them in your pigeonhole.'

'Thank you. I will be here most of the weekend, I expect, so if you get them, come up to my office with them first, if you will.'

Naish went on inside and having ordered a mug of tea from the desk sergeant he went up to his office.

'Your tea, Inspector,' said the sergeant, as he came in to Naish's office. 'I have this message for you as well, which was phoned in by a Miss Whiting at half past nine last night.'

Naish took the note and the sergeant placed his mug of tea next to the ashtray on his desk. The message was short and to the point. The catalogue was being delivered to her that morning and she would be in the Victoria Art Gallery between half past nine and two o'clock, because she was hosting a symposium for a society of artists.

'I have to go out in a while, sergeant, but I need you to telephone Miss Whiting just after half past nine and tell her that I will be pleased to meet her at one o'clock, as she suggests,' said Naish. 'Get a car for me, will you, out the front at half past eight. I will be back about noon.'

Having dispatched the sergeant, Naish rolled himself a cigarette and took his mug of tea over to the evidence table. As he smoked, he picked up the canvases recovered from Ted Lynch's flat and examined the wooden frames that he was now convinced that Emery had made. Naish scratched at the surface of the wood with his penknife to see if the wood was period timber or stained to look aged. As far as he could make out, it was not a stain and from what he could remember, these frames and particularly the joints at each corner were identical to the frame that he had seen on the workbench at the Byfield Gallery the previous evening. He measured the frame and the canvases with a steel ruler and made a note of the dimensions in his notebook. Given the almost identical nature of the pieces of work, and that Miles had stated clearly that the frames built from reclaimed timber were externally sourced, it was inconceivable to Naish that Emery was not the supplier of the frames to the Byfield gallery. He picked up the ledger that had been recovered from Emery's shop and took it back to his desk. The ledger went back five years but, given the low volume of trade that Emery did, it did not contain a huge amount of entries. After half an hour and three cigarettes, Naish had read it through line by line. There was, however, no mention whatsoever of the Byfield Gallery. Emery had entries for repairs to frames that he had done, and he had clearly sold a number of frames to other private clients, but no mention of the Byfield. Naish closed the ledger and rolled yet another cigarette. He was deep in thought when there was a knock at his door and Constable Miller popped his head in to say the car was ready for him outside.

Naish and Miller went up the steps at Emery's house and located the constable who had been detailed to the task of nightwatchman.

'You two can go and have a smoke for ten minutes,' said Naish. 'I will call you if I need a hand.'

Naish went inside and made a careful inspection of each of the ground-floor rooms, opening each wall cupboard that he found. He then looked under the stairs but was unable to find an entrance to the cellar which he knew to be there. Having exhausted the inside, he went out into the garden and walked around the house looking for an opening. At the side of the house he found, if not exactly what he was looking for, then something that was at least evidence of the cellar as it had been described to Hancock. The land on the left of the house was lower on that side and in the wall was a doorway that had been infilled with Bath stone blocks, in keeping with the rest of the house. It was a tidy job, and a Virginia creeper had been grown over the wall with the clear intent of covering the infill. It being autumn, the creeper was free of leaves, leaving a clear view. Naish stepped back a little to orientate himself to the house and realised that the doorway must have led to a cellar which was under the kitchen area. He went back into the house and called the two constables to come in and move back the kitchen table and chairs, which stood on a square of carpet in the middle of the room. Once the furniture was removed, Naish told the constables to roll up the mat.

'I am going to call this the trapdoor case,' said Naish. 'This is the third one, so far.'

'Sorry, Inspector, I don't understand.'

'Never mind, lad. Just a joke to myself,' said Naish, kneeling by the side of the trapdoor. 'Now, one of you get on the other side and the other pull up on that ring there, recessed into the wood.'

The trap was hinged on one of the shorter ends and Naish and the constable lifted it up beyond the vertical where two chains, one on each side, prevented it falling all the way back on to the floor behind.

'Pass me your torch,' said Naish, and he shone the beam down into the cellar below. A set of wooden steps ran down into the cellar at a steep angle and Naish made his way down.

'Do you want one of us down there with you, Inspector?'

'No, just stay there for now. Ah, that's better. A light switch.'

The bare bulb that hung from the ceiling immediately flooded the void with light. The cellar was about the size of the kitchen above and although a little dusty, it was otherwise clean, and the walls whitewashed. Other than a cupboard door at the end opposite the foot of the steps, it was empty. Naish reached into his coat pocket and pulled out a ring with the two keys he had taken from under the floor in the second-floor room. He placed the smaller of the two keys in the lock and it turned effortlessly. The door opened out into the room and there behind it and recessed into the stone wall was the door of the Chubb safe, with exactly the proportions that the locksmith had described to Hancock.

Naish was surprised to detect a slight thrill running through him as he placed the second key into the lock of the safe door and turned it. Again, the key turned with ease and he pulled the door open. He was not sure what it was that he was expecting to find in the safe, but all that confronted him were a number of shelves spaced up through the height of the safe, about eighteen inches apart, and on each shelf were brown cardboard boxes about the size of a shoe box, three boxes to each shelf.

None of the boxes appeared to be marked in any way to indicate its contents other than on the end of each box was a year written in what appeared to be pencil. The dates went back to 1925. There were twelve boxes in all, and the dates were in chronological order, although there were gaps in the years with no apparent regular interval between each. The latest date was 1950.

Naish took one of the boxes off the shelf and placed it on the floor. Kneeling down, he lifted the lid off. Inside were what appeared to be historical documents, the papers yellow. Naish lifted the top few documents out of the box. They were letters, all in the same elegant hand and all addressed to the same person. The date on the box was 1935, but the postmark on the three letters that Naish was looking at was 1849.

Naish replaced the box on the shelf and, despite his curiosity to understand what he had found, he was conscious of the need to treat the contents of the safe as potential evidence and have it examined and catalogued in the correct manner. He therefore closed the safe door and locked it, together with the cupboard door. He put the keys back in his pocket and climbed back into the kitchen.

'Right, there is nothing more that I need to do here for a while, so I will leave you back on your watch, constable. If I can find someone suitable, I may send him up here to start making an inventory of the safe contents. Right then, back to the station.'

As he got out of the car back at Orange Grove, Naish glanced at his watch and was pleased that it was still only half past ten. As he was going back through the foyer, he heard his name called out and, turning, he saw Burton still in his tramp disguise running up the front steps to catch up with him.

'Calm down, lad, and catch your breath,' said Naish, coming to a halt. 'What's so urgent?'

'I have just seen him, Inspector,' said Burton, still catching his breath.

'Seen who?'

'Emery, Inspector, it was Emery, and if I am not mistaken, he was chatting with the second thug.'

'What,' exclaimed Naish, 'where was this?'

'In the gardens, Inspector, in Parade Gardens. I was making my way back from Swallow Street to here, but I take a longer route than necessary just in case I am noticed, and I was walking along Grand Parade and I looked down into the Gardens, and over by the riverbank I saw what I thought was Emery. He had his collar pulled up but I was sure it was him, so I paid my entry fee at the top and made my way towards him as fast as I could, while still maintaining the demeanour of a tramp. By this time, he had sat down on a bench facing out on to Pulteney Weir. I relaxed my pace and began to shuffle along slowly, looking in the bins and picking up dog-ends and the like. It was my intention to get right up to him, and perhaps even ask him for a couple of pence for a cup of tea, so that I could be sure it was him. But while I was still ten yards from him, I noticed the thug coming towards him. I was not sure what to expect – was it a planned meeting, or had the thug ambushed him with the intent to cause him harm and were his associates nearby, even. Luckily, I was dressed as I am, so I got to a bench nearby and laid on it as if I were asleep.'

'It seems a very public place for Emery to be taking the air,' said Naish.

'The benches down by the weir are quite secluded and well away from being overlooked. Anyway, I was relieved to see from the corner of my eye that the thug sits down next to Emery, and by Emery's calm reaction to his presence, it is clear that he is expecting him.'

'Were you able to make out anything they were saying?'

'No, not a thing I am afraid, Inspector, but by their manner it was clear that it was not aggressive. I don't say they were slapping each other on the back or anything, but there was clearly a businesslike understanding between them. Anyway, after ten minutes or so they get up and walk off in opposite directions.'

'Where did they go? Emery, in particular.'

'I held back so as not to arouse any suspicion, and by the time I got up to follow him, Emery was already going up the steps from the gardens back to Grand Parade. I could see the thug on the other side of the gardens still following the longer path back round to the steps. I took a chance and ran over to the steps, but by the time I had got there he was over at the taxi rank and he was gone in a cab.'

'Didn't you get a cab to follow him, then?' asked Naish, a little irritably.

'Unfortunately, that was my downfall, Inspector. I had no more money on me, being in my tramp costume, and I thought it would cause a lot of unnecessary confusion and attention if I tried to persuade the cab driver I was a police officer.'

'You could have come over here and got a car.'

'I am afraid it was all too late then, Inspector. Emery's cab was already out of sight by this time.'

'What about the thug then, where did he go?'

'I am so sorry, Inspector, but in focusing on Emery, which I thought to be the right thing to do, by the time I had lost him and run back to Parade Gardens, the thug was nowhere in sight. I ran and looked down a few streets, but he was gone. I do apologise.'

'Don't fret about it, lad, you did your best,' said Naish, trying to focus on the positives of the situation. 'If it had not been for your keen eye, we would never have known about the meeting at all, would we? And it is very significant that he has met up with just one of the trio, in my view. Don't beat yourself up, lad, you did the best you could, given the circumstances. Did you get the taxi's registration or plate number?'

'No, I am afraid I didn't manage that, either,' said Burton, looking even more wretched now. 'I know it was a black Ford, that is all.'

'Sergeant,' called out Naish abruptly to the desk sergeant. 'Get over the road to the taxi rank and find out the name and number of the black Ford taxi that left the rank in the last twenty minutes with one male occupant. There can't be that many gone off the rank in the last twenty minutes. Even if no one saw him, he should be back on the rank in the next hour, I would think.'

'Right, Inspector, I am on it now,' said the sergeant.

'Go and freshen up and get back into your uniform, lad. Then go and join the sergeant over at the taxi rank. What time do you finish today?

'Five o'clock, Inspector.'

'Good. Right then, I will be back in my office just after two o'clock, all being well. Meet me there with an update then, and bring a tray of tea. Oh, and well done, lad. You did well,' said Naish, with a smile.

As Naish climbed the stairs up to his office, he reflected just what the purpose of the meeting between Emery and the thug was. He sat down at his desk and, having rolled a cigarette, took a piece of paper and began to map out the thoughts going through his mind. The most telling aspect of the meeting in Parade Gardens as described by Burton, in Naish's opinion, was that it was clear that the two had met before, even if only briefly to agree where they should meet. Clearly, they had some shared understanding, since their meeting was at least businesslike, if not even cordial, from Burton's description of their manner. It was also plain to Naish that the thug had no interest in restricting Emery's movements, nor was he interested in following him to find out where he was living.

Naish drew out dots on the paper representing the trio and Emery, and drew various connections between them as he created theories to justify what was going on between them. Each theory he created had elements that were plausible, but each one, when subjected to counter argument, fell apart.

After an hour and a half, he felt able to claim three reasonable suppositions to be true. Firstly, that they had met before. Secondly, that, although their motivations may well be different, some common reason or purpose had brought them together. Thirdly, that it indicated a tension or even a fracture within the trio. What that was, he had no idea at present.

His only slight concern was that the trio, through thug two, were working some kind of double-cross on Emery, perhaps to gain his confidence and get him to reveal to thug two some secret he had that the trio needed. What was also emerging in Naish's mind was the strong sense that it may well have been thug two who had tipped off

Emery about the trio's visit to his home on Thursday night. What was said or agreed was impossible to deduce, but it worked in with the notion that the two must have met before. Clearly, Emery must have known they were going to his house, since the coincidence of his being there and at such an unusual hour was impossible to believe. He clearly was not interested in removing the paintings that the trio removed, unless he was unaware that they were the focus of the trio's visit. No, thought Naish, the only logical answer is that he knew that they were coming, and, in all probability, he knew that the paintings were the target. Therefore, the only logical reason for him coming to the house after the trio had left was to check that something else was still there, and that whatever it was had not fallen into their hands. As far as Naish could deduce with the current evidence before him, the only logical thing that this something else could be was the two keys under the floorboards. And therefore, the focus of Emery's concern was for the contents of the safe in the cellar, since the keys were simply a means to its contents. Yet, for some reason, he appeared to have not moved the keys, given the dust and the cobwebs, nor had he gone into the safe, given the fact that the contents that Naish had inspected earlier appeared to be completely intact, with no spaces on the shelves. The only other item that may have been removed was something that might have filled the void with the keys. Naish doodled a few more lines but was unable to produce any hypothesis of what might have been in the void with the keys.

The clock on the abbey suddenly chimed a quarter to one and it brought Naish up smart. Checking the time on his own watch he gathered up his coat and hat and set off for his meeting with Miss Whiting.

'Good afternoon, Inspector Naish,' said the elderly guard that Naish had encountered the previous day. 'Miss Whiting asked me to give you her apologies as she is running fifteen minutes late.'

'Thank you, that is not a problem,' said Naish. 'They have got you working on a Saturday as well then, I see.'

'It's a rota, Inspector. I share the job with two other gentlemen, so we take the weekends in turn.'

'Sounds good to me,' said Naish, with a smile. 'I will have a wander round while I am waiting and see if I can improve my mind a little.'

Naish wandered around the room, pausing for the customary short period in front of each painting. Naish was surprised at how popular it was. The majority of visitors were following his own method of progress around the exhibition but a few sat on the benches down the centre of the room. Naish was not sure if their purpose was to give deeper scrutiny to an individual piece or to prolong their time out of the cold. Looking at them closely he decided that it was probably a fifty-fifty split of the two. There was also a third category of visitor: they were only two in number, but they intrigued him most of all. One appeared to be a student and was sat on the floor opposite one of the paintings, and the other, a lady, was more elderly and was sat on one of the benches. They were both sketching their painting of choice and Naish thought that, even with his untutored eye, they were making a reasonable fist of it. He wandered on, half concentrating on the paintings that passed before his eyes, half watching the people in the gallery, and interspersing both with occasional glances at his watch.

'What is the script with our friends doing the drawings?' asked Naish, as he wandered back to the place where the guard had resumed his chair.

'Oh, them over there,' said the guard, with a nod in their general direction. 'We get a fair few of that sort in here. Some are art students making sketches of the old masters or of paintings of a particular genre. Some, like our lady over there, are what I always think of as frustrated artists, copying a painting or genre. Often, they are brilliant, but I always think that if they were any good, they would draw from their own inspiration rather than copying another person's work. Still, each to their own, I always say.'

'You're a deeper thinker on these matters than I imagine folk give you credit for,' said Naish. 'Perhaps deeper than I gave you credit for.'

'Well thank you, I am sure, Inspector,' said the guard, with a tone somewhere between sincerity and sarcasm.

'I didn't mean to give offence,' said Naish.

'None taken, I am sure, but sitting here all day is an excellent cover for some detailed people watching. I sit here, all innocuous like, and people behave as if I am not here at all. It's amazing what they do when they let their guard down. Anyway, to answer your original question, they sit and draw the paintings, mostly in pencil or charcoal but occasionally in coloured pencil, nothing more. I think Miss Whiting would draw the line at them getting the watercolours out. Talking of whom, I will go and give her a knock up. She is later than she promised.'

'No, honestly,' said Naish. 'I am happy to wait.'

'I am sure you are, Inspector, but it does not do her good to get too high-handed with people. Besides, she doesn't frighten me like she does the others,' he said, as he walked off to his task with a wink to Naish.

Chapter 17

Naish returned to his absent-minded viewing of the paintings. It was as he wandered back towards the entrance doorway that something caught his eye. It was a painting in a broad gilt frame and the colours of the painting, although vivid, were, to Naish's mind, a little out of focus. But there was something about it that stirred him, and he could not put his finger on it.

'Good afternoon, Inspector, I apologise for the delay. I see you are admiring a painting by one of our local artists,' said Miss Whiting, breaking in on Naish's thoughts.

'Yes, I was,' said Naish.

'It is by the painter Walter Sickert. When I say local, he was local in the sense that he lived here in the later part of his life and was buried out at Bathampton. We have three paintings by him. The one before you is a view of the Assembly Rooms in Bath. Perhaps you know the scene?'

'May I use your telephone, Miss Whiting?' asked Naish, as he looked more intently at the picture.

'Of course, Inspector. If you go into my office you will find the telephone on my desk. I will go and arrange for a cup of tea and join you in a minute.'

As Miss Whiting entered her office, Naish was just replacing the receiver, having completed his call to the station.

'Right then, Inspector,' said Miss Whiting, handing him a cup of tea, 'shall we make a start on the catalogue?'

'Yes, that would be ideal,' said Naish. 'I have just asked a constable to bring round something that I would value your opinion on, after we have finished with the catalogue – if you can spare me a few more minutes of your time?'

'Of course, I am free for the rest of the afternoon,' said Miss Whiting, spreading the catalogue on the desk in front of them. 'Now, here are the paintings in question, Inspector – three views of Bath Abbey by Turner.'

'They are undoubtedly the same three views as the paintings that hung on the wall in St Mark's Road,' said Naish.

'Really? Are you sure, Inspector?' said Miss Whiting, politely incredulous.

'Absolutely. They are the same views, as far as I can remember. The colouring is very similar, as is the style. Forgive me the correct technical phrasing, but misty, I would call them, perhaps even blurred.

'This is most interesting,' said Miss Whiting, ignoring Naish's layman's adjectives.

'But they were smaller than these,' said Naish. 'Looking at the dimensions here in the catalogue, the paintings at the auction were twice as large as the ones at St Mark's Road, as you saw yourself. The ones at St Mark's Road were the same size as the watercolour you have in the gallery outside.'

'Yes, you are right, Inspector,' said Miss Whiting, peering at the catalogue, 'a very similar if not exact size. I will just pop out and check it for you with the information on the panel next to the painting.'

As she disappeared, Naish turned back to the front of the catalogue and began to flick through the pages. It was indeed a very high quality catalogue, just as he would have imagined such a thing to be from a high-end London gallery. As he turned to the preface on the second page, he scanned the overview from the gallery about the exciting and rare nature of the paintings for sale and then, to his surprise, he saw that the preface was signed off by Mr Walter Williams.

'Yes, Inspector, the sizes of the three paintings at St Mark's Road are the same as the one in our collection.'

'Excellent,' said Naish, with little attention. 'This man Walter Williams – was it he who managed the sale?'

'Yes, indeed it was. Another local man, one might say. Walter runs the Byfield Gallery in Wood Street, having moved down from London a few years ago.'

'That is interesting' said Naish. 'Well, thank you for taking the trouble to get hold of this catalogue. It has been invaluable. I will get someone over to photograph the pictures and make some notes about them, if you don't mind. That will probably be on Monday.'

'That will be fine, Inspector,' said Miss Whiting, as there was a knock at the door.

'Bring it over here, constable,' said Naish, as the constable came into the room carrying a parcel that he handed to Naish.

'Right, Miss Whiting. If you will come with me out into the gallery, I wish to seek your opinion on one further matter,' said Naish, taking a sketchbook out of the brown paper. He led Miss Whiting out into the gallery and sat down next to her on a bench opposite the Sickert painting. 'If I hand you this sketchbook, I would like you to thumb through each page and when you have finished, tell me if anything occurs to you.'

Miss Whiting turned the pages slowly and looked with greater intent after the first few pages, as the sketches became more detailed.

'It is quite remarkable, Inspector,' she said when she was only a third of the way through. 'These are clearly sketches of the Assembly Rooms but of the three other elevations, from what I can make out.'

'That is exactly what I thought,' said Naish, with an air of satisfaction. 'It's quite a coincidence, is it not, that we have another scene of Bath by a famous artist displayed in this gallery and once again we have three new views of that scene that were previously unknown.'

'Are there three such paintings of the Assembly Rooms?' asked Miss Whiting, clearly surprised at the information.

'I think not, but there almost were,' said Naish, cryptically. He rose from the bench and went over to where the guard sat. 'Have you ever seen this man?'

'Why yes, Inspector, he comes here on and off. I haven't seen him for a while, but before that he was here quite regularly. He is one of those "drawers" that we joked about earlier.'

'When he came here most recently, where was he sat? Anywhere in particular?'

'Oh yes, he came for a few hours every day for a fortnight, I would say – given my shifts – and he was always sat just where Miss Whiting is now.'

'Thank you,' said Naish, replacing the photograph in his inside jacket pocket. 'I will have to send an officer round next week to take a statement from you to that effect. In the meantime, I would be grateful if you kept the matter just between ourselves.'

'Certainly, Inspector, you can rest assured.'

Naish returned to the bench where Miss Whiting was closing the sketchbook and sat back down beside her.

'It's an interesting conundrum, isn't it?' he said. 'I will have to ask you to keep the matter confidential for the time being.'

'Of course, of course,' she replied.

'Certainly, Inspector. It will be change of shift in a couple of hours and I will detail some men to the task.'

'Thank you. Where are we with the artist's impressions that our tramp was helping us with?'

'He rang in, a few minutes before you got back, Inspector. He wants a bit longer to get them right. They will be here at nine o'clock tomorrow morning at the latest, he promised.'

'Perfectionists,' said Naish, with a sigh of frustration. 'Either way, I don't suppose a few more hours will make a lot of difference. Right, you get on with the tasks in hand and when you go back down, ask the driver to have the car out the front at five o'clock. I want to go out to Bathampton.'

'Is he in?' asked Naish, removing his hat.

'No, Inspector, he is down at his allotment. You have only just missed him – he went down about ten minutes ago to light a bonfire. Knowing him, he will be down there till it's out. Is there a message?'

'No. I will wander down and find him. Good evening to you, Mrs Hancock.'

Naish opened the gate to the allotment and made his way towards a column of smoke that was rising against the dark sky at the far side. As he approached, he could see Hancock sat in an old armchair by the side of his shed, smoking his pipe contentedly while superintending the fire.

'Like children, bonfires,' said Naish, as Hancock turned suddenly towards the unexpected voice. 'Need constant supervision, serious matter.'

'Good evening, Inspector,' said Hancock, with a broad smile. 'What can I do for you – I take it that this is not a social visit.'

'I wanted to pick your brains, if you don't mind.'

'Not at all, wait here a moment.'

Hancock disappeared behind a neighbouring shed and emerged carrying a wicker chair.

'There you go, make yourself comfortable,' he said, before disappearing into his own shed and returning with a small bottle of whisky and two tea mugs.

'It's a regular home from home here,' said Naish, lighting a cigarette.

'You need to rest between digging, and it's good to contemplate what you're going to do with an allotment. No point rushing these things,' he said, with a smile. 'I was going to come in tomorrow and see what you were up to. I understand you have been hard at it today.'

'You and your network,' said Naish. 'You are right, I have been at it. I can't let it rest until Monday. The good news is that it has been worthwhile, and I have made some progress.'

They sat and smoked in the glow of the bonfire while Naish gave him an overview of his activities that day.

'Events really have developed today and no mistake,' said Hancock. 'This meeting between Emery and thug two, I agree, is particularly intriguing. You are certainly correct in your supposition that they had met before, if the encounter was how Burton describes it. I understand your line of reasoning that thug two is potentially being used as a tool to get Emery to reveal some secret, but it doesn't work for me I am afraid. For a start, it is too subtle, not perhaps for our controlling mind to have devised, but certainly, in my view, for thug two to be able to carry out. That sort of thing needs tact and guile and I don't see it in him. I know that appearances can be deceptive but, in my book, thug two is what he looks to be, plain and simple as that. I think this liaison is linked to your perception of a fracture within the trio. I think that thug two has got the wind up with how things are panning out, which is interesting, because if – as we suspect – the murders of Lynch and Edwards are down to them, then they are professional hard men, and professional hard men don't usually flinch unless they think that things are getting out of control.'

'You think that he sees these murders as something that has gone too far, then?'

'Yes, I think I do. Clearly, they gave Lynch a professional working over, and the tortures that they perpetrated on him were the work of men who do not usually flinch at such violence. Even if they had not intended or thought that Lynch would end up being killed, I think that, being professionals, they would have considered it an unfortunate outcome. But it would not in itself be enough for them to break ranks.'

'So, what do you think has spooked him?'

'Perhaps another killing is planned, do you think?'

'It could be, but who? I can't see that it could be Emery. As we have discussed before, if they wanted to do away with him, they have had more than sufficient opportunity. The other reason may be that he sees these two killings as their having gone too far. Lynch was perhaps planned or, as we said, an unintended outcome, but that Edwards is one murder too far.'

'I have thug one down as the one who knifed them both at the end. It would account for thug two having lost his nerve. He now fears being convicted for being party to double murder, when he was only expecting to be at risk for grievous bodily harm or attempted murder, at worst.'

'That rings true,' said Naish, holding out his mug for a refill. 'The controlling mind has a firm grip on thug one, who is perhaps the more callous and violent man, and thug two is the more intelligent and less violent henchman. It does stack up as a theory to some extent. The only thing I don't see, at present, is why does he fall in with Emery?'

'Perhaps he mistakenly thought that Emery was at risk of being the next corpse. It would account for Emery's disappearance for no apparent reason.'

'And because he was mistaken, we end up with Emery on the run and living up at Camden Crescent, but still alive and not being pursued, as far as we can tell. It sounds reasonable.'

'Camden Crescent is one of the houses that Emery owns, is it not?'

'He certainly has two houses up there that we identified he had purchased. I need to go back and check the numbers, but it's a fair assumption he is in hiding in one of his own rooms, yes.'

'What really intrigues me,' said Hancock, after a moment's silence 'is this. If we are right in our perception that thug two has got the wind up because he sees these murders as, in some way, disproportionate to the wrongs committed by Lynch and Edwards, there must be someone who does not consider them disproportionate.'

'I agree with you completely. To my mind, the controlling mind who is commissioning these thugs clearly perceives a risk to himself or his business that is worth murdering two men for, yet the thugs – and you and I, for that matter – are unable to see that risk. We are therefore not seeing the whole picture, are we? On the surface of it, Lynch has burgled a number of premises on the night in question, one of which is Emery's shop. The controlling mind and or Emery are, as far as we know, only linked to that series of crimes by the break-in at Emery's shop, so it must be this that makes the link between the trio, Emery and Lynch. I can see the bare framework that that relationship hangs on, but I can't see what Edwards has done that is so heinous that he deserves to be murdered.'

'All we can suppose is that he betrayed Lynch to the trio, so he must, in some way, have double-crossed them. Perhaps he got too clever and tried to blackmail them.'

'I can't see the blackmail. Professional thugs would not torture him first, not even for revenge. They would have just knifed him, plain and simple, in my view,' said Naish.

'So where are your thoughts going about this Byfield gallery, then?'

'There is something there, I am sure about that, but I need more time to firm up my suspicions. That is one of the reasons I am holding off searching the Swallow Street garage and pulling in Emery. Those brown storemen coats in the locker at the gallery are not much in themselves – although Miles told you that none of their men used such a coat – but, to my mind, it potentially links the thugs to the Byfield gallery. However, those frames in the workshop are, to my mind, a clear link between Emery and the Byfield – but I need to prove it. The workshop itself looks a genuine set-up, carrying out genuine repairs and restorations, but it is that link to Emery that doesn't sit comfortably with me. Then there is Williams. There is something about his association with the sale of the paintings in London – they are so similar to the miniature versions that were taken from St Mark's Road – that I need to get to the bottom of. Then there is the connection made by Cotman Holdings between Emery's old shop in Lambeth and the Swallow Street garage. It is very tenuous at present, both in my head and in the evidence that we have before us, but there is a clear link between Swallow Street, Lambeth and Williams somewhere in those brown coats that we have seen thug one and thug two in, while they travel round in the blue Bedford that is garaged in Swallow Street.'

'So, are you putting this Williams in the role of the elegant gent that the tramp saw with the thugs in Swallow Street as they set off for St Mark's Road?' said Hancock.

'It has to be a possibility, don't you think? I mean, there is some work to do on it in terms of evidence, but it has the makings of a credible theory, in my mind.'

'In light of the evidence, it has to be looked into, if only to discount it, but I can see where you are coming from,' said Naish.

'So, what do you want me to do tomorrow, then?'

'If you are coming in, then I would like you to get up to St Mark's Road and make a start working through the contents of that safe. I need each box examined and the contents recorded. More importantly, I need someone to give me some idea as to what relevance, if any, these documents have on this case. It's going to be a bit laborious, I am afraid, but it's got to be done.'

'If I am inside, in the warm, and can smoke my pipe, then I am more than happy to get it done. I will meet you in your office at eight o'clock, if that suits you. Then you can take me up there and show me where you want me to start.'

'Eight o'clock will be fine,' said Naish. 'Now, I thank you for your hospitality, but neat whisky on an empty stomach is all very fine, but I think I need to get off now and get something to eat.'

'It's good to know that you do eat occasionally,' said Hancock, with a smile. 'Watch your footing on those pathways back to your car. I will see you in the morning, Inspector.'

It was nine o'clock when Naish returned to Orange Grove. He had gone with Hancock in the car up to St Mark's Road to show him the safe and its contents and give him a briefing on what he wanted doing with the documents. He had agreed to return at midday to see what progress had been made.

'Any news from Camden Crescent?' he asked the desk sergeant.

'Only a message for you to say that there is no sign of him. Burton is in the general office. I think he was going up later on this morning.'

'I thought he was off duty today?'

'He was, but this case has got them all pouring in to be involved.'

'I hope we make some progress – the overtime bill is going to need explaining to the superintendent. If Burton is in the office, send him up to me, will you. Oh, and ask him to bring me a mug of tea.'

'Good morning, Inspector,' said Burton, opening the office door and struggling with the handle, a large manila envelope and the tea mug. 'What can I do for you?'

'Firstly, pass me that mug,' said Naish, putting his cigarette in the ashtray. 'Are those the artist's drawings in that envelope? Yes, then hand them to me.'

Naish withdrew three A3 size pieces of heavy gauge paper from the envelope and, picking up his cigarette, laid them out on his desk and scrutinised them.

'They are very unusual sketches,' said Burton. 'More like paintings of a scene rather than the usual head and shoulders mugshot type of thing.'

'They are, but that is what our tramp could see from his vantage point in the gutter. It was pitch-black apart from a couple of street lamps, and from what he told me, this is very like the scene he described. This one is a partial view of the man's face, but it is the stance and outline of this man here in this picture of the general scene that we are most interested in,' said Naish, pointing at the silhouette of the well-dressed man in the centre of the picture next to the Bedford van.

'I am glad it is what you were expecting.'

'It is better than I expected, because that man is the spit of someone I am very interested in. However, before I get too excited, you need to get our Swallow Street friend back in, and we can check that he is happy with the drawings. If he is, he can sign a witness statement to that effect.'

'Do you want me to get him in now?'

'If you can manage it. The sooner the better for me.'

'Give me an hour and I will have him in the interview room for you, Inspector. There was something else I was going to ask of you. Do you mind if I can get up to Camden Crescent later on and see if I can get into the front hallway? I want to try and establish which part of the building Emery is in, if I can.'

'You can, but on no account take any chance with being found out – Emery knows you, remember. How are you planning to do it?'

'Being that it is Sunday, I was going to put on a dog collar and make out that I was collecting for a mission in the city. Just knock up one of the occupants and then see the names on the pigeonholes. It might not get anywhere, but I though it worth a try.'

'Yes, it's worth a try. You are quite the man of disguise. Are you an amateur dramatist by any chance?'

'No, Inspector, nothing like that. But we have a collection of stuff in the basement for surveillance work. The minister is easy – black suit, dog collar, earnest expression, and there you are.'

'All right, but let's get the tramp in and sorted out first. Let me know when he is ready, and I will come down.'

Naish dug around in the drawers of his desk and eventually, having found a ruler, he went over to the evidence table. He measured the canvases that had been recovered from Lynch's lodgings and compared them with the notes that he had made on the dimensions of the Sickert painting in the Victoria Gallery, and was pleased to see that they were exactly the same. He also reviewed the notes that he had made on the frames he had seen at the Byfield gallery and at Emery's shop. Although he had not had the opportunity to measure the frame he had been shown by Miles on Friday night, he was as near to certain as he could be that they were the same size. There was also a strong resemblance between the styles of the gilt frames he had seen in almost all the paintings he had observed. Perhaps a coincidence of personal taste, he wondered, but he would need to get all the examples he had seen in one room to make an accurate and evidential comparison, and that would only be possible once he was in a position to begin making arrests.

Naish returned to his desk with his notes and sat, deep in thought, until a knock at his door roused him and he realised that Burton was back with the tramp.

'Anyone covering Swallow Street?' asked Naish.

'Yes, I have a plain clothes man there for an hour. There wasn't time to get someone else done up in all the costume. I thought it should be all right for a short while.'

'Yes, that's fine. Now, let's speak with our friend the tramp.'

Naish sat down at the table opposite the tramp but sat back in his chair as far as was possible, as the tramp was exuding a rich aroma of rough sleeping.

'Are these pictures that you helped the artist to draw up a reasonable representation of the scene you saw that night?'

'They are better than reasonable,' said the tramp, with an articulate voice that surprised Naish. 'They are almost like a photograph. It is as if I was led there looking up at the scene now.'

'Excellent,' said Naish, passing the tramp a rolled cigarette. 'Now this partial view of the face of the main man – here in the centre of the scene – is just as you saw him?'

'Yes, that right.'

'There is no way at all that you could give any more detail about his features?'

'No, not a chance, given the shadows. It was just as I have described to the artist.'

'That's fine. So, am I to take it that the outline of the man here is representative of what you described?'

'It certainly is. He is the image of the man. Your artist has captured the stance and almost his manner in the pose. We spent a lot of time on it as I knew that you were after capturing it. An odd cove – masterful, as it were, but with that effeminate air to him. As they say, pictures are sometimes worth a thousand words, and this is a case in point.'

'That is good news. Now, if you will sign a witness statement with the constable here, you can be getting back to your place in Swallow Street. Thank you for your assistance in this matter once again,' said Naish, putting a few shillings on the edge of the table as he got up to leave.

Naish returned to his office and a few minutes later Burton joined him with the signed statement that he placed in the file on the evidence table set aside for statements.

'Good work,' said Naish. 'Right then, you are off to Camden Crescent, I assume?'

'If that's still all right with you, Inspector?'

'It is, just be careful, and don't take any chances at all. I don't want Emery getting the wind up and disappearing again. I am off to catch up with Sergeant Hancock but I will be back later in the day. If you are about, look in, but otherwise just leave me a note with an update.'

Chapter 18

'To judge from the fug down here, you have been at it non-stop since I left you here,' said Naish, as he climbed down the steps into the cellar.

'It helps to focus my mind,' said Hancock, taking his pipe from his mouth and looking round. 'Although, as you say, it has got a bit thick down here.'

'So, what have you found?'

'I am not sure that I have found anything, but I think that I understand what all this is. Sorry to be cryptic. What I mean is that these papers don't reveal anything in themselves, but they are part of something bigger, I think.'

'Go on then, explain,' said Naish.

'Each of these twelve boxes contains documents, letters and notes on scraps of paper. The content of each box is independent of the others. The correspondence is random – some of it consists of a series of letters between individuals, some of it is diary notes, picture postcards of holidays or cities. There appears in each to be a central correspondent to whom the letters and papers belong, although some of the papers – in particular, the letters – refer to the individual. For example, there are a number of letters and diary notes between individuals that mention the main player – we had so and so here for the weekend, or we saw so and so in Venice, or wherever it might be – do you get the gist?'

'Yes, I understand what you are explaining, but is there any indication as to why this correspondence exists?'

'Well, I have a theory, but let me finish off the facts first. As you noted, the dates on the twelve boxes bear no relation to the dates of the documents in each of the boxes, although the dates of the correspondence within each box are from one period only. For example, in this box marked 1932, we have a collection of correspondence and papers from 1875. In this box marked 1927, we have a collection of documents and papers from 1775. So, to be clear from an evidence point of view, we have twelve boxes which – it is to be inferred by the dates on the boxes – have been amassed over time between 1925 and 1950. Each box contains a similar collection of documents and the documents in each box are all from the same period. However, the dates of the documents in each box bear no resemblance to the date on the outside of the box.'

'So, those are the facts. What is your theory? Is there a common theme to these collections of documents? If it's a hobby or an interest, then there should be a common theme, I would have thought.'

'There is a common theme and I believe that it is the world of art. But if it is a hobby or interest on the part of Emery, then clearly these documents have a value greater than I can perceive in them. Why else keep them in a safe, and a safe that is hidden away, more to the point?'

'Are any of the correspondents famous people? Is that their value?'

'I don't know enough about the world of art, but I do recognise the names of some famous artists, hence that is what gave me the common theme of art. I assume that if I were an art historian and I knew the names of more painters than I do, then the contents of the other boxes would become equally obvious.'

'Well, give me the name of one that you do know, as an example.'

'Well, there is a box about Constable – I have heard of him. There is a box about Renoir, and I have heard of him, and then there is this one here, which I would not have known but for you mentioning him the other day – Turner. J.M.W. Turner, to be precise. This latest box, the one dated 1950, contains papers and documents all about him –

from him, to him, and about his activities at the time. The papers are all dated between 1798 and 1812.'

'Pass me that box, then. Let me have a look at the papers,' said Naish. 'Let's get it up into the kitchen and we can spread it all out on the table.'

'What do you think, then?'

'I am not certain, but it all appears to relate to Turner and a series of paintings he was planning of the abbey. I have seen the painting of his in the Victoria Gallery, but that was dated as being prior to 1793,' said Naish, referring to his notebook. 'These documents are all after that date, so they might refer to the time that the paintings in the catalogue that Miss Whiting showed me were painted.'

'So, what are you thinking?'

'I am thinking, why has Emery amassed this collection of documents? If he is a collector, I can see, given the artists concerned, that they may be of historical interest and therefore of some significant value. However, the risk here is that we are getting into waters deeper than we understand. I think that we need to secure all of the documents back in the safe and hope that next week we can bring Professor Andrews up here and let him give us his thoughts on the collection.'

'That sounds best to me,' said Hancock. 'I have collated everything that we need from an evidence point of view. If the professor has anything to add, I can amend my notes and, if necessary, get him to give us a statement.'

'Right, let's get this locked up and leave the place with the constable upstairs. Then, I think it is back to Orange Grove. You may as well get on home. I don't see that there is much more for you to do today. There is no point wasting your Sunday afternoon.'

'How about you, then? Are you taking the afternoon off?'

'I am going to finish off a bit of paperwork and set a few tasks and then, yes, I think that I may wander home and put my feet up for today.'

'What are the tasks that you refer to?'

'Just some odds and ends. I need to arrange for the catalogue loaned by Professor Andrews to be photographed, we need a statement from the guard at the Victoria Gallery about his observations of Emery, and I am hoping to hear from Miss Whiting that the Professor will be able to come over and meet us as soon as possible.'

'Well, I am happy to take the first two off your hands. Mrs Hancock has gone off with the ladies' group from church this afternoon, so I am not going to be moaned at for being another hour or so late. That's all it will take me, then things can get started first thing in the morning.'

'All right, that would be helpful,' said Naish, as the car drew up outside the station. 'If I don't bump into you again today, I will see you in my office first thing tomorrow with Newton.'

Naish hung his coat and hat up and as he sat down at his desk, he picked up an envelope that had been left in his absence. Having read it, he sat back, satisfied. Professor Andrews would be at Orange Grove at two o'clock on Monday afternoon.

Despite what he had said to Hancock about putting his own feet up, Naish had remained in his office for some hours after reading the note about Professor Andrews. He enjoyed the quiet solitude of the station on a Sunday afternoon, and spent the time reading and re-reading notes, reviewing the information on the blackboards. He had been working on some theories about Cotman and Derwent Holdings, and it was only when he leant back in his chair to stretch himself that he realised that it had got dark during his deliberations and, looking at the clock, he saw that it was half past seven. He surprised himself at the level of his own concentration, since the abbey clock usually broke in on his thoughts with a subliminal reminder of the passage of time. He decided that he had achieved all that he wanted for today and decided to set off for the Circus and an evening meal. He was just about to switch off the light in his office, when the phone rang and, despite his better judgement, he returned to answer it.

'Yes, this is Naish, who did you say it was? Oh yes, put him through right away,' said Naish, as he put his hat on his desk and sat down waiting to be connected to the caller.

'Is that you, Inspector?'

'Yes, this is Naish. How can I help?'

'It's George Jenkins here, Inspector.'

'Hello, George. Why didn't you say it was you?'

'I didn't want anybody to know that I was contacting you, Inspector. I don't want any trouble, you see.'

'All right, George, your secret is safe with me,' said Naish, with a grave yet reassuring tone in his voice. 'What's going on? Are you all right?'

'Yes, I am fine, but I need to be quick. I am in a pay phone around the corner from the pub – I thought it best to come out of sight.'

'Come on, George, what's wrong? Explain whatever it is to me.'

'He is back, Inspector. That thug bloke you were looking for – he is in the Fleece now.'

'Listen to me, George – you just make your way back to the pub and carry on as usual. I will deal with this. You won't see me, but I will deal with it. One last thing – where is he sat? Just so that I don't go and peer in at the wrong window.'

'At a small table in the far corner of the bar. If you look in at the right-hand front window, you should be able to see him.'

Naish picked up his hat, switched off the light and headed across the abbey churchyard. It was dark on the green outside the pub. A cobbled street ran around a small central green that gave the place its name, and the canopy of an enormous tree filled the space, making the night even darker. There were only a couple of street lights that gave light to the gloom cast by the tree canopy. The other source of light was the yellow blaze that came from the front windows of the Golden Fleece. The pub was packed and, given the sound emanating from within, the locals were having a fine night of it and clearly not of a disposition to be worried that it was a Sunday.

The sound from the pub occasionally rose briefly as a customer entered or left and the front door opened and closed. Naish walked around the perimeter of the green so as to give his movements a natural appearance, and then walked slowly up the pavement past the pub's front windows. He paused outside the right-hand window and feigned to search in his pockets for an elusive item, and in the time that it took, he was able to cast a quick glance inside where he was able to see that the thug was still sat at the table where George Jenkins had described him to be.

His dilemma was what to do next. There was no other entrance to the pub other than the main doors that led out into the green. However, the green itself was not only a small place but it was also deserted, and anyone lingering in its vicinity would quickly draw attention to themselves. Naish glanced at his watch. It was eight o'clock – another two and a half hours to go until closing time. Naish realised that his best hope of being able to take up the trail of the thug would be if he left at closing time and came out into the green amid a crowd of other drinkers. It was not an attractive prospect to be kicking his heels around the green for the next two and a half hours, but there appeared to be little alternative. He considered ringing George back and asking him to ring him at a nearby call box when the thug made ready to leave, but he was concerned not to replicate the blunder that Burton had made in following the thug and Emery and letting him slip through his fingers. He could stand outside and watch the thug, and it was unlikely that he would be seen out in the dark by someone sat inside in the bright lights but, again, it didn't sit comfortably with Naish. It was essential that he was not seen by the thug as he left the pub, not even if he were just a shadowy figure in the alleyway opposite that led to North Parade. Naish wandered around the green once again, contemplating his options, when he noticed that one of the buildings opposite was a guest house. The front door was closed and there was no sign to indicate if there were vacancies or otherwise. There was a light on in the ground floor front room, and so Naish, with few other alternatives, he felt, decided to try his luck and knocked at the door.

As he stood in the porch the sound from the pub rose again and Naish instinctively glanced over his shoulder to look. He looked away, pushed himself into the corner of the porch to take advantage of its shadow, and sensed that he was almost holding his breath. It was the thug leaving the pub that had caused this latest sound wave, and Naish knew that the next few seconds would be crucial. His first concern was the door in front of him opening and his presence being illuminated in the green against the light from the hall. His only possible solution to this risk was to grip on to the door handle and pull it towards him as best he could. His second concern was the direction that his quarry chose to take. He glanced round again and saw to his relief that the thug was heading away from him towards York Street. Naish released the door handle, and after a suitable interval to allow the thug a few seconds start, he set off after him.

Naish was conscious of the difficulty he faced in these nearby streets. They were a constant mass of turns, and it would take considerable skill to not lose the thug but at the same time maintain a discreet distance from him. As Naish came up into York Street, his plans nearly fell apart immediately. The first turn on the left was Swallow Street, and there was an unusual noise of voices shouting and laughing coming from it. The thug had stopped at the top and was now shouting at what appeared to Naish – given the nature of the thug's comments – was a group of boys kicking a football against some garage doors. Naish retreated back out of sight and, having allowed a few moments for the thug to presumably watch the boys disappear from view at the other end of the street, he glanced round the stone edge of the building and saw the thug wandering off towards Stall Street where he turned right, out of view. Once out on Stall Street, Naish's task became a little easier. The road was long and straight, there were a few people about to mask his presence, and there were ample shop doorways that he could dive into if the necessity arose. Naish paused from time to time to look into a shop window or light a cigarette, to give himself the opportunity to look about him. He was also anxious that, while he was following the thug, he was not being followed himself.

As the thug came into Milsom Street, he turned left into Quiet Street and Naish was intrigued, as Quiet Street led into Wood Street. However, just at the end of Quiet Street the thug turned right into a narrow lane and stopped. Naish was able to look through the shop windows that formed the corner of the street and saw the thug unlock a side door in the wall and disappear from view. Naish waited for ten minutes and walked on to the doorway. It was difficult to discern which of the collection of buildings on the corner that the door served, but a small brass plate to the side of it provided the answer. Engraved on it were the words: Byfield Gallery. Tradesmen and Deliveries.

Naish walked around to the front of the gallery in Wood Street, but there was no light showing. So, clearly, the thug could be assumed to be out in the back of the premises. He walked around the block into Queen Square and back along Wood Street, but the premises were exactly the same. Naish was concerned that, despite the lack of signs of occupation, there may be a face up there in the dark rooms above, watching his movements out in the street, and so he decided to take a break and walked around the corner into the Raven and ordered himself a pint.

After half an hour, Naish wandered around the block past the Byfield gallery one last time, but the scene was as it had been earlier, and so, reluctantly, Naish decided to make his way home to his flat in the Circus and cook his belated evening meal.

'There is a mug of tea on the desk ready for you, Inspector,' said Newton.

'You two are keen,' said Naish, as he took his hat and coat off.

'I get a sense that we are going to have a busy week, so I thought it best to make an early start,' said Hancock. 'I took the liberty of going round to Newton's home last night to apprise him of the developments. Have you anything else to add?'

'The only addition is that I took a call from George Jenkins yesterday evening because thug two was in the Fleece. The long and short of it is that I followed him when he left, and it looks very likely to me that he is lodging somewhere either at the back of or on a floor above the Byfield galley. Oh, and he also appeared to have a proprietorial interest in the garages in Swallow Street, sending some kids on their way who were hanging around there.'

'Another piece of the puzzle falls into place, then,' said Hancock.

'I am not sure that it fits into place as yet. We need to tidy it up with some proof and statements, but without a doubt it looks very interesting. Right, is there any other news?'

'Yes,' said Hancock, 'that Cotman Holdings has turned up again. The ratings department left a hand-delivered envelope for me on Saturday morning, and the upshot is that Cotman Holdings own the freehold on the Byfield premises in Wood Street and they pay the business rates on it. They have apparently followed up all the other property types that we gave them on that list but there are no other links to Cotman or Derwent.'

'Well, it is, to me, a convincing link that ties Emery and Williams ever closer together,' said Naish.

'Convincing proof, I would say,' said Newton.

'I agree that it is convincing, but it is only proof of an association. It is not in its own right proof of any criminal wrongdoing,' said Naish. 'I gave the Cotman and Derwent matter an hour of my thoughts while I was sat here yesterday afternoon, and I am left with two thoughts, inconclusive and ironic.'

'Go on,' said Hancock, looking puzzled.

'Well, unless we get someone up to Companies House, or some other such body that regulates or registers these holding companies, I don't see that we are ever going to make much progress on understanding their precise relevance to this case. Clearly, if we knew the directors or the principal players then we might see the light, but to me, the fact that they form these loose links in this case is sufficient for me at the moment. So, as I say, other than knowing that Derwent and Cotman Holdings are registered abroad and that they link our main players, our understanding of them is inconclusive at present. But I don't see that as a major stumbling block to us.'

'You think that their role will become clear when we have cleared up this case, as opposed to it being fundamental to our solving it?' asked Newton.

'Exactly,' said Naish.

'And the irony is?' asked Hancock.

'That came to me in the Green Street art shop the other day. Cotman and Derwent are both manufacturers of artistic materials – paints, pencils, paper and the like. I think that they were chosen by someone who needed to create these holding companies and chose the names as being unremarkable to the layman but with a hint of irony behind them.'

'A joke you mean?' asked Newton.

'A joke, yes. But in the irony they have perhaps undone themselves. To me, it was an unnecessary flourish of arrogance that has formed the link in my mind, at least between the controlling mind of Cotman and Derwent and someone related to the world of art. They had no need to do it, but in doing it, they have unwittingly let their guard down and revealed this small chink of light.'

'Burton left a note to say that he thinks that Emery is in the attic flat at Camden Crescent. There has been no further sign of him since he went in from the taxi, so I guess that he has decided to lie low for the time being,' said Newton.

'That sounds plausible. Have we still got a man watching the place?'

'Yes, that is all in hand. Fortunately, he is near to a public telephone box, so he can ring in reasonably quickly if anything happens.'

'Excellent,' said Naish, as he finished his tea and began to roll a cigarette. 'This afternoon we have our meeting with Professor Andrews, and I am hopeful that we will have a better understanding of some of the convolutions related to the world of art as a result. That leaves us with about five hours to go, so unless you have anything pressing, I have something that I want us to try and achieve in the meantime.'

'Go on then,' said Hancock, with a glance at Newton, 'tell us what you have in mind.'

'Let me just make this call, then I will be able to tell you,' said Naish, picking up the receiver of the phone. 'Good morning. Is that the Byfield gallery? This is Mr Bennett. Ah, Mr Miles, it is you. I thought that I recognised the voice. I was wondering if it would be convenient to call in today and meet with Mr Williams to have that conversation with him about the selection of a painting. Good, so his diary is free this morning – what time would he be free? I see, so he will be coming in at half past ten this morning. Well, I have an appointment that I must keep at half past one, so perhaps if I look in at about eleven, that would be convenient? It is, oh excellent. Then I will see you at eleven o'clock.'

'You are quite the impersonator, Inspector,' said Hancock, with a smile.

'It's odd how he can find the time, at the drop of a hat, to meet a man with fifteen hundred pounds to spend on a painting, isn't it? It just goes to prove that money talks,' said Naish. 'Anyway, my meeting with him was not the main purpose of my call, although it will be interesting to chat with him and see if I can find out a little more about him without raising any suspicions. No, the main purpose is that I now know when he will be walking to work.'

'Go on,' said Newton.

'Because I want you to get down to Swallow Street now,' said Naish, looking at his watch. 'It's half past nine now, so that gives you plenty of time to get our tramp from his doorway and take him along to Wood Street. Get him sat against the railings on the opposite side of the road to the gallery. That should give him an adequate opportunity to watch Williams walking along the pavement opposite him and going into the gallery.'

'We already have an artist's impression provided by the tramp of the man we suspect to be Williams,' said Newton.

'Indeed, we have but it is more of an impression of his figure and a partial view of his face. The main crux of the identification rests on the tramp's view of Williams in silhouette and the impression he had of his stance and mannerisms. So, I think, just so that we can be certain about the identification, that if the tramp can by a fortuitous coincidence see the man again, then it will hopefully confirm that Williams is our man.'

'Would it help if Hancock or I were to interrupt him on the pavement and ask the time, or for directions? It might get a bit more movement for the tramp to compare with what he saw in Swallow Street that night.' said Newton.

'Yes, that would be a good idea, as long as it is done well. Nothing must look clumsy or contrived, but I trust you to judge that to a nicety. Directions would be best, I think, they encourage movement and gesticulation, don't they? So, if you are both happy, I suggest that you get on with it and have him in place by ten o'clock. If one of you hangs around to accost Williams and the other keeps an eye on the tramp, that should work out nicely.'

'Keep an eye on him?' said Hancock.

'Just in case someone comes along and tries to move him on before we have our task completed.'

'I understand. Then I think that I would be best doing the minding and Newton can do the accosting, if that suits you, Sergeant,' said Hancock, with a friendly glance at Newton.

'What about the surveillance of Swallow Street in the meantime?' asked Newton.

'Get a plain clothes man to hang around. If all goes to plan, the tramp should be back at his post by half past eleven.'

'You are going in at eleven in the guise of Mr Bennett, then, Inspector?' said Newton.

'That's right, and so, if we should see each other for whatever reason, remember that you don't acknowledge me in any way at all. Right then, if all goes to plan, I will see you both back here about one o'clock, ready for our meeting with the Professor at two.

When Hancock and Newton had gone, Naish rolled himself some cigarettes and made some notes for himself on his planned discussion with Williams. Casual as it was intended to be, Naish didn't want to be wrong-footed, and he also wanted to work in a couple of references to Turner in the hope that Williams might open up on the subject of his role in the sale of the rediscovered Turners in the catalogue. He wanted to ask about Sickert but felt that it was too close to the knuckle, given the state of the investigation.

'Did you manage to get our tramp a good view of Mr Williams then?' asked Naish.

'Yes, it worked out pretty much as you suggested,' said Newton. 'I even managed to accost him and ask for directions to the abbey, which gave him ample opportunity to gesticulate. The tramp is one hundred percent certain that the man in Swallow Street and the man he saw this morning are one and the same person.'

'That is excellent,' said Naish. 'I had a most interesting hour with Mr Williams, myself. He was extremely courtly with me, giving me the old oil and charm – as I say, fifteen hundred pounds focuses the mind – but I felt, all the time, that he was not quite at ease.'

'Did you manage to get into any detail regarding the investigation?' asked Hancock.

'No. He appeared a little uneasy this morning, so I thought it best to play safe and avoid provoking any suspicion on his part.'

'So, are we in a position to move in and arrest him,' asked Newton, 'given the tramp's identification this morning, and the fact that you believe that at least one of the thugs is lodging somewhere on the Byfield premises?'

'We are not far off from it,' said Naish. 'I think that the three of us need to sit down and plan out an arrest strategy. We need to plan the sequence of events in great detail – timing will be crucial. We also need to make a list of premises that we need to make applications for search warrants for, as part of that plan. We haven't got the time this afternoon, as our meeting with Professor Andrews is a priority.'

'Newton and I can rough out the strategy while you are with Andrews, if you wish,' suggested Hancock.

'No, I would prefer for you both to listen in on what the professor has to say. If you are both able, I suggest that we spend an hour or so on the strategy this evening once we have finished with him.'

'Fine with me,' said Hancock.

'Me too,' said Newton.

'Right then, we are all set. I have sent a car to collect the professor from the station. His train gets in at ten to two. I think our first move, after the pleasantries of introduction have been done, is to take him up to St Mark's Road to see the paintings and the documents in the safe. After that we can come back here for further discussion. Given that the professor and Miss Whiting need a seat in the car, it may be as well if you two set off now and walk on ahead to St Mark's Road, and I will meet you there.'

Chapter 19

Naish was not sure what to expect of Professor Andrews but was reassured to find that, while he was clearly an aesthete, he was not condescending or given to affectation. He was courteous and well-mannered, and Naish was reassured of the extent of his scholarship. In the car on the way to St Mark's Road he gave an overview of his expertise which was in no way arrogant but which Naish thought a little odd, as if he were anxious to demonstrate his credentials. It was only when he became aware that Miss Whiting was less ebullient than usual that he suspected that the purpose of the professor's resumé was perhaps intended to remind her who was the expert here, although his manner towards her was marked by its politeness, treating her as if she were a promising postgraduate student. She appeared accepting of the implied academic hierarchy, for which Naish was relieved. The last thing that he wanted while trying to make progress on the matters in hand was any needling between learned colleagues.

'On this wall, Professor, are the pictures of which I have spoken and which I believe Miss Whiting has given you an overview. On these three hooks hung the three oil paintings that were signed J.M.W. Turner. You can see their size by the marks left on the wall,' began Naish.

'I do not wish to be pedantic, Inspector, but I cannot see the size of the paintings. The mark on the wall is an indication of the size of the frame. Can you estimate what size the canvas itself was?'

'I would say that the canvas was the same size as the remaining six paintings. The frames and the canvases were all almost identical in proportion, I would say,' said Naish.

'Thank you, Inspector, that is most useful,' said Andrews, who had now closed in on the first painting of the nine on the left of the group. 'I will be some little time, if you will excuse my silence, as I wish to make a detailed examination of the remaining six paintings one by one, so please don't feel you have to stand and watch me.'

Naish and Miss Whiting went over and sat on a settee while Hancock and Newton went off to the kitchen to open up the cellar in readiness for the professor.

Andrews scrutinised each painting in turn, then removed each in turn, and made a detailed examination of the back of the frame and canvas. He rehung each as he finished with it, and then spent another quarter of an hour flitting from one to another, as if making comparative notes in his head as he went. At the end of half an hour he turned to Naish and Whiting.

'Very interesting, very interesting, indeed,' said Andrews.

'What can you tell me, Professor?' asked Naish.

'Well, the most remarkable fact is that they are all forgeries,'

'Forgeries,' said Naish, glancing at Miss Whiting to see how she was taking this contradiction of her opinion of the works.

'I am afraid so. They are, however, brilliantly executed, and are clearly the work of a most gifted person. The perpetrator may be male or female, but I suspect them to be male.'

'How can you tell,' said Naish, 'I mean, that they are forgeries rather than by a male hand?'

'I can answer both points for you, Inspector, as one, in a way, is linked to the other. As I say, they are remarkable forgeries, probably the best that I have ever seen. Each of the artist's styles – in terms of the subject chosen, the palette of colours used and the brushstrokes used – are almost imperceptible from an original. Indeed, the subject and the palette are, in fact, imperceptible. It is in the nature of the brushstrokes that the forger has betrayed himself. It is hanging them together that has undone him, you see.'

'I must appear dense' said Naish, 'but can you explain that to me?'

'As I said, the brushstrokes are extremely painterly and in keeping with the style of the individual artist. However, even with the most studious forger, the occasional lapse into their own style will occasionally occur. If you come and look closely at the sun in this painting here, you can see the brushstrokes left by the artist in the paint. They are, to me in the world of art, as indicative as a fingerprint may be to you in the world of crime.'

'With your expertise you are able to tell an artist by his brushstrokes?' asked Naish.

'In some cases, I can, but in general terms I can certainly see the similarity of brushstrokes that occur in a series of paintings by a single artist. As I say, these forgeries are masterly, but the brushstrokes on the surface are not quite in keeping with the brushstrokes used in the rest of the composition. Now, if you take this area of water in this painting and the glass in the windows of this house in this painting, for example, it may be imperceptible to you, but I can see that the brushstrokes are the same in each of the paintings, but they are acutely at variance with the rest of the brushstrokes that replicate those of the artist.'

'Do you think that these areas that you have shown us could be areas of restoration by the same restorer, perhaps?' asked Miss Whiting, possibly hoping to recover her reputation as an arbiter of painting.

'No, no, my dear, I am afraid not,' said Andrews, sympathetically. 'I can see your point, but, having identified these common areas to each picture, I revisited each painting as a whole in conjunction with a close examination of the frames and canvas and I am satisfied that they are forgeries. If you look for example at the carpentry of the frame on which this canvas is stretched, I should say that the joint is not quite right for the period. I would need to have the painting removed from its frame to make a thorough examination to prove my theory conclusively, but I am all but certain that I am right.'

'So, when you say that the forger has undone themselves by hanging the pictures together, you suggest that the forgery might have escaped even your learned notice?' asked Naish.

'Yes, I do. One minor deviation in brushstrokes might be overlooked as an anomaly, carelessness or tiredness on the part of the artist, but seeing the replication of the fault across the collection leaves no doubt at all.'

'A true schoolboy error, then?' said Naish.

'It may be so, but it is not necessarily so. If the forger hung these pictures here for his own pleasure, it would be of no concern to him if he did not intend anyone else to see them. At least not anyone with the discernment to detect the forgery – I mean you no insult, my dear,' said Andrews, turning to Miss Whiting with a smile. 'As I say, if it had not been for the hanging of the pictures together, I would, in all probability, have been deceived myself.'

'Excuse my ignorance, again,' said Naish, 'but when you talk about the scenes chosen for these paintings, are the forgeries also copies of original artworks or are you suggesting that the subject is new?'

'It is not an ignorant question, Inspector,' said Andrews. 'As you suggest, some people make copies of famous works of art. There is no harm in that as long as the intent is not to deceive, of course. However, the accomplished and serious forger chooses an original scene. It may well be a scene that the artist has never painted before. In these circumstances, the known movements of the artist or some letters, for example, that point to his being in a location may support the hypothesis that he may have painted this unknown work while on holiday or visiting family or friends. The other ploy is to paint a famous scene by the artist but in a different season, in snow, for example, or perhaps even at night, or it may be as simple as painting the scene from a different angle.'

'The points you raise are bringing clarity to some of the matters that have troubled me in my investigation,' said Naish, glancing at Hancock and Newton as they returned from the cellar. 'What you have to say is fascinating.'

'I am glad to be of service, Inspector.'

'So, given that the three paintings attributed to Turner that hung here were presumably by the same hand, is it safe to assume that they are also forgeries?'

'As you say, Inspector, I am in no position to pass comment in the absence of the works. But if I were a betting man then I think it highly probable that, if the man who produced these paintings had replicated the works of these other artists, it is almost certain that he tried his hand at a trio of Turners.'

'Thank you, Professor. As I say, your observations have been more than enlightening. I am afraid that I may have to ask you to encapsulate them in a formal statement at some point in the future.'

'That is no problem at all, Inspector. I have to say that I have found the examination extremely interesting myself, anyway.'

'As I explained earlier, I have another request to make of you. In a safe downstairs in the cellar, I have discovered a number of documents that I believe are relevant to this case, and I have to say that, having listened to your comments about the work of the forger, they are now of particular interest to me. Would you care to take a break or are you happy to continue?'

'It would be pleasant to take a pause for a smoke, but I appear to have left my cigar case in Bristol.'

'I am afraid that I can only offer you a hand-rolled cigarette,' said Naish, holding his tin towards the professor.'

'That is most kind of you, Inspector,' said Andrews, not quite recoiling, 'but in that case I think that I will press on, if you don't mind.'

Naish showed Andrews to the cellar. Hancock had placed a couple of the kitchen chairs in front of the safe together with an occasional table that he had found in the drawing room. Andrews appeared content to begin his trawl of the documents with Miss Whiting in the role of willing assistant, so Naish left them there and joined Hancock and Newton out in the sunshine on the front steps.

'You will need to change your smoking habits, Inspector,' said Hancock, with a smile, 'if you are going to move in these more exalted circles.'

'Not me,' said Naish, with a glance at the front door to make sure he was not overheard. Rolling tobacco is good enough for me, and it has the advantage, of course, as I found with the professor, that you can offer it about but few take you up on the offer.'

'It appears to have been invaluable getting the professor in on the case,' said Newton.

'I agree, it has been a real eye opener for me, and it begins to make some sense of this business for once. If Emery is a forger and we can place him in this case as such, it would begin to answer a lot of questions for me.'

'I see that it answers a lot of the questions about the things we have discovered since the murders of Lynch and Edwards, but I am not sure that it adds much to how their deaths link to the rest of the case,' said Hancock.

'I see your point,' said Naish, putting a match to his cigarette, 'but for me it does begin to provide a solution, at least in the case of Lynch.'

'Care to elucidate?' asked Newton.

'Not at the moment. I need to think it through myself, really, but I am hopeful.'

'Why didn't you mention to Andrews the similarity of subject between the paintings that you saw on the wall in the sitting room and the paintings that were in the catalogue that he has lent you?' asked Hancock.

'It was on the tip of my tongue to say it, but I didn't want to lead him, at the moment. You see, I think that when he begins to read through the papers in the box related to Turner that he may be in for a shock.'

'You think that he will relate the documents to the paintings he validated as being genuine Turners before the sale?' said Hancock.

'I should be extremely surprised if his mind does not make that connection, especially as I have a fancy that some of the documents in that box may well be ones that he has already read during his deliberations over the provenance of the paintings at that time.'

'If he gets to that one early, how can you hope to focus his attention back on the other boxes?' said Newton.

'Because I have been guilty of a slight subterfuge,' said Naish. 'I placed that box out of sequence and repositioned it on the right of the lower shelf in the safe, so he will come to it last.'

'Cunning,' said Hancock with a smile. 'Never mind a smoke, I should think he might need a stiff drink when he has read it.'

'Maybe, maybe not,' said Naish. 'I cannot see that he will not see the relevance of the documents, as we have done, but the manner in which he takes it is not easy to predict. He doesn't strike me as the sort who is given to hysteria.'

'No, but it's going to be a bit of a dent to his pride and professional standing, isn't it? Especially in front of Miss Whiting.'

'Then it's a good job he was so magnanimous about her mistaken attribution of the paintings wasn't it.'

'Yes, but this has potentially got national repercussions for him I would think.'

'Well, we will have to wait and see, won't we?' said Naish, looking at his watch. 'Right they have had three quarters of an hour. Give them another half an hour and I think we had better rustle up some refreshments for them, at least a cup of tea. Go and see what the constable can sort out for us.'

Ten minutes before Naish had planned to go down to the cellar to see what progress the professor was making with the papers, he emerged from the kitchen door squinting slightly in the sunlight.

'I was just about to come and see how you are getting on,' said Naish. 'Is Miss Whiting not taking a break with you?'

'No, no,' said the professor, in a vague manner, as if his thoughts were elsewhere. 'She is continuing with her note taking, which is proving an extensive piece of work.'

Naish was not sure what to make of the professor's manner and, not wishing to break his train of thought, if indeed it was thought rather than distraction, he left him to himself and waited for him to continue the conversation.

'That is a most aromatic tobacco you have there, officer,' said Andrews, turning to Hancock. 'Might I try some, if you don't mind my presumption? I have found the last hour or so most perplexing and it might go some way to helping me gather my thoughts.'

'Of course you may, Professor,' said Hancock, offering him his tin. 'Have you a pipe?'

'No, no I have no pipe,' said Andrews, continuing his absent-minded air, as if the fact should be obvious.

Hancock glanced at Naish with a shrug of the shoulders, and Naish touched his finger to his lips as if to say, wait and see.

'Have you a paper, Inspector?' asked Andrews.

'A paper, Professor,' said Naish, in a mystified tone.

'Yes, a cigarette paper. You hand roll your cigarettes, do you not?'

'Of course,' said Naish, reaching into his pocket to locate his tin. 'I apologise for being obtuse. Here you are, Professor.'

'No need of an apology, it is I that is being obtuse, Inspector,' said Andrews, with a vulnerability that Naish found reassuring.

'May I?' said Andrews, holding his hand towards Hancock.

Andrews sat on the low stone wall that edged the top of the steps which led up from the street and, opening Hancock's tin, he rolled himself a cigarette using the pipe tobacco with an expertise that impressed Naish.

'You have an expert touch, Professor,' said Naish.

'Yes, I was a smoker of hand rolled cigarettes in my youth,' said Andrews, taking a deep drag on the cigarette and inhaling deeply.

Hancock and Naish both watched him smoke with every expectation that his next action would be to break into a coughing fit, given the strength and coarseness of the pipe tobacco, and exchanged an impressed look of respect as he simply exhaled the smoke and finished it off with a small smoke ring.

'So, what do you make of the documents so far, Professor?' asked Naish, keen to return to the subject in hand.

'It is both fascinating and deeply troubling at the same time, Inspector, I have to say.'

'Go on,' said Naish, keen not to break Andrews' train of thought.

'From an academic point of view, they are fascinating documents, and my first impression was that they are genuine. That was, of course, until I examined the last box.'

'The last box?' asked Naish' innocently. 'What is it about the last box that altered your first impression?'

'Because it is the last box that takes me into the aspect of this matter which is deeply troubling. If I deal with the first eleven boxes, first of all, I might be able to better explain myself. I have not read every word of every document, but I have given the contents of each box a sufficiently thorough examination to enable me to understand the significance of the contents. The documents, as you pointed out, are varied in their nature, ranging from letters to postcards to bills from suppliers of artistic goods to diary entries. Without any shadow of a doubt, these documents have been gathered together to produce a provenance for a painting, or in some cases a collection of paintings, three or four in number but no more. These collections of documents, together with the dates on the outside of the boxes, are significant to me, given my own knowledge of the world of art, since they are clearly the provenance documents that would have supported the authentication of important works of art that were discovered at that time. How the documents come to be gathered together here is another matter that is deeply troubling.'

'You mean that you would have expected them to have remained with the respective paintings that they authenticated?' asked Naish.

'Not necessarily, but I would not have expected the documents to have all been gathered together in one location, not even in a museum, let alone a suburban villa in a minor city. That would of itself make me uneasy but, as I say, it is the contents of the last box that is of grave concern and may cause me some personal and professional embarrassment.'

'Please go on, Professor,' said Naish, keen to get to the gist.

'As you may be aware, a number of years ago three paintings by J.M.W. Turner came to light, having spent a considerable time in a private collection. It was thought that they might have been in this collection from very soon after they were painted. Anyway, the newly discovered pieces were put on display at a gallery in London and, as you may imagine, they generated considerable interest, not only with those in the serious art world but among the general public, given the popularity of Turner. As part of the process of authentication, I was among a number of academics who were invited to examine the paintings and give an opinion as to their authenticity. It was during this process that I was also given access to a number of documents that supported the claim of their authenticity and which sought to calm any doubts in the market. I have to tell you, Inspector, that the documents in the final box are the documents that I viewed at that time.'

'I am sorry to appear dense yet again, Professor, but, other than the incongruity of the documents being here, what is it about the contents of this last box that has caused you to be concerned? If the documents contained in this box were not a cause of concern when you first examined them, what has caused you to change your view?' asked Naish.

'The fact of their being here with these other boxes of documents has, as I have said, made me feel uneasy, but what compounds my concern is that I now believe the documents to have been forged.'

'What is it in particular that leads you to that conclusion though, Professor?' asked Naish, sounding a little frustrated.

'It is that a number of the documents are duplicated, if you study the contents carefully. At least two of the letters and one of the diary entries, among others, appear to have what I might describe as drafts that replicate the contents.'

'But might that just not be the case,' asked Hancock. 'Might that not be a genuine draft, as one might do with an important letter?'

'I agree that it might be the case with a letter, but not with a postcard. Not even the most fastidious correspondent drafts a postcard, surely.'

'Postcard,' said Naish. 'Perhaps if you can explain your thoughts with the documents before us, it might be of assistance. Newton, go down and get the box up here, will you.'

'So, let me explain,' said Andrews, as he spread the documents in question out on the kitchen table. 'Now, I don't know how you go about drafting a letter, gentlemen, but I would start my draft in the assumption that it was not going to be sent. That is to say, that I would fully intend before I started the draft to have to rewrite the content in its final form ready for posting. So, I would not go to the extent of writing my own name, address and the date at the top of the draft. I would simply rough out the contents of the paragraphs and, as I went, I would expect to make a couple of crossings out as I reflected on my thoughts and revised the construction of sentences or phrases, for example.'

'Yes, I can see the sense of what you say,' said Naish.

'Exactly, of course you would. It is the whole purpose of the drafting process,' said Andrews. 'Yet in these drafts, the writer started off with his name, address and the date written in a carefully crafted hand.'

'It is also unusual for a draft to be written in one's best hand, in my experience,' said Naish.

'Exactly,' repeated Andrews. 'This letter does not look like a draft to me. It looks like a first attempt at a letter that was intended to be sent, but the writer just stopped the composition midway through a sentence.'

'But is that not a credible thing that might have occurred?' interjected Hancock. 'The writer began a letter, made a mistake or lost the thread, and just started again.'

'And what would you do with that piece of paper?' asked Andrews. 'You would screw it up or tear it up and put it in the fire or the waste basket, I imagine. You would not keep it with your private documents, I suggest.'

'Yes, I see the sense of that,' said Hancock.

'Now, if you compare the draft with the final letter, in both cases you find that the content is exactly the same up to where the draft breaks off. So the writer didn't make a mistake or rethink the contents, it was something else that made him or her discontinue their first attempt, and it was this. If you look carefully, what changes is the handwriting. I think that the writer looked back and realised that the handwriting he was attempting to replicate was not as he wanted it, as if he lost his concentration on the formation of the font as he got distracted by thinking about the content.'

'Replicating?' said Naish.

'Replicating or copying, Inspector, they are all synonyms for forgery. That is what I believe these discontinued letters show. You can see, here and here, that the handwriting has become less regular in the draft, but in the final version it continues fully formed in a coherent style.'

'And the postcard? asked Naish.

'As I say, who drafts a casual note to a friend sent in a postcard? Only someone who is keen to ensure that the handwriting they are forging is formed convincingly.'

'So your personal and professional concerns stem from your belief that these documents that you viewed at the time – that reassured you in your opinion that the works by Turner were authentic – are, in fact, forged and that the logical conclusion must be that the paintings themselves are forged.'

'I would need to examine the paintings again to make a final judgement but, yes, it is a real concern for me, Inspector. I face both personal and professional ridicule. There is the remote chance that it is only the documents that are forged, in an attempt to bring any doubts about their provenance to a quick end, but I fear that I am just clutching at straws.'

'By a logical extension of thought, it is to be implied that all the other documents in the other boxes are also forged, then,' asked Naish.

'I am convinced of it, Inspector, although I quite understand that you may need to take a second opinion on the matter. You see, in the same way that the forger of the paintings in the sitting room over there betrayed himself by hanging these paintings together, these documents, when put together in close proximity, also reveal some commonalities that are not obvious when they are viewed in isolation. When we have the documents together, I can give you a number of examples.'

'You may rest assured, Professor, that I do not doubt your word, but from an evidential point of view, I will need to take another opinion from an expert in the field to ensure that my case is robust. As we discussed earlier, it will be important for you to set out the examples of forgery within the collection of documents in a formal statement, with the relevant documents cross referenced. I have no wish to be over dramatic, Professor, but from what you suggest it is probable that all the other paintings related to the other documents are open to the suspicion of forgery.'

'It is more than likely, Inspector, it is a certainty. Doubt will instantly be cast on the authenticity of these works and I have to say that, in all likelihood, it will be proved to be well founded. There may well be other paintings in circulation that we are unaware of, as yet.'

'Other paintings, Professor?'

'It may well be the case, yes. In two or three of the documents there is reference to the artist working on a canvas in a specific location – Constable is one example. One of the letters suggests that he is working on a scene at Flatford Mill. He painted several scenes around this area but, from his description of the scene, I can say that, as far as my scholarship is concerned, the painting he refers to has never been seen. The implication being that he has produced a painting that, as yet, we have not discovered.'

'So, there may be other forgeries out there in addition to the ones that have already come to the market, then?'

'It plainly has to be considered to be the case. We are looking at the prospect of a major scandal within the art world, Inspector, of a magnitude that is unimaginable. I simply do not know what to do.'

'Well, with the greatest respect to you, Professor, you will do absolutely nothing for the time being. This is a police matter and what you have been able to explain, painful as I know it is to you, has enabled me to make sense of a case two elements of which I have been unable, until now, to make sense of.'

'I understand your satisfaction in being able to progress your case, but I am facing professional ruin over this matter, so with the greatest respect, police matter or not, I have to consider myself.'

'I apologise, Professor, I did not mean to sound officious. I merely meant that you do not need to worry about how to progress or conclude this matter,' said Naish, in a genuinely conciliatory tone. 'I am certain that we can deal with the furore of interest that this case will cause when it comes to the public's attention and your own professional integrity with sympathy. If what you suspect about these documents is true, you will not have been the only academic to have been deceived by these documents. Clearly, other people over the past thirty years or so have all been taken in in the process of passing off these paintings as genuine works.'

'Unfortunately, it is of little or no comfort to be among a group of fools any more than it is to be regarded as a fool in one's own right, Inspector. But I appreciate your sentiments,' said Andrews, in a forlorn tone.

'Right, then,' said Naish, in a brisk tone. 'I think that we have achieved all that we can here for now. I suggest that my two sergeants secure the documents in the safe and tidy things up here while I take you and Miss Whiting back to Orange Grove for some refreshment. Newton, can you get Miss Whiting from the cellar and tell the constable to get the car started.'

'You have been extremely generous with your time, Professor, and your presence has also been invaluable, Miss Whiting,' said Naish, as they got out of the car outside Orange Grove. 'I have one last favour to ask of you and that is to examine two sketchbooks and some drawings made on canvases. What time is your train?'

'I have not booked a return ticket as I was uncertain how long I should be with you.'

'In that case, I will have the constable drive you back to Bristol. No, I insist,' said Naish, as Andrews protested. 'After all that you have done to assist me, it is the least I can do. I extend the invitation to you as well, Miss Whiting.'

'Thank you, Inspector,' said Miss Whiting. 'If it is in order, I should like to accompany Professor Andrews back to Bristol and be dropped at my home on the return journey, as there are a great many things arising from this afternoon that we wish to discuss.'

'Of course you may, Miss Whiting. As I said, it is the least I can do.'

Chapter 20

'Well, Inspector,' said Andrews, pushing back his chair from the evidence table and looking over to Naish's desk, 'it is my opinion that there was about to be another box added to the safe at the villa that we have just visited.'

'That is very interesting,' said Naish. 'Although I do not have your academic knowledge, the same thought was beginning to dawn on me by a process of logical deduction.'

'Do you have any theory as to what these sketches are working towards?'

'My guess is that the sketches have been produced as part of a plan to produce some paintings in the style of Walter Sickert, based on his painting of the Assembly Rooms in Bennett Street. To be precise, it is my theory that the forger intended to produce two or three paintings of the other facades of the building.'

'I have to say that I concur with your theory, Inspector,' said Andrews, as if pleased by a promising pupil. 'I think it is obvious that the sketchbooks have been produced to give the forger some sketches to work from during the composition of the canvases themselves. But given the attention to detail and the style of the sketches mimicking Sickert's style, I think that they would then have been included in the provenance documents.'

'In light of your observations earlier, it makes complete sense to me,' said Naish. 'Do you think that these canvases were about to have been developed into the final paintings, Professor?'

'No, I do not think that they were. These very faint outlines giving just the barest impression of the building are certainly in the style of Sickert, but I don't think that they are the final canvases, for two reasons. Firstly, they have been done in ink, and that is not in line with Sickert's technique. Secondly, if you look at the proportions of this canvas, they are not quite right. It is as if the artist has started off sketching the composition and then realised that he has not left sufficient space for the upper portion of the elevation to be painted. Given these two factors, I think that these canvases were discarded.'

'They were discarded, in the sense that they were not continued with,' said Naish. 'Yet they were clearly not discarded in the sense of being thrown away.'

'No. I imagine that the forger would have kept them nearby as he began the actual canvases, to use them as a sort of guide or prompt, perhaps.'

'Do you think that the forger had begun his work on the final canvases, Professor?'

'He may well have done so. If you look on the back of this canvas, just where the canvas itself is pinned to the frame, there is a mark of what I take to be a smudged finger mark. It would need to be examined, of course, but I strongly suspect that the substance that caused the smudge was paint. I am straying into the world of complete conjecture here, of course, but I don't think it too fanciful to imagine that the forger, while at work on the final canvas, might have picked up this draft canvas to check some detail or other. Complete speculation, of course, on my part. Where did you find them, may I ask?'

'It is a convoluted story, Professor, but in essence I believe that they were taken from the building in which the forgery may well have been undertaken. I also suspect that they were taken from there by an opportunist thief, who saw no value in them other than that they might be useful to a friend of his. However, when he examined them in the light of day, he saw that what he had taken for blank canvases had in fact been used and so he set them aside to dispose of them himself, fearing that they would link him to the crime.'

'The forgery?'

'No just the opportunistic theft,' said Naish.

'Are there any signs of the provenance documents that would accompany the final forgeries, Inspector?'

'No, I have found nothing other than these two sketchbooks and the canvases that you have examined. They may have existed, but I believe that if they did then they have, in all probability, been destroyed along with the canvases, and I think that I know where.'

'It is all becoming a bit confusing for me, Inspector, I am afraid,' said Andrews, wiping his forehead with his handkerchief. 'I am afraid that I don't have anything else to add so if you don't mind, I think that I will take my leave. It has been a cerebrally and emotionally challenging afternoon, and I think that I would appreciate an hour or two at my own fireside with a glass of whisky and my own tobacco to reflect on these events and their ramifications.'

'I completely understand, Professor. I hope you find your whisky brings you a sense of calm. As I have said, I will do all that I can to prevent these revelations being a cause of embarrassment to you, you have my word for that.'

'I appreciate your sentiments, Inspector. It is very considerate of you.'

'I would just remind you and Miss Whiting of the need to maintain complete discretion and secrecy in these matters until I advise you otherwise. I am sorry to sound officious, but it is vital if I am to close the net on the perpetrators of all the crimes that are tied up in this case.'

'I understand, Inspector, and you have my word. If you make arrangements with Miss Whiting, I am more than willing to set out my observations and findings in a formal statement to one of your officers.'

'Thank you and good night, Professor. Good night to you, Miss Whiting. I will be in touch to arrange the statements,' said Naish, as he held the door open for them.

'Right then, it is a little later than I had imagined it would be, but we need to press on with the plans for arrests and search warrants,' said Naish.

'I will make a list of who and where, then,' said Newton.

'Right. For the warrants, I want the Byfield Gallery, the garage in Swallow Street, Emery's house in Camden Crescent and Williams's home address – you need to find that out, by the way. Once you have got the applications drafted and submitted to the court, I will need to take them to the Chief Superintendent for sign-off.'

'Who's for the arrest list, then?' asked Newton. 'We will need a plan of which order we arrest them in, as well.'

'The list is simple – Williams, Emery and the two thugs – names to be formally confirmed at the time they are charged. As for an order, I want them all taken at the same time, so we will need to have plenty of men on hand, particularly for the group dealing with the thugs.'

'Are we assuming that the thugs are in hiding at the Byfield gallery?' asked Hancock.

'That has to be the assumption. I think that in order to give ourselves the best chance of finding them there, we need to make the arrests in the early hours of the morning. I would suggest five o'clock.'

'Sounds sensible to me,' said Hancock. 'I suppose that's why you want Williams's home address – take him there rather than at the gallery.'

'To give ourselves the best hope of getting the thugs, we need to be going in at an hour when they most likely will be there. It has the additional advantage, of course, that they will hopefully be asleep and off their guard. To avoid giving any warning to Williams and Emery, we need to take them at the same time.'

'What if the thugs are not at the gallery? What's the fallback plan?' asked Newton.

'Pile the pressure on Williams and Emery that they are going to carry the can for the forgery and the murders if they don't give us the information on the thugs' whereabouts.'

'Suppose they don't know the thugs' whereabouts?' said Newton.

'I can't see Williams losing contact with them, even if they are in hiding somewhere else. He needs to keep an eye on them to make sure that they stay onside.'

'You are linking the forgery and the murders all in one, then?' said Hancock, with mild surprise.

'Yes. I think that I have got it straight in my mind how the whole thing links together and how the events unfolded,' said Naish.

'Care to elucidate?' asked Hancock.

'Not right now. I am sure that you have enough information to put it together, but I want to get the approval of the Chief Superintendent before I make my final move.'

'Can I suggest that we get permission for someone to be carrying a firearm for the arrests at the gallery,' said Newton. 'Given his skills with the knife, I don't think that we want to risk one of our men getting a blade between his ribs.'

'Good point,' said Naish. 'I will sign it off with the Chief.'

'I am happy to carry it,' said Hancock. 'I have the necessary certificate and I don't mind going in first at the gallery.'

'Thank you,' said Naish, 'it will be good to have you armed and covering my back.'

'Your back?'

'I will be leading on this,' said Naish, emphatically. 'Now, it's getting on for eight o'clock, so I suggest that we call it a day. I will see you back here in twelve hours and hopefully we can finalise our arrest plans and all that sort of thing.'

At half past eight Hancock came back into the foyer of the station carrying a portion of fish and chips wrapped in newspaper.

'Supper, sergeant?' enquired the constable on the front desk.

'Not mine. They are for the Inspector, but if he is on his way home then you can have them on me,' said Hancock, with a smile.

He wandered up on to the first floor and saw what he was expecting to see, a light shining from under Naish's door.

'I thought that you might fancy something to sustain you other than tobacco,' said Hancock, as he came into the office. 'I saw the light in your office window as I was walking past.'

'What were you doing walking past at this hour?'

'I had been round to the Ale House for a quick one with Newton to compare notes, and I saw the light as I was heading for home. Come on, eat up and I will go and make you a mug of tea. Then you can tell me what you are mulling over.'

'That was just the thing,' said Naish, pushing back his chair and lighting a cigarette. 'As for mulling things over, it is the attic that I have been giving some thought to.'

'At Emery's house, you mean?'

'Yes. You see, it occurs to me that, now that we realise the significance of the works undertaken by the builders in the cellar, it seems improbable that works that were undertaken in the attic are not also relevant to this case.'

'I see where you are coming from. "Can you please install a secret safe in my secret cellar, oh, and while you are at it, just floor-out the attic." Yes, I suppose that there may be some significance to the works in the attic, but what are you imagining that they are?'

'It is a long shot, but if the safe in the basement contains the documents of provenance, is it possible that he has concealed the paintings that he was working on at the time of the burglary in the attic?'

'He may have done so, but there is no link to his intention to have the works in the attic done and these latest paintings, is there? The works in the attic were undertaken years ago – the evidence from the locksmith confirms that.'

'All right, but you see there is something playing on my mind about the three Turners taken from Emery's house the other evening. Those three oils are the same size as the watercolour at the Victoria Gallery – I know because I have measured them. I think that Emery painted them as his preparation for the larger versions of those scenes that were then sold on by Williams as new discoveries.'

'So, he liked the three preliminary paintings so much that he kept hold of them and hung them in this house?'

'Well he must have also been pleased with their quality. We know that they were probably good enough to fool Miss Whiting, since she was taken in by the others.'

'Although not by someone as accomplished as Professor Andrews,' said Hancock.

'Yes, it is interesting that. I have a funny feeling that despite being deceived by the paintings, she will be dining out on her association with this case for some time to come. Her reputation isn't tainted by her association with the case as the poor professor's is,' said Naish, with a wry smile. 'Anyway, he was pleased enough to keep hold of them, so he must have valued them.'

'I wouldn't mind something like that salted away to top up my pension,' said Hancock.

'A pension. You may have hit on something there, Sergeant.'

'Surely the last thing that our friend Emery needs is more money to his name. We know that his bank balance is already very healthy, and his property portfolio is enormous. How much money does a man need?'

'You know the old adage – how much money is enough? Just a little bit more than you already have!'

'I know, but he is a boring sod. It's not as if he is a playboy is it – gambling, drinking, women, or a vice like that.'

'Avarice is a vice. For some men the acquisition of wealth itself is a driver, whether or not they have a need for the money.'

'So, you think that three paintings added to what he already has will motivate him?'

'If they were passed off as Turners then it is possible that their value could be such that they alone could double the value of his total assets. However, it may simply be that it was the sheer thrill or pleasure of pulling a fast one on Williams, or in fact the whole artistic world, that drove him to it, and money was not a motivating factor.'

'So, somehow, when Williams found out about them, he decided to secure them to protect his business?'

'Yes, and I think we know how he found out about them, don't we?'

'The thug dressed as the milkman,' said Hancock.

'Yes, either that, or else thug two just disclosed the details of a confidence that Emery had shared with him during a meeting prior to their meeting in Parade Gardens.'

'But why was Emery apparently so unconcerned about their removal, given their potential value?'

'Because I believe that he has a number of other similar paintings up there in the attic. Hence, he went up there that night after the trio had been, to check two important things. First, that the keys to his safe were secure, and second, to make sure that the attic had not been disturbed.'

'And having found that both were safe and sound, he went on his way.'

'Yes, and he was as pleased as punch, in my view, because he thought that Williams was now off his back, having secured the three Turners – while he still had all the provenance documents and, I believe, some other paintings up there in the attic.'

'More Turners?'

'No, I think that what he had been doing over the years was making an additional painting surreptitiously behind Williams's back.'

'Paint two or three for Williams and one for himself, you mean?'

'Exactly, and that all makes sense of the undiscovered paintings referred to in the provenance documents that Professor Andrews alluded to earlier. It also accounts for why Emery appears now to have been left alone by Williams and the thugs.'

'Williams thinks he has secured all the additional works?'

'I think he does, although I am not sure where he thinks all the provenance documents are.'

'It's just as well he isn't aware of the attic contents, then, isn't it?'

'Potential attic contents. We need to get up there first thing tomorrow morning and examine the scene. We will have a couple of hours while the warrants are being processed.'

'I will get a couple of uniformed men to assist us and make sure that they bring along a selection of woodworking tools – screwdrivers, saws, that sort of thing. Shall we say ready to leave here at half past eight?'

'That will be fine with me,' said Naish. 'Right, its ten to ten, so I suggest that we get some sleep. It's likely to be a long day tomorrow as well.'

Naish and Hancock stood in one corner of the attic and watched as the two constables cleared the empty trunks and boxes stored there out on to the landing.

'That's the last of the boxes, Inspector,' said the older constable.

'I am no builder,' said Naish, kneeling down on the floor, 'but I think that plywood sheets are an unusual wood to use for a floor, wouldn't you say?'

'Yes, I would have thought that traditional floorboards would have been the favourite thing to use, particularly given the limited access to the attic through that door. I should imagine that it was a struggle to get these eight sheets in here.'

'I would also have expected to find that the boards would have been nailed down using floorboard nails, wouldn't you? These appear to have been screwed down, if you look here, and here.'

'It's not a very good job either, to my eye. This row of four boards that run across the floor here are, I would say, four foot by three foot. The four in the row behind them are the same size but they stand proud of the others, so they must be a thicker board.'

'Anyway, I suppose it what's underneath them that intrigues us, that may explain the screws being used – more precise. If there is an old master underneath them, Emery wouldn't want a nail being driven through it by some chippy, would he? If you lads have got a couple of screwdrivers, then the sergeant and I will step outside for a smoke. Just get all the screws out for now, but whatever you do, don't start lifting the boards just yet.'

Half an hour later, the younger constable came down to the front porch where Naish and Hancock were sat in the sunshine to announce that all the screws had been removed.

'Right, then,' said Naish, as he stood in the attic doorway. 'If you can get that nail bar under the corner of that first board in the front row, just ease it up gently and let's see what there is to see.'

'That's the last of the front-row boards, Inspector. Shall we start on the back row?' asked the constable, as he stood astride the exposed rafters.

'Yes, let's get them up. Although I am beginning to think that perhaps we are in for a disappointment with this theory,' said Naish, drawing on a cigarette.

'These boards are definitely thicker than the first row, Inspector, and a sight heavier as well,' said the older constable, as he strained to lift the board upright.

'Well, let's hope they are protecting something worthwhile,' said Naish, without a great deal of conviction.

'Well, there is nothing under it, I am afraid,' said the older constable, as he peered back under the rafters.

'Well, keep lifting them. We may as well finish the job so we can at least close off this line of thought,' said Naish. 'Stack it over there with the others from the first row and then do the same with the other three.'

'That's the last of them,' said the older constable, as he placed the last board against the stack. 'I can't say I'm sorry that's over – it's playing hell with my back.

'Get over here and have a breather,' said Naish, 'while I have a final look around, just to be sure.

'This is interesting,' said Hancock, as Naish balanced his way back across the exposed rafters.

'I am glad that you think something is,' said Naish. 'It strikes me as having been a wasted couple of hours, personally.

'Look at these last four boards. The reason that they are thicker is simply that they are three boards screwed together,' said Hancock. 'It wasn't obvious at first because the heads of the screws holding the boards together were on the underside.'

'Let me have a look,' said Naish. 'Yes, that is very interesting. Constable, get yourself a screwdriver and take out the screws around the edge of this board, will you. Here, let's lay it flat on the floor out on the landing, it will make it easier to work.'

With the board laid out on the landing, the constables set to work removing the line of screws around the edges of the board.

'They were clearly not short of screws,' said the older constable, looking up from where he knelt. 'That's fifteen that I have taken out of this long side alone.'

'Same over here,' said his younger colleague. 'And I have counted ten along the top edge already.'

'That may be why it's so heavy,' said Hancock, with a smile.

After another ten minutes of unscrewing, the constables both sat back on their haunches.

'Right, let's separate the three boards and see what we have, if anything,' said Naish.

'That's interesting,' said Hancock, kneeling down beside the long edge. 'I don't think it's three boards at all. Look, this piece of timber sandwiched in the middle is a piece of half-inch by half-inch timber running along the edge of the sandwich. It has slipped slightly out of place now the screws are out.'

'Right, let's get one of us at each edge and lift the top panel off,' said Naish.

As they lifted the top panel clear and set it to one side, it was clear that Hancock had been correct in his supposition. The sandwich, as he termed it, was in fact two sheets of plywood separated by four lengths of half-inch by half-inch square beading that ran along the four edges. The screws had then passed through all three pieces of wood around the outside edge, securing the sandwich together.

'What's this in the middle, then?' said the younger constable, reaching out.

'Hold it,' barked Naish. 'Let me have a close look before you move anything.'

The void formed by the edging timbers was filled almost to the full square area by something wrapped tightly in brown paper. Naish knelt down, removed the pieces of timber around the edges, and then peered closely at it with his face only a few inches from the surface.

'Right, then, Hancock. Let's see what we have got, shall we? You get on the other side and let's lift it into that room over there and place it on the rug on the floor.'

With the parcel on the rug, Naish took his penknife and carefully cut the brown paper along the fold made in it as it passed over the edge of the parcel. Once he had freed enough of the paper covering, he was able to peer inside. Having satisfied himself it was safe to continue without causing any damage, he gently pulled the top covering back across the surface of the parcel and whistled.

'It's the back of a canvas, by the look of it,' said Hancock, glancing at Naish.

'I think that you may be right. Let's stand it up and get the rest of this brown paper off.'

'Look at that there – it's fantastic,' said the older constable.

'Well, I never did,' said Hancock, as they set the picture against the wall and all stepped back to take it in.

'Emery's pension,' said Naish, with satisfaction. 'Just as we thought.'

'It's a masterpiece,' said Hancock.

'Indeed it is, Sergeant, and unless I am mistaken, it is a masterpiece by Velázquez.'

'Val who?'

'Diego Velázquez, 1599 to 1660, to be exact – the leading artist in the court of King Philip the fourth of Spain.'

'You have been doing your homework, Inspector.'

'I most certainly have, Sergeant. Once I knew the contents of those boxes and the artists they referred to, I have been burning the midnight oil at home, learning all that I can about them. Although I value Professor Andrews as an expert witness, it never pays to abdicate your own responsibility for understanding the facts that underpin a case. Yes, this is an – as yet – undiscovered masterpiece, the only known reference to its existence being the mention of it being painted by Velázquez in the documents in the safe. If you refer to the documents in the box marked 1929, you will find that he makes reference to a painting that he made about the time he painted his famous work "Old Woman Frying Eggs" in 1632. We will need to do some comparisons, but I suspect that the old woman in this scene of ours will be the exact likeness of the "Old Woman" herself.'

'A forgery that is not a copy but is so like an existing painting that it will be accepted as authentic,' said Hancock.

'That, and a few documents to confirm its provenance, also forged by our friend Mr Emery.'

'Shall we open up the other panels?' asked Hancock.

'No, just unscrew the top edge of each and remove the top spacing timber. If, as we suspect, we see the edge of a brown paper parcel, I think we get on and get all four back to Orange Grove and we can deal with them back there. You two will need to repackage this one back in its sandwich as well, so that it doesn't come to any harm,' said Naish, taking his tobacco tin from his pocket.

'The car is here, Inspector,' said Hancock, ten minutes later.

'Right, you two can have a smoke break. When I get back to the station, I will send the van up here to collect the paintings, put them in my office as they are, and we can open them up later on,' said Naish, as he got into the front seat of the car.

'It looks unlikely that any of those sandwich panels contain the latest forgeries, from my reading of it, Inspector. It's my bet that those panels and their contents all went down about the time that the works in the attic were completed.'

'I tend to agree with you, but we need to get them opened up later and confirm exactly what they are.'

'It shouldn't be too difficult. I assume that the paintings will be signed, and it will be easy enough to check them off against the names referred to in the documents in the boxes.'

'It will, and I think that we will find that the paintings are all linked to the boxes. It's my hunch that they will be more or less equally spread out over the last twenty-five years or so. Rather than risk his sideline coming to light, I imagine that he only did one every now and again.'

'So where are the ones that he was working on for Williams at the time of the burglary?'

'In that bin at the back of Emery's shop. I believe that those burnt fragments that we found when we searched the back yard were all that was left. I imagine that the provenance documents, if they had been begun, went into the bin at the same time, all on the instructions of Williams in his bid to clear the evidence.'

'But what provoked the destruction of such a valuable fraud?'

'Ted Lynch,' said Naish, emphatically, as the car drew up at Orange Grove. 'That's what.'

'Good morning, Newton,' said Naish, as he came into his office and hung his coat and hat up. 'Where are we with the arrest and search warrants?'

'All here and signed off, Inspector.'

'Who was on the bench this morning?'

'Just old Major Bowden from Wellow.'

'That's good news. The Major is of the old school and, being from a village, it's unlikely he will have any association with Williams and the artistic set, I imagine. Did he ask anything?'

'Only who was leading the case. I mentioned your name, he looked up at me, nodded approvingly, signed all the papers and sent me on my way.'

'Right, then. Give them to me and I will pop up and show them to the old man. In the meantime, you and Hancock can be getting the plans for the early hours drawn up. You can have as many men as you want – and you will need vehicles – and make sure that we have space in the cells here. They each need a separate cell, so if we get inundated with drunks or other minor stuff, then send them out to Shepton Mallet prison or some such place. I also want to see the names of the teams that we will be sending to each location and I want a briefing at two o'clock in the canteen for everyone involved. Oh, and you had better get that revolver issued to yourself, Hancock. When did you last use one, by the way?'

'I had a refresher about six months ago but, being that this is Bath, you don't get a lot of opportunity to use one, do you,' said Hancock, with a smile.

'Then once you have it issued, I suggest that you run out to the woods for half an hour and let off a few practice rounds – I don't fancy being shot by accident just because you haven't got your eye in.'

Chapter 21

'Any news on thug two as yet?' asked Naish, as Hancock and Newton came into his office with the tea tray.

'No, but the ambulance officer I spoke with thought that he would live. I sent two constables to sit with him at the hospital in case he tries anything. They are going to ring here as soon as there is any news,' said Hancock.

'I thought that you might have to shoot thug one, at one point,' said Naish, blowing out the match that had lit his cigarette.

'I thought so as well,' said Hancock. 'He was up so fast when we busted in there that I think he was not fully asleep. If he had not been so intent on getting the knife into his mate, then I think one of us might have been in trouble. I was just about to squeeze the trigger when young Jones laid him out with that blow from his truncheon.'

'Has he come round yet?' asked Naish. 'He's no use to us in a coma.'

'Yes, he came round in the back of the van on the way back here' said Newton. 'Luckily we had cuffed his hands and feet and put another set of cuffs through the chain and around the seat uprights on the floor. It took four men to get him out of the van and into the cell, but now he is in there he appears to have calmed down a bit.'

'He knows the score,' said Naish. 'He knew it was his last chance to escape before the cell door closed behind him. He was bound to give it a go.'

'He must have had a deep suspicion of his mate, though, to have gone for him so suddenly,' said Newton.

'I think he has been suspicious of him for some time but has not dared to do what he wanted and do away with him. I think his lust for vengeance just got the better of him when he realised that this might be his last chance to take his revenge on a suspected traitor.'

'It just sounds very illogical to me. I mean, I get the revenge idea, but to murder a bloke in front of us is suicide, in effect,' said Hancock.

'As I say, the lust for revenge blanks out any thought of logical reason – assuming, of course, that he was capable of logical reason in the first place. I believe that he is the more culpable of the two. I think he knew he was at risk of being set up because, foolishly, he had committed the two murders and possibly conducted all of the torture. Being a sadist or psychopath, I know not which, he had enjoyed the role offered to him by Williams, but he was not intelligent enough to think through the consequences. Not of what would happen if he got caught, but understanding that he was placing himself at risk of carrying the can for everything if Williams and thug two decided to side together and sell him down the river, which, unless I am very much mistaken, they will try and do as soon as we begin to interview them. How is Mr Williams, by the way?'

'Indignant, I think would best describe it,' said Newton, 'playing the "I can't possibly imagine what this is all about role" at the moment, but I think he is worried.'

'Well, unless he is remarkably stupid, he has every reason to be worried. I imagine that he probably only thinks that we are on to his association with the thugs and the murders of Lynch and Edwards, although he will obviously begin with stout denial. He may have already contrived a plan with thug two to stitch up thug one. Thug two exonerates Williams in exchange for the promise of a substantial amount of cash to compensate him for a prison sentence for complicity to commit GBH, rather than life for murder.'

'Do you know something we don't?' asked Newton.

'No, it's just an assumption based on human nature and their individual circumstances,' said Naish.

'Why would thug two take a prison sentence for Williams?' asked Hancock.

'Because he is going inside either way, isn't he? Williams must have explained to him that the alternative is that he, Williams, says that both thugs were equally complicit in the murders and they both book a trip to the gallows. A jury would probably believe Williams's explanation of events over two thugs who, in all likelihood, would be quarrelling even in the dock.'

'And no one is going to believe that Williams committed the murders with those two henchmen there at the time. The worst that could happen for him if thug two doesn't exonerate him is that he goes inside for complicity,' said Newton.

'Exactly,' said Naish. 'How is Mr Emery reacting to his arrest by the way? Defiant and indignant, like Williams?'

'No, he is remarkably calm,' said Newton. 'He is refusing to say anything until he has spoken to his solicitor but appears almost resigned to the situation.'

'Whatever else he purports to be, he is clearly nobody's fool, and I wouldn't be surprised if he has realised the true extent of what we may know about his and Williams's activities. Given our involvement with him over the past couple of weeks, I think he may have a better idea than Williams,' said Naish. 'Other than his being aware of our interest in Emery and his shop, and the activities of his two thugs and Hancock calling at his gallery to ask about blue vans and brown coats, he is completely unaware of our interest in him.'

'It will be interesting when he sees Mr Bennett – erstwhile purchaser of works of art – come through the door of the interview room,' said Hancock.

'Yes, I am looking forward to that moment, as well,' said Naish. 'Although I have contempt for all of them involved in this business, I have the greatest antipathy for Williams.'

'Why is that, then?' asked Newton surprised.

'The two thugs are what they claim to be – I suspect they make no secret of their trade, despicable as it is – and Emery is what he is, a forger and a conman. In a way, Williams is no worse than Emery, in that he is a conman and a deceiver, but somehow it's the cold, calculated and merciless way that Williams orchestrated and oversaw the murder of Lynch and Edwards that I find most evil.'

'I see your point, but he has played a clever game in keeping himself at arm's length from this business over the years while pulling all the strings,' said Hancock.

'Indeed he has. But now it's over, and it is our job to bring this case to a satisfactory conclusion and get the appropriate convictions in the court. And I, as much as either of you, need to realise that we are not going to do that by getting emotionally involved at this late stage,' said Naish.

'Who do you want to interview first, Inspector?' asked Newton.

'Before we get on with the interviews, I want a full briefing of what was found at Swallow Street,' said Naish. 'Was it the place where Lynch and Edwards met their ends?'

'I think that it was, Inspector,' said Newton. 'I went around there after I had got Williams and Emery in the cells, and I am happy to take you round there now, if you wish to see it for yourself?'

'No, I am happy to take your findings as read.'

'There was no evidence in terms of an area of bloodstaining on the floors, but I imagine that they would have had the sense to have scrubbed that away.'

'Being professionals, I imagine that they sat their victims on a sheet or tarpaulin and wrapped up the body and the associated gore in it at the conclusion of the session,' said Naish.

'The main thing is that we found a chair with a high back, consistent with the injuries that were caused to the inside area of the upper arms of both Lynch and Edwards. There are two eye bolts screwed into each of the rear legs low down that I suspect the rope securing the victims was passed through, to hold them firmly. There was also a brazier made out of a dustbin which contained the residue of a coal fire, which would be consistent with what was needed to heat the poker that was used on Edwards.'

'How about the poker, hammer and other implements of torture?' asked Naish, impatiently.

'In a toolbox in a cupboard we did find a number of tools, including pliers and a hammer. The wooden handle of the hammer appeared to be darkened by what could be bloodstains. I could not find a poker, but I did find three lengths of iron rod which, looking at the end of one of them, appeared to show traces of having been heated in a fire – there was soot on the end and what may well be traces of flesh or skin on the very tip. I have arranged for all the tools to be sent away for analysis, if you are happy with that, Inspector?'

'Yes, that will be fine. Get them off as quickly as you can. Anything else?'

'Nothing linked to the torture, but there were a number of items that looked to have been cleared out from Emery's studio.'

'What were they?'

'Two artist's easels and a lot of small tins of paint, but no paintings or artworks.'

'No, I imagine that they went into the fire at the back of Emery's shop. They probably thought that the two easels were too chunky to risk putting in the brazier, in case they didn't burn right down to ash, so they took them back there in the van to dispose of later.'

'When you say tins, do you mean tubes?' asked Hancock.

'No, small tins about a quarter of a pint each, all marked up with handwritten labels. I thought it odd as well, as the only artist's paint that I have ever seen comes in those metal tubes. I suppose they would not have burnt either,' said Newton.

'The reason that they are in tins is because, I suspect, that they contain the handmade paints mixed by Emery to exactly replicate a paint mixture specific to the time of the painting that he was working on. Get them sent off for analysis to the people who looked at the paint samples we found on the top floor of Emery's shop. Anything else?'

'No, that was about it, Inspector, other than the blue van, of course.'

'Right, well, it is compelling enough evidence to put our suspects under some considerable pressure, even if we have not had it formally validated as yet. Right, then – back to the interviews. Get Emery in first. Has his solicitor arrived yet?'

'He was due in at seven, having been summoned from his bed. I was in the room when Emery called him,' said Newton.

'Good, then bring him up to the interview room at eight o'clock and I will be down to make a start,' said Naish.

'My client will be maintaining his right to silence, Inspector, until such time as he has been made fully aware of the charges that are being made against him. Furthermore, my client protests himself innocent of any wrongdoing,' said the solicitor sat beside Emery.

'It could be said that, despite your client's claim of innocence, his position of waiting to hear what he may be charged with rather suggests that he has got something to hide.'

'I categorically reject your interpretation of his lawful position in this matter.'

'Very well, Mr … ?'

'Sanderson.'

'Very well, Mr Sanderson. I accept your client's position, but I think it would be more helpful if he were to engage. However, I can do this either as dialogue or monologue, so, for the time being, I will begin a monologue. I think that you have been telling me fibs, Mr Emery,' began Naish, leaning forward on the table.

'Are you trying to lead my client into comment, Inspector?'

'No, I have clearly stated to you that I am beginning a monologue and, as such, any questions I put are merely intended to be rhetorical. But they may also be matters that your client may wish to reflect upon with you later in private, back in his cell. You see, Mr Emery, I am very strongly of the opinion that the second floor above your shop has, for a considerable period of time, been used as an artist's studio – and a most interesting artist's studio, at that. I believe that two substantial easels were set up opposite each other under the skylight in the roof. I am confident of there being two, confident of their location and confident that they were there for some considerable period of time. After the unfortunate fire that occurred at your premises, I made an examination of that second floor, and when I removed the newly fitted floor covering, I found heavy deposits of paint on the floorboards, the amount and position of which, I believe, will evidence my theory. Now, I can produce a couple of different theories of how somebody – let us call them the artist – came to be there every evening of the week in the hours after your shop closed for business. However, each theory is more convoluted and difficult to reconcile than the simple fact that the artist is you, Mr Emery. If I place you in that role, you see, everything fits into place naturally, and without any clever add-ons having to be incorporated to explain the presence of someone other than you. It ties in with the known facts of your movements connected with your business, as witnessed by your neighbours in Broadway Parade, and your domestic arrangements, which have also been witnessed by your housekeeper. So you see, Mr Emery, I am forced into the position of believing that you were being untruthful when you told me, on a number of occasions and in a formal witness statement that I have on file, that you possess no artistic talent whatsoever. You do remember saying that, don't you, Mr Emery, when we were discussing those sketchbooks that I recovered following the burglary at your shop?'

Naish paused and sat back and took a sip of water from a glass to let his words resonate with Emery and Sanderson. Having glanced at them both as if to confirm their lack of appetite to respond, he leant forward again and continued.

'Now, let us return to that unfortunate burglary committed on Tuesday the ninth of October, just over three weeks ago today. You may remember that, following that occurrence, I came to your shop to discuss a number of items that I had recovered from an address in the city that I believed to have been stolen from your premises. Although you denied any knowledge of either the two A3-sized sketchbooks or the canvases, I am now convinced, as a result of my enquiries, that they had indeed been at your premises. The precise semantics of whether they belonged to you or another individual is of no matter. They were there on the second floor in the vicinity of the easels and they were stolen by Edward Lynch on that Tuesday night. The sketches made in those two books were features of the elevations of the Assembly Rooms in Bennett Street in Bath. The complete address is pertinent because it is also the title of a painting by Walter Sickert that hangs in the Victoria Gallery. I believe that these sketches were intended to be used in the composition of two or three other paintings that were to be created of the other facades of that building, to fraudulently give the impression that they had been painted by Sickert as part of an – as yet undiscovered – series of paintings complementing the known work. I can see from your body language that my comments strike a chord with you, Mr Emery.'

'I protest. The insinuation that you can place an interpretation on my client's posture that leads to a conclusion that is to the detriment of his good character is farcical, Inspector.'

'Let me also point out, and entirely without any detrimental insinuation as to your good character, that I have witness testimony of your repeated visits to the Victoria Gallery, where you were observed making sketches of the work by Sickert of the Assembly Rooms.'

'My client's interests in the world of art are in no way an implication of guilt or involvement in whatever it is that you are attempting to insinuate, Inspector,' said Sanderson, becoming more animated.

'Very well, let us leave that matter for a moment and focus on another area,' said Naish, sipping at his water. 'Interesting as all these matters related to forgery in the art world may or may not be, the more important investigation that I am conducting concerns the brutal murder of two men – Edward Lynch and Thomas Edwards. As you will have gathered from my recent monologue, I have a view about your involvement in the forgery of artworks and I am confident that, with a little more work, I can prove beyond reasonable doubt that you were complicit in that crime. However, I can prove that the abduction, torture and murder of Ted Lynch, and probably Thomas Edwards, was consequent on the theft from your shop, and I can place you in direct association with the gang of murderers. In fact, I have witness testimony that you were seen meeting with one of the two men I suspect of perpetrating the murders in Parade Gardens. Now, I suspect that the examples of forgery that I have set out here are but a small part of a much larger and highly sophisticated operation that will require an in-depth investigation by experts, and, as such, I intend to pass my preliminary findings on to Scotland Yard's fraud squad. However, matters that occur in this city are my responsibility to pursue and mine alone and, as such, I am responsible for bringing the abductors, torturers and murderers of Lynch and Edwards to justice, and I will do that if it is the last thing that I do.'

'Are you threatening my client, Inspector?'

'Your client can take it how he wishes, but since he does not wish to enter into dialogue, I am setting out my case, to be open and transparent. If I wished to, I could choose not to disclose any of this information until due process requires it to be disclosed, and let your ill-advised client wait for formal charges to be placed and him enter pleas that he might live to regret. So, as I say, you and your client can take my monologue in any way that you choose, because it really is of no matter to me. Whilst the evidence of his association with the gang that committed these crimes is potentially damning, I have a view that, despite his association with these men, he is innocent of complicity in abduction, torture and murder. However, unless he is prepared to offer some comment on these matters, there is every possibility that he could find himself facing charges for these capital crimes.'

'We have been here for an hour and a quarter, now,' said Naish, looking at his watch. 'I am going to make one or two more observations – rhetorical observations, let me stress – and then I am going to leave you both to confer and consider your position. It may well be, Mr Sanderson, that some of what I have to say in conclusion turn out to be matters that Mr Emery has forgotten to mention to you when he briefed you. First, you may wonder why I am confident of your involvement in the wider undertaking to produce forged works of art. As you know, I have been to your home in St Mark's Road. What you may not know is that, when investigating those forged works of art on your sitting room wall, including the three Turners removed by Mr Williams and his thuggish associates, I found what you had managed to keep hidden from Williams – namely the safe hidden in your covert cellar containing a large number of forged provenance documents relating to a series of forgeries going back over a number of decades. In addition, I have found four examples of forged works of art hidden between sheets of plywood flooring in the attic of your home in St Mark's Road. The works in the cellar and the attic were carried out by a local locksmith and builder, and I have witness evidence that supports these facts. I see from the astonished look on both your faces, gentlemen, that you will need time to digest and then discuss this information. So, in parting, let me reiterate my position. I will pass the matters of fraud to Scotland Yard and you will have to answer for your role in that at another investigation, but if you are prepared to give me a detailed statement regarding your relationship and involvement with Mr Williams and his activities, it may well assist me in bringing him and his thugs to account and remove you from any risk of charges in connection with the crime of abduction, torture and murder that I am pursuing as matters pertaining to my direct area of responsibility. Do I make myself clear? Good. Then I will leave you to consider your position. If you wish to discuss the matter with me further, please let the constable know.'

Without further word or eye contact, Naish got up from the desk and left the interview room.

'Well, Powell,' said Naish, sitting back from the desk in a relaxed manner. 'If you want my honest opinion, I think that you are going to hang.'

The thug said nothing. He was sat next to the duty police solicitor and was cuffed at the wrists and the ankles. In addition, two constables stood behind his chair on either side, should he make any sudden movement.

'I mean that, while attempted murder is not a capital crime – even when inadvisably committed in front of half a dozen police officers – it is going to carry a life sentence, in my humble judgement,' continued Naish. 'But I have the suspicion that it is not that crime that I saw you commit an hour or so ago that will put you on the gallows. It is the other crimes that I suspect you to have perpetrated, namely the cold-blooded murder of Lynch and Edwards. I know what you were thinking, which is that you needed to silence your colleague, no matter how desperate the attack may appear, in order to prevent him telling us everything about those murders in order to save his own skin. Your desperation is, to me, a sign of the desperate situation you are in. You see, in that moment that we burst in I think that your true nature came through. I think that you suspected what was not, in fact, true – that your colleague had shopped you to us – and your anger and desire for revenge was so strong it blinded any common sense from your mind and you went for him. Probably driven by revenge for what you perceived as treachery, you grabbed your knife and went for him and, I have to say, very nearly succeeded. Now, I have not had the opportunity to ask him, as yet, but I think we both know that he will be making a full and frank confession of what he knows of the two murders as soon as he is sufficiently recovered. And when he does, that is you in the dock for double murder with menaces.'

Naish paused and looked from Powell to the solicitor. Powell sat with his head down, as if accepting of Naish's summary of the situation. The solicitor shrugged his shoulders as his eyes met Naish's, and so he continued.

'Now, I can understand that you may not wish to make any statement at all, as, no matter how cooperative you might choose to be, we both know it is not going to alter your eventual appointment with the hangman, but I will say this: your colleague will undoubtedly make a full and complete confession and will, in all probability, get a reduced sentence, but that is not a given. Emery, the forger, as you know, has no direct role in the matters surrounding these two murders. However, I have sufficient information and evidence of his activities in association with Williams to prompt a full investigation to be carried out by Scotland Yard regarding a matter of fraud. Now, although your colleague will make a full confession, I have a suspicion that what he may well do is only implicate you and play down, to the absolute minimum, the role of Mr Williams.'

Powell's head rose for the first time and he fixed Naish with a quizzical stare behind which Naish could see that anger bubbling just below the surface.

'Ah, I see I have interested you,' said Naish, calmly lighting a cigarette. 'You see, I know that it was you that drove the knife into Lynch and Edwards and, after what you did to your colleague, no jury is going to believe you if you tried to argue otherwise. He knows that, and I can imagine he is working on the theory that if he can get his own sentence reduced by putting all of the chilling events of the tortures on to you, he may very well succeed. He will get a sentence, there is no doubt of that, because when the cold horrifying detail of those tortures is read out in court, action by action, it will turn the jury against the pair of you, probably more than the murders themselves. Now, you think he won't get away with that because Williams has to testify as well, and you think he will explain how the two of you carried out the torture, both playing an equal role in the brutality while Williams directed the operation. But think on this. If your colleague can minimise his own role to that of a supporting one in the treatment of Lynch and Edwards and paints Williams out of it completely, saying that he was not there but set out instructions as to what was to be done, then that's you carrying the can for them both, isn't it?'

Real anger flashed into Powell's eyes, and the two constables made to move as he flinched as if to try and stand up. Naish sat calm and took a deep drag on his cigarette.

'I can see that even you have worked it out now. Your colleague puts everything on you and paints Williams out of it in the assumption that, when he has completed his sentence, Williams will be there waiting for him with a pay-off at the prison gates as his reward for protecting him. Now, that may be a bit naive on his part but, either way, it's a better alternative to a life sentence for just taking what's coming to him as his just deserts. Because I know he is as guilty as you in terms of the torture – there is no way that what was done was not done by two men acting together – but with a good barrister and a sympathetic jury, he may well pull it off. So, I will leave you and your solicitor to think it over. If you want to discuss anything with me just let one of these officers know.'

'You have a talent for sowing the seeds of doubt and double-crossing in their minds,' said Hancock, with a smile.

'What I told them was no more than a perfectly likely scenario based on the facts. I appreciate that it is not the only scenario that can be constructed from the facts, but it is none the less honest. The fact that it may get them to double-cross each other is a pure coincidence. In fact, the beauty of it may be that we get the truth out of all of them as a result of their individual motivations to do down the others.'

'And save their own skins?'

'Emery will, thug two might, but Powell is already on his way to the gallows, in my opinion. As for Williams, we will find out when I have had the chance to interview him. However, even if Emery and Williams dodge the bullet on this one, I can't see then evading a spell in prison once Scotland Yard have trawled through the facts that we have surrounding this forgery enterprise.'

'Shall I get Williams up to the interview room, Inspector?' asked Newton.

'It's getting on for twelve now,' said Naish, glancing at his watch. 'I prefer to take an hour to review my notes before I sit down with Williams and his brief, so if you two want to get yourselves some lunch I suggest that you do that, and get Williams ready for me in the interview room at one o'clock sharp.

'If I am going over to the market to get some rolls, do you fancy one, Inspector?' asked Newton.

'No, I am fine with this,' said Naish, holding up his tobacco tin with a smile, 'but a mug of tea would be appreciated when you make one.'

Chapter 22

'Mr Bennett?' exclaimed Williams, in an astonished tone.

'Ah, I see that I need to offer an explanation to you, Mr Williams,' said Naish, with a smile.

'What is going on here?' asked Williams's solicitor.

'My name is Inspector Naish, gentlemen. I have been making some investigations into a number of crimes which I believe that you, Mr Williams, are involved in. As part of my investigation I posed as a Mr Bennett and made a number of visits to your client's Byfield Gallery in Wood Street. You are Mr … ?'

'I am Mr Stone and I represent Mr Williams,' said the solicitor, 'and I have to say that this is most irregular, and I object to this interview continuing until my client and I have had the opportunity to consider this extraordinary situation. In my view, it may seriously compromise any case that you have against my client.'

'Extraordinary yes, irregular no,' said Naish, emphatically. 'I checked the legality of my position before I assumed the role of Mr Bennett and I am confident that it in no way compromises the case against your client. You see, the crucial matter is that I did not lead him into making any confession or revealing anything about his involvement in this case – that is the role of this interview. All that I did was to ingratiate myself into his society and learn a little about his business and activities. He told me no more than he would have revealed to another client, had he been asked. So, I am confident that there is no obstacle to this interview continuing. We can take an adjournment if you wish, but the direction of my interview will be exactly the same either way. What do you wish to do?'

'We will continue, but I want a note made that I have raised my objection none the less,' said Stone, after a brief, whispered conversation with Williams.

'Very well, then,' said Naish, sitting down and taking out his tobacco tin and placing it on the table. 'Where to begin? How about you explain to me your relationship with Mr Emery and his work for you at his premises in Broadway Parade.'

'My client has no comment to make at this time, Inspector,' said the solicitor, having conferred with Williams.

'Everyone I want to enter into dialogue with about this case is giving me the cold shoulder,' said Naish. 'You want to play the wait and see game as well, then – wait and see what it is I know about you all, hey? I could be difficult, but the approach I am taking is to be open and honest and set out what I know about the crimes that have been committed and outline the consequences that each of the players faces.'

'My client is not in association with anyone with intent to commit crime, Inspector.'

'Maybe, maybe not,' said Naish

'What do you mean by that remark?'

'Let me continue,' said Naish, ignoring the comment. 'Just to be helpful, let me embark on a little monologue that sets out what I think your relationship with Emery is in connection with his shop in Broadway Parade. On the morning of Wednesday the tenth of October, Emery arrives at his shop as usual but soon realises that the front door has been forced open during the night. I think that he goes in and makes a quick appraisal of the situation and concludes that he has been the victim of a burglary and fortunately, from what he can ascertain, nothing other than his tools and some petty cash from the till has been taken. However, I think that he then telephoned you to report what had happened before he even rang the station, as he was requested to do in the note left by the beat constable who had discovered the crime.'

Naish paused, sipped his water and looked at Williams and Stone to see if they wished to comment, and then continued.

'Now, that is interesting isn't it? Why would a small-time shopkeeper in an unfashionable part of the city telephone you, the owner of probably the most exclusive gallery in Bath? A shopkeeper who, in all normal circumstances, you would probably not give the time of day to? That's the question that I keep asking myself.'

'Is this a fishing expedition, Inspector, or do you base these ludicrous accusations on the testimony of witnesses?' barked Stone.

'As I say, I am trying to be open and honest with you,' said Naish, inwardly pleased at having provoked such a response. 'However, I am not revealing what has or has not been said to me by any of your associates in this business, I am afraid. Open and honest I may be, but foolhardy, no, particularly as you are choosing to be so taciturn.'

'My client is doing no more than his rights permit him, Inspector.'

'And I am doing no more than my rights allow me. So, the answer to myself is that Mr Williams must have some interest in this shop. I think that you make your way round to Broadway Parade to see the situation for yourself, because I think that you have a particular interest in what is going on up on the second floor of Mr Emery's shop.'

'There is no evidence of any such connection as you insinuate, Inspector,' interrupted Stone again.

'Oh, but there is,' said Naish, cutting him off. 'There is the matter of some very interesting wooden frames on which canvases are stretched. You see, I may be no expert in the field of art but I am something of an expert in the field of detection and I see an uncanny similarity between the handcrafted frames in the workshops at the Byfield Gallery and those in the workshop of Mr Emery there in Broadway Parade. Now, I accept that I will need to have that similarity tested by experts, but for now I am satisfied that they will endorse my suspicion. Anyway, back to the monologue. You arrive at Broadway Parade and you conduct your own inspection of the premises and it is while you are doing this that you and Emery notice that two A3 sketchbooks and some canvases that have light sketches on them have been stolen during the burglary, and it is at this point that I believe you make your fundamental and fatal mistake. Fatal, that is, not only for you, but more importantly for Ted Lynch.'

Naish paused again and glanced first at Williams and then at Stone. Both, however, remained implacable and so, having sipped his water for effect as much as refreshment, he continued.

'You see, my theory is that up there on the second floor, on two easels set up opposite each other under the skylight, were two of three paintings that Emery was working on from the sketches in the two A3 books, and that those paintings not yet completed were of three elevations of the Assembly Rooms in Bennett Street in the style of Walter Sickert. You made the unwarranted leap of imagination to assume that the burglary had been perpetrated by someone acting for a gang who had compromised your forgery business, or else someone who intended to possibly blackmail you over the matter. I don't think that you could decide which it was, but you knew that it was imperative to track down the perpetrator of the crime, get the truth out of him and dispose of him. So, you immediately brought in the two thugs from outside Bath that you retained to do any dirty work that may arise in connection with your illegal activities and set them on the task of tracking down this unknown burglar. I don't think it took them long to establish themselves in the city and get to know where to ask around within the criminal fraternity and, within a short period of time, they soon spotted Ted Lynch – not the most discreet of characters in his new suit and a bit flash with his newly acquired cash. So, probably after a few follow-up conversations, accompanied by suitable threats of violence, they had the confirmation that they needed. Now, it was probably during those investigations that they identified Lynch's new-found friend Thomas Edwards who, I suspect, not only told them everything they wanted to know about Lynch's recent criminal activities but also agreed, probably under coercion, to deliver Lynch into their hands. I suspect that he did this not only because he was under threat but, in fairness to him, to protect Lynch's landlady from getting involved in any danger. So, six days after the burglary, on the night of Monday the fifteenth of October, Edwards, dressed in his clerical costume, calls on Lynch at his lodgings and – probably on the pretext of taking him for a drink – leaves the lodgings and sets off with Lynch to take him to a preordained location where your two thugs abduct him and take him to a garage in Swallow Street. Any of this strike a chord, gentlemen?'

'My client is wisely not going to be provoked by outrageous provocations in, what I have already identified, as your fishing expedition, Inspector. But, pray, continue to relate your fantasy if you wish. It is of no matter to me or my client.'

'I will say that your client appears particularly attentive to what I have to say, to my mind, but that is of no matter for now. Anyway, back to my monologue. It is just an interesting coincidence, I am sure, but later on that Monday night I have a witness statement that Edwards is seen back at his lodgings in the company of one of the thugs and, interestingly, he is passed a brown envelope by the thug before they part company. Now, it's also odd, isn't it, that I find in Edwards's lodgings, after he subsequently goes missing, twenty-five pounds in five pound notes tucked into his post office savings book. I know he hadn't withdrawn it, so he must have acquired it and been going to pay it in. And the most interesting part of it is that I have the serial numbers of those notes.'

'However, back with Ted Lynch. You have him brought to Swallow Street where he is bound in a chair and subjected to a horrifying process of torture over which you presided, Mr Williams. It was you that watched as he was first punched across the face, and I suspect that you let two or three land before emerging from the shadows to pose a series of questions as to what he had seen and why he had stolen the sketchbooks and canvases. He had been up there on the second floor, I know that for a fact – the paint in the treads of his shoes matched the paint that I removed from beneath the newly laid linoleum on the second floor. He saw everything on the second floor, but he understood nothing of its purpose. So when he told you that he knew nothing, he was telling the truth, because you didn't know what I have always known about Ted Lynch – that is he is no more than a petty thief, nothing more nothing less. And I know why he stole those sketchbooks and canvases – because he wanted to help out a friend. Your paranoia about some plot to infiltrate your forgery business must have been overwhelming. Surely it must have dawned on you that Lynch had not gone in there to abstract items to use to either blackmail you or in some other way compromise your operation. Clearly, he had not the intelligence to conceive such an operation himself, and on top of that you must have questioned why a man commissioned to break into your premises and remove incriminating items would have stopped to steal a few coins and some worthless tools in the process. In addition to that, did it not enter your mind that as this man screamed for mercy and pleaded that he knew nothing of what you were suggesting he was actually telling the truth? He would have sung like a canary before the first punch was landed, I know that to be a fact. I find it unimaginable that, at some point in that cowardly and sickening process of torture, it did not occur to you that he knew nothing at all and that was the reason for his silence. He was, however, braver than any of us probably realise because this is where he turned the tables on Edwards. He clearly knew that he had been betrayed by Edwards and so he managed to do two clever things. He decided to tell you that Edwards had the sketchbooks and the canvases. His first purpose was, in all probability, to protect his landlady from receiving a visit from your thugs, since that is where he had secreted them. His second purpose was so that you would get hold of Edwards and, in all probability, do exactly what you did – torture him to find out what he had done with the sketchbooks he, in fact, never had possession of. And Lynch knew that the consequence of that would be that you would torture Edwards to death trying to get him to reveal something he did not know. You did, and so you and your two thugs delivered to Edwards the revenge that Lynch wanted. Not such a fool after all, was he? Anyway, back with Lynch. At the end of this sadistic and pointless torture, your head thug, Powell, drove a knife between his ribs with the precision of a hitman and that was the end of him. You then have a corpse on your hands, and, in its disposal, you went on to make another mistake.'

'You are frustrated because, despite the violence and the terror you have perpetrated, you are no nearer understanding who it is that you mistakenly believe to be behind this intrusion into your business. So, instead of taking him out into the countryside and burying him in a field in the middle of nowhere, you decide to string him up publicly, to try and ward off whoever it is that is behind Lynch. So you take him along to Widcombe – probably in the back of the blue Bedford van – and you have him suspended from his neck beneath the footbridge. It was your misjudgement in that act that made me first suspect that there was something more to this case than at first met the eye.'

Naish paused and took time to look long and slowly at Williams and he did not divert his gaze as he opened his tin and took out a pre-rolled cigarette.

'Are you attempting to intimidate my client, Inspector?' asked the solicitor.

'With my gaze or with the considerable number of facts that I have laid before him?' asked Naish, without taking his eyes off Williams.

'You have produced nothing to substantiate any of your comments, as I will call them, to demonstrate that they are capable of being classed as facts, Inspector,' said the solicitor, angrily.

'I am under no obligation to do that at this stage, but I can prove them, and I will prove them. And the few pieces of evidence that I am missing I will have as soon as Mr Williams's associates have given me their formal statements setting out their version of the events,' said Naish, turning to Stone and lighting his cigarette. 'As I said at the beginning of this interview, I am being open and honest with you as to what I know. It is up to you if your client wishes to take that opportunity to set out fully his role in these matters if he wishes to mitigate the consequences of his crimes and limit his exposure to only what he has done, rather than find himself the scapegoat for the collusion of his two thuggish employees and Mr Emery. As I say, it is your choice, it really makes no odds to me. Now, I could go on with another monologue about the abduction, torture and murder of Thomas Edwards but I really see no point in that, other than to point out that I have as many facts as to that matter as I have about Lynch. Now, I think it is time for a break. I suggest that we adjourn for an hour and then reconvene, as there are some other matters I need to discuss with you. It may be another monologue, but I would hope that, after some reflection, you decide to at least contribute to the process, if not completely cooperate.'

Naish got up, picked up his tin from the table and left without another word or another glance at Williams.

'I am going for a walk,' said Naish, out in the corridor. 'There is something about Williams – that simpering smugness and the air of superiority – which gets under my skin. I need to take a breath of fresh air before he angers me into doing or saying something that I will regret.'

'Do you want me to come along with you, in case you want someone to rant at?' asked Hancock, without any hint of levity.

'No, I will be fine on my own, thanks. Make sure that he and his solicitor are given every facility so that we cannot be criticised and tell them that we will reconvene the interview at three o'clock sharp.'

'Right, gentlemen. If you have had the time to refresh yourselves and consider the matters that we have begun to examine, I will recommence, unless you have anything that you wish to make observations on?'

'My client does not wish at this stage to alter his position of refraining from comment until you have concluded what I think we can agree to describe as your monologue, Inspector,' said Stone, in what was a noticeably more conciliatory tone. 'However, having had the opportunity to discuss the matter in detail with my client during the recess, we may, having heard the conclusion of your monologue, wish to offer a statement setting out my client's position on the matters that you have raised.'

Naish betrayed no emotion but smiled inwardly as he realised that the pressure was beginning to tell on Williams.

'That would be a useful development in moving the case forward,' said Naish, dispassionately. 'In light of that, I will set out a short summary of each of the other concerns that I have which I think that your client needs to address in connection with this matter.'

'I have to tell you now, Inspector, that my client is confident that we will be able to produce witness testimony that will show that he was in no way involved in the process of abduction, torture and murder that you have described.'

'I assume that the production of that evidence depends on thug two surviving the injuries inflicted on him by his opposite number,' said Naish. 'I see from your reactions that you were unaware that he had been a victim of such an assault. Yes, he is at this moment gravely ill in hospital. I am advised that he is expected to make a recovery, but you may wish to have a second string to your defence bow should he not.'

'When did this occur?' asked Stone, after a whispered conversation with Williams.

'It occurred in the early hours of this morning when the pair were arrested in the rooms at the back of your client's gallery in Wood Street. Anyway, back to my monologue,' continued Naish, pleased at the unease his statement had roused in the two men opposite him. 'Mr Emery is a very extraordinary man, is he not? A man of apparently modest means, given the nature of his business in Broadway Parade – a good business – and I am sure it returns a reasonable income, but I cannot see how it generates the wealth needed to match the purchase price of seven – if you include his home in St Mark's Road – substantial houses in this city. The conundrum to me is, if you owned such wealth, why work in such a modest business? Personally, I would sell up and retire rather than work all hours for such meagre returns, unless, of course, there was something else beneath the surface of my modest business that was generating more substantial sums of money.'

Naish paused and took a sip from his glass of water whilst looking first at Williams and then to Stone. Pleased to see the unease in their eyes, he continued.

'He is, of course, not new to this sort of business. I am reliably informed that he ran a similar business in London some years ago, in Lambeth to be precise, and the oddest fact is that the premises were owned by a company called Cotman Holdings who, by some coincidence, pay the business rates on a garage in Swallow Street where Lynch and Edwards were murdered. Odd things, these holding companies,' said Naish, continuing calmly, having noted again the unease his comments had provoked. 'Particularly as some of them are registered overseas – you know, Switzerland and places like that. Derwent Holdings, for example, is such a company and again, by some coincidence, Derwent Holdings was the previous owner of each of the houses that Mr Emery purchased in this city. Not long-term owners, as one might expect from an investment company – they owned each of them for only a matter of months before Mr Emery purchased them. Now, these are deep matters and I have not got the resources or the inclination to look into all the facts behind these coincidences beyond where they impinge upon my own enquiries. As I have said before, I am concerned with the solving of crimes perpetrated within this city, but I have no doubt that when I pass all of what I know to Scotland Yard's fraud department they will quickly get to the bottom of what I believe to be a sophisticated conspiracy to commit fraud. Now, that takes me back to Mr Emery, you see. I should probably not disclose what I am about to say to you, but I am fairly confident that you know some of the details already. You became aware that Emery may have some works of art that would be of interest to you at his home in St Mark's Road. I think that you were tipped off by thug two who, for one reason or another, had formed a connection with Emery. Either because he was instructed to do so by you to gain his confidence on the pretext of his losing his nerve due to how the matters related to Lynch and Edwards had played out, or because he genuinely had turned to Emery in desperation of the situation he found himself to be in. Further information about what was inside the house may also have been obtained from Emery's housekeeper by the bogus milkman who one of my officers had the pleasure of meeting. Whatever the motivation was, you were taken by the two thugs in the blue Bedford van that was garaged in Swallow Street up to Emery's house last Friday night at about two o'clock in the morning to find out what was there for yourself.'

'Again, Inspector, I must protest,' said Stone. 'My client has offered, in good faith, to consider making a statement, but this provocation will prove counterproductive.'

'Let me tell you something in good faith,' said Naish, leaning forward across the desk with a dark look on his face. 'Your client's statement is of no weight to me. I don't need his cooperation to prosecute my case. It will only serve to support his defence, and if it is honest then it may serve to tidy up a few loose ends that I may have, but they are nothing more than loose ends. I am confident I have all the facts that a jury will require, including witness testimony, to put your client in that van in the company of the two thugs on the night in question.'

Naish sat back and took a cigarette from his tin and without asking if he may, he lit up, took two deep drags and, in light of the silence from Williams and Stone and having composed himself, he continued.

'I will offer you these last observations and then I will leave you to consider your position. It is my belief that in the drawing room of Emery's house you discovered nine small oil paintings. You realised that they were all forgeries by Emery. Six were minor artists, possibly done by Emery for practice or for his own pleasure, but three of them concerned you because they were smaller versions of paintings that Emery had produced and which you subsequently sold to the public as the miraculously discovered Turners – the ones that Professor Andrews was so unfortunate to be deceived by. Oh yes, I have spoken with the Professor at length. You removed them and, having secured them, you presumably decided to take up with Emery – when you eventually tracked him down – whether they were just for his ill-judged amusement or evidence he had double-crossed you, and had kept them as an investment for himself. It was, of course, vital to you that there were no other paintings than the ones you controlled, as any others turning up could destabilise your enterprise. It was this paranoia to control that had led you to overreact in the case of Lynch. Anyway, you left with the three paintings, presumably content that you had negated any risk to your operation. Well, for what it is worth, you didn't. Don't bother to protest or interrupt me, I am nearly done. In the basement was a safe and in the safe are a collection of papers, and possibly additional documents not used at the time, that were produced by Emery as the provenance documents for each of the frauds that were perpetrated. In addition to which I found in the attic four paintings that I believe Emery painted surreptitiously. Every now and again he would paint an additional painting in one of the series that he was painting for you. So, there it is. He was playing you and, no, you didn't secure all the evidence that evening.'

'Now I have done what I said I would do and set out some of what I have uncovered in my investigation, being, as I said, open and honest. You now need to consider your defence and any statement that you may wish to make. Oh, and before I go,' said Naish, as he rose from his chair and put his tin in his pocket, 'think on those bank notes and the serial numbers that I have. I am awaiting the definitive information as to whom they were issued, and I will be interested to have my suspicions confirmed.'

Naish wandered along the corridor to the foyer with Hancock and Newton following silently.

'Before we finish for the day, I want one last word with Emery,' said Naish. 'Bring him up to the interview room but before you get him, I want you to go up to my office and bring down the painting that we got from the attic that has the label with Constable on it. Put it on a chair in the interview room and then bring him up.'

Naish lit a cigarette to help gather his thoughts and made his way back to the interview room.

'Ready for us to get Emery and his solicitor, Inspector?' asked Newton.

Naish nodded in the affirmative and Newton and Hancock disappeared to the cells.

'I had understood that you were not proposing to interview my client until we had considered our position,' said Sanderson, formally, but without the combative tone he had previously employed.

'It is with a view to allowing your client to better understand the evidence that I have against him that I have decided to offer you this additional information,' said Naish, calmly. 'It appeared to me at the conclusion of our last interview that some of the facts that I had set out left you surprised as to the extent of what I had learnt. However, on reflection I think that I want to go over one matter again in greater detail. I will explain why once I have concluded my remarks.'

Naish got up and went over to the painting on the chair and removed the blanket covering it.

'Now this is a very interesting painting, in my opinion,' said Naish, 'from the point of view of a detective rather than a student of art, you understand. It is signed John Constable and, as you gentlemen will appreciate more than I, the style is unmistakably that of the celebrated English artist. It is dated 1822 and from my recent but limited studies of art that suggests that it was painted a year after he completed his celebrated painting "The Hay Wain". Interestingly, I can find no record of this painting in any of the books on Constable that I have been able to study in the past few weeks. Now, that may be because my studies are very limited, but I have a suspicion that even if I were to seek the opinion of Professor Andrews or one of his learned colleagues they would come to the same conclusion – that this work was unknown.'

Naish paused and looked at Emery and Sanderson before resuming.

'The most interesting points of this painting, as I am sure you will appreciate, are that the scene is of Flatford Mill on the river Stour, a regular setting for some of Constable's most celebrated works. But this particular view of the mill and the river is, as far as I can tell, not one that has featured in any of his works before. It is also interesting because, on the far side of this ford, we have two horse-drawn carts, or, as they should more accurately be described, hay wains, about to cross the river. A very interesting scene, I am sure you will agree. It is untitled, but an accurate title might just be "Flatford Mill Meets

The Hay Wain" – a true Constable highbred. Now, I chose this particular painting from the collection in the attic at St Mark's Road because I was reminded of some comments that Professor Andrews made following his examination of the documents that were found in the safe in the cellar. The Professor stated that all the documents in the box that was marked 1949 dated from around 1822 and referred to the artist John Constable, and, while ostensibly about the two celebrated Constables discovered by Williams in 1949, they also alluded to another painting that was as yet undiscovered. Now, once again my knowledge is strictly limited, but I am confident that, if the documents were reviewed in greater scrutiny with this painting beside them, it would be apparent that this was the painting hinted at in those documents – the documents that would provide the provenance required to convince any sceptical members of the art establishment, or, more importantly, any nervous investors in the art market. Because these documents, like this very fine painting, are all forgeries and forged by a highly talented forger working for a highly polished and efficient business headed by Mr Williams with you, Mr Emery, in the role of forger.'

Emery and Sanderson conferred in a whisper but said nothing to Naish.

'Returning to my earlier comment, Mr Emery, my intention is to set out the completeness of my case against you, in the hope that you will produce a complete statement as to both your involvement in this business and what else you know about how it was operated and run by Williams. You may choose to construct a defence that seeks to distance you from the role of forger but, in my view, the evidence that I have will not allow you to do that, and, once your lies are exposed in the court, the jury will, of course, have little faith in the rest of your testimony, no matter how honest it may be. If I am honest with you, I am certain that you are looking at a term of imprisonment, but your associates in this matter – Williams and his two henchmen – are looking, in all likelihood, at the gallows. So, rather than seeking to avoid a sentence which I think is unrealistic, I am suggesting that you might wish to make a full and frank confession which, in all likelihood, will result in your sentence being as lenient as the judge can allow.'

'Would you be prepared to make a statement as to my client's cooperation with a view to a reduced sentence, Inspector?'

'Yes, I would consider that, but only once I have read your client's complete and signed statement.'

'What guarantee can we have that once you are in possession of such a statement you would not subsequently renege on this offer?' said Sanderson.

'You will have to accept my word. You have seen how I have proceeded in this matter. I am afraid it is for you and your client to decide whether you prefer to trust me or not. It is getting late so I will add one other thought in closing. Professor Andrews made an interesting comment when he saw the paintings hung together in your drawing room, Mr Emery. He said, no matter how well a painting is forged, it is when they are hung together in close proximity that insignificant but tell-tale signs appear – those little brush marks that seen in a single painting excite no comment but seen replicated in a series of paintings reveal the hand of the forger. I am very confident that, when the paintings that you have forged over the years are compared along with these four paintings from your attic, Professor Andrews and his learned colleagues will make the link between them that will lead all the way back to you, Mr Emery.'

As Naish got up to leave, Sanderson rose from his chair and followed him into the corridor.

'Inspector Naish, might I have a word?'

'Of course. What do you wish to discuss?'

'Clearly, my client is in a very grave position. I did not mean to cast doubt on the sincerity of your word in there just now, it was clumsy of me. But I would like to know how we may best proceed with my client's statement?'

'It is very simple, Mr Sanderson,' said Naish, leaning up against the corridor wall. 'Firstly, your client produces a statement that sets out the history of this business as far back as his days in the Lambeth gallery right through to today. Secondly, he sets out all that he knows about the break-in at his shop perpetrated by Edward Lynch and how Williams and his henchmen tracked down and murdered Lynch and Edwards. I know that he was not involved or even an accessory, but I am clear that he knows something. You get him to set all that out in a comprehensive statement. You hand it to me to read and consider. We will then meet and discuss it. If I am satisfied then I will provide the statement regarding Emery's cooperation with the police and a request that his cooperation be considered by the judge when handing down his sentence. I think that is fair?'

'I think it fair as well,' said Sanderson, reaching out to shake Naish's hand. 'It will take me most of tomorrow, but I would hope to have a draft for your consideration by late morning if that is in order?'

'That will be fine,' said Naish. 'I will be in the station all day.'

Chapter 23

'Good morning, gentlemen,' said Naish, as he came into his office and hung his hat on the stand. 'What are you two up to?'

'We were reviewing the statements and evidence to see where we needed to tie up any loose ends,' said Newton.

'Excellent,' said Naish. 'You must excuse my late appearance, but I have been up at the hospital interviewing Rodgers.'

'Rodgers?' enquired Hancock.

'Better known as thug two,' said Naish.

'Was he very informative?'

'He was not only informative but also very cooperative. As I had thought, he is prepared to tell us what he knows about Williams and Powell, hoping that his cooperation might get him a life sentence rather than face the gallows. Oddly enough, he was very frank about his own involvement.'

'Do you believe him?' asked Newton.

'Yes, I do, at least in the substance of what he says. He may have revised the odd detail to his advantage, but he knows that if the main features of his statement are at odds with the others' then his credibility is damaged, and thereby his chances of a reduced sentence.'

'So, what have you learnt?' asked Hancock.

'I need some time to reflect on it all. It is getting on for half past ten now and I am expecting a draft of Emery's statement at about noon. If we meet here at two o'clock, I will be in a position to tell you my conclusions.'

At two o'clock, Hancock and Newton returned to Naish's office and sat opposite him across the desk.

'Right, then. Let's make a start. I have finished reading Emery's draft statement and I have to say that I am satisfied with it. It also supports the interview that I have had with Rodgers and, to a lesser extent, Powell. So, I think we are as near to the truth as we will probably get. According to Emery, he first met Williams in London in 1923. Williams was working for an auction house and was looking for a skilled restorer to retain on the books, as they had had an occasional need for such services. Having seen the quality of Emery's work, Williams floated the suggestion that he would make a better income as a forger. Emery agreed and produced his first forgery – nothing major, just a simple forgery of a minor Victorian artist who was popular among collectors at that time. Once the work was finished, Williams took it along to the auction house and showed it to the director claiming that a woman had brought it along for sale. He was uncertain as to how the work would be received and nervous that it might immediately be identified as a forgery by the director. To distance himself from the painting, he created a false name and address for the lady together with a typed letter of authority for its sale signed by Emery, mimicking the signature of an aunt of his. To his amazement, the director waved the painting through and put an estimate on it of ten pounds. On the day of the sale, Williams was again nervous that, once scrutinized by the collectors attending the sale, the forgery might be exposed or at least questioned. However, he had nothing to fear, and the painting went into the auction and sold for eighteen pounds. Williams collected the money on the strength of the letter of authority, saying he would deliver the proceeds to the old lady. He returned the following day with a receipt signed by Emery. Emery and Williams split the proceeds fifty-fifty and their career as partners in crime began.'

'Emery continued to produce the works and Williams passed them off through his employer's establishment but increasingly through other auction houses. As his confidence in Emery's skills began to grow, he dispensed with the need of claiming to be acting on behalf of a third party and sold the paintings as his own property, developing the persona of an art collector.' 'As their income grew, Williams established Cotman Holdings as the financial entity that managed the assets of their enterprise. In 1925 Williams resigned from the auction house and set himself up in the art gallery in Westminster that Newton tracked down and set up Emery in his workshop in Lambeth.'

'The partnership continued to flourish, although they limited their forgery to the works of minor artists, still hesitant of pushing their luck too far. Williams didn't pass off any of the forgeries through the gallery, but he used his growing reputation as a dealer and an expert in fine art to validate the forgeries, passing them off to other dealers and through auction houses. It was when a minor challenge was put as to the authenticity of one of Emery's works that Williams recalled how Emery had copied the signature of his aunt on the letter of authentication. Working together using Williams's knowledge of art history and Emery's skilled hand, they produced their first forged provenance document – a letter from the artist offering the painting in question to a friend as a gift. Williams produced the letter to support the picture and all doubts immediately passed, to the extent that the painting made three times the estimate at the auction.'

'In 1925 they decided to make their first big play with a large painting by a significant artist. Emery set to work on a painting in the style of Gainsborough while Williams drafted some documents to support its provenance. By the end of 1925 it was completed and Williams, with some trepidation, brought the painting to market. To mitigate the risk to themselves, he reverted to his original ploy of acting on behalf of a third party who wished to remain distant from the sale. The plan was that if the painting was exposed as a forgery the main risk to Williams was only that his reputation as an art historian and dealer would be tarnished for having been taken in, while the phantom seller would, of course, have vanished without trace.'

'Hence the first dated box being 1925,' said Hancock.

'Exactly, and the painting passed off without question. The financial returns were enormous, and Williams and Emery were set on their path of forging significant works of art. It was at this time that Williams established Derwent Holdings to manage the profits from the crimes so that the income would not feature in the accounts of Cotman Holdings, the entity fronting their allegedly legitimate business.'

'All went well until the beginning of 1931, when an organised crime syndicate began to take an interest in Williams's new-found wealth. At first, they were only seeking protection money, but Williams, in particular, was concerned that their interest might lead them to discovering the means by which they were making their money. He was particularly concerned that if they got hold of Emery, he would, under threat, reveal all.'

'So, he found his two thugs, Powell and Rodgers, to counter the protection men, but organised crime is too big for a small business to fight, no matter how brutal your henchmen may be. Williams grew increasingly concerned when Emery's workshop was broken into by the protection men and their pushing of a simple protection racket turned to threats of blackmail. So, Williams devised a plan before things could go any further. He agreed to pay the blackmail and met with the leader and his henchman who had carried out the burglary. The meeting took place at a disused warehouse in Lambeth, but the meeting was in fact an ambush organised by Williams. Powell and Rodgers emerged from hiding and murdered the blackmailer and his henchman.'

'Williams realised that while he could stem the interest in his business by this one gang, he could not stave off the attention that his actions would incur from the other organised crime gangs in the capital. So, he timed his liquidation of the gang with his exodus from London. Overnight, he left his gallery and Emery left his premises in

Lambeth and they disappeared for six months, hiding in a hotel in Bournemouth until things had cooled down. In the meantime, Cotman Holdings had sold its London-based interests and eventually Emery relocated his business to Bath, replicating on a slightly smaller scale the set-up he had had in London.'

'So, by the end of 1932 everything was perfect once more. Williams and Emery continued their successful forgery enterprise and after two years Williams was satisfied that he had shaken off the London crime gangs, who had either lost interest in tracking him down or had given up the challenge as soon as he had left London. Either way the business thrived.'

'Williams's big mistake was to use Cotman Holdings to purchase the properties in Bath in which he established his new business – Wood Street for the gallery and Swallow Street as a base for Powell and Rodgers, who Williams had brought with him as his own insurance policy against any further unwanted interest in his affairs. Had he set up another holding company or changed its name, Newton may never have made the link that he did.'

Derwent Holdings continued its function for channelling the profits of the business to Williams and Emery. No doubt Scotland Yard will get to the bottom of how and where Williams syphoned off his fifty percent of the proceeds, but we know how it was achieved for Emery. Derwent purchased the property and six months later it was, so to say, bought by Emery. I suspect that no money ever changed hands, and so the capital in Derwent Holdings was passed on to Emery in the form of bricks and mortar – a very sound method and an excellent investment strategy all rolled into one.'

'What about the income from the tenants he had in his properties?' asked Newton.

'I was wondering that myself,' said Naish. 'Once you read Emery's explanation it is very simple. He employed a rent collector who collected the rents in cash. A very neat strategy, I would say. It also explains the relatively small number of personal transactions on his Lloyds bank account.'

'So why did Emery get greedy and start forging the additional art works?' asked Hancock.

'He says that he got jealous. Initially, it was clear that, in terms of risk, Williams was taking all the risks in passing off Emery's work to the art market and so a fifty-fifty split seemed reasonable. However, as time went by, Emery clearly began to resent the fact that it was his skills – in both making the forgeries and, indeed, the documents that supported the forgeries – that were the source of the income while Williams's role became less and less risky, in his view. He clearly began to believe that he should be getting more like a seventy-five to twenty-five percent split. However, he never had the courage to tackle Williams on the matter, given his propensity for violence and the presence of Powell and Rodgers.'

'Emery was trapped. He was a man in his sixties, probably hoping to retire with the profits from his crimes, yet he could not escape Williams's clutches, not only due to the implied threats of violence, but also because Williams no doubt reminded him that if he became uncooperative then he could be exposed as a forger. This might also go some way to explaining why he was so unmoved at the theft of the canvases and sketchbooks – perhaps he hoped it would be the beginning of the end of Williams's forgery business. Williams had an ongoing lust for more and more wealth and an ego that thrilled at the crime he was continuing to perpetrate. Emery, by contrast, had more wealth than he knew what to do with but could not escape into retirement because of Williams. So he contented himself with pulling the wool over Williams's eyes, producing the additional works more out of some strange anger than anything else. I also do think that there is a degree of arrogance in Emery as well that kept him, reluctant or otherwise, focused on the task of forgery.'

'Powell and Rodgers returned to London in 1938. They were anxious to avoid conscription and thought that the capital provided greater anonymity, as well as a wider market for their particular talents. Williams was content to see them go, having realised that the absence of organised crime in Bath did not require their presence. He had run out of things to occupy them and did not want them attracting the attention of the police if they tried to establish themselves in criminal activity in Bath. He called them in on those occasions when Emery's works needed to be transported about the country for sale but, other than that, they disappeared from the world that Emery inhabited. So, the business carried on very successfully for twenty-one years until the fateful night that Ted Lynch chose Emery's shop as the location for one of his speculative petty crimes.'

'Emery reported the burglary to Williams who immediately went round to the shop. Emery showed Williams the note that the beat constable had put through the letter box requesting the occupier to contact the police at Orange Grove, as a record had been made of the break-in. According to Emery, Williams was focused on two main concerns. Firstly, he was concerned that, at any moment, the police might turn up, and secondly, who was it who had perpetrated the crime. Williams telephoned Powell and Rodgers in London straight away and told them to come directly to the shop as quickly as possible, as he knew that he needed to get Emery's studio on the second floor cleared away before the police came to investigate. Emery was content that he could explain it as a private studio where he dabbled in some amateur painting in his leisure hours, but Williams was having none of it. He wanted nothing to do with painting to be associated with Emery or his business, not only at that time, one assumes, but also should suspicions be raised at some future point and linked back to Emery and his shop. Powell and Rodgers were going to take three to four hours to reach Bath and so Williams began to discuss with Emery how they could make a start on the clear-up themselves. At that moment they had a lucky break. To Williams's horror, a beat constable appeared at the doorway to follow up on what his colleague had handed over to him from the night shift. Williams excused his presence as being a neighbour and thanked the constable profusely for the police's assistance. They were told that Sergeant Dodd was going to follow up the case that morning but had been delayed with another case from the previous day. Telling the constable that Emery was naturally shaken by the crime, Williams agreed with the constable that, rather than Dodd rushing round, he would assist Emery to secure the premises that morning and get an inventory taken in the afternoon, so that Dodd would have a complete list of anything taken in the burglary. The constable checked the proposal with Dodd, who was grateful for the assistance, and agreed that he would meet Emery at the shop at nine o'clock the following morning. Williams was exultant, according to Emery, as he now had the whole of the next twenty-four hours to get the second floor cleared.'

'Powell and Rodgers arrived in the afternoon and the second floor was cleared. The canvases and other combustible materials were burnt in the brazier in the back yard, and the larger items like the easels and the paint tins were taken to Swallow Street to be disposed of later on. Dodd arrived the following morning and when he made a tour of the second floor, it is just an empty room with nothing in it to attract his attention. Emery handed Dodd the list stating that the only two items stolen were the cash from the till and some of his tools and Dodd took it at face value, understandably.'

'Once Emery told Williams that the four canvases he had used to rough out the compositions, together with the two sketchbooks containing the detailed drawings, had been stolen, Emery states that Williams became consumed with paranoia that his old adversaries from London had tracked him down and were going to try and blackmail him. Williams decided to take pre-emptive action and set Powell and Rodgers to work to track down the perpetrator of the break-in.'

'According to Emery, that is the last he was told of the matter by Williams and he saw virtually nothing of him or the thugs for a week. I believe Emery, as it would tie in with the statement of Rodgers of their activities tracking down Lynch, his abduction, torture and murder. On the following Wednesday, Emery states that he had opened his shop at nine o'clock as usual, and at half past nine got a call from Williams to say that Powell and Rodgers were coming round to his shop to redecorate the second floor to eradicate any last traces of evidence that a studio had been there. I have to say that they are cool customers. Having murdered Lynch sometime on the Tuesday night, they had taken his body in the small hours of Wednesday morning and hung it from the bridge in Widcombe. Then, some five or six hours later, they roll up at Emery's shop and start decorating.'

'So, when did Edwards get murdered, then?' asked Newton, as Naish paused to light a cigarette.

'Well, we know from the landlady at the Rose and Laurel that Edwards left there at half past one and wandered off down Lansdown View, opposite the pub. According to the landlord of the Old Jupiter, the thugs were at Emery's shop all day on the Wednesday, but he only knew they were there because he saw their van out the back of Emery's shop. According to Rodgers, he and Powell told Emery they were taking a break for lunch at one o'clock and took the van to Jews Lane, which is at the bottom of Lansdown View, to a prearranged rendezvous with Edwards. Williams had sent Edwards a note at the Rose and Laurel on the Tuesday evening in the name of Rodgers saying that he wanted to meet up to check he was all right and assure him that Lynch was safe and well. I suppose that Williams assumed he had at least twenty-four hours before any formal announcement was made as to the identity of the corpse found hanging from the bridge. The van pulled up alongside Edwards who was waiting as instructed in Jews Lane under the railway bridge and was told to get in which, apparently, he did. It appears very naive to me, but I suppose the full horror of what was going on is apparent to us in hindsight but to Edwards it was all a bit of a mystery. That combined with the significant hangover he had acquired, drinking off his guilt in rough cider. Again, in a manner that I find very cool but which, I suppose, is the hallmark of professional heavies, they took him to Swallow Street, secured him in a room at the back of the garage and left him there for twenty-four hours. They returned to Emery's shop in the afternoon and continued the decorating job. They returned again on the Thursday and, as we know from the statement of the landlord of the Old Jupiter, they finished up at three o'clock in the afternoon. That ties in with Rodgers' statement that they went back to Swallow Street, secured the van, had a clean-up and waited for Williams to arrive. He arrived at half past seven, at which point Edwards was dragged from his improvised cell, tied in the chair and his torture was begun.'

'What about the screams?' asked Hancock.

'As we know, Swallow Street is not a popular thoroughfare during the day. Once evening has fallen, the chances of being overhead are remote. However, I did ask Rodgers about this in my interview with him this morning and, according to him, the room that they used was at the back of the garage and with the door locked, the sound insulation was almost perfect. Apparently, the brazier to heat the poker was moved out into the main garage, as the fumes from it were overpowering in the inner room with the door shut. According to Rodgers, the torture matched exactly the deductions of the police doctor who conducted the autopsy, and once he had been killed, they wrapped him up in the tarpaulin that he had been sat over during his ordeal and put him back in his improvised cell until the early hours of Sunday morning, when he was dug into the gravel in the trench in Monmouth Place.'

'Hence the decomposition,' said Newton.

'It accounts for it exactly. By chance, Williams had been walking through Monmouth Place on the Saturday morning when he saw the workmen and, on the pretence of being a local businessman, he asked when the works might be completed. When he was told that the trench was being filled that evening with a view to tarmacking on Monday morning, he believed he had hit on the perfect hiding place for the corpse and set Powell and Rodgers to the task.'

'Then we come to the fire. According to Rodgers and Emery, Williams was becoming increasingly concerned about our visits to Emery's shop, unsure what it was that was driving our interest. You see now why I was keen to minimise our interactions with Emery. However, it was the information from Rodgers masquerading as the milkman that really spooked him, and he decided to act and do whatever he could to attempt to destroy the last remaining pieces of evidence. Fortunately, as Hazel pointed out, they were professionals but clearly not experts in arson.'

'Does Rodgers explain his friendship with Emery?' asked Newton.

'Emery had always been aware of Powell and Rodgers on the periphery of his world, but his role in the operation rarely brought him into direct contact with them. His main interaction with them prior to the Lynch affair was their coming to his shop to collect the completed paintings and transport them wherever Williams directed. He knew that Williams had brought them in to get to the bottom of the break-in but saw little of them. It was when the redecoration of the second floor was taking place that he began to speak with Rodgers, who was clearly the more articulate of the two. Emery sensed that he was uneasy, as if he were almost seeking a confidant. From Rodgers' own testimony, it is clear that he was, indeed, uneasy at the way things were playing out and, clearly, from what we know now he had every reason to be. At the time of the redecoration they had just tortured and murdered Lynch and had Edwards in a cell at Swallow Street, about to get something of the same. While Powell was clearly relishing the situation, Rodgers had realised that things were spiralling out of control and wanted someone to confide in.

Since Emery was, as he saw it, a member of the gang, he became the only person he could share his concerns with.'

'The upshot was that they shared confidences and Emery invited him to his home on the Friday evening after the redecoration works were completed. From what we know, Edwards was dead at this point, and his corpse in storage at Swallow Street prior to its burial in the trench at Monmouth Place the following night. Emery offered Rodgers a drink, which he says he desperately needed at that point, and one drink turned into another and since, clearly, Rodgers had a greater capacity for alcohol than the usually abstemious Emery, he was soon drunk. Emery awoke the next morning in a panic, uncertain as to how much he may have revealed to Rodgers, but he could not recall the majority of their conversation. Hence, later on in the chain of events, when he went to his home in the early hours of the morning, he went up and checked that the two keys were there and was relieved to learn that, whatever his indiscretions might have been while under the influence, he had not been so foolish as to reveal his secrets about the safe in the cellar or the contents of his attic.'

'The exact detail of what was discussed and of who was lying to who is uncertain to me, but at some point, Williams realised that there was a confidence being shared. Fearful that Williams might set Powell on him, Rodgers told Williams of the paintings that he had seen on the wall at Emery's house in an attempt to re-establish trust with him. While no intellect, he told me that he did recognise the three scenes by Turner since he had handled the larger works when they had been collected from Emery's studio and taken to the gallery. Rodgers clearly did not realise the extent to which Emery was being kept in the dark about the tracking down of Lynch and Edwards and when he alluded to it, Emery was horrified at what he subsequently learnt had happened to Lynch and Edwards. He began to consider making a break from Williams but was not sure how to achieve it. However, he left St Mark's Road and moved into the flat of his house in Camden Crescent, hence his absence, as noted by Mrs Carson.'

'Williams sent Rodgers along to St Mark's Road on a fishing expedition in the guise of the milkman. From what he tells me, primarily to see what the opportunities were for them breaking in and recovering the paintings. However, it was at that point that he unexpectedly encountered Jones. Nervous as he was, he decided he had to try and bluff his way out of it, and so the conversation that we have already had recounted by Jones occurred and it was the essence of this that made Williams decide, as we suspected, to send Powell and Rodgers around to Emery's with the petrol.'

'Powell and Rodgers arrived unannounced to Emery, who was bundled out of the shop at lunchtime and who decided at that point to go to ground completely at Camden Crescent. He had no idea whatever as to how he could make a break from Bath, let alone escape the wider clutches of Williams. So he got a message to Rodgers, knowing that he was also keen to make a break for it and seeing him as his only hope, hence the meeting in Parade Gardens. They had decided to leave things to cool off for a while before making a move, and so Emery returned to his attic in Camden Crescent and Rodgers went back to his lodging at the Byfield Gallery. As far as I can tell, Rodgers kept Emery's confidence on this occasion and did not divulge this meeting with Emery to Williams, as he had now decided where his best interests lay.'

'The next outcome of the information Rodgers fed back to Williams was the late-night trip to remove the three small Turners. Unaware that Emery had already decamped to Camden Crescent, Rodgers admits that he did tip Emery off about their intentions, as he didn't want him to be there and come to any harm. He said he was intrigued that Emery did not appear to be perturbed about the intended theft of his paintings but, as we know, they were a minor matter to Emery.'

'Emery, as we know, had the paintings in the roof and his safe in the cellar, which, after the drinking session with Rodgers, were the primary focus of his concern. He knew that all he had to do was wait until he saw the blue Bedford drive off down the street before he would be able to check that both were still secure and reassure himself that, in his cups, he had not revealed their existence to Rodgers.'

'Do we know any more of the details surrounding Lynch's abduction and murder?' asked Hancock.

'Powell and Rodgers began to circulate around the bars and low haunts in the city frequented by the criminal fraternity and identified Ted Lynch as the likely suspect. They also identified his associate Thomas Edwards, who was occasionally passing himself off in his clerical garb committing small scale confidence tricks. Powell and Rodgers reported back to Williams who told them to pick up Edwards and get him to reveal if, in fact, Lynch was the burglar. Edwards, under the threat of violence, revealed that Lynch was the burglar, and so his fate was set. Edwards was then instructed to bring Lynch to the Golden Fleece for, what he was led to believe, would be a friendly meeting between himself, Lynch, Powell and Rodgers. Thinking it was unlikely that things could turn unpleasant in a public place, Edwards, probably under coercion, did as he was asked. However, when he and Lynch got to the bottom of Oak Street, Powell and Rodgers emerged from the blue Bedford van. They bundled Lynch into the back and drove off, taking him to Swallow Street.'

'Before they drove off, Edwards was told to be outside The Lamb and Lion pub at ten o'clock. The pub is just around the corner from Swallow Street where, unknown to him, Ted Lynch was being held. Having secured Lynch at Swallow Street, Rodgers drove round in the van to drop a note at Williams's home to say that the goods had arrived as planned. Then, at about ten o'clock, he drove round to The Lamb and Lion and collected Edwards and took him back to The

Rose and Laurel on Williams's instructions, as he was keen to make sure that Edwards was under instruction to stay put and hold his tongue on what he knew. As the cellar man confirmed, Rodgers walked Edwards round to the back of the Rose and Laurel and paid him the twenty-five pounds that Williams had provided to keep him sweet, together with threats of violence should he try and abscond. Edwards's knowledge now posed a potential threat to the gang. Rodgers says he was uncertain whether Williams would have bumped him off at some future point but, clearly, the focus of their attention for the time being was on Lynch. The mistake was to have abducted Lynch so brutally in front of Edwards. Had they got Edwards to leave Lynch somewhere where they could subsequently abduct him, then Edwards would have known nothing of their actions but, either way, that is the series of events. I believe that Lynch probably heard Edwards in conversation with his abductors through the side of the van, and it was at that moment that he realised that Edwards had stitched him up. It was that thought that, later on during his torture, gave Lynch the idea to tell the gang that he had passed the canvases and sketchbooks to Edwards, thereby condemning him to his own torture and subsequent murder – an event that may well have followed inevitably if Williams eventually decided he need to be silenced.'

Chapter 24

'The process of torture was uncannily similar to our speculations informed by the autopsy reports. Powell took the leading role and administered the punches to the face, the injuries to the hands and delivered the coup de grâce with the knife between the ribs. Rodgers was there throughout and assisted in restraining Lynch, holding his head up for Powell to land his punches in the last desperate part of stage one of the torture. He also assisted in pinning down Lynch's hands so that Powell could break the joints with the hammer and extract the nails.'

'And what of Williams's role in the torture?' asked Hancock.

'He was there throughout, according to Rodgers, and this is supported by Powell. In phase one, he was stood right next to Lynch, leaning down and whispering in his ear that it would be best to come clean, then leaning back just a foot or so as Powell delivered another barrage of punches, almost enjoying the sadistic pleasure of taunting the man. To facilitate the second stage of the torture, Lynch was retied in the chair and sat up to a table. Again, the statements of both Powell and Rodgers state that Williams sat opposite Lynch with the pliers and the hammer on the table between them and explained to the terrified Lynch what was about to happen. He remained sat opposite Lynch throughout the process, repeating the same series of questions demanding Lynch reveal the names of the people who had sent him to commit the crime and where the canvases and sketchbooks were. Powell and Rodgers worked on Lynch from the other two sides of the table. After his first nail was drawn, he told Williams that he had given the sketchbooks to Edwards but that did not satisfy Williams, at first. Rodgers says he could tell that Lynch was not going to say any more than he had because it was clear that he was not working for anyone at all. He was what he claimed to be – a small-time crook chancing his arm with an opportunistic crime. Rodgers sensed that Powell knew that as well but, either way, Williams refused to halt the process, almost revelling in it, according to Rodgers. Eventually, as we suspected, Lynch passed out and they untied him and threw him back into his cell. They were surprised to find that after thirty minutes he was still unconscious and could not be roused. Despite Powell gripping one of his injured hands, he did not even flinch. Williams and Powell murmured something to each other, and then Williams told them to drag Lynch back out on to the tarpaulin, where Powell rolled him on to his back and pushed the knife between his ribs. There he stayed until they took him in the van down to Widcombe. Later, the tarpaulin and the instruments of torture were put away and got out again to deal with Edwards.'

'So, we appear to have all we need to charge them, but do we have all the evidence that we need to be confident of getting the appropriate convictions in court?' asked Newton.

'Yes, I think we do now,' said Naish. 'After the fire at Emery's shop I posed three questions. Who is the artist? What is Emery's involvement? And how long ago was this last used as an artist's studio? Hancock added a fourth question. Where are the paintings that have been produced? Well, we now have the answers to those questions, and, for me, the process of acquiring those answers has, in itself, produced the majority of evidence we need.'

'We know what happened to all the paintings forged up there on the second floor – that they were passed off into an unsuspecting art market,' said Newton. 'I suppose that Scotland Yard will eventually identify whose possession they are in.'

'I believe they will,' said Naish. 'It is the fate of the last pictures that he produced there that interests me, however, from an evidence point of view. Once those fragments of canvas that we found in the makeshift brazier in Emery's yard are analysed and the paint samples compared with the ones we have from the floor and Lynch's shoes, I think we have the scientific proof that links the production of a forged work of art to the shop and, by implication, the gang.'

'Will it hold up in court? The implication of their involvement, I mean,' said Hancock.

'I think it would be an unusual jury that failed to see that, on the balance of probability, the burden of proof is convincing,' said Naish. 'However, our focus is on proving the case against the murderers of Lynch and Edwards, and I am content that we can do that. The world of art forgery is the motivation behind the crimes and the backdrop against which those crimes played out. The final prosecution of the forgery case and all its ramifications is now a matter for Scotland Yard.'

'Well, Newton and I are planning to spend tomorrow reviewing all this evidence and cross-referencing the statements one last time to make sure we have not overlooked anything. So, hopefully by this time tomorrow, we will be as sure as we can be of our case against them.'

'That will be very helpful,' said Naish, looking at his watch. 'Well, it is getting on for half past five now and I am tired of hearing my own voice, so I am sure that you two are as well. While you two are going over the evidence, I am going to have a final interview with Emery and then Williams. When can we expect the analysis of the items from Swallow Street and the analysis of the paint from Emery's shop to be ready?'

'Both will be here at nine o'clock,' said Newton. 'I telephoned the laboratories at lunchtime to make sure that we would have it as a matter of urgency.'

'That will be fine. In that case gentlemen, I suggest that we take what counts for an early finish, given the hours we have been keeping in the last few weeks. I am off for a couple of pints to ease my parched throat. I suggest you also make your way homewards. I will see you in here at eight o'clock in the morning.'

'I find this whole business appalling in its brutality but I find Williams to be the most contemptible and sickening of all of them, to be honest,' said Naish, looking up from the notes on his desk as Hancock came in carrying the tea tray.

'I agree with you. It is unimaginable the terror that Lynch and Edwards must have gone through,' said Hancock.

'To some extent, Edwards got what he deserved, in my view. Be done by as you would, so to speak. It is Lynch I feel for most of all.'

'Have you been here since dawn?' asked Hancock.

'No, I got in at seven. I have just been reading through Emery and Williams's statements in fine detail, mapping out the inconsistencies.'

'Well, I will let you get on in peace. I am going to work at the evidence table, if that is all right with you? Newton will be in later, as he has taken the statements from the staff at Lloyds bank around to Milsom Street for them to sign.'

'Excellent, I want to read them through as well before my second interview with Williams,' said Naish, putting a match to his cigarette.

The abbey clock striking ten jolted both Naish and Hancock from their studies, and as they looked up, Newton came in.

'I have the last of the evidence that you requested, Inspector,' said Newton, placing three envelopes on the desk in front of Naish. 'The two large manila ones have the analysis of the tools found at Swallow Street and the paint samples found at Emery's shop. The smaller white one contains the statements from the staff at Lloyds bank.'

'Thank you,' said Naish. 'Give me an hour or so to read through all of this and then I would like Williams brought up to the interview room for half past eleven. Telephone Stone at his office now so that he has some notice to prepare.'

'I believe that you have been provided with the statement that my client has produced in order to set out transparently his entirely innocent but, I agree, unfortunate association with the matters that you have set out to us?' began Stone, combatively, as soon as Naish had sat down. 'Before this interview begins, therefore, I wish to know what your response to his statement is, and an indication of when we can expect to see the formal charges brought – if, indeed, any are forthcoming – as a consequence of any minor error of judgement my client may have committed as a result of his misplaced and naive association with these men. I would also expect some indication of the mitigation you will offer in the unlikely event that any minor charges are brought against my client, as an acknowledgement for his cooperation with your investigation.'

Naish stared expressionlessly at Stone while he spoke, and calmly made himself comfortable. He took his tobacco tin and matches from his pocket, one by one, and arranged them on the table. He then poured himself a glass of water from the jug, all done to give the suggestion that he was uninterested in what Stone had to say. Once Stone had finished, Naish paused, looked at Williams and then back at Stone, before taking a sip of water and replacing the glass on the table in a measured manner.

'Mr Stone, I have read your client's statement very carefully and I can tell you now that I can drive a coach and horses through it. Not only does it fail to account for the substantial body of evidence that I have, but it also conflicts with everything that the three other protagonists agree on in their statements,' said Naish, as he raised his hand to stop Stone from interrupting. 'Before you say anything more, let me explain a few facts to you and your client. Let me take the removal of three forged paintings purporting to be by J.M.W. Turner as an example. You, Williams, were seen by a witness getting into a blue Bedford van in Swallow Street on the night in question. That witness, unnoticed by you, subsequently identified you in Wood Street. As you made your way to your gallery on Monday morning, you were stopped by a gentleman who asked you for directions – you do remember that don't you, Mr Williams? You may be interested to know that, while you were at St Mark's Road, you were only feet away from a safe that was in the cellar of the house. It was in that safe that Emery had kept all the provenance documents which he had produced for you to support the numerous forgery projects that you had both worked on over the years.'

Naish paused and looked at Williams who was clearly moved by the information. Stone looked at Williams, as if asking if he wished to make comment, but Williams remained silent.

'I suggest that his primary motive was that they provided an insurance for him should you ever threaten him. If you did, his counter would be to produce the documents as forgeries, and every fraudulent painting you had ever sold would be exposed for what it was. Emery knew you would never kill him, as you regarded him as the goose that kept laying the golden eggs, but he clearly did not trust you completely to not sell him down the river if it ever suited you to do so.'

'I have, this morning, received the results of some analysis that I commissioned which you may be interested to hear. I sent a selection of tools that I found in the garage in Swallow Street – the one that your holding company Cotman Holdings pays the business rates on – for analysis. Of particular interest to me was a hammer with a wooden handle that was deeply stained. As I suspected, the staining was blood, and I am certain that it was the blood of Edward Lynch, since it was the hammer that Powell used to smash his fingers as you sat callously opposite him across that table. The second items of interest were some metal rods, one of which had traces of human flesh on the tip. I am certain that those traces of flesh came from the body of Thomas Edwards, since it was used by Powell to burn holes in his chest as he was tortured at Swallow Street.'

'The other analysis confirms that the charred section of painted fabric that I found in an improvised brazier in the back yard of Emery's shop was, in fact, a piece of painted canvas, and that the paint on its surface was exactly the same composition as the small tins of hand-blended paint that were found in Swallow Street, along with the other items that you had ordered Powell and Rodgers to remove from Broadway Parade when they cleared out the traces of the forgery of the Sickert paintings that Lynch had seen.'

'None of this in anyway provides direct proof of my client's involvement in these matters,' said Stone, in a voice lacking the previous aggression and confidence that it had had.

'That may or may not be the case,' said Naish, coldly. 'Either way, what I know is that it helps me to weave a web of steel around your client that I believe will place him rightly at the very heart of these crimes. However, for what it is worth, let me detail to you one last piece of evidence I received this morning. It is a series of statements from staff at Lloyds Bank in Milsom Street along with copies of your bank statements. This evidence clearly shows that it was you who entered the bank on Monday the fifteenth of October and drew out twenty-five pounds in sequentially numbered five pound notes. It was these notes that were given to Edwards by Rodgers in the rear yard of the Rose and Laurel in Lymore Road at around half past ten that night, as payment for his betraying his old cellmate Edward Lynch to you. Now, whatever you may have to say about the other evidence, I believe that that is convincing proof that implicates you directly in these crimes, and I am confident that a jury will see it the same way.'

'So, going back to your client's statement, Mr Stone, as far as I am concerned, it is a worthless tissue of lies. I don't know if you were expecting, or had even prearranged, that Rodgers would produce a statement that would agree with your version of events and thereby exonerate you, but I can tell you now that he has not done so. He has very sensibly seen that his best interests lie in working with the police. His statement matches Emery's version of events and even the account given by Powell – yes, even Powell has been forthcoming. I thought that would surprise you. You see, he knows he is going to hang for what he has done, but he is not going to see others who are equally complicit attempt to walk away scot-free, and so he has produced his statement which also tallies with everything Emery and Rodgers say and also with the evidence that I have gathered in the investigation of these crimes. So your lies have been your undoing, Mr Williams. I told you at the start that I was going to be honest with you in my approach and Mr Stone, here, heard me say it. I gave you the chance to cooperate and you have chosen to ignore that opportunity, and so I will hang you out to dry. But, in effect, you have done that to yourself with this arrogant and contemptuous document, which will condemn you in the eyes of the jury since it is so at odds with the testimony of the others that it exposes you for the liar and the self-serving opportunist that you truly are. I have to say, Mr Stone, that I am amazed that you associated yourself with such a strategy but that, fortunately, is a matter for your conscience and not mine.'

Naish picked up his tobacco tin and matches and put them back in his pockets as he rose from his chair.

'Unless you have anything that you wish to say, I think our interview is over. I shall not be needing to speak with your client again, Stone. He will be formally charged later today, and I can inform you now that the police will be recommending that your client is remanded in custody. Good day to you.'

'Good afternoon, gentlemen,' said Naish, as he entered the interview room in the afternoon. 'I have called this interview, Mr Sanderson, so that I can formally respond to the statement that your client has made concerning his involvement in the matter under discussion. I have read the statement and I am content that your client has set out a full and frank account of his actions and the history surrounding the origination, planning and execution of the crimes perpetrated by himself, Williams and his associates Powell and Rodgers. I am also content to state that I am satisfied that he had no knowledge of, or any involvement in, the abduction, torture or murder of either Edward Lynch or Thomas Edwards. He will therefore not be facing any charges in connection with those two crimes, although he is clearly a key witness for the prosecution. However, I cannot speak for the investigation that will follow when I pass the file of evidence that I have accumulated regarding the forgery operation to Scotland Yard. They may wish to apply to have you remanded in custody and so, until they have made that determination, I will be applying to the magistrate's court to have you remanded in custody pending the consideration of charges.'

'I have here in this envelope a letter signed by myself which sets out my request that your cooperation and assistance given to the police in the prosecution of these two murders is taken into account by the court, if and when you are eventually charged in connection with the crimes of forgery and deception by Scotland Yard. I have also asked that that consideration be used in mitigation of any sentence that you are handed down. If you would like to read it through now, I think that you will agree that it more than fulfils my side of the agreement that we had.'

Naish pushed his chair back from the table and lit a cigarette as Sanderson read through the letter and then passed it to Emery for him to read. They then conferred for a few moments in a whisper.

'My client and I would like to thank you for this document, Inspector Naish, and we can confirm that its content more than covers our expectations.'

'In that case we can conclude our interview,' said Naish, rising from his chair, and he left the room without saying any more.

Naish returned to his office where Hancock and Newton were sat waiting for him with a tray of tea.

'Have you finished your interviews with Williams and Emery?' asked Hancock.

'Yes, I have, but it has not made any difference to our position. I told Williams that his statement was a pack of lies and that I would throw him to the wolves as a consequence.'

'What about Emery?' asked Newton.

'I just wanted to confirm that we would provide him with a statement that he had cooperated with us, which he hopes will go some way to mitigate his sentence. He is a slightly tragicomic figure, in my opinion. He has, at long last, found the freedom that he sought from Williams but will, in all likelihood, have swapped it for a different form of incarceration,' said Naish.

'I have no sympathy for him at all,' said Hancock.

'No, I agree,' said Naish, 'but he was not in the same league as the other three. Anyway, I think that we three can congratulate ourselves. It is three weeks and two days from Lynch being found hanging under the bridge to us sat here, with those responsible for his death downstairs in the cells. I bumped into the Chief Superintendent on the stairs just now, and he was most complimentary. He wants the charges to be laid formally before we finish for today.'

'I think we are in a position to do that,' said Newton. 'We have the paperwork here. Do you want to take it upstairs to the Chief Superintendent?'

'No, you two can take it up to him. If he is happy, then get down to the cells and complete the formalities with Williams and Powell, and I will take a trip up to the hospital and deal with Rodgers.'

'What about the charges related to the fraud?' asked Newton.

'I have told Emery that we will be applying to the magistrates to have him remanded in custody, so he knows where he stands. I have also had an informal telephone conversation with Chief Inspector Hobbs about the process of passing our investigation over to him. He is confident that with some additional work at his end he will be in a position to bring charges.'

'Not a bad end to the week, then,' said Hancock.

'Indeed. Now, I suggest that you two get the charges sorted, tidy your desks and go and enjoy your weekends,' said Naish, lighting a cigarette.

It was a relatively bright day for late autumn and Naish was strolling through the city on his way to Orange Grove. He had allowed himself a lie-in until eight o'clock and had sat quietly in his flat, able for once to enjoy his pot of expresso. As he came into the High Street, he decided to take a quick detour and walked round the front of the abbey to his tobacconist in Church Street.

'Good morning, Mr Naish,' said the proprietor. 'Would you like a couple of ounces of your usual?'

'Not this morning,' said Naish, with a smile, 'I would like to see what coronas you have please,'

'Ah, so the case is over at last, then, I take it?'

'It is indeed,' said Naish, peering into the glass-fronted cases that contained an array of cigars.

'I have some excellent Cuban coronas in stock,' said the proprietor, taking an example from the case and offering it to Naish to examine.

After some discussion, Naish made his choice and, with the cigar in his inside coat pocket, made his way over to Orange Grove. He had one last piece of unfinished business on his mind that he wanted to complete before he could sit down and enjoy his cigar with complete peace of mind.

As he crossed the foyer, Naish nodded to the desk sergeant, who was in conversation with a member of the public, before making his way to the stairs that led down to the cells. He made his way along the corridor to the iron-framed gate that secured the cell block, where a constable sat at a small wooden desk.

'Good morning, Inspector,' said the constable, rising in deference to rank. 'I didn't expect to see you here today.'

'I have a matter that I need to attend to,' said Naish.

'Well, I will make a note of your visit in the ledger, Inspector, and let you in.'

'There is no need to enter anything in the ledger,' said Naish, as the constable opened the gate. 'This is a matter between you and me. Now, take this half crown and go and get yourself a bacon roll and a cup of tea on me. You leave me with the keys to the cells and be back here in twenty minutes.'

'I am not sure that I can, Inspector,' said the constable, nervously.

'Of course you can, lad. Now get along, and I promise you that you have nothing to be concerned about.'

The constable left, reluctantly clutching the coin for his breakfast in his hand. As he looked back along the corridor, he saw Naish closing the gate behind him.

Naish looked through the spyhole in the cell door before turning the key in the lock. Williams sat up on his bed with a look of surprise.

'What do you want?' Williams demanded, with a tone that combined anger and anxiety. 'Is my solicitor here?'

'There is no need for a solicitor, Williams,' said Naish, pulling the wooden upright chair towards the bed with its back towards Williams. Naish sat calmly down and, leaning over the back of the chair, stared intently at Williams.

'What do you want, I tell you?' demanded Williams again, 'I will call for the guard.'

'Call all you want,' said Naish, coldly, 'he has gone off for a while, so you see, it is just you and me. I always find men like you contemptuous. Stripped of your status and without your henchmen you are revealed to be nothing more than a conniving and spineless coward. I know you, Williams – not the polished you, but the real man behind the façade. You loved the adoration of the art world whilst at the same time sneering at it as you deceived it. Yet now, whatever your pretentions were for yourself, you will be forever associated with your crimes and be remembered as a partner of the homicidal sadist, Powell. I have no illusions about Ted Lynch, he was nothing more than a petty criminal, and not a very successful one at that, but he was, at least, honest about himself. You can reflect on that, can't you, in the short time that you have left to live.'

Williams face turned ashen as he stared at Naish.

'Oh yes, you are going to hang, Williams, I am certain of that,' said Naish, looking deeply into Williams's eyes. 'I am going to apply to the court for permission to be a witness at your execution. I want to be there in the gallows chamber and look into your eyes, and see the terror in them, as the hangman places the bag over your head. Then I will know that you truly understand what it was that you did to Ted Lynch, that moment as you share in his terror, as what you brought upon him is done unto you. You will remember that when you see me on that day, won't you?'

Naish rose, pushed back the chair and locked the cell door behind him. Outside in the corridor, the constable had returned and was looking apprehensively through the bars of the gate. Naish unlocked the gate and handed the bunch of keys back to him.

'Is everything all right, Inspector?'

'Yes, everything is fine, but I want you to go and look through the spyhole of each cell and make sure that all the prisoners are all right.'

The constable returned and nodded to Naish.

'Thank you for sharing this confidence with me, young man,' said Naish. 'I can assure you that nothing untoward went on here, but I needed to settle something in my own mind.'

Naish made his way back up into the foyer and made his way out into the sunshine. He crossed the road and headed to The Volunteer Rifleman where he intended to pass the rest of the morning in solitude with his cigar and a couple of pints.

Postscript

The trial of Williams, Powell and Rodgers was scheduled for three weeks at Bristol Crown Court. Naish always found the ritual of attending court a tedious process that, combined with the daily commute on the train, the lack of cerebral stimulation away from the world of detection and the limitations it placed on his consumption of tobacco, did nothing to improve his humour.

However, his fortitude was repaid when, having taken just two days to conclude their deliberations, the foreman of the jury declared that they found Williams, Powell and Rodgers guilty of the charges against them. The judge then handed down to Rodgers two concurrent life sentences, having noted that he would have faced execution had he not cooperated with the police to the extent that he had.

Williams stood ashen at the realisation of what was coming next, as Powell, stood alongside him in the dock, stared dispassionately ahead. Then, in the ominous silence, the clerk to the court placed the black cap on the judge's wig, as the judge pulled on his black gloves before telling Williams and Powell the sentence of the court: that they would be taken from the court to a place of lawful execution and there be hanged by the neck until they were dead, concluding, may God have mercy upon their souls.

As soon as the judge had risen, and without glancing at the men in the dock, Naish rose from his place and made his way to the station to catch the train back to Bath.

'The Chief Superintendent asked for you to look into his office when you were back,' said the desk sergeant, as Naish walked into the foyer.

'Fine, is he free now?' asked Naish.

'He is, as far as I know, Inspector.'

'Right, then I will go on up.'

Naish climbed the stairs to the second floor, an area he avoided as far as was possible, and paused outside the Chief Superintendent's office to straighten his tie before he knocked at the door.

'Come in, Naish, and take a seat,' said the Chief, in a genial manner. 'I have received some information from the Assistant Commissioner of Scotland Yard this morning about the Williams and Emery case and I thought you may wish to hear it.'

'Ah yes,' said Naish, 'I had put a note in my diary for around now to remind me to see if there were any developments.'

'As you know, Williams's sentence of death was deferred until the Scotland Yard enquiry into the forgery case had been finalised. However, Williams has refused to cooperate in any manner and – with Emery making a full and detailed confession about the entire matter – the Judge has ruled, given Williams's lack of cooperation, that the deferral is no longer required. Therefore, he is to be executed at Horfield Prison at nine o'clock next Monday. I thought you should know as I had understood that you were attending as a witness.'

'Yes, the judge gave me permission to attend as a witness if I so wished,' said Naish.

'Well, there you are, that is all that I know at the present. I will, of course, keep you informed when the investigation reaches its conclusion. Oh, and well done once again on a very thorough and efficient investigation.'

'Thank you, sir,' said Naish.

'What are you working on at the present?'

'I am just off to Green Park Station, sir. A body has been discovered on the train from Bournemouth.'

'Ah, good. Keeping you busy, I see. Oh, and when you are free, can you make an appointment to meet me so I can go through your budgets with you?'

'I will do that, sir,' said Naish, with a supressed sigh before he closed the door behind him and set off to Green Park Station.

On Monday morning, Naish paused as the heavy wooden door closed behind him. His leather-soled shoes sounded bleakly in the silence, as he walked across the tiled floor. Above him in the half-light, the clock began to strike the hour. As the first stroke of nine sounded, Naish dropped to his knees in the pew before the Lady Chapel and closed his eyes.

'Holy Mary, Mother of God, pray for us sinners, now and at the hour of our death,' murmured Naish, as the remaining eight strokes sounded in the silence of the church.

He remained on his knees for a while in prayer, conscious of how long his absence from this place had been. Then, as the front door of the church closed behind him, he made his way out into South Parade and back to Orange Grove.

Printed in Great Britain
by Amazon